LT TAYLOR
Taylor, Brad,
All necessary force :a Pike Logan
 thriller /

ALL NECESSARY FORCE

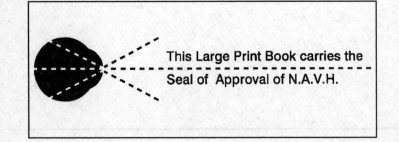

A PIKE LOGAN THRILLER

ALL NECESSARY FORCE

BRAD TAYLOR

THORNDIKE PRESS

A part of Gale, Cengage Learning

Detroit • New York • San Francisco • New Haven, Conn • Waterville, Maine • London

GALE
CENGAGE Learning®

Thorndike Press® Large Print Core.
The text of this Large Print edition is unabridged.
Other aspects of the book may vary from the original edition.
Set in 16 pt. Plantin.

LIBRARY OF CONGRESS CATALOGING-IN-PUBLICATION DATA

Taylor, Brad, 1965–
    All necessary force : a Pike Logan thriller / by Brad Taylor.
        pages ; cm. — (Thorndike Press large print core)
    ISBN 978-1-4104-4710-4 (hardcover) — ISBN 1-4104-4710-3 (hardcover)
    1. Special forces (Military science)—United States—Fiction. 2. Special operations (Military science)—Fiction. 3. Large type books. I. Title.
PS3620.A9353A45 2012b
813'.6—dc23   2011051910

Published in 2012 by arrangement with Dutton, a member of Penguin Group (USA) Inc.

Printed in the United States of America
1 2 3 4 5 6 7 16 15 14 13 12

To Sergeant Richard Thomas,
United States Army Special Forces,
KIA Cambodia, 1970,
and to the men of MACV-SOG,
unsung heroes of the original Long War

That the President is authorized to use all necessary and appropriate force against those nations, organizations, or persons he determines planned, authorized, committed, or aided the terrorist attacks that occurred on September 11, 2001 . . .

Joint Resolution of Congress,
September 18, 2001

Whoever fights monsters should see to it that in the process he does not become a monster. And when you look long into an abyss, the abyss also looks into you.

Friedrich Nietzsche

1

April 1970
Cambodia
Target Kilo 8: The Fishhook

Slithering the last fifty meters on his belly, Staff Sergeant Chris Hale reached the edge of the depression where the engine noise was coming from. Slowly parting the jungle growth to his front, he had his first clear view of the hollow. The sight caused his gut to clench.

Milling around as if they were about to start a parade were at least fifty North Vietnamese Army regular soldiers. Behind them was an elaborately camouflaged structure that looked like a large lanai that Hale had seen on his R&R to Hawaii, complete with wicker chairs and a ceiling fan lazily turning. Which explained the noise. There was a generator somewhere close by.

Hale continued to scan, peering intently at another intricately camouflaged structure about a hundred meters away. Trying to stitch together what he was seeing, like a jigsaw puzzle with missing pieces, he realized it wasn't a building, but a helicopter. A Soviet Mi-4. He couldn't believe it. What's more, he knew nobody at MACV-SOG headquarters in Danang would believe it. He inched up his camera, hoping the lens was good enough to make out the chopper from this distance.

After a couple of snaps, he turned back to the lanai, now full of NVA officers. *The mother lode,* he thought. Looking closer, he saw they weren't NVA, but something else. They were taller than Vietnamese, and wore a different uniform. *Shit, they're Chinese.* He watched them all turn at the same time and look toward the rear of the room, where another man entered dressed in civilian clothes. With a start, Hale saw he was a Caucasian. *A fucking Russian. No way will the FOB buy this.* He'd heard many strange tales about what recon teams had seen across the fence inside Cambodia or Laos, including Chevy station wagons with Texas plates or Soviet armor, but this compound was taking the cake.

The Caucasian walked to the edge of the lanai and stood with his hands on his hips, surveying the activity before him in the hollow. Hale snapped as many pictures of him as he could, no more than thirty meters away. When the man returned to the group, Hale continued to photograph, fired up with the thought of providing evidence of both Chinese and Russian advisors helping the NVA in supposedly neutral Cambodia. When he figured he'd pushed his luck enough, he slithered backward to Houng, the Montagnard native he'd left pulling security to his rear. After a brief exchange of hand and arm signals, they began creeping back to the Remain Overnight Position, or RON, where the rest of the five-member team waited.

They crept very slowly, covering only ten or fifteen meters before stopping to listen. Such movement required extreme patience, as Hale fought the urge to stretch the fifteen meters into fifty. They had to cover only about a football field, but it took them close to an hour to reach the team.

Moving inside the small security perimeter of the team, Hale signaled his one-one, Sergeant Dickie Thomas. Second in command, Thomas carried the team radio, their only lifeline if anything went wrong.

Thomas crept up and whispered, "What about Cummings?"

Specialist Cummings was the only other

American on the team. The remaining four men were Montagnard mercenaries recruited for their fighting prowess and their fierce hatred of the Vietnamese. All belonged to the Ground Studies Branch of the U.S. Military's Studies and Observation Group, more commonly called SOG. The cover name made it sound like they were a bunch of scientists out taking soil samples to improve the South Vietnamese rice crop. In reality, they were Special Forces soldiers who'd volunteered for top-secret cross-border reconnaissance missions into the countries neighboring Vietnam to develop intelligence on enemy movements down the Ho Chi Minh Trail.

Specialist Cummings was new to SOG's Command and Control South — the element responsible for Cambodia — and was accompanying Hale's team as an orientation before assuming one-one duties of his own on another team. Hale had forgotten he was there. He motioned Cummings over.

Speaking in a whisper, he told the two men what he had found. As expected, they were skeptical, which aggravated him. How was he going to convince the boss at CCS if his own team doubted him?

"I got fucking pictures. I'm telling you, there's a head-shed meeting going on between the NVA and a bunch of foreign advisors."

Thomas grabbed Hale's arm as his voice began to rise.

"Shhh. Jesus, remember where we are?"

Hale abruptly became quiet, with the entire team straining to hear anything out of the ordinary in the jungle growth. His team was on day four of a five-day mission, and the strain of working alone deep inside enemy territory was wearing them down, with last night bringing them to the breaking point.

They had pulled up into the RON just as the sun began to set. After the darkness had descended, a black curtain that was claustrophobic in its intensity, they had noticed fires all around them, winking like fireflies and extending off into the distance. Cooking fires. For a large number of people.

Somehow, they had managed to penetrate inside the perimeter of a large enemy base camp without either them or the enemy realizing it. As the one-zero, or team leader, Hale had made the call to use the RON instead of trying to thread their way back out in the darkness, then thread their way back in during daylight for the recon. The night had been sleepless, but the decision had paid off big-time. All they had to do now was live to talk about it.

Hale whispered, "Let's get the hell out of here. Before some idiot out to take a shit stumbles over us. We've still got a day's walk before we exfil."

Thomas grimaced at the thought of walking all the way back to target area Lima 7, but understood why. Lately, it seemed as if the NVA knew the SOG Recon Teams were coming. Even if they managed to insert across the border, the NVA found them within hours, forcing a running gun battle for survival. Several teams had vanished without a trace, the last contact by radio simply saying they were okay, then nothing. The rumor going around was that there was a mole somewhere within higher headquarters. A plant that was feeding information to the enemy.

This, coupled with the importance of Team Anvil's mission, led their commander to use a little misdirection, hiding the team's true objective. The operations plan was fake, detailing the team moving northeast into target area Lima 7 after infil. Instead, they had walked southwest into Kilo 8 for their real objective, but due to the sensitivity of this undeclared front, they would need to return to Lima 7 for pickup.

Hale waited for the team to ruck up, then

gave the signal to move. They had gone no more than seventy meters when the point man signaled enemy to his front. Shortly, Hale heard the sounds of movement from their left flank. A lot of movement. He felt his adrenaline spike, the blood flooding into his muscles in preparation for the fight. He looked at Thomas with an unspoken command. Thomas prepared to call the Forward Air Controller flying somewhere nearby to let him know the situation, as seconds would be precious.

Hale waited until he could clearly see the first five men of the platoon-size patrol before he opened up with his CAR-15. Immediately, the rest of the team began firing, killing man after man as the surprised NVA tried to understand how they were being attacked in their own backyard.

Hale gave the order to break contact, and the team began an intricate dance to the rear, with half firing while the other half moved. Hale could hear Thomas trying to remain calm on the radio.

"Covey, Covey, this is Anvil, contact. I say again, contact."

"Anvil, this is Covey. I copy. What's your location?"

While still on the move, Hale pulled out his signal mirror and sighted into the sky.

15

Changing magazines, Thomas said, "Using a shiny. Do you see it?"

"Roger. Got you. Stand by."

They had managed to break from the engagement but were moving in the wrong direction due to the contact, perpendicular to where they needed to go. Hale knew they were on the verge of bumping into another enemy element and that everyone in this world would do whatever it took to kill them. The team was holding up, but he could feel the fear surrounding each man like a physical thing. He felt it himself. Abruptly, they were hit again, from the direction of the lanai.

The team began to pour fire out again, repeating the dance, but they had lost the element of surprise. The NVA came in looking for a fight.

Hale screamed, "Claymore!"

Cummings ran over and took a knee, firing at the enemy while Hale tore into the rucksack on his back, pulling out a claymore mine rigged with a thirty-second time fuse and a white phosphorous grenade taped to the front. He jammed it into the ground and set the fuse while Cummings provided cover, then both bounded back to the team.

The ball bearings of the claymore shredded the lead NVA element in pursuit, with the white phosphorous grenade spewing out a blanket of fire that incinerated anything it touched. The enemy response died off, replaced by the screams and moans of the wounded.

The team continued running, everyone panting. Hale did a head count and saw he was missing his tail gunner.

He shouted, "Where's Houng?"

"I don't know," Thomas said. "He was right with me when we started to break."

They both knew there was no way they could search for him. To do so would cause the entire team to be annihilated. Hale strained to see some indication in Thomas's face, but it was his decision to make.

Hale paused for a moment, torn, then said, "Fuck. We can't go back in. Call Prairie Fire."

He got the team up and moving again, hearing Thomas relaying the call to Covey. Prairie Fire was the code word for a team about to be overrun. It was used only in absolute need, because everything available was dedicated to that team. No one-zero wanted to call Prairie Fire and have another team die because he had taken their support.

Thomas said, "Covey's got two Thuds inbound with some ordnance left from a run to Hanoi. No idea what they're carrying."

The flight of F-105 fighter/bombers would help, but only if they got to the team soon. Hale knew it would be a matter of minutes before the NVA gained control and began a methodical hunt, using what appeared to be an entire regiment around them. After what he had seen at the lanai, he was sure they wouldn't quit until the team was dead, and maybe not even then. He could see the team knew it as well, the fear pulsing off them, the whites of their eyes stark against the camouflage greasepaint on their faces. He was reminded of a treed raccoon from his youth, hissing and snarling while the dogs barked in a frenzy below. He'd often wondered how the raccoon felt right at the end. Now he knew.

Still on the move, he heard Cummings empty a magazine at the rear of the formation, screaming, "B-40 rocket! B-40 rocket!"

An explosion lifted Hale off of his feet. Momentarily stunned, he saw his right side covered in blood. The team lay scattered, some still firing, others in a daze. Shaking the haze from his head, he moved from man to man. Reorganizing the defense, he was relieved to see that, despite various wounds, everyone with him was still alive and ambu-

18

latory. In front of him he saw nothing but khaki uniforms darting between the trees, perhaps a hundred NVA advancing toward them. The sight caused him to momentarily freeze, the sheer magnitude of their situation sinking in.

We're dead.

The enemy unleashed everything they had, the rate of fire preventing the team from moving, the bullets snapping through their small perimeter like a swarm of angry bees and shredding the vegetation around them. Hale scrambled through the fire to Thomas, intent on breaking the NVA momentum before they realized they had it. He took over the radio, talking directly to the inbound F-105 pilots, giving them instructions on where to drop their load.

He dropped the hand mike and shouted, "Hug the ground! Danger close! Danger close!"

No sooner had he said it than the earth rocked violently, literally lifting the team into the air, the shock wave of the ordnance hammering them. The firing from the enemy slacked off to nothing.

"Let's go! Let's go!" Hale said, urging the team forward before the enemy could recover. He heard Thomas asking Covey for an exfiltration LZ, and heard Covey reply that the closest one was two kilometers to the north.

We aren't going to make it two klicks through this. Hale said nothing out loud.

After ten minutes of movement without contact, Hale began to think that maybe they'd broken through. That now it was just a footrace, with only the team knowing the location of the finish line. He began to hope. Five seconds later, something slammed into his chest, knocking him to the ground. The air around him erupted in pops from incoming rounds. The team immediately returned fire, with someone grabbing his combat harness and dragging him forward. The Yard pulling him was hit, causing him to let go. Immediately, another took his place, continuing to drag Hale to cover.

Amazingly, the enemy fire grew fainter the farther they ran. After the experience with the claymore, the NVA were pursuing cautiously, not wanting to charge into another wall of ball bearings and fire, giving the team some much needed breathing room.

Hale shook the hands off of him and tried to stand up, then sank back to a knee. He felt like he couldn't get any air, like he couldn't inflate his lungs.

Thomas checked him, then began to work, putting a plastic strip over an entrance and exit wound on his breast. He said, "You got an in-and-out. It's sucking."

Hale saw the look of fear on his face and nodded. He slowly stood up, adrenaline alone willing him forward.

"Let's keep moving. Those fuckers will be back on us soon."

To confuse the enemy tracking them, they took a right turn, walked for about a hundred meters, then continued toward the LZ, now moving at a much slower pace. Hale was struggling to keep up, the gap between his diaphragm and left lung filling with air and preventing him from inflating it. He heard Thomas get confirmation that three helicopters were five minutes out, two slicks with gunship escort. Hale figured the team was at least thirty minutes from the landing zone.

It dawned on him that with the loss of Houng, they were down to a normal team of six men, which could be extracted by McGuire rig — a simple sling seat that was dropped from both sides of the aircraft, three to a side, allowing exfiltration without having to land.

"We aren't going to make it to the LZ," he said. "We get hit again, and we're done. Tell Covey to pick us up here, with strings."

Thomas relayed while they moved. Minutes later, he was talking directly to the helo, coordinating the extraction with the team spread out in a perimeter around him.

"I'll pop smoke. You identify." He pulled the pin and tossed the grenade, knowing it would be a beacon for the NVA but vital to get them out.

The pilot's voice came back calm and mechanical. "Roger. I see green smoke."

"Roger. That's us."

The team could now hear the chopper and smell salvation. The first Huey was sliding into position when a 12.7mm heavy machine gun opened up from the camp, strafing the tail. The gunship immediately obliterated the fire with its miniguns, but the damage to the first helo was done. Hale watched it pull off and begin limping back toward the South Vietnamese border. He prayed it would make it.

The second Huey came overhead and dropped the rigs, the rotor wash beating the brush around them in a mini hurricane. As the men were frantically getting inside the slings, one of the Yards began screaming and pointing. Out of the wood line, Hale saw Houng stumbling toward the hovering aircraft, weaponless, one arm dangling uselessly at his side, his face a bloody mess. In the distance behind him, he saw swarms of

NVA drawn by the smoke and noise of the helicopter. He slipped out of his sling to give it to Houng.

Thomas shouted, "What are you doing?"

Hale looked at him with sadness and said, "You know what I'm doing."

Thomas started to leave his sling as well, tearing at the slip noose around his wrist. Hale stopped him.

"No. You're not getting off. Remember what I told you about the camp. Get that information back to the FOB."

"Fuck that! No way! You die, we both die."

Hale pointed to his chest and side, both freely bleeding from the multiple wounds. "I'm already dead. Go."

Without waiting for an answer, Hale turned and assisted Houng into the last sling. Thomas helped as tears left tracks through the greasepaint on his face.

The NVA began running forward and firing through the trees in a desperate attempt to stop the extraction. Doing figure eights overhead, the gunship unleashed its twin miniguns, knocking soldiers down by the dozens as if they had been swatted by a giant hand.

"Go, go, go!" Hale screamed. He turned and stumbled away, wobbling toward the brush while firing his last magazine into the advancing soldiers. The enemy paid no attention to him — not even realizing he was there. Instead they focused all of their fire on the helicopter as it lifted off. Hale crawled forward underneath a tree that had been shattered by lightning, pulling brush over his body in an attempt to hide himself, the fear of death coiling in his belly like a snake. Wheezing from his destroyed lung, he watched the team lift off, dangling beneath the helo like spiders on a web, heading toward safety. Toward home.

He remembered he still had the camera in his rucksack, with the proof of the meeting. Intelligence of tremendous value to the war effort. He cursed himself at the oversight, knowing the information would die out here with him. Disappear as if it had never existed. At least Thomas would pass the basics along.

As the helo got smaller, another heavy machine gun opened up. The tracers arced through the sky and cut into the aircraft, punching through the thin skin to the avionics beneath. Hale watched the bird lose tail-rotor function and begin spinning out of control, the team now flung out on the end of the ropes like a pinwheel from the centrifugal force. He watched in disbelief as the helicopter slammed into the earth in a fireball. He heard the NVA cheering.

The fear left his body, replaced by despair at the futility of it all. He closed his eyes and drifted into unconsciousness.

2

Two Years Ago
Central Sudan

Brett Thorne's head jolted forward, snapping him awake, as the decrepit Japanese pickup hit another rut. He gazed at the stars above his head as they drove through the Sudanese desert, the sky infinitely brighter than anywhere he had been in the States.

He nudged a form in front of him with his boot. "How much longer?"

The man, a tall, lanky member of the Zaghawa tribe from the Darfur region of western Sudan, said, "Another hour, maybe less. Are you regretting your decision to ride back here with us? I can have him pull over."

Brett shook his head. As a CIA operative, he could have easily traveled in the cab of the pickup, but he wanted the ability to fight — and run — without restriction. The cab was too confining. Even if it meant being crammed in the back with five other men, all smelling like they hadn't bathed in over a month. It was like riding in a basket of clothes that had been dipped in sour milk.

Brett leaned out into the wind, catching the dust from the truck ahead of them but enjoying the escape from the fetid air. He sat back down and reflexively patted the rucksack at his feet.

If they fight half as ferociously as they stink, we might not need this anyway.

The truck abruptly slowed, shutting off its headlights and driving with parking lights alone. Brett stood up and noticed the lead truck had done the same. He heard excited murmurings from both trucks in the tribe's native tongue, something he couldn't understand.

He turned to the tribesman who spoke English. "What's going on? Why are we stopping?"

"Janjaweed. Over there."

He pointed to the north, and Brett could make out several sets of headlights bouncing across the desert, moving closer.

"You don't know they're Janjaweed, and even if they are, this mission is more important than killing some low-level militia. If any get away, we're screwed."

"Nobody else drives around in convoys at night. It's Janjaweed." The tribesman smiled, his teeth gleaming white in the moonlight. "And I agree with you, Mister Brett, but I cannot make the others agree. They have suffered many times at the hands of the Janjaweed and will not be denied. We just need to make sure we kill them all."

Brett muttered under his breath, cursing his boss at the Special Activities Division in Langley and cursing his poor, dumb luck to be born African American. Because of it, he was always chosen for any mission in Africa that involved infiltrating with the natives, regardless of the fact that he was a five-foot-five-inch fireplug of solid muscle, and the Zaghawa were all six-foot string beans. He looked nothing like them, although he'd known that before he'd crossed the border at Chad. At the time, he'd laughed about it because all of his buddies in SAD had been denied a seat on the trip based on the color of their skin, no matter how hard they bitched that Brett looked about as native as they did. Bigotry at its finest.

Now, as he often did when plans started falling apart four thousand miles from help, he was wondering about his career choices. He tried one last time.

"We lose a single man, and I'm aborting the mission. The refinery is much, much more important than a random militia patrol. Think about that. You're risking a strategic gain for a tactical one."

The tribesman didn't answer. He simply slipped over the side of the truck and faded into the darkness, along with everyone else. Brett cursed again and jumped over the side himself. Instead of following, he hunkered down next to the cab of the pickup, intent on hauling ass if things went bad.

The Janjaweed, an amorphous group of militias comprised of nomadic tribesmen, were responsible for a campaign of terror in Darfur, committing atrocities as a matter of course in an effort to run out all of the sedentary farming tribes, such as the Zaghawa. In response, the farmers had banded together, forming militias of their own. The Zaghawa tribe belonged to the Sudanese Liberation Army and had formed ostensibly to take the fight to the Sudanese government for the perceived injustice of the government's lack of effort to stop the Janjaweed from raping and pillaging. The plan had backfired. Instead of stopping the Janjaweed, the government, fearful of the threat, began arming them.

As has happened throughout history, the conflict had escalated out of control until it was genocide, with civilians bearing the brunt of the damage.

Brett knew all of this, but he wasn't emotionally involved in any way. He was simply, as Clausewitz said over a century ago, the continuation of politics by other means. In this case, Chinese means.

Over the past decade, China's appetite for resources had grown along with its economy, until it was now a rapacious beast. China had begun pouring money into Sudan, becoming the largest investor in Sudan's petroleum industry, and the largest consumer of Sudanese oil. Thus, China had more influence in Darfur's war than perhaps any other country.

Unfortunately for the victims of the genocide, China had little interest in Sudan's conflict. Chinese arms kept the Sudanese government and the Janjaweed fighting, and because of it, a symbiotic relationship had been created: Sudan favored the Chinese for their support, and China used its sway within the UN Security Council to prevent any meaningful UN action.

Brett hoped to change that equation, if he could keep these backwater natives focused on the mission.

He patted the rucksack again, ensuring the device was with him, then crouched next to the cab of the pickup, hearing the tick of the engine and the clink of weaponry around him as the men deployed in a half-assed tactical manner. Eventually, he heard the groan of the Janjaweed vehicles, steadily growing louder.

The Zaghawa tribesmen had tucked inside a small wadi, preventing him from seeing the approaching vehicles, which was the only tactical thinking that Brett could spot. There was no security to the flanks or rear, no discernible ambush line, and no way they would ever know if anyone escaped. He sighed. *Another kindergarten fight.*

He prayed the Janjaweed were just as bad. He pulled on a pair of night observation goggles, the darkness immediately replaced with an eerie green.

He saw the glow of headlights against the brush on top of the wadi, bouncing in and out and growing stronger, along with the Zaghawa tribesmen waiting to ambush the convoy in a formation that guaranteed failure. The lead Janjaweed truck reached the edge of the wadi and stopped, its headlights silhouetting the Zaghawa formation. He heard the shouting of the men in back, then the night erupted into gunfire.

It seemed that the Zaghawa had surrounded the trucks and were now firing wildly into them, regardless of the friendly men on either side. Tracer fire arced through the air, most of it harmlessly over the heads of the Janjaweed. Miraculously, they began pouring out of the trucks unscathed, shooting just as wildly as the Zaghawa tribesmen.

Jesus H. Christ. Fucking idiots.

Brett threw his AK-47 to his shoulder and began firing controlled pairs, dropping everything he aimed at in the dim glow of the headlights, his NODs giving him an unbeatable edge. An RPG sputtered through the air and managed to find the lead Janjaweed truck, exploding the gas tank into a fierce ball of fire and throwing Brett backward.

He rolled to the rear of his pickup, still snapping rounds, then realized he no longer had the rucksack. No way could he allow the Janjaweed to get it. If they lost this fight, he needed to ensure it was destroyed.

He sprinted bent over, losing the depth perception in his NODs, forcing him to pat the ground until he hit the rucksack. He snatched it up and continued forward, climbing the wall of the wadi. Rounds were blasting from all sides, going both in and out, the tracers and the fire from the exploded truck causing his NODs to white out. He ripped them off and surveyed the damage.

He was outside the ring of the fight and

saw his intrepid Zaghawa tribesmen leaping forward, spraying rounds, then leaping back again. From all sides. *Jesus. A circular ambush. Are they retarded?*

The Janjaweed were more disciplined, controlling their fire in a synchronized manner. And they had an edge: Using their trucks for cover, they could fire indiscriminately out three hundred and sixty degrees without worrying about hitting anyone friendly. With the Zaghawa's poorly chosen formation, the fire would devastate any ability to mount an assault. In an instant, Brett saw they were going to lose. They had maybe a minute to gain the upper hand before the Janjaweed men began a systematic attack on a flank and rolled up the entire crew. Brett knew his men would either die or throw down their weapons and run off into the darkness.

The second pickup of Janjaweed militia shifted attention to his side of the perimeter, the flames from the burning vehicle negating any edge his NODs would have provided. He could hear the second truck yelling to the third truck, and knew the assault was close. Rounds ripped the air around him, forcing him to push his face into the desert floor, worming backward for any low ground that would protect him. Bullets snapped through the fabric of the rucksack on his back, causing him to freeze and wonder if he would even feel the devastation should the device go off.

The shooting shifted to his right, and up the line, he saw the men from the third truck massing to flank, unmolested because of the protection provided by the fire from truck two. *Need to intercept them.*

He jumped up and raced through the darkness, screaming at any man he saw to follow him. None did. *Shit . . . No English speakers.*

He reached the apex of the perimeter just as the men from truck three began to move. He had run far enough to put the assault element from truck three between him and the covering fire from truck two. He dropped to a knee and began pulling the trigger, his aim much, much more devastating than any of the tribesmen around him. He hit five before the assault was broken, the men retreating back to the safety of the vehicles, unsure of who was killing them.

He followed at a sprint, needing to finish the job before they could regroup. He reached the trucks in the confusion of the enemy running back, with nobody realizing he was among them. He dropped the AK and pulled out his Glock 19, firing so close to the men that they didn't realize he wasn't shooting out. Within seconds, truck three was dead.

Not wanting to lose momentum, he grabbed a PKM machine gun and sprinted the forty meters to truck two, mowing men down from their unprotected rear like he was working a scythe. The last two men realized that someone other than a jittery tribesman was after them, and turned to face the threat just as the belt ran out on his machine gun.

Brett threw the heavy weapon into one man, knocking him to the ground, while he dove into the other. He grabbed a fistful of hair and pounded the man's skull into the rocky ground until he felt no resistance, then turned and jumped on the other Janjaweed recruit, using his knee to crush his face. He rolled off and drew his Glock again, looking for another threat. None came, and the fire had slacked off to nothing from outside.

Slowly, men came forward, looking incredulous at his actions. The English speaker found him, his eyes wide.

"You are truly a lion among men."

The adrenaline still burning, Brett spit on the ground and grabbed him by the chest. "Get me the leader."

He saw that the tribesman's grasp of English wasn't strong enough to follow, so he got belligerent, like an ugly American tourist. He raised his voice, speaking slowly and distinctly.

"Get. Me. The. Fucking. Leader."

Forty-five minutes later, he dropped down from the bed of the pickup truck, the land around him glowing from the myriad of lights emanating from the refinery. The tribesmen themselves were milling about with little thought to security, making Brett antsy.

This refinery was built with Chinese dollars, manned by Chinese engineers, and guarded by Sudanese government troops. He had no doubt they were better than the Janjaweed he had just fought, which meant they were exponentially better than the men who accompanied him. He needed to find the critical components of the refinery and trigger his device, then get the hell out. If the tribesmen here wanted to continue attacking, so be it. He wasn't going to stop them, since it would help him escape to the south, where his exfiltration vehicle was staged.

He pulled in the English speaker, reiterating what he had said before. "Nobody fires until I initiate. When you hear my explosion, start tearing it up. You understand?"

"Yes, yes. We will wait. Where will you go?"

"I'm going to cross the fence. You guys wait out here. Whatever you do, don't initiate. Got it?"

"Yes. We are lions too. We will wait."

Brett smiled and patted him on the shoulder, thinking he was about to take his life into his own hands. He turned and scaled the chain-link fence, then scampered into the first area of darkness he could find.

He put on his NODs and scanned the refinery one hundred meters away. He'd learned all sorts of terms when studying the critical components of the average refinery — from atmospheric and vacuum fractionating towers to fluid catalytic crackers — but the key wasn't learning how they worked, only what they looked like. He had determined that the fractionating towers were the components to attack, given the parameters of the device he intended to use.

He saw a row of narrow columns to his front, four in a parallel line perpendicular to him, hissing steam out of the top. *The target.*

All he needed was to take out one, and the refinery would be put off-line for weeks. The end state would be a rebel success against a government facility, which would cause the Chinese to rethink their tepid efforts at stopping the civil war. Rethink their support for the Sudanese government because their own bottom line would now be affected with the loss of oil imports. They couldn't help but wonder if this wasn't a precursor to another successful attack by the rebels.

Brett gave no thought to whether the strategy would work, only about the tactical method of engagement. The device he had brought was a test item. Something that should take out a tower with little effort, but he had no real idea if it would work. One thing was for sure: If it didn't, the clowns he was with would get nothing done.

He low-crawled forward until he was within eighty meters of the first column, then opened his rucksack. He pulled out a tripod and a device that was the same size as a gallon stewpot. He was preparing it for initiation when he heard gunfire outside the fence.

Dumb-ass bastards.

He frantically began aiming the device as the gunfire grew in volume. He saw men spilling out of buildings next to the columns, thankfully drawn to the sound of the guns. He rose up to check his aim and was caught in the headlights of a vehicle screaming down the perimeter fence, just to the right of the columns.

He hit the ground, breathing hard, wondering if he'd been seen. He glanced up and saw the headlights swerve toward him.

Holy shit. . . .

He grabbed the initiation device and rolled away, frantically jabbing the button. The device exploded, sending its deadly payload toward the column.

He looked up and saw the first tower buckle. Then the second. And the third. All spewed out an enormous amount of vaporized fuel in various stages of distillation. A split second later, the gaseous cloud erupted in a violent explosion, the shock wave slamming him to the earth.

He rolled around, his ears ringing, his conscious brain screaming at him to find the truck. Eliminate the threat.

He rose to his knees and saw the truck on its side, burning furiously, knocked out by the fuel-air explosion. The entire refinery was on fire, the battle to his rear now silent.

What the hell did I just use? What did they give me?

He began running flat out to the perimeter fence and his exfil to the south.

■ ■ ■ ■

Two days later, Han Wanchun studied the reports on the demise of the oil refinery. As a partner in the Great Wall Industry Corporation, purportedly a Chinese technology consortium, there was no reason for him to be privy to the secret satellite data showing the destruction wrought by the rebel band. No reason for him to be allowed to read the sensitive firsthand reporting from the Chinese workers on the ground. But as a colonel in the People's Liberation Army, Han had access to whatever information he needed to conduct his mission, which, unlike the false statement propagated by the Great Wall corporation, wasn't to develop technology. It was to steal it.

Reading the reports, Han realized that something more than a motley band of rebels was involved. There was no way the tribal members could wreak the havoc shown with small arms alone. He cared not a whit about the genocide occurring in Darfur, or about the loss of the refinery. Not his job to do so. But whatever had caused the damage was something to be concerned about. Maybe something to covet.

The strike on the oil refinery was designed to get Chinese attention. As often happened in the hazy world of covert operations, it had accomplished the task, but not in the way the United States intended.

Han put the reports back into the classified sleeve on his desk, the germ of an idea beginning to form.

3

Present Day

Jennifer Cahill noticed her speedometer had crept past seventy miles an hour, causing her to reflexively glance into the rearview mirror and pull her foot off the gas. It wouldn't do to get pulled over by some North Carolina redneck sheriff after all she had been through. *Too close to finishing. No need to rush. Plenty of time.*

No cops appeared out of the tree line. The only thing she saw on the desolate road behind her was a pickup truck. It was a monster four-by-four, and gaining fast. She felt a little spike of concern but quelled it when she remembered all of the other trucks she had seen driving around the outskirts of Boone over the past seven days. *Way to go. You've fully converted into a paranoid. Even farmers cause you to flinch.*

The adrenaline subsiding, she felt the weariness seeping back through her like waves rolling into a beach. She had been operating on little sleep for days, and she knew she would either finish this today or she wouldn't finish it at all. No way was she going back to The Hole again. No way on earth. For the thousandth time, she wondered why she was stupid enough to agree to this. *I could be on a dig in South America. Or in grad school, sleeping all I want. Instead, I'm out here playing Jane Bond.*

The pickup had gained considerably in her rearview mirror, appearing behind her after every second bend or so. She knew that like every other local, he'd pass her in a cloud of dust, daring anyone to appear in the blind spot around the curve. She decided to let him pass, then track behind at his speed. Let him get the ticket.

The truck drew close enough to allow her to see the farmer behind the wheel. A great big bear of a man with a full beard and the ubiquitous baseball cap. He pinned up right behind her bumper, apparently waiting on the road to straighten out long enough to allow him to test his luck. When it did, Jennifer slowed down and pulled a little to the right to let him to pass. She saw him signal and veer out, then returned her eyes to the road. A second later, she knew something was wrong.

43

He should have shot right by her. Instead, he was matching her speed in the oncoming lane. The benevolent farmer was gone, replaced by a scowl that was concentrating intently on the rear of her car. *Shit. He's going to PIT me.* She knew the truck was about to slam into her rear quarter panel and push her sideways, spinning her into the ditch. The minute she lost traction on her rear tires, she was done. She knew this because she had just learned to do it a month ago.

She looked for an out, and saw nothing but trees blurring by on her right. She was trapped. *And I helped him do it. Idiot.* She seized the initiative, jerking the wheel to the left and slamming broadside into the truck in an attempt to get him out of position. Her little sedan did nothing to alter the truck's trajectory. Instead, she ricocheted back into her lane, weaving left and right, making her manhandle the steering wheel to regain control. She felt the truck kiss the rear of her car and saw the driver crank the wheel to the right, forcing her rear end to begin to slide. She turned into the spin in a last desperate attempt to break the skid. She failed. A split second later, her car was rotating out of control. In a blur, she saw the truck rocket past and disappear as her car continued to spin into the right-side ditch.

Her travel was brought to an abrupt halt when the front of the sedan hammered into a tree, causing her to crack her head into the driver's-side window.

Woozy, she fumbled with the door latch, desperate to get the package from the rear seat and run. She had no plan other than to get away from here. Away from the bearded truck driver. A memory flitted across her consciousness. Her hanging from a beam, naked. The room freezing cold. A woman with a foreign accent hosing her down with water, demanding answers. A man behind the woman leering, waiting his turn. *Not going back to The Hole.*

She fell onto the ground, turned to the passenger door, and found herself facing the bearded man. Much bigger outside of the truck. Showing not a whit of compassion.

"Where is it?" he said.

She decided to keep to her cover, acting like she couldn't believe this idiot had just run her off the road. Anything to buy herself some time.

"Are you crazy? You just wrecked my car! You're not even asking if I'm all right. Jesus. I ought to call the police right now. You'd better have some insurance —"

He cut her off by slapping her hard across

the face with a hand the size of a ham, knocking her to the ground.

"I don't have time for this bullshit. Tell me where it is or I'm going to get rough. It's over. Don't make it any worse."

On her knees, Jennifer looked up at him and stammered. He drew his hand back again, causing her to throw up her arms and shout, "Don't!"

The bearded man smiled at her reaction and said, "Tell me."

Jennifer dropped her head to her chest and began to cry. In between the sobs racking her body, she said, "It's underneath the front passenger seat."

The man turned away without another word, bringing a phone to his ear.

"It's Radford. She's done. I've got the package."

He listened for a second, then said, "No, it didn't end well. She's sitting here crying like a baby. Or like a woman. I told you this whole experiment was stupid. No way is any girl going to be able to do operator shit. I'll be back in ten minutes. Send someone out for her. The car's pretty fucked up and I don't think she can drive."

Still making sobbing noises, Jennifer watched him circle around to the passenger side, tracking his movement like a predator.

She waited until he bent over and disappeared from view before trotting lightly around the car. When she reached the door, she saw him facedown in the footwell, craning his neck to see beneath the seat, his right arm down in the well but his left arm holding on to the seat itself. Right in front of her. As if it were day one of combatives all over again and her instructor was giving her an easy gift.

4

Keshawn Jackson pulled next to the white coupé in the small parking area for substation 117. He stared at the vehicle for a second, making up his mind. The car was not supposed to be there. The substation was supposed to be deserted. For what he needed to do, it *had* to be deserted. On the other hand, he couldn't come back here a second time. The Baltimore Gas and Electric Company truck he drove had a built-in GPS to facilitate recovery operations after a storm or other disaster. It would register him being here. Once could be explained away, but twice would invite scrutiny.

As an ex-con, he was a low-level worker. A cable dog. Someone who did the manual labor of getting power back on, supporting the more experienced linemen, not someone who had any reason to be at substation 117.

It dawned on him that he was about to break the law for the first time in over five years. He felt no shame. Before his job at BGE, he had been a gang member and a career petty criminal, in and out of jail for everything from drugs to assault with a deadly weapon. His last stint had been at the infamous Attica prison in New York, where he had found religion. As for many inmates before, God had saved his soul. He had identified what had been wrong with his previous life and found a reason to belong. And a reason to blame. Since then, he'd been on the straight and narrow, a model citizen, waiting to give back something for what his newfound faith had given to him. There were three others from his prison prayer group just like him, working in electrical companies in Washington, D.C., Pennsylvania, and Virginia.

Making up his mind, he decided to go inside the small concrete-block house. He was in his BGE uniform, so he wouldn't be completely out of place. If he saw someone, he'd throw out an excuse and leave. If not, he'd get to work.

He dialed the combination on the chain-link gate and passed through, walking underneath the lines heading in and out and ignoring the myriad of transformers. What he wanted was inside the building. Substation 117 was one of a handful that had a server inside that allowed access into the BGE network. They were sprinkled throughout the service area to allow monitoring of the grid without having to travel to a central control node.

He scanned the facility inside the fence line, but didn't see a soul. *Maybe the guy just parked here and went somewhere else,* he thought, although the chances of that were unlikely, since the substation was out in the boonies, in a rural area west of Baltimore, Maryland. Not a whole lot of places to go from here.

He punched in the combination on the metal door and entered the concrete structure. It was small, only two rooms with a closet. Most of the area was filled with analog equipment and circuit breakers to pull the substation off-line in an emergency. He didn't see anyone inside the building, which caused him to let out his breath. He also didn't see the server, which made him wonder if his information had been wrong. He opened the closet door and smiled. Inside on a desk was a normal-looking desktop computer. The screen was off, but he knew it was running by the blinking hard-drive light. He looked around once more, then pulled out a thumb drive and stuck it into a USB port.

He had no expertise at all in what he was doing, but then again, he didn't need any. His contact from the prayer group had told him to simply stick in the thumb drive and it would do the work. The mass hysteria and multiple news reports of cyber threats and the vulnerability of the U.S. system to hackers had caused a phalanx of firewalls and other security measures to be implemented in the BGE power grid. All were directed outward, at the access points to the Internet, where the threat was supposed to live. Nothing had been done to protect from an attack on the inside, using BGE's own hardware. A lesson they would learn the hard way.

Watching the erratic blinking LED on the thumb drive, Keshawn was startled by light spilling in from the outside door. Before he could react, he heard, "Hey, what are you doing?"

He turned around and saw a smallish man in a coat and tie. *Shit. Management.*

Blocking the view of the computer, he said, "Nothing. A buddy of mine did some work here yesterday and thought he'd left his sunglasses. My route was over here today, so he asked if I'd look."

The man cocked his head suspiciously. "And he left them inside this building?

What's he do?"

"He's a cable dog. Like me. I don't know what he did at this substation. Look, they ain't here anyway, so I'll just go."

Keshawn could tell the man was still suspicious, but the fact that he worked for BGE seemed to be tipping the scales. He turned to close the closet door, which was a mistake. The man saw the blinking thumb drive.

"What the hell is that? What are you doing with the server? Do you know how bad you could screw things up?"

Keshawn said nothing. He simply reached out and clamped both of his hands around the man's neck, squeezing with all of his might. The man fought back, at first trying to pull Keshawn's hands away with brute strength, then resorting to ineffectual hitting. When his face went bright red and his eyes began to bulge, he seemed to realize he was truly in a fight for his life. He began clawing at Keshawn's face, scratching gouges on his cheeks. Keshawn maintained the pressure until the man passed out, then continued on, kneeling on his chest and squeezing until he was sure the man was dead.

Keshawn slowly let go, looking deeply into the half-closed eyes of the body on the ground for signs of life. He saw none. He smiled and whispered, *"Allahu Akbar."*

Finally, after years of waiting, he had begun his part of the jihad.

5

I heard Radford's transmission in disbelief. I just couldn't picture Jennifer completely breaking down. Then again, she had never been placed under so much pressure in so little time. Even given her experiences last year.

Turbo, the guy in charge of this section, said, "Well, that's it. Let's wrap this up and go get a beer."

"Wait a second," I said. "We don't do anything until we get a debrief from Radford. Let it continue."

Turbo rolled his eyes and said, "Pike, are you shitting me? You think your chick's going to come through that door? Radford's right, and you know it. This whole thing was a waste of time and money."

Like most of the men inside the Taskforce, Turbo was a he-man woman hater. Any thought of a woman encroaching on his meat-eater world caused a fit. He wanted

Jennifer to fail, with all of his heart. I used to be just like him, but after she saved my life, I became a believer. I had convinced her to do this, and wanted her to succeed more than I was willing to admit. Even if it looked like it was going to go Turbo's way, I wasn't doing anything until I spoke to Radford.

"Another couple of minutes won't hurt. She's only got eight minutes left anyway. Let it ride."

Turbo grimaced and stomped away. Knuckles, the man to my right, finally spoke up.

"You sure you want to continue? You think she can handle the RTL again? Even if she says yes, do you think it's fair to put her through that?"

I said, "She can do this."

"Pike, I know she did some amazing shit overseas last year, but maybe this is just too much. She came pretty damn close, and that's going to mean something to the boys."

Knuckles was somewhat of a woman hater as well. He had been my second in command before I left the Taskforce and was now in charge of my old team. He'd gotten mixed up with Jennifer and me in a chase for a terrorist in Bosnia last year and had seen Jennifer operate a little bit. Not as much as me, but he'd seen enough to wonder. If Jennifer made it through this, he'd be a believer too.

Even so, Knuckles might have a point. Maybe I was overambitious in asking Jennifer to attempt Assessment. She wasn't coming onboard as an official operator. She was just a partner in our business — a cover organization designed to *support* Taskforce activities, not execute them. Given that, she would be the first Taskforce female who came even tangentially close to the sharp end of the spear. We had plenty of female intel analysts and a smattering of case officers, but they all exited stage left when we did an Omega operation. I knew the meat eaters would need to trust Jennifer, sometimes with their lives. They wouldn't do that unless she earned their respect, and I figured there would be no better way than to make her go through Assessment just like the males.

All of the Taskforce operators were invited to the unit by word of mouth through the Special Mission Units of the Department of Defense or the Clandestine Service of the CIA. As such, we didn't need to run a full-on selection process. We let the SMUs handle that, then picked the cream of the crop. Even so, every meat eater loves a challenge and wants to feel like they did something to earn admittance, so the commander of the Taskforce had invented Assessment.

It was basically a seven-day gut check, starting out in the RTL — the Resistance Training Laboratory — where the prospective candidate resists interrogation for a couple of sleepless nights.

If he succeeds in not giving anything away, the candidate is given a mission that involves obtaining a package from a contact. From there a scavenger hunt from hell begins, all with a hostile security force trying to capture him or retrieve the package. If he does everything right, he continues. If he screws up, he goes back to the RTL, or The Hole, as the guys called it, and starts over. Knuckles was asking if maybe having Jennifer start over was just cruel.

I was thinking about my answer when I heard Knuckles say, "I don't fucking believe it."

"What?" I said, running around the desk to see the monitor for myself. My face split into a smile.

Jennifer had just entered the building.

Inside his office, Colonel Kurt Hale grinned when he heard the radio transmission from North Carolina. As the commander of the

Taskforce, he ordinarily didn't pay much attention to any single evolution of Assessment, mainly because he'd already hand-selected the men who would try out. He knew they'd do fine and had only invented the damn thing to give them some bragging rights for leaving their previous units. This assessment, however, was a little different. This one had someone who was really trying out, with a ton of people hoping she would fail. Kurt didn't hold that same hope.

Two years ago, Pike had been one of the best operators the Taskforce had ever seen — until his family had been brutally murdered while he was on an operation. Blaming himself because he'd volunteered for the deployment, he'd fallen apart. Kurt had tried to help him, but Pike had continued self-destructing until he posed a threat to the very existence of the Taskforce. A classified organization operating outside the bounds of U.S. law, it couldn't risk having a loose cannon as an operator. At Pike's request, Kurt had cut him free.

A year later, after Pike had averted a terrorist threat, Kurt asked him to return to the Taskforce, but he had refused. Instead, he had broached a crazy scheme of starting a business with Jennifer as a partner. A business that the Taskforce would use to facilitate their operations. It would be just another cover organization, like the myriad of other ones the Taskforce used on a daily basis — from corporate air charters to shell boating companies — but with a distinct difference; this one would be run by operators. Kurt had thought the idea of a cover organization with a full-on operator at the helm had merit, and had agreed.

Once that happened, Pike had sprung the Assessment request. Kurt had drawn the line at that, but Pike was relentless. Kurt had finally given in, and Pike had spent the better part of a year teaching Jennifer a host of skills to get her ready.

At first, the men had all just grumbled. When Pike finagled her into the same hostile environment tradecraft course that the men attended, the grumbling got louder. Teaching her some hand-to-hand was one thing. Pushing people out of the way so she could do HETC was something else. When he began to teach her to shoot, it grew into a howl. *If she makes it through the next ten minutes, people are going to scream like a baby.* Kurt smiled at the thought, glancing up as a man entered his office.

"What's going on, Mike?"

Kurt knew Mike was tracking the Assessment just like he was, probably down to the second.

"You tell me, sir. Where's Pike's protégé?"

"She made it to the house of pain. The last hurdle."

"Jesus. Pike must have swayed it in her favor." When Mike saw Kurt scowl, he back-pedaled. "Just kidding. I know it's legit. . . . Uhh . . . You got a call on the unclassified military line in the Ops Center."

"Who is it?"

"Some colonel from the embassy in Cambodia. Want me to transfer it?"

"Yeah. Go ahead."

Kurt picked up the phone, wondering who on earth would be calling him from Cambodia. The line was rerouted from the Pentagon, so whoever was calling was dialing Kurt's cover job as a staff weenie in the J3 Special Operations Division of the Joint Staff. It could be anybody with a Pentagon phone book.

He identified himself and asked how he could be of assistance. After the first sentence, he forgot all about Assessment.

6

Jennifer stopped in the doorway to let her eyes adjust to the gloom of the sleazy roadside saloon. It wasn't that impressive. Just a large open area with a smattering of chipped tables and the overpowering smell of stale beer. To her front was a cheap pine bar that ran down the length of the room, dead-ending into the wall. The ceiling had no tiles, just open rafters made of two-by-fours. The wall behind the bar didn't even extend to the top, looking like it had been made as an afterthought, with a four-foot gap between it, the roof, and the room beyond. Not counting the bartender, there were five other people in the bar. All men. And all staring at her.

One of these guys should be the contact. She waited for a pregnant second, hoping someone would approach. She really didn't want to use her vetting phrase on a stranger. When nobody stood up, she went up to the bartender and got his attention. He looked at her like he'd just wiped something off his shoe, but came over.

"You lost?"

"Uh . . . I don't think so. I'm looking for someone."

The bartender simply stood mute. One of the men ambled over and took a seat next to her. *Shit. I'm going to have to say it. Stupid, stupid Taskforce humor.*

She glanced at the man on the barstool, then back at the bartender. Swallowing hard, she said, "Maybe you can help? I'm looking for an inbred redneck with shit for brains?"

She immediately knew neither was the contact when both of their eyes went wide, no recognition of the bona fides at all.

"I'm sorry. I didn't mean to say that. It just popped out."

The man on the barstool stood up. "You think that's fucking funny, cunt?"

"No, no," Jennifer said, her mind racing to spit out an excuse. "I was told I was playing a prank by a guy outside. He said you'd laugh. I'll go get —"

Before she could finish her sentence, the man punched her hard above the right temple, snapping her head back and causing an explosion of light. He clamped both hands onto her neck and began to squeeze, bending her over backward. The strike rattled her for a split second, long enough to feel her windpipe start to crush. She felt a sliver of panic and uselessly tried to pry his hands away. She began thrashing violently, the fear growing until it blotted out any logical thought. Realizing she was about to pass out, she forced the panic away and focused on what she needed to do.

Rotating to the right, she raised her arm and brought it straight down against his elbow joints, breaking the stiff-arm. Sliding forward, she used her weight to fold his arms, getting within striking range of her attacker. She began to see sparks of light, the man's grip relentless. She raised her right leg, lodging her foot against the top of the patella on his left knee. She shoved outward with all of her might, praying it would crack the hold.

The strike broke the support of the man's knee, triggering it to buckle and causing him to blessedly let go of her neck as he fell off balance to the floor.

Jennifer fell with him, scrambling to wrap up his wounded knee in a leg lock. She grabbed his ankle and brought it to her chest while extending his leg. Rotating her legs over his body, she leaned backward, thrusting forward with her hips against his knee while twisting the ankle, desperately trying to damage him enough so that he couldn't catch her when she ran. If done right, she knew he wouldn't be catching anything without help for the rest of his life, but she was out of position. She couldn't get the leverage to break something and was about to be in a stalemate, unable to let go but also unable to hurt him. She heard him yelling from the pain and slapping the ground over and over, the noise finally penetrating her survival instincts.

Oh my God. He's tapping out. He's Task-force. She let go and warily rose. The man slid backward, remaining on the ground.

She backed up a step, then turned to run out of the bar, only to be confronted by the remaining five men, all advancing toward her.

In the room next door, I lost control when Jennifer got whacked in the temple, jumping up and yelling at Turbo.

"What the hell is that? You know the rules. No head strikes to the candidate. What's he doing?"

Turbo backed up, recognizing that I'd kick his ass all over the room in the next few seconds. No question of whether I could or not.

"Whoa. Wait. I know . . . Cleary just gets emotional. He's a little pissed to be supporting this. You know head shots happen every single evolution."

I advanced on him, my fists balled up. "Not on the first fucking punch. Maybe in the heat of rolling around, but he deliberately hit her."

Knuckles yelled from behind me, "Let it go, Pike. Don't stop the evolution. She's doing okay."

Still glaring at Turbo, I said, "What do you mean?"

"He tapped out."

Turbo and I both said, "What?" and ran over to the monitor.

I saw the remaining five men advancing on her and went ballistic again. "What the fuck are they doing? Jesus Christ!"

The house of pain was the final hurdle to Assessment, a beat-down where a candidate had to fight six people and win. Not six at a single time, though. The candidate was supposed to take on one, then two, then the final three. Of course, after the week of hell he had been through, there was no way he could defeat six operators just as good if not better than him. We didn't expect him to. As long as he kept fighting, kept plugging away, he'd eventually win. It was a little secret only exposed after he was through, and then only if he supported Assessment in the future — when he got his instructions as cadre. Make no mistake, though, it wasn't a gimme. The candidate had to use every skill he possessed to survive, with the cadre pushing him to the limits.

In this case, I didn't think the men were going to let Jennifer do that. They were going to end this right now. Teach her a lesson, five on one.

I started toward the door that led into the bar area, intent on stopping the fight. Knuckles grabbed my arm.

"Don't do it. You don't know what's going to happen. You stop it now, and it's over. Let her go. They aren't going to permanently hurt her, and we both know Turbo's team screwed with the conditions."

I glared at Turbo for a second, then sat back down. "Yeah, well, I screwed with the conditions as well."

"What's that mean?"

"I picked this place for a reason. It favors Jennifer. She has something those guys don't."

"What's that?"

"She's a damn monkey."

66

All of the training I had given Jennifer was for one reason: to give her an edge to escape if she found herself in trouble. The Task-force guys all groaned at the shooting and hand-to-hand, but they missed the point entirely. She was learning the skills to survive, not to replace them. Last year I had seen firsthand how someone could get wrapped up in a dangerous situation no matter what the reason for being there. If Jennifer had had the skills then that she did now, a lot fewer people would have died.

Here in the bar, she didn't need to beat all six men like a male candidate. She just had to get away from them. I knew she'd figure out how — if she had enough time.

I watched Jennifer throw a chair at the group of men and race to the door leading outside, a thermos on a sling bouncing against her back. I knew the door was locked.

They closed in on her as she violently ratcheted the knob. At the last second, she ran to the other end of the room, the men right behind her. She reached the wall and sprang up, planting one foot and pushing off. She clawed the air for a rafter, but came up short, landing on the other side of the men.

That a girl. "She's found a way out. She'll

be here shortly."

"What are you talking about? All she's doing is running in circles. They'll catch her sooner or later."

I pointed to the gap between the roof and the wall, the bar on the other side. "She'll be coming through that hole in about a minute."

Jennifer hit the ground running, putting a table between her and the men. They slowly circled around. When she had two on each side and one in the middle, she leapt up on the table and split the gap, jumping full force into the single man. They hit the ground together, with her springing to her feet and running to the bar. We watched her leap onto the bar and race to the end, where she repeated her wall-jump maneuver. This time, she was high enough to snag a rafter.

She began going hand over hand toward the gap. The men saw what she was doing and tried to block her, one jumping up on the bar himself and swatting at her legs. Without breaking speed, she flipped underneath the rafter, swinging her legs up and over it, until she was crouched on top. She moved with astonishing speed on the two-inch beam, scuttling right to the gap.

I saw her poke her head through the hole, then fall to the ground on our side of the wall. She advanced to the table warily, recognizing me and Knuckles but unsure if that was good or bad. Our faces were stoic.

She didn't sit down. Without fanfare, she said, "I'm looking for some inbred rednecks with shit for brains."

I replied, "I can understand why. They can be quite handsome."

The correct answer caused her to visibly sag. She pulled the strap over her head, set the thermos in front of me, and collapsed into a chair, her head coming to rest on the table.

I leaned over and rubbed her shoulder. "Congratulations. You're done. I was beginning to worry about our trip to Angkor Wat. Looks like you get to go after all."

She looked up, but said nothing, the exhaustion on her face giving me a pang of guilt. And a little pride.

"How'd you get past Radford?" I asked.

She smiled, the blood between her teeth and gums making her look feral. "He slapped the hell out of me. Just about knocked me out. I started faking, crying and blubbering, and that chauvinistic son of a bitch actually turned his back to me and walked away."

I glared at Turbo, who was studiously studying a computer monitor. "Where's

Radford now?"

"Unconscious in the rental car. You might want to get a medevac to him. His arm's out of socket."

That's one I won't have to deal with.

Turbo came over and shook her hand, which must have pained him, but not as much as the pain I was going to bring to him in the next few minutes.

"Jennifer, why don't you go clean up," I said. "There's a trailer out back. I'll come get you in a minute."

When she was gone, I said, "Turbo, go into the bar and line up your team. I'd like to talk to them about following instructions."

Turbo looked at the door, then back at me. "Uhh. I can handle that."

"No, I don't think you can. If they'd like to put on protective gear, I don't care, although they didn't give Jennifer the same chance."

He looked a little incredulous. "You think that piece of ass is worth taking on my whole team by yourself?"

Out of the corner of my eye, I saw Knuckles scowl at the verbal slight, then slowly rise like a wraith. *That's got to look scary.*

He said, "I want the asshole that hit her first."

Hassan Rafik booted up his Skype account and clicked the call button for a cell phone in Montreal. When a man answered, all Rafik said was, "Call me back on your computer."

Five minutes later, he was hooked up via voice-over Internet protocol through his laptop. It was completely unsecured, but with the enormous amount of digital traffic on the Internet, it might as well have been encrypted by the NSA. There was no way the Great Satan would be able to randomly pluck this call out of cyberspace, even if they were already listening to Rafik's cell phone. Discovery would have to be luck because Rafik changed locations — and thus his IP address — every time he called. He had the contact do the same. It was like having a cell phone that changed numbers every time he dialed, thwarting the ability to monitor it.

The contact gave Rafik good news. All of the cells had managed to penetrate their respective electric company's security and plant the virus. It had not gone without incident, however. He relayed what had happened to Keshawn.

Rafik frowned. "Yet you said all were successful. How did he prevent the discovery from getting out?"

The contact paused for a minute, then said, "He killed him. Don't worry, though. Keshawn knew what to do with the body. He's experienced in law enforcement techniques. It'll look like a robbery in a poor section of Baltimore. One near another substation that the man had visited earlier in the day, so it fits."

Rafik grinned. He felt like shouting in triumph. Al Qaeda had been trying for years to recruit members who didn't look, talk, or act Arabic. Men who could easily pass into the lands of the Far Enemy and wreak havoc. All that had gotten them so far was a couple of fat Americans who created a lot of press but couldn't fight their way out of a baby's crib.

Rafik had taken a different tack. Instead of trying to get non-Arabs to come to al Qaeda, he went to them. The idea came to him when he learned that Richard Reid, the so-called shoe bomber, and José Padilla, the so-called dirty bomber, had both converted to Islam in prison. Planting a Muslim chaplain in the New York prison system, he began to recruit in earnest, using America's own freedom of religion against it.

The prison had turned out to be the perfect recruiting ground. All of his converts could blend in anywhere precisely because they were Americans, born and raised. The recruits also had no compunction about breaking the law and were used to using violence to obtain their goals. Finally, they came to his chaplain already despising their country's authority. There wasn't a lot of quibbling over innocents.

At the core, they were all looking for someone to blame for their own failings, something to identify with that would provide them honor and a reason to exist. It was no different from a Palestinian living in squalor in a refugee camp. Rafik had gladly provided that something, first through the pacifist teachings of Islam, then, when he had culled out the potential mujahideen, through the concepts of jihad in a smaller prayer group. No one in the prison system monitored his chaplain's preachings.

His idea wasn't just to convert as many as he could to the jihad but to build a cohesive fighting cell for a spectacular attack. It had taken years, but now it was paying off in unexpected ways. No infiltrated transplant could have averted discovery as Keshawn had done. The mission would have been over.

The contact asked, "When will we insert the real virus? Like I said before, we should have done that initially, instead of this test case."

"That is the real virus," Rafik said. "We won't be risking a second insertion. You can initiate it remotely, right?"

The contact's voice became agitated. "Yes, of course, but that virus will only disrupt their early-warning software. It won't do anything to the system itself. What good is that? Was I supposed to give the men a different one?"

"Calm down. You did what I asked. Computer attacks can be fixed in hours. Worst case, they go without power for a day or two. We need to physically destroy parts of the system to cause a long-term effect."

"That's the same problem. They'll just put in repair parts. That'll take less time than cleaning out a virus. Why on earth would you risk such a complicated plan? I can do the same thing using my computer."

"There are some components that don't

have spares. Some critical components."

The contact persisted. "If it's so critical, it will be heavily protected."

"You'd think so," Rafik said, "but the Americans don't do anything until *after* an attack. I found the components in their own vulnerability assessments."

"How will you attack them?"

"I'm working on that now. It's why I'm in Egypt. Just be prepared to receive an airplane in the next couple of weeks. I'll give you the details when you need them."

Rafik could hear the disbelief in his contact's answer. "We have worked together for a long time, but now I fear you're misleading me. I won't continue like this. You have never kept things from me before."

"It's for your own safety. You live inside the Far Enemy. If you get captured, I want to be able to continue. Maybe not immediately, but soon enough. It's bad enough that you know all the names of the cell. Trust me, I have found an Achilles' heel. Just leave it at that."

Kurt paced outside the Oval Office, hoping to catch five seconds of the president's time. He had never done anything like this before, only coming to the White House when summoned. The phone call from Cambodia had changed that.

He knew it was incredibly frowned upon to attempt to ambush the president, but he really didn't have a choice. He was about to divert the next Taskforce mission for personal reasons, and he needed the president's approval. He also needed a little of the president's big stick to cut through some Army bureaucracy.

"You sure he's coming back here before his meeting with the finance committee?"

Sally, the president's secretary, smiled. "Yes. He always comes back here before heading out again. Gives him a breather without interruption."

Kurt inwardly winced. "I won't be long. I promise."

"What I can't figure out is how you got past the chief of staff in the first place. Nobody else gets to ambush the president."

Nobody else runs an organization that can bring down his entire administration with one mistake. "I don't know. Just lucky, I guess."

Sally was rolling her eyes when President Payton Warren entered the reception area, talking with a scrum of people bringing him up to speed for his budget meeting. He did a double take when he saw Kurt. Without waiting for Kurt to speak, he said, "Okay,

76

everyone have a seat out here. I'll be back in . . ."

Kurt said, "Five minutes, tops."

After closing the door and shaking hands, President Warren said, "This must be bad news. Did Jennifer get sent to the hospital or something?"

When Kurt had agreed to let Jennifer attempt Assessment, the biggest obstacle had been that she was a civilian. They could camouflage the death or injury of any military or CIA member simply by claiming a training accident, but a civilian would be exponentially harder. Friends and family would have to buy the story, something that would be very, very difficult to control.

"No. Nothing like that. Believe it or not, she passed with flying colors."

President Warren smiled. "Good for her. I'll bet that's caused a little barking."

"Yea, it has, but they'll get over it. In the end, they all respect ability, and she has it. Actually, she *is* part of the reason I'm here."

"Okay. What do you have?"

"Well, Pike's taking her, along with Knuckles' team, on a cover development trip to Cambodia in two days. Get the business ready for operations. I need to divert them."

"And you came to me? Sounds like Oversight Council business."

President Warren was referring to the council that supervised Taskforce activities. Made up of thirteen people, including the president, they were the only ones who knew of the Taskforce's existence, and they approved every mission as a single body. All the council members were either in the executive branch of government or private citizens. None came from the legislative branch.

"It's personal. And not worth the council's time. I got a call from the defense attaché at the embassy in Cambodia. He's a friend of mine." Kurt paused a second, then continued. "Apparently, someone turned in some artifacts that belonged to my father. It may lead to his body."

Because of the Taskforce bond, the president was as close to Kurt as to any of his advisors. In some ways closer, since Kurt wasn't part of the political machine. The president could relax around him, be himself without being on stage as the head of the most powerful country on the planet, or worrying about leaks for political gain. After getting used to being in the president's presence, Kurt had relaxed as well. One night, late, after an Oversight Council update, Kurt had told him the story of his father becoming MIA on a secret mission during the Vietnam War. The Army had recovered the remains of the entire team minus Chris Hale, the team leader. No one knew why he wasn't among the others in the wreckage of the helicopter. Kurt had been ten years old at the time. It had eaten at his soul every day since. He knew the president would understand.

"That's great news . . . isn't it," President Warren said. "What did they find?"

"It's not great news yet. Just good news. They found a rucksack pretty much destroyed by the elements. Inside was a Nikon SLR camera, a recon journal, some rotting Army T-shirts, and other odds and ends. The Nikon and the journal were packed in a waterproof rubber sack. They were the only things marginally serviceable."

"What makes you think they were your father's?"

"They were able to make out his name written in one of the T-shirts."

The president nodded. "Okay. Sounds like it might be real. What do you need Pike's team for?"

"Sir, I'd like to send him to the embassy to get the stuff. I know it's breaking the rules, getting his team involved with a defense attaché who has nothing to do with his cover, but he's headed there tomorrow, and JPAC is going to take forever. The equipment won't help them find my father. Whoever turned it in will do that. I really want that camera and journal before it ends up lost in bureaucratic limbo."

Kurt knew that the Joint POW-MIA Accounting Command would do everything they could to recover his father, as they did for all investigations into MIAs from America's wars overseas. He also knew that they were understaffed, and that for every person's remains recovered by the command, there were probably three hundred bogus stories to investigate. Chris Hale was now at the bottom of that heap, with the camera and journal — the only thing left of Kurt's father — tied up waiting its turn.

President Warren said, "That's it? You just want Pike to swing by the embassy while he's in-country?"

"Uhh. Well, no. My buddy can't release the gear to Pike. There's a huge trail of custody that has to be followed. Eventually, it ends at me, but I was hoping you could make some calls and cut through the red tape."

The president smiled. "That's easy. I'd be glad to do it, but I think you're a little paranoid. Nobody's going to give a shit about a camera from 1970."

8

The man testifying before the House Foreign Affairs Subcommittee on Terrorism, Nonproliferation, and Trade droned on and on about some obscure prohibition against a technology transfer that was destroying the GDP of some obscure country, of which, apparently, the United States had some obscure but important reason to remain engaged. It was all Congressman Richard Ellis could do to even pretend to care. He had much more important things on his mind. At least important to him. He was thankful that this hearing was taking place in the Rayburn House Office Building, where his workplace was located, instead of the secure compartmented information facility buried underneath the Capitol Visitor Center, where the House Intelligence Committee met, his other committee obligation. It meant he could steal away to his office on the breaks.

A large, jovial man, he had a classic patrician's face. He looked like a politician should, at least from the left. The profile on the right was marred by a three-inch birthmark that rose from his right eye and ran up into his hairline, like he'd smeared lipstick on his brow. He did his best to cover it with hair, and was always particular about camera angles.

Ellis was well liked on both sides of the aisle, but this conference was testing even his patience. *He must be breathing from his ears.* Finally, the man shut up, allowing Ellis time to whisper some nothings into the chairman's ear and bolt.

As he arrived at his office, his secretary handed him a list of calls he'd missed. He thumbed through them until he found one that simply said *Oakpark Industries* with a number. The number was new, as expected. Every time he called Oakpark, he would dial a new number. Those were his rules, not theirs. Rules learned from a lifetime of practice. It was why he was still around.

He told his secretary to hold all calls and closed the door. Pulling open a drawer, he withdrew a brand-new pay-as-you-go cell phone. His number would be new as well. After this call, the phone would go in the trash. Ellis knew that the only way anyone was listening to phone calls either from him or from Oakpark was through a court order, which would dictate in no uncertain terms the number to be monitored. There was no way they could monitor a new phone every time he dialed the company. Well, they could, but nobody would let them. *Call it a business expense.*

A man answered on the third ring. Ellis wasted no time on pleasantries, not wanting to remain on the line any longer than necessary.

"Did you get the cargo?"

"Yeah, we got it. No issues."

"Is it properly packaged? Like you were instructed?"

"Yes. I told you, no issues. Nobody will be able to tell what it is. We broke all the kits down into separate components, then lumped the like parts together. It looks like a bunch of metal plates and plastic containers. Just like the bill of lading says."

Ellis relaxed a little bit. He'd facilitated the game many times, but this would be the first time he was a player.

"What about the landing on the far end? For the transfer. Is the coordination complete?"

"Hey, come on, we're leaving tomorrow. Do you think I'd fly if I didn't have it squared away?"

Yes, for the money you're getting, I think you would. Ellis wished the man on the other end knew he was dealing with a United States congressman, but a little impertinence was worth the security. "Last time we spoke, you had mentioned complications. Have they been resolved?"

"We're good. It wasn't a complication. It was just a matter of finding the right guy. We've got the airport to ourselves for three hours. Plenty of time. It's not in Cairo, but it's close enough."

Ellis couldn't believe the man had just said a location. He wanted to scream into the phone, but he knew that would only attract attention to the mistake — should anyone be listening. He let it ride.

"All right. Go ahead and stage. When I contact you, you need to be on the ground in the following forty-eight hours. Don't get boozed up on European beer with my per diem."

Rafik left his hotel room and exited onto the crowded streets of Alexandria, Egypt. It was hot here, but the breeze off the ocean made it much more bearable than the heat around Cairo. He walked north along the shore, passing a coffee shop just off El Gaish

Road and entering the Roushdy food court. He cared little about eating at one of the Great Satan's hegemonic restaurants, but the food court allowed him to watch the café unimpeded, looking for threats before his meeting.

Taking a seat in a Kentucky Fried Chicken, he grimaced at all of the Egyptians waiting to scarf down the infidel's recipes. He turned toward the window facing the café, disgusted.

Already crowded, the coffee shop had several small round tables underneath an awning, all holding men smoking the ubiquitous shisha water pipe. His contact was a member of the Egyptian Muslim Brotherhood.

Once an underground organization that had been hunted relentlessly by the Mubarak regime, it was now the strongest political party in Egypt, torn between an old core responsive to its radical roots and a new, egalitarian base. Even as the party struggled to decide its vision of the future, the radical elements continued. They cherished their heritage as the umbrella group that had spawned and connected just about every Islamic terrorist organization in the world, including Rafik's own organization, al Qaeda in the Islamic Maghreb.

Originally called the Salafist Group for Preaching and Combat — or GSPC — al Qaeda in the Maghreb was formed during the civil war in Algeria, a particularly brutal conflict.

Rafik had decided to join the GSPC at the young age of fourteen, when he and his parents had been ripped off the streets by Algerian authorities in a random cordon and search. He was tortured unmercifully for four days, then released. He never saw his parents again. Consumed by rage, all he wanted was revenge. The GSPC provided that outlet.

As he grew older, he proved himself for higher training. In 2001 he was sent to Afghanistan, where he met the sheik himself, Osama bin Laden. He was there for the glorious strike on September 11, and also there for the fire that followed. Rounded up by the Northern Alliance and the Special Forces team with them, he was on his way to Guantanamo Bay when the prison he was in outside of Mazari Sharif — called Qala-i-Jangi — erupted in a riot. While most of the prisoners satisfied themselves by cowardly beating a CIA man to death and generally running around like lunatics, Rafik escaped, knowing how the riot would finish. He found out later that most of his brethren had died in the massive retaliation of U.S. firepower that followed.

Returning to Algeria, he was a different man. The sheik had shown him that their fight was global. He now saw that the Near Enemy, like the government in Algeria, existed at the pleasure of the Far Enemies of the West. That's who needed to be destroyed. They were the ones crushing Islam all over the world. Even now, with the shifting landscape of change sweeping the Middle East, the Far Enemy continually thwarted any attempts to return to the one true faith, instead championing a system of debauchery cloaked as democracy.

Try as he might, he couldn't convince the GSPC leadership. By 2006 he had at least convinced them to pledge loyalty to al Qaeda and change their name. He knew they did it for the publicity and that they had no desire to enter the global fight. They preferred pinprick strikes against the government of Algeria to any strategic global attack in the name of Islam.

He had set out on his own, bringing with him a select number of trusted men. He'd worked nearly five years, patiently building his plan, while al Qaeda in the Maghreb remained somewhat of a joke in the fight

for Islam. During that time, Osama bin Laden had been martyred, and al Qaeda in
the Arabian Peninsula had become the
prominent group. That was okay by him. In
less than two weeks, he would make sure
that al Qaeda in the Maghreb would cause
more damage to the Far Enemy than all
other attacks combined.

9

Jennifer came into the office as I was digging through a scattered pile of outdoor gear, looking for my neck light. I was hoping to be done packing before she arrived because she'd just give me shit about procrastinating. When I looked up, she was leaning against the doorjamb with her arms crossed.

I said, "Did you put my neck light back in my duffel after you borrowed it?"

We both knew she hadn't touched the neck light, but it was worth a shot. As usual, I was packing on the fly. She, of course, had packed her stuff perfectly in one small suitcase before she even left for Assessment in North Carolina.

"Pike, if you'd plan ahead more than five minutes, you wouldn't be flinging stuff all over the office tonight."

Yesterday afternoon, we'd flown straight back to Charleston, South Carolina, to our

little business called Grolier Recovery
Services. Situated in an office complex on
Shem Creek just outside of Charleston, we
specialized in facilitating archeological work
around the world. Jennifer had the anthro-
pology degree to talk scientist, and I had
the military background to talk to anyone
who had an issue with the scientists. We did
everything from laying the groundwork with
the host nation and U.S. embassy to providing security on-site. A one-stop shop, so to
speak. Just add pencil necks. It was a great
cover, because it gave us a plausible reason
to travel anywhere that had something of
historical significance. Which was just about
anywhere on earth.

You'd think that a business plan with
those parameters would be dead on arrival
— I mean, really, how many Indiana Jones
expeditions could there be at any given
time? — but we already had real requests
for quotes. Our splashy publicity hadn't
hurt.

We had started the business with the
proceeds we earned from finding an ancient
Mayan temple in Guatemala. For about
sixty seconds, we were all over the news,
but much longer for people who actually
cared about such things. Because of it, we
now had respectable people beating a path

to our door. Not that we needed the work, since we could count on a Taskforce pay-check.

I quit trying to find the neck light and shoved everything back into the duffel bag, slinging it into the closet on my side of our small office.

Jennifer came inside and took off her sunglasses, exposing the bruise around her right eye. The sight caused a confusing mishmash of emotions in my gut, making me feel guilty, angry, proud, protective, and shameful all at the same time

I said, "Want me to screen your bag? Make sure it's clean?"

She knew what I was asking, saying, "Yeah, I guess, but this is my first trip. How could it have anything compromising in it?"

"Good point. Just force of habit. I'll have to get used to a permanent cover. You could check my bag, though, just to be sure there's nothing left over from my past."

She took the backpack and zipped it open, going through the pockets, looking for receipts, business cards, or anything else that could cause a question on this trip. Our purpose was to camouflage Taskforce activi-ties, so everything on us had to support our business, with nothing leading to the unit. It would be bad form to have an ATM receipt from a military post when you were claiming to be a civilian. When I was operational, the hardest thing was making sure my real life didn't intrude on my cover. I couldn't believe the clutter I'd accumulate. Just check your wallet to see what I mean. I no longer had to worry about that, because my life and cover were now the same. I was no longer ping-ponging back and forth pretending to be something different every mission.

The people who came with us were different. We would be the skeleton that the Taskforce would fall in on. We had a roster of TF operators who were included as our "employees," but we'd only see them when we were tasked with an operation. Knuckles and Bull — our employees on this trip — would be the ones with the risk. Lord knows where they had been in the last six months.

In a nutshell, that was the purpose of our travel. As a company, we had to build a record with Taskforce personnel acting as employees, so we were doing what we called a "cover development" trip. Otherwise known as a "boondoggle" or "vacation on the government dime." Basically, we just wanted to start populating air travel databases, getting our passports stamped, and collecting business cards from overseas, all of which would support that we were who we said we were. It was a really sweet gig because we'd be forbidden to do anything that wasn't part of our cover. And it was truly necessary if we wanted to fool anyone with an Internet connection for more than five seconds. Jennifer, who was really into what our business did, had picked the temple of Angkor Wat in Cambodia, so that's where we were going for a week, with Knuckles and Bull as our employees.

As Jennifer worked through my bag, she asked, "How many companies are there like us?"

"Honestly, I don't know. A lot. So many that probably only the comptroller or Kurt Hale knows for sure. None have a business like ours, though. All the other companies that I know of are just that — companies full of corporate types. We're the only one founded and run by operators."

Jennifer reflexively touched her eye, looking at me with a sad, wistful expression, like a child who had saved forever to buy a toy only to be disappointed in the reality when it arrived at the door, a pale imitation of the TV commercial promises.

"I don't think anyone in the Taskforce thinks about me that way."

I regretted my choice of words, because

she was right. It would take more than some training and assessment to win them over, but she was on the way. In truth, I respected her abilities greatly, but deep down, even I still harbored a sliver of doubt. I covered it up.

"Bullshit. Knuckles doesn't feel that way anymore. He's a believer now. Anyway, who cares what those assholes think? It only matters what you think."

I changed the subject. "Knuckles will be here any minute. Where do you want to take him for dinner? He's never been to Charleston."

"I just figured you'd take him to Red's Ice House. It's why you rented this office space in the first place." She smiled. "So you could walk home."

She was partly right. I had snapped up an office on Shem Creek in the town of Mount Pleasant because the depressed economy made it a steal, but being a stone's throw from my favorite haunt hadn't hurt the sale.

"We can go wherever you want. No bars. I'll even dress up."

She zipped up my bag and stared at it for a second like she was trying to figure out what to say. What came out took me completely by surprise.

"Pike, I've already got plans tonight. I'm

meeting someone downtown. I figured you'd want a boy's night out."

"Plans? Tonight? With who?"

"Nobody. Just a college friend I haven't seen since I graduated."

"A guy?"

She didn't have to say anything. Her expression told me it was. I started shoving all the loose gear I wasn't taking back into a duffel bag, using more force than was necessary. Before it could get any more awkward, Knuckles came through the door, dragging a backpack.

"Hey, workmates. Ready to do some sightseeing on the government dime?"

He saw our expressions and said, "Did I interrupt something?"

Jennifer pulled out onto Coleman Boulevard headed toward the Ravenel Bridge, feeling a little guilty. She really *was* just meeting a friend from college, but she'd hidden it from Pike because she'd known it wouldn't be taken that way. She knew him better than he thought. She knew the terrible history and had seen the demons he constantly fought. She had simply wanted to protect him from any pain, but had failed. She had seen it in his eyes, and the hurt had boomeranged right back into her.

She knew Pike's emotions were still ragged from the loss of his family, and gave him space because of it, but the truth was she had her own confusion to deal with. There was no doubt she felt drawn to Pike, but she wasn't sure if it was real. Last year he had been willing to sacrifice his life for hers. Not once, but twice in selfless acts that had touched her core. She couldn't tell if that was affecting her feelings. If maybe she wasn't projecting a debt she felt she owed.

The idea of going to Assessment and launching the company had been intriguing, but initially she had shied away. Pike had been insistent, and she'd acquiesced simply because he'd asked. Well, mostly. She couldn't deny that some part of her had enjoyed the excitement and satisfaction of success. And Pike had promised that it wouldn't all be Taskforce business. She'd get to do some real research with real scientists. She knew it would just be to keep the cover intact, but that was good enough. Where Pike fit into all of this she was unsure.

She realized that they were going to have to talk. To get it out in the open, for real. For either good or bad.

She was broken out of her thoughts by her cell phone. Looking at the screen, she saw it was a call from Texas. She didn't recognize the number but did know the area code. As soon as she answered, she wished she hadn't.

"Hey, baby. How're you doing?"

Immediately sick to her stomach, she was taken back to the fear, like she'd never left.

"What do you want?" she said.

"Nothing. I just wanted to catch up."

"You're not supposed to contact me. Ever. Your dad promised. *You* promised."

Her voice quavered, and she hated herself for it. *You're not the same girl he beat on. You're better than that.*

"Well, Dad and I have sort of . . . fallen out. So, no more money from the trust fund, and no more agreements that he made for me."

"I've got nothing to say to you. Good-bye."

"Wait! Okay, so we can skip the small talk. I saw you found some sort of temple last year. Made a little money."

"Yes. So what."

"Well, I was hoping you'd be willing to share a little of your good fortune with me. Not a lot. Just enough to get your ex back on his feet."

She couldn't believe the audacity. "Chase, forget it. Forget this number and forget we were ever married. You're not getting a dime."

His voice went from silky to rabid. "You little bitch! I'm just asking for a little help. Consider it payback for all of my money you spent when we were married. It's only fair."

"I hear you, and I'm hanging up. Stay away."

She cut off his screaming and threw the phone in the passenger seat, shaking. The voice of her ex-husband had released a kaleidoscope of images and feelings, all competing for attention in her mind. The beating, the blood and vomit. But mostly the terror. Something she'd run from and thought she'd left behind, but his voice was enough to take her back.

It dawned on her that she had felt this same way in the saloon. Not as extreme, but a knife edge of terror facing a roomful of men all intent on beating her. Just like her ex-husband. Maybe even taking joy in it like her ex-husband. The difference had been that she had learned how to fight back. She'd been so intent on survival, she hadn't made the connection. Now it left her a little disgusted.

The Taskforce was supposed to be made of heroes. Pure, with her being Tonto to the

Taskforce Lone Ranger, both only doing what was necessary for the defense of the nation. She'd seen Pike's selfless side but had also seen him act in ways that were borderline homicidal. She'd put it down to the torture of his past. Now, she wasn't so sure. Maybe the difference between the black hats and the white hats was simply the interpretation of the artist. *Maybe they're all like my ex-husband, but they've just found an outlet for the violence.*

She wondered again if she'd made the right choice.

10

It was a little bit early, but Congressman Ellis told his secretary good-bye and left the Hart Office Building. He still needed to pack for tomorrow's travel to the international trade fair in Cairo, Egypt, and the hearings had worn him out.

He strolled at a leisurely pace up Delaware Avenue, away from the Capitol. When he reached Union Station, his heart picked up a bit. He'd either see that his instructions had been passed, and the meeting in Cairo was set, or he'd see that he'd wasted six months' worth of work.

While in D.C., he lived in a luxury condominium complex at Judiciary Square, just inside Interstate 395 on Massachusetts Avenue. It had taken quite a while to find a location close enough to a Metro station that allowed him to walk to work, and he'd looked hard. His business had to be put on hold until he could, which was a distinct motivator. There was no way he was going to attempt contact with a driver watching his every move, and going out for a walk every day would have raised someone's suspicions.

Walking home from work, however, was just a congressman judiciously using the taxpayers' money. No driver for him. No, sir. He'd rather use his God-given legs.

He went straight through the station and took the escalator down to the food court. Walking toward the Union Station Metro stop, he scanned the wall of the up escalator. There were three food-court tables against the wall, and between the second and third table, both occupied with tired tourists eating a hasty meal, he saw a Chinese character scribbled in chalk. He recognized it as the character for victory, and felt the tension leave his body. The transfer was a go.

If he'd seen the character for fail, he would have known the transfer was off. No character at all meant his Chinese contacts hadn't gotten the instructions.

He had worked for the Chinese for close to forty years, and found them just as confusing now as when he'd first made contact. They insisted on this archaic method of communication, as if it were still the seventies. Originally, they had simply used different colored chalk to denote messages, but there was so much intrigue going on in Washington that, once, they had actually confused signals with some other group. The Chinese had settled on chalking characters from their language and had steadfastly continued doing so while everyone else had gone high tech. They would order food, sit at one of the three tables, and sometime during the meal scribble out the message. Invariably, the tile of the wall would be wiped clean within twenty-four hours.

Ellis found the old-fashioned tradecraft ironic because his job involved transferring cutting-edge U.S. technology to China. He had asked to change tactics, to begin using the very technology he was transferring, but the Chinese had refused. He assumed it was because they knew nobody could hack a chalk mark, and that they liked him taking all the risks. He didn't really mind. He had to walk through the food court to get to the Metro, so it was a natural movement he took every day to get home. Nearly impossible to prove he was doing something else. So far, the risk had been worth it, with only one close call, and it hadn't involved chalk messages.

In the 1990s, three separate Chinese

rockets with U.S. satellite payloads had crashed. The U.S. satellite companies, in an effort to prevent future losses, had helped the Chinese with their rocket systems — without going through the proper channels in the State Department for release of possible military technology.

The ensuing political carnage had spawned a select committee on Chinese industrial espionage, which had caused Congressman Ellis a great deal of concern. After all, he knew that the crashes were done on purpose. The transfer of technology had been the satellites themselves, supposedly obliterated by the explosion. While they were, in fact, destroyed, the specific computer chips that regulated their functions were not.

Unwittingly, the satellite manufacturers had almost caused his downfall with their stupid release of data, all in the name of profit. Of course, the Chinese had gleefully accepted the information, getting a two-for-one deal. Ellis had managed to become a member of the investigating committee and had diverted attention away from himself, but it had been close.

He didn't consider himself a spy. Well, not in the traditional sense. He would never sell U.S. military or diplomatic secrets to the

Chinese. Only technology, letting them sort out how they would use it. He wasn't naive. He knew the information could enhance China's military systems, but in his own mind he had to draw the line somewhere.

He had started out as a case officer in the CIA during the Cold War and had become jaded at how the game was played. And to him, it was just that: a game. Friends one day, enemies the next. And it hadn't ended with the Cold War, either. It had just carried over. *Arm the Afghans with stingers to defeat the Soviets, then invade the country twenty years later, fighting the same damn Afghans we had cultivated as friends.* It was just a game, and he'd make a profit on it, just like Raytheon, Loral, or Halliburton.

Going up the elevator in his condominium complex, he reflected on the risks of this latest venture. In the past, he'd simply worked in the shadows. A key vote here, a corporate nudge there, a little information passed on locations, times, or meetings. Now he was the middleman, and it made him both excited and uneasy.

The Chinese had contacted him a little over a year and a half ago, irate, claiming he had failed to warn them about a covert action in Sudan. At the time, he'd told them the truth: He had no knowledge of any covert act against Chinese interests. While on the Intelligence Committee, he wasn't a vaunted member of the "Gang of Eight," so he wasn't privy to anything considered extraordinarily sensitive, which an attack on Chinese assets would most certainly be. The Chinese had abruptly gone silent at his protest, then come back a few months later with a request: Find them a weapon they knew existed. Obtain samples and transfer them to the Chinese.

He'd never, ever been tasked before. In fact, he didn't even consider himself an "asset" of the Chinese. More like an entrepreneur. When he'd balked, he'd received a veiled threat — something else that had never happened. While the threat irked him, he had decided to go ahead because of the money involved. He was given parameters to research by his handlers, and begun to dig, using his Intelligence Committee standings. He'd found what they were looking for in the Defense Advanced Projects Research Agency, and now was within a month of transferring the technology.

He had no idea how the Chinese knew what to look for, knew how to point him in the right direction. Maybe there were more like him in America, but he didn't think so. If there were, and they were feeding the parameters to the Chinese, why wouldn't they just feed them the device? Why make him dig, and risk exposure? At the very least, why not just tell him where to look? One thing was for sure; he was out after this. The risk was just too great. And the Chinese were now treating him a little like a doormat instead of the rock star he had been. He'd had enough of their ungrateful shit.

Opening the door, he felt his BlackBerry chime with a message to check his e-mail. *Probably a change in the flight schedule.*

He connected securely with his congressional account and saw a note from his aide, short and to the point: "You said to keep tabs on this guy." Attached was a report from the Joint POW-MIA Accounting Command detailing possible information regarding the location of Christopher Hale, MIA in 1970, Cambodia. The name brought a flash of nostalgia, a comfortable blanket he found himself wanting more and more as he grew older. *So they finally found him.*

He remembered the disbelief he had felt when the North Vietnamese had said a reconnaissance team was in the area. At first, he had dismissed the alarm, since he knew for certain where every recon team was targeted and had routinely passed that information on to the NVA. The nearest one was a full day's walk from the camp. After the gunfire erupted, he had fled with his Chinese counterparts, desperate to beat the bombing that was sure to come.

Returning to his job as CIA liaison to MACV-SOG, he had been relieved to learn the team had died, then mortified to hear one man was MIA. He had lived in absolute terror for weeks, waiting for Chris Hale to pop out of the jungle and finger him. As time went on, and the man never appeared, the terror faded, only spiking briefly in 1973 when the POWs were released by North Vietnam. Chris Hale wasn't among them.

Returning to the United States, he had forgotten all about the man, until the drive for MIAs in Vietnam had reached a fever pitch in the U.S. consciousness. He'd used his position as a newly minted congressman to be updated on the status of Hale and had done so every year since, more out of a perceived connection to the man than anything else.

He opened the report and felt a small sliver of fear. The only items listed were a reconnaissance journal and a camera. He immediately willed himself to calm down. *No way any film has lasted this long, and even if it has, the odds of it having anything besides some bamboo bunkers is nil.*

Just to satisfy his curiosity, he Googled "processing old film," and felt the fear return. Apparently, it not only could be done, but it was done routinely. There were whole Web sites dedicated to finding old cameras at garage sales, developing the film, then trying to determine who is in the picture. Several companies were solely dedicated to developing outdated formats, and claimed success with film from the early 1900s. A roll of film from 1970 was well within the art of the possible.

He returned to the JPAC report, seeing the items were currently located in the U.S. Embassy in Cambodia and that the investigation was labeled INITIAL, which meant JPAC wouldn't get to it for at least six weeks.

He closed out his account. He had too much on his plate to worry about it now. *Just have to beat JPAC to the camera when I get back.*

11

Peering out of the grimy Kentucky Fried Chicken window, through the growing throngs of Egyptian tourists, Rafik saw a young man wearing a white shirt enter the café and look at his watch. At precisely one o'clock, he sat down and removed his sunglasses. Rafik waited. The man pulled a tattered paperback book from his pocket, thumbed through the pages, then placed the book facedown on the table, still open. *So far so good.* Rafik had never met the contact from the Muslim Brotherhood and didn't know what he looked like. The only way he could be sure he wasn't walking up to a stranger or into a trap was if the contact followed his instructions to the letter.

When the man crossed his legs, the final signal, Rafik started to rise, then abruptly sat back down, a spike of adrenaline coursing through him. *Left leg over right. Not right over left.* To protect himself, he had given the contact an emergency signal. If the man was compromised and was making the meeting under duress, he was to cross his left leg over his right. If everything was fine, it would be right over left.

Rafik stared in disbelief, running through his mind all of the connections that could have lead to compromise. He came up with very, very few.

He saw the man give a small start, then recross his legs right over left. Rafik debated. *The idiot probably just screwed up.* Rafik knew he should leave and reestablish contact, but he was running out of time. A new meet might take another week to set up.

There was one more check he could do. The book was supposed to be on page 100. Anything else, and he'd leave. Approaching was a risk, but a small one. If the contact had been turned, the authorities would want the meeting to continue for the information they could glean. They wouldn't make a hasty arrest.

Rafik left the KFC and circled around to the contact's blind side. Walking as if he had another destination, he slipped into the seat next to the contact at the last second. He grabbed the book before the man could react and saw it was on page 100. He tossed the book on the table and said, "I'm the falcon. Follow me."

He stood up without looking back and wound through the close-packed alleys surrounding the food court, getting lost in the Dumpsters and garbage. When he was sure they couldn't be seen from any street, he turned abruptly, pulling a knife and thrusting the contact up against a grimy cinderblock wall.

"Empty your pockets."

The man struggled for a second, until the knife bit into his neck. Then he sagged, doing nothing.

Rafik backed off a foot. "I said empty your pockets. And open your shirt."

In short order, Rafik had determined that the man had no recording or transmitting gear.

"Why did you swap your legs?"

The man clasped his hands as if he was praying. "It was a mistake. I made a mistake. I didn't mean to do that. I'm with you. I'm one of you."

"You make a mistake like that again and we might all die." Rafik raised the knife until it was a millimeter away from the contact's left eye. "Understand this: If it happens again, one person will die for sure."

The man twitched his head vigorously, attempting to nod without putting out his eye.

Rafik said, "I'm told that you are the man who can help me get into El Nozha Airport."

The contact nodded his head but said nothing, apparently afraid to speak.

"And that there is a plane coming with special cargo."

The man nodded again.

Exasperated, Rafik said, "Tell me something I don't know. How are you, a mistake-prone child, capable of this?"

"It's coming in at night. We don't know when. My boss will get a call twenty-four hours before. I'm in the Army unit that provides security for the airport. Nobody checks anything there. I could dress up my mother in a uniform and put her on the gate. It's a closed airport, after all. Nothing really to protect."

Rafik knew that the aging El Nozha Airport had been closed for close to a month, with all commercial traffic diverted to Borg El Arab Airport outside of Alexandria. Whether this was for renovations or was a permanent condition, Rafik could never determine.

"And how is this plane landing at a closed airport?"

"I don't know. Someone was given baksheesh, I guess. I only know that we're being paid to turn on the runway lights for a period of three hours. The plane will land, do whatever it's going to do, then take off again."

Rafik already knew everything being said except the three-hour window. That would make things tight.

He knew that an American private air contractor had leveraged the chaos of the current Egyptian government by bribing several government departments to use the decrepit airport without any official knowing. Well, at least any official who was not on the payroll. He also knew the cargo, something this low-level foot soldier did not. Somewhere, during the six months of complex secret negotiations, using intermediaries throughout the Egyptian government, the cargo had been revealed. This knowledge meant little to most of the people involved, but one man, another member of the Muslim Brotherhood, had understood the significance and had sent a message to al Qaeda. Rafik had been lucky enough to be one of the many in the nebulous chain of the reporting used by the terrorist network. He was supposed to pass it along in its complex path to the al Qaeda leadership, but he instead chose to use it for his own plan.

For six months he had wondered if the message was real. If maybe he was basing a plan on a chimera. Sometimes, lying awake at night, he hoped it was fake. The mantle of responsibility was enormous, weighing him down like a wrought-iron chain around his neck. He had no grand organization like bin Laden's. Outside of his small circle, men who would follow him into hell, he had to rely on others for help. Algerian contacts in Montreal, prison recruits in the United States, and radical members of the Egyptian Muslim Brotherhood. And he still had to convince another organization to provide him with an aircrew for the plane.

Today, though, all of that was forgotten. The aircraft was real, which meant the cargo was real. Soon, *insha'Allah,* his victory would be real.

12

Bull and Knuckles were waiting for us when we returned to our hotel in Phnom Penh.

"Any issues with the embassy?" Knuckles asked.

"No," I said. "They didn't even want an ID. It was strange. Like they couldn't give me the stuff quick enough."

"They probably just figured there was no way someone would fake a name like Nephilim."

"That's what I mean. Usually, I spend fifteen minutes trying to sort out the message traffic because some idiot changed my name to Nicholas or Nestor. This time Nephilim was right on the sheet, and when I said that was me, they started throwing the stuff my way."

"Let me see it."

I pulled the Nikon SLR out of my bag and tossed it to him. Jennifer began packing her suitcase, saying, "If we get out of here quick enough, we can catch today's bus to Siem Reap. This little detour won't cost us a day at Angkor Wat."

Knuckles turned the camera over in his hands, then put it to his eye like he was taking a picture. He cocked the film lever and said, "Hey, I think this thing's loaded."

"Really?" I went over to him. "Careful. Don't break it."

He held it away from my hands. "I'm not going to break it. I'm going to get it out."

He unfolded the rewind lever and began to crank, with me hovering around like a nervous hen.

Jennifer put her hands on her hips. "Come on, guys, let's pack. We've got plenty of time to mess with that camera on the bus. Bull, can you pack up the laptop?"

"Don't force it," I said. "If it won't crank, let it go."

"I'm not forcing it. Calm down." He continued winding until we both heard the lead spin inside the camera. He smiled. "See. It's done."

Opening the back, he pulled out a roll of black-and-white Kodak TRI-X film. Exasperated, Jennifer said, "Pack up your stuff. Please. We're going to miss the bus."

From behind her, Bull said, "Yeah, pack your stuff. But don't worry about the bus."

He was looking at our corporate Web site, pulling up our e-mail through a VPN.

"What's up?" I said.

"We got a mission."

Twenty-four hours later, I was sitting in a coffee shop in Jakarta, Indonesia, playing with my smartphone. Jennifer was sitting across from me, looking a little peeved. I guess I didn't blame her. We had left Cambodia immediately, without going to Angkor Wat, and chances were we wouldn't be going back.

She said, "I thought we weren't allowed to do this stuff until we had the business established."

"Well, ordinarily that's true, but it's the risk that counts. This can't be too much adventure. Probably something simple that Johnny would rather not do for whatever reason."

All the message on the VPN had said was that Johnny — meaning Johnny's team — needed some help and had given the location of the coffee shop with a time. Because of our separate covers, Johnny wouldn't contact us directly but would use a digital dead-drop instead. We'd never even see anyone from his team. Someone would just walk or drive by and launch the message from their smartphone to ours, using an encrypted Bluetooth connection. When it was done, there'd be no history of the transmission that would connect us, unlike a cell phone text message, e-mail, or a call.

Jennifer said, "What if it's not something simple? Maybe it's something that could jeopardize our company. Are you going to do it?"

"It depends. I won't know until I see it. Anyway, you know how I feel about that. The company's just a means to an end. Not an end unto itself. You start worrying too much about that shit, and you end up paralyzed, never doing anything for fear of burning something."

A long time ago, I had had a teammate almost die because another government agency refused to help. He survived, but in the after-action review, I found out that we'd been left high and dry because the other agency was afraid of blowing its cover. The method that facilitated the operation had superseded the operation itself. I had decided then and there that I'd never let cover stand in the way of a critical mission. I wouldn't do anything stupid, but I also wouldn't let it paralyze me.

She said, "Yeah, I remember what you told me, but we haven't even started yet, and we might be destroying what took six months to build. That's something to consider, isn't it?"

Apparently, she was still wondering if I was a loose cannon like I had been when we first met. Before I could answer, my phone vibrated.

"It's here."

Jennifer looked a little startled, then glanced around trying to spot the teammate, which I knew was a losing proposition.

The message was a location for a physical dead-drop. I called Knuckles and relayed the directions.

Jennifer said, "Did it even say 'should you choose to accept it' or anything like that?"

I smiled. "Nope. Let's get Bull and Knuckles their coffee orders and see what this is about."

By the time we returned to the hotel, Knuckles had serviced the dead-drop, retrieving an encrypted thumb drive. He had it in our computer and was reading the screen.

"Well," I said, "what's the mystery?"

"Nothing big. Looks like Johnny's tracking a guy named Noordin Sungkar. He's supposed to be a facilitator for Jemaah Islamiyah and runs a travel agency here in

Jakarta."

Jemaah Islamiyah, or JI, as we called them, was an Indonesian terrorist group affiliated with al Qaeda. Like every other fanatic associated with AQ, they wanted an Islamic state based on Sharia law and were constantly blowing shit up to accomplish it. They were responsible for the Bali massacre in 2002 that killed more than two hundred innocent tourists.

"Okay," I said. "What's that mean to us?"

"Well, they've been trying to get a handle on this guy for a while. They've been watching his travel agency for over two weeks now. So far, nothing. All they want us to do is go inside and see if we can confirm or deny he even works there. If eyeballing the place is a waste of time, they want to know."

"I still don't get why they called us. Just go in there, for Christ's sake."

"There's CCTV cameras all over the building. They're afraid of pulling a Dubai if they have to hit the guy here in Indo."

A couple of years ago, someone had whacked a Hamas leader named al-Mabhouh in Dubai. Since he'd freely admitted to the stone-cold killing of two Israeli soldiers in 1989, the odds-on favorite was the Israeli intelligence service, Mossad. Whoever it was did it pretty smartly and had successfully exited the country, but the Dubai police unraveled the plot by looking at every CCTV video in the entire city, piecing together who had done what, starting with the dead guy's hotel. It had turned into a huge diplomatic row when it was discovered that the killers had used falsified passports from European Union countries. Dubai had also spread the killers' faces, taken from their passports, all over the worldwide news. Johnny was afraid of the same thing happening to them and wanted to avoid any CCTV footage linking anyone on his team to the target. Which made sense to me.

"So all he wants us to do is go in there and confirm or deny his presence?"

"Yep. And I don't want to do it, for the same reasons as Johnny. I could end up with this target two months from now."

"I don't want you to do it either. I want Jennifer to go."

Jennifer jumped up. "*Me?* I'm not an . . . I'm not in the Taskforce."

"You're not what?" I said.

Knuckles said, "I think that's a great idea. It's a travel agency, so you can just do what we were already doing. Find some old shit here in Indo that we can go look at. That should make you happy."

She looked from Knuckles to me, then at Bull, who nodded his head with a grin.

"Jesus Christ. What a bunch of babies. Let me see the instructions."

13

Congressman Ellis looked at his watch. He had rushed over to the Cairo convention center to meet his contact while the rest of the delegation got over jet lag at the hotel, but he couldn't spend a great deal of time here before the delegation began to wonder where he was. He expected a quick meeting, and now didn't like the answers he was getting.

"What do you mean you can't do anything?" he said. "This guy has a camera that might have my picture on it with Chinese officers. It could destroy our relationship."

Han Wanchun gave a little shrug. "What on earth do you want me to do? I'm a simple businessman. I cannot help it if you get in trouble."

"Don't give me that shit. I have a copy of his passport and his last itinerary. He's in Jakarta right now. That's close enough for your people. We need to get that camera."

Han was attending the international trade fair in Cairo as a representative of the Great Wall Industry Corporation, hiding his association with the People's Liberation Army.

"You wish me to track someone down in Jakarta while I'm in Egypt? I think you're growing a little paranoid. Is there something else I should be aware of? Something to do with our business?"

"I'm not paranoid. Just careful. The camera was in the U.S. Embassy in Cambodia. It should have stayed there until I could get to it, but somehow this man managed to get them to hand it over, against regulations. I did some digging on him, and he owns a company that has no history. No travel, credit purchases, or anything else. It stinks."

Han smiled. "So you think this company is fake? A costume for something else?"

Exasperated at the dance, Ellis said, "Yes, just like your damn company. I'm not asking you to fly to Indonesia. Get some friends in the MSS to do it."

Han looked at the booths to his left and right, making sure nobody next door had heard the outburst. Ellis realized he'd overstepped. While they both knew how ludicrous the pretending was, Ellis had never outright called any of his Chinese contacts liars or mentioned their association with the Chinese Ministry of State Security, the organ that conducted foreign espionage.

"Watch yourself, Mr. Ellis. You fear what's on the camera when the real danger is in front of you. If I *had* contacts with State Security, I might be inclined to call them for other reasons."

Ellis backpedaled. "I just meant you have a lot of pull with the Chinese government and could probably help. Nothing more. It would be conducive to our business."

"Let's discuss that first. When and where will we transfer the equipment?"

"Here in Cairo. I'll give you specific instructions later. A plane will land at the airport in Alexandria, and I'll transport the equipment here. From there, I'm out of it. It's up to you to get it out of the country."

"When? We are only here for one week."

Ellis passed him a local cell phone he'd purchased. "I'll call you twenty-four hours before the transfer. It'll be within a week."

He glanced at his watch. "Look, I have to get back to my delegation before they wonder what happened to me. I don't want to meet again. Are we good?"

Han said, "Yes, up to a point. If I haven't heard from you in five days, I'm going to find you. You won't have to worry about the

126

camera."

Ellis felt sweat trickle down his sides. "Hey, no need for threats. I've always been good. Ask your other folks. We go back a long ways. The proof may be on that camera."

"I'll make some calls. Forget about the camera. Focus on the transfer. Give me the information on the man."

Ellis gave him all he knew and left, winding his way back through the maze of booths. As he walked, he replayed the conversation in his mind. He realized the power scale had shifted. Somewhere along the line, he had fallen from a valued asset to a tool to be used. He had always called the shots, with the Chinese accepting whatever he offered. Now he was being outright threatened to produce. Even with the risk of the camera, an uncomfortable truth settled in: His greatest danger was no longer his own country discovering his activities. He'd never seen that coming.

14

Keshawn walked through the woods around the substation, sketching what he could see of the interior. This one was a distribution point, one of the substations around the state that took the power from high-voltage lines coming from the generation plants and stepped down the voltage to something the residents and businesses could use. He was looking for the piece of equipment that made the step-down possible — an extremely high voltage transformer. He didn't know why, but he'd been tasked to gather information on every substation that housed an EHVT. So, when his daily rounds took him by one, he stopped and sketched. Not many of them did, but enough to keep him busy.

He'd been specifically told to look at the line of sight, to find a vantage point where he could clearly see the transformer from outside the chain-link fence. A position where the view wasn't blocked by the myriad of other components inside the substation. The contact had said, "See where you could attack it from the outside with a rifle."

He knew that a rifle would do little damage to the transformer, since each one weighed over twenty tons and stood fifteen feet tall, but he liked the sound of the tasking.

Attack.

15

After pushing Jennifer to enter the travel agency, I had worried like a grandmother until she was out. Not about her safety, but about whether she'd get the information. It was a simple task, but the repercussions would ripple through the Taskforce grapevine if she failed. Precisely because it *was* a simple task. I should have known the worrying was a waste of time. After all, I'd trained her.

Jennifer had had no trouble inside the travel agency. She found out that the JI guy maintained an office there but was out of town for another week. Maybe more. She'd spent most of her time setting up a trip to Solo on the eastern part of the island, where archeologists had found one of the earliest known hominid skeletons. Whatever the hell a hominid is.

After passing the information, we spent a day and a half at a UNESCO world heritage site, Jennifer running around like a child while the rest of us wondered if the hotel had a bar. Fortunately, before Jennifer could find other sites to go explore, we got another message. Which meant another mission. Johnny was really wearing out his welcome, but it did get us out of the jungle and back to Jakarta.

Knuckles got the coffee this time. "He wants to meet to talk about it. I didn't get any instructions."

"Where?"

"A place called the Bar Fly Club. It's on Jalan Jaksa. Apparently, it's where all the expats hang out, so we'll blend in fine."

Contacting Johnny or his team face-to-face was a risk because it would tie our two covers together when they had no business meeting, like a Wall Street banker having lunch with a pimp. It would have to be carefully managed.

"What's the plan?"

"Pretty simple. He'll be playing darts. We'll get a beer, then go play darts with him. Introduce ourselves as fellow Americans, bullshit a little bit, then get down to business."

It was plausible. Expatriates naturally congregated, so our actions wouldn't draw too much attention. As long as neither of us was being targeted, it should work. Knuckles read my mind.

"He's sure his guys are clean. They've done nothing to spike. He'll have the team wash us. Once we get to the bar, we just get a table and wait. If we see another teammate join Johnny at darts, it means we're clean and the meeting's a go. If nobody shows by seven thirty, we walk out, meeting canceled."

We spent the rest of the day scouting the area. At precisely seven, we entered the bar. It was a seedy little place, consisting of outdoor seating and a small inside area with a pool table and a dartboard. It was already crowded with backpackers staying in the hostels on Jalan Jaksa and expats from all over the world lined up at the bar. Johnny was at the dartboard, throwing with another man I didn't recognize.

We got a few beers and took the only inside table that was open, trying to talk over the groan of the overworked and useless air conditioner.

Jennifer watched the dart game for a minute, then said, "Is Johnny religious?"

Knuckles laughed. "Hell, no. Why?"

"His baseball cap has a Bible verse on the back."

Knuckles looked at me, passing the ball

for the answer. I said, "Uhh . . . That's just an inside joke. A Taskforce joke."

Before I had to explain further, a man I did recognize joined Johnny's group. I couldn't recall his name, but he was Taskforce.

Knuckles said, "That's our cue."

We got up and sauntered over to the dartboard, spending twenty minutes introducing ourselves, throwing darts, and generally playing the "where you from" game like expats always did. Finally, Johnny said, "You're clean. Let's get a table outside."

We were assaulted by the heat as soon as we exited. Even at night, the humidity caused my clothes to stick. Johnny found an isolated spot and didn't waste any time. "I want you guys to do a B&E on the travel agency and get into Noordin's computer."

The task caught me by surprise. Breaking and entering wasn't a risk-free proposition, and he already had the experts here for that. I couldn't understand why he wanted to even enter in the first place.

I said, "We've got the best hackers in the world in D.C. Why take the risk of breaking in?"

"Yeah, I know, and we've already cracked the network, but there's close to a hundred computers in that building, all on the same

ISP. The guys have to go through each one, line by line, to see if it's the right one. It'll take a month."

Knuckles chimed in. "So? That's what we do. Slow and patient. You push the issue, and you'll burn the Taskforce."

"I know, but there's a lot of chatter right now. Something big is going on, and the boss is willing to push it. Nobody has any leads, and this guy might be involved. CIA, FBI, and DOD are all pinging red, but with nothing concrete. It's coming from all sorts of groups. JI, GSPC, AQ — everyone's talking about a hit."

"Why us?" I said. "You've got the Taskforce team. We've only got a couple of operators and a cover organization."

"Because you've already seen the inside of the building. You know the layout."

"Bullshit. Jennifer's the only one that's been inside."

"Right."

He didn't say anything else, and it dawned on me that he wanted *Jennifer* to do the B&E.

"Whoa. Wait a minute. We're just the cover organization. You guys do the operations. We just facilitate."

"Pike, come on, don't feed me that shit. You're the only cover organization in the

Taskforce that's run by operators. What did you think was going to happen when you started traveling? You expect me to believe you wanted to sit on the sidelines?"

I looked at Jennifer and saw she had caught the reference. He had said operators. Plural.

He continued, "You know this makes sense. Why send in someone who doesn't know the floor plan when you can send in someone who's already been inside?"

He had a valid point. It's exactly what I'd do — if I had my own team. But I didn't, and Jennifer was brand spanking new. She'd never done anything like this outside of training, and it was my fault she was in this position. I'm the one who had forced her to go inside in the first place. This was a much bigger risk, and Knuckles saw it the same way.

He said, "Johnny, I agree with what you're saying, but I don't know. Jennifer's not ready for this. She's never done a live operation."

"Jesus," Johnny said. "She's not going in alone. She'll have my team there with her. I just want to use her knowledge of the floor plan. We'll do the hard work."

Jennifer spoke up. "I'll do it."

We all looked at her as if we'd forgotten

she was there.

"I'll do it on one condition. My guys go inside with me. No offense."

I scowled and she mouthed *What?* I looked at Knuckles and Bull. "What do you think?"

Bull said, "If someone's going in regardless, might as well be us getting the high adventure."

Knuckles nodded, saying, "I'm game, but I think it's a bad idea all the way around. Not Jennifer or us going in, but anyone going in. Too risky. Especially for a fishing trip."

Johnny was smiling, knowing he'd won. "It's not my call. Someone getting paid the big bucks wants it done, so don't fret over it."

I said, "Okay. What was your plan?"

"Well, we haven't seen any security guards — even with the jewelry wholesaler on the third floor — so that's not a threat. Basically, the place is wired with CCTV cameras and an alarm system, but they're all linked into a central hub. Unfortunately, it's a closed network. We can't find an access point on the Web, and we've looked hard. We can still gain control of the SCADA system if we can just get to a wire anywhere on the network."

SCADA stood for supervisory control and data acquisition and was an egghead phrase for the computer system that controlled the security of the building. It came from industrial processes where a computer monitored all aspects of production to ensure efficiency. More and more commercial facilities were networked this way, with one overarching computer controlling everything from the air-conditioning to the lighting — sometimes in a location hundreds of miles away from the building.

I said, "Where were you planning on gaining SCADA control?"

"There's a blockhouse out back. We're pretty sure that's where the lines are feeding. Once we had control, one team would enter while another pulled security, using the cameras all over the building."

"How sure are you about the blockhouse?"

Johnny grimaced. "Well, not one hundred percent. I was going to crack that first, put on a slave unit, then crack the building. If we couldn't figure it out, or the blockhouse was bad, we'd just pull back."

Knuckles said, "You just need a data line that's in the network?"

Johnny nodded. "Yeah. We only need about two inches for the slave unit to function. It's got a broadcast range of about a quarter mile, so anywhere nearby's good enough."

"Why not just use one of the wires coming out of the cameras?"

"We thought about that, but they're all on the exterior of the building above the second floor. I thought it would be easier to crack the blockhouse than climb the building. We don't have any climbing gear."

"But if you tagged the camera, you'd *know* you had the network, right?"

"Yes," Johnny said. "But I just told you, we don't have any climbing gear, and I'm not risking a guy trying to do that freehand. If he fell, the whole operation would be shot. On camera, no less."

I saw where Knuckles was going. "But what if you had the climbing gear? That'd be a better choice, wouldn't it?"

"Yeah, it would." He squinted at me. "Don't tell me you guys brought climbing gear."

"Something better. We brought a monkey."

16

Jennifer was halfway up the drainpipe to the third floor when she heard movement below her. She saw three men milling around the corner of the building, half in and half out of the shadows. Her foot slid against the pipe, making a soft clanking noise. She held her breath. *Please don't look up.*

When Pike had made the monkey comment, she knew they were talking about her. At first, she had violently disagreed, saying that Johnny was right. There was just too much risk. Pike had worn her down until she eventually agreed to at least see if she could climb the building before she made a decision. She knew it was a simple four-story square from her earlier visit, but she hadn't really looked for a way up on the outside.

It turned out to have a solid drainpipe on the back corner, which was hidden in the shadows from the street. Each floor had what looked like a foot-and-a-half ledge circling the building, with a six-foot alley separating the target from the buildings next door. The cameras in question were on the third floor.

She knew she could climb the building with ease. Pike knew it too and had worked on her until she agreed. In truth, she had secretly been a little thrilled by the challenge. Now, twenty-four hours later, her hands becoming slippery in the cloying humid air, she wondered what the hell she'd been thinking.

Her earpiece crackled, and Pike's voice came through like a megaphone. "Koko, you set yet?"

Jesus Christ, that was loud. She looked down and saw that there were only two men now. Neither glanced up. She clicked twice for no, then clicked rapidly four times. She heard the crackle again while still fumbling with her volume control.

"I understand you have a situation."

She clicked once for yes.

"Roger. I copy. Do you need assistance?"

She thought about it, knowing assistance would cause the mission to be scratched. She didn't want to be the reason for that. *If they didn't hear the first transmission, they won't hear me move. As long as I'm careful.*

She clicked twice, and slowly began to climb.

Five minutes and two near-slips later, she was on the third-floor ledge, looking at the cameras seventy feet away.

"Pike, this is Koko. I'm on the third floor."

Stupid call sign. While at Solo, Jennifer had explained to Knuckles the importance of the Java man hominid and his possible link between apes and humans. She had made the mistake of talking about Koko, a lowland gorilla that could communicate in sign language. Knuckles had then given her the name as her call sign for the mission. It had done no good to explain that lowland gorillas weren't monkeys.

"Roger," Pike said. "Standing by."

Movement inside the building caught her attention. She could see the glass cases of the jewelry wholesaler in the security lighting, full of samples for retailers to peruse. Just outside the door, behind the bars, stood a man.

"Pike, there's someone inside the building. At the jewelry store."

There was a pause, then, "Roger. Security guard?"

"No. Stand by."

The man had bent down and opened a duffel bag. He pulled out a hammer and a canvas sack, setting them carefully on the ground next to the door. Then he pulled out a cordless drill.

"He's a thief. He's got a drill. He's breaking in." Her voice came out rushed and panicky, embarrassing her.

Pike's came back like he was ordering doughnuts. "Roger all. Break-break, Johnny, we're aborting. I say again, we're aborting."

"Roger. I copy."

Jennifer cut in. "Pike, I can't get down. There's two men at the bottom of my drainpipe. I can't jump from this height."

Pike's voice reflected urgency for the first time. "I copy. What's the guy inside doing?"

The man had placed his duffel bag by the stairwell and was kneeling in front of the door, working a drill bit into the drill. The canvas sack and hammer were by his side. Clearly, he intended to defeat the lock, set off the alarm, then use the hammer to smash the glass cases in the jewelry store, stealing whatever he could before the police arrived.

"He's preparing to drill the lock. When he gets through that, the alarm's going to go off."

"Roger. Johnny, how'd he get in? Has he already set off an alarm?"

"I won't know for sure without the

SCADA, but I don't think so. My bet is that alarm is pretty damn loud. I doubt they'd have just a silent one."

The man had finished with the bit and began working the lock.

"Pike, he's drilling."

Pike came back immediately. "Go to the camera. Initiate the slave unit. Johnny, shut off the alarm. Don't let it go off."

Jennifer had begun moving before he was done, reaching the camera in seconds. She heard Johnny say, "Then what?" followed by Pike's "How should I know? One step at a time."

She found the wire with the red stripe leading out of the camera. *Should be the data line.* She pulled out the slave unit, a device the size of an average pager with a small antenna on the side. On the bottom were two claws designed to cut through the insulation to the metal beneath. She clamped the unit onto the wire, seeing a blinking red light. *This is great. The alarm's going to go off and I'm going to have a spotlight on my ass like a bad King Kong movie.*

She watched the man drill, her stomach knotting up. She saw the slave unit begin blinking alternately green and red, meaning it had the data line and was doing an encrypted handshake with Johnny's receiver. She knew once it went pure green, it would take a few seconds for the hacking team in Washington, D.C., to gain control. *Come on, come on.* The man pulled back, shaking his hands and resting for a couple of seconds. Then he returned to the lock.

Knuckles, Bull, and I were just outside the front door, where I could see the leads to an alarm system. *How the hell did that guy get in?*

Knuckles was grinning a little. "I told you this was a bad idea."

I nudged Bull. "Time to beat your record."

He pulled out a lockpick kit and selected a couple of tools. We could have used something like an electric rake gun, but those types of things left marks, and we were supposed to be in and out without any evidence. Luckily, Bull was the fastest I had ever seen at cracking an unknown lock mechanically. He could go through five doors in the time it took me to do one.

While he inserted the tools into the bolt lock, Knuckles and I slid a piece of Kevlar fabric that looked like a deflated tube balloon between the joint of the door and wall, just underneath the knob. Once Bull opened the bolt lock, we'd inflate the balloon using a compressed CO_2 cartridge, which would separate the joint far enough apart to spring the doorknob with a screwdriver.

We waited for the all-clear from Johnny, like a NASCAR pit crew. I heard Jennifer say, "I've got green. Shut it off. Shut it off. He's leaning into the drill. He's close."

Johnny said, "We're working it. Hold on."

Not enough time. I whispered to Knuckles and Bull, "Get ready to run to the drainpipe. Looks like a hot exfil."

Jennifer came back on. "Shit. He's in."

17

Jennifer watched the thief kick open the door. She tensed, waiting for the earsplitting sound of an alarm. She started when she heard Johnny through her earpiece instead.

"I have control. The alarm's off. I can see both the two outside and the asshole inside."

She sagged against the wall, watching the man run inside with his hammer and sack. After a few steps, he stopped, looking at the ceiling and wondering why the alarm hadn't triggered. Then he sauntered over to the first glass case and smashed it with a hammer. Reaching inside, he began stuffing his sack.

Pike came on. "All elements, we're going to take care of the burglar, then get Jennifer inside the building through a window. We'll exfil together out the front."

Seeing the bars on the windows of the jewelry wholesaler, Jennifer said, "Pike, the windows here are sealed for security. I can get down to the second floor without those guys seeing me. Then you wouldn't have to mess with the burglar."

"Sorry. I'm not helping these assholes clean out that jewelry store. We shut off the alarm for them. Find another window while we deal with him."

Huh. Didn't expect that. She looked up and saw a window above her cracked a few inches. "The fourth floor's good. I see an open window."

"Okay. We're inside. Wait until I call again, then meet us in the jewelry store."

Johnny cut in. "Koko, didn't you say the travel agency was on the fourth floor?"

Jennifer clicked once, not stopping her climb.

"You still have the thumb drive?"

Now on the fourth-floor ledge, she stopped and said, "Yeah. I'll see what I can do."

She snaked through the window and retraced her steps from a few days ago. Within short order, she was inside Noordin's office, waking up his computer. When it came to life, she saw a password screen. She shut down the computer, inserted the thumb drive, and rebooted. When the screen came back up, she was inside his system.

She accessed the Internet and typed in the Web page Johnny had given her. The only thing on the screen was a button that said Enter. She clicked on it. Nothing appeared to happen.

"Johnny, I'm inside and clicked on the Web page, but it didn't do anything."

"It's not supposed to. We got it. We're good."

She left the office exactly as she found it, rebooting the computer to bring up the password screen. She reached the stairwell and was about to head down when her radio crackled again.

"Pike, the other two assholes have entered the building. They're in the stairwell headed up."

We had just finished tying up the first thief when the call came in. *Shit, Jennifer's going to run into them.* A second later, I was thinking that wasn't a bad idea.

"Koko, this is Pike. Come down the stairs until you see them. Let them get a good look at you, then haul ass to the jewelry store. Come right through the door. You copy?"

After a pause, I heard, "Uhh . . . Okay. You'd better be right there."

"We'll be there. Hurry."

Bull and Knuckles looked at me like I had started smoking crack.

"Bull, get over by the counter. Knuckles, grab that chain."

Knuckles got the idea and laid it in front of the door, me on one end and him on the other.

Jennifer came on, out of breath. "I'm on the way! And they're right behind me!"

Seconds later she came flying through the door. Once she passed, we raised the chain to ankle height. Both thieves hit it at a dead sprint, sending them sailing across the floor and crashing headfirst into the wall. Bull was on them immediately, but it was unnecessary. Like their partner, they were out cold.

Knuckles stood up, surveying the damage. "Man, what a clusterfuck. It's great being back with you, Pike."

Jennifer was sucking in oxygen as if she'd just run five miles, her hand on her knees, still pumped by the adrenaline, but the comment brought out a laugh. "Look at the bright side. At least we accomplished the mission."

Bull stared at her for a second, apparently sizing her up for the first time. "Yeah, I guess you did."

I winked at Jennifer. *Another believer.* She

grinned.

"Well," I said, "if you guys think I can get us out of here without a lightning strike, I say we take these assholes out and drop them off somewhere. When they wake up, they won't come back here and certainly won't be going to the police about a bunch of gringos."

Bull said, "What about all the damage in here? This wasn't too clandestine."

"Let 'em think Batman showed up. Nothing's missing. We're not on camera and neither are they. Johnny's replaced that footage."

It was a little bit of work, but forty minutes later, I opened my hotel room door, completely spent from the adrenaline of the last couple of hours. When I turned on the light, I saw my room had been ransacked.

Jesus, this place is full of thieves.

Luckily, I had nothing of value that couldn't be replaced. Jennifer had our laptop, and the only thing I cared about was Kurt's camera. With a start, I realized it wasn't where I had left it. The journal was there, but not the camera. I ripped through the small room to no avail, finding the film in my shirt pocket on the bed, but not the camera. It was gone.

Shit. Kurt's going to have my head.

18

Kurt Hale quit listening to the director of Central Intelligence, since the man was saying the same thing he had already heard from a score of other officials, including his own team of analysts. Hell, even the DEA was reporting on it. A hit was coming. Potentially a big one. The indicators spiked from all sources, HUMINT, SIGINT, everything. And despite all of the intelligence, there wasn't a single concrete thread of when or where. The only unique thing, which wasn't a comfort, was that at least four different terrorist groups were discussing it.

Kurt watched the facial expressions on the Oversight Council members and saw that some weren't convinced. As the Task-force commander, he wasn't a voting member of the council, so he waited until he was asked to speak. Waited and watched the debate.

When the DCI finished, Anthony Brookings, the secretary of state, said, "We get this sort of intel all the time. It doesn't mean something catastrophic is going to happen in the next few weeks. It doesn't even mean it's going to happen at all. I don't think loosening the reins of Project Prometheus is the answer."

The DCI threw his briefing folder on the table. "No, we *don't* see this all the damn time. We did see it once before, though. In August and September of 2001. It's coming, and we can sit here and watch it, or try to prevent it."

"Quit being so melodramatic," said Secretary Brookings. "We heard this same level of chatter at the turn of the century. There were going to be these massive terrorist attacks on the millennium, and we got nothing. Nada. Zip." He turned to President Warren. "Sir, letting Prometheus run riot is asking for trouble. What happened with the team in Indonesia is a prime example. I was against that, and I'm against this. I was hoping that incident would have knocked some sense into people."

Kurt bristled at the comments about the Taskforce. He was also against pushing the issue in Indonesia, preferring to let the hackers work it out, but he'd sent in the

152

team when told to by this very council. *Quit blaming the guys on the ground, you chicken-shit.*

The secretary of defense cut in. "Hang on, nobody's saying let 'em run riot, but something needs to be done. We're getting nowhere with traditional intel. If there's another 9/11 on the way, then the risks have increased."

"Risks? Risks! What do you think's going to happen if word gets out that we're running some sort of secret assassination squad around the world? This whole administration's going down. Congress will dismantle our entire counterterrorist apparatus. You think that's good for America? We won't get any intelligence next time."

President Warren's voice was cold. "Tony, I never want to hear you categorize Project Prometheus like that again. I understand your misgivings, and I welcome your insight, but I won't tolerate you belittling the men that we put into harm's way. Those same men saved your ass last year."

Secretary Brookings flushed, but pressed ahead. "Sir, remember it's an election year. Now is not the time to get more aggressive."

President Warren said, "What the hell does that have to do with anything? I don't think the terrorists care about my campaign, and

I'm certainly not going to let an attack occur because of politics."

Brookings said, "That's not what I meant. It's not your choice. The opposition probably has a hundred people trying to dig up dirt on you. Your greatest strength is on national security. They'll be digging hard to find something to turn that strength into a weakness. They don't need to worry about domestic issues, because the economy's in the gutter. All you have going for you is national security, and they'll be looking to put a stake through your heart. We should be getting more cautious, not less, because they might stumble on the Taskforce."

President Warren turned to Kurt. "What do you think?"

Kurt paused, then said, "I think it's a moot point right now. We don't have anything to go on, so there's not anywhere we can 'run riot' anyway." He locked eyes with Secretary Brookings as he finished.

President Warren said, "But you think it's coming?"

"Yes. I do. In my mind, the question isn't whether it's coming, but how big it will be. All of the groups talking about it have subordinate affiliations with al Qaeda. That indicates they're cooperating, which is something we haven't seen on this scale.

Cooperating with AQ, yes, but not horizontally with each other for a single attack. They do unilateral acts, then claim it was done on behalf of AQ."

"Does that help us in any way?"

"Maybe. With that much chatter, we should have some leaks somewhere, which is what really concerns me. How can all of these groups be talking about it, yet we never get anything we can sink our teeth into? Whoever's the head honcho is very, very good. Compartmentalizing everything."

"Or," said Secretary Brookings, "there isn't an attack on the way."

President Warren ignored him. "What did you get out of the Indonesia Op?"

Kurt said, "The guy's a facilitator, no doubt about it, but he's pretty small-time. His travel company has some airframes that I'm sure have been used for bad reasons, and he's got offices in Prague and Bangkok, along with a ton of financial information we've turned over to the FBI, but nothing related to this."

The secretary of defense said, "What about rolling him up? The team's still there, right? We do an Omega operation and then wring him out. If he's a terrorist facilitator, he needs to be gone anyway."

"Johnny's team's there, but he's not. He's

in Cairo at some international trade fair. If you guys give me Omega authority, I can lay the groundwork for when he returns."

Secretary Brookings said, "Cairo? We've got a congressional delegation there right now." He looked at President Warren. "Attending an international trade fair."

The DCI said, "Shit. Maybe that's the target."

Kurt said, "Wait. Noordin's not a big player. He's certainly not a hitter."

"But he could be facilitating someone else who is."

President Warren said, "Can you shift Johnny's team in Indonesia to Cairo? At least keep an eye on this guy?"

"Not without a large amount of risk. They're supposedly contracted to an Indonesian company for cellular phone infrastructure. If they get investigated in any way while in Egypt, starting with customs, they'll last about twenty minutes."

President Warren said, "Maybe we lean on the Egyptians if that happens. Get a little something for all of the money we give them."

Kurt smiled. He knew that Egypt receiving more U.S. monetary aid for defense than any other country on earth, including Israel, grated on President Warren. Especially after the fall of Mubarak. "I have a better idea. Pike's company deals with archeological work. I can get him to Egypt with little trouble. There's no better place to look at old shit."

"Pike?" said Secretary Brookings. "Isn't he the one who just caused the incident in Indonesia?"

"Uh . . . no," Kurt said. "He's the one who *prevented* an incident in Indonesia."

Twenty minutes later the meeting wrapped up, with Kurt jotting down some final notes for the movement of Pike's team. President Warren stopped by him before leaving.

"How did it work out with the Cambodian Embassy? Did you get your father's things?"

Kurt grimaced. "Yes, sir, but believe it or not, someone broke into Pike's hotel room in Indonesia and took the camera."

"You're kidding."

"Nope. I appreciate the pull you used, but I guess I should have just let nature take its course."

"I'm sorry to hear that. I know how much those articles meant to you."

"It's not all bad. The camera had some film in it, which is more than I would have hoped. Pike's mailing it to me. With any luck, there'll be something interesting on it from my father."

19

Congressman Ellis laughed politely at the banter of his congressional brethren as they stood in a circle waiting for their transportation. Glancing across the lobby of the Conrad Hotel, he visibly blanched. Walking purposely across the floor was a man who looked remarkably like the passport photo of the guy from Cambodia.

He watched the man all the way to the elevator, only pulling his eyes away when he felt someone tugging on his sleeve. "Hey, you all right?"

"Yeah, yeah, I'm okay. Sorry. I thought I saw someone I knew."

"Well, you have any input on where we go for dinner? Jack here wants to go to some belly-dancing place the consulate recommended."

Ellis felt queasy, wanting to run. "That sounds fine. Could you hold the limo? I left something in my room."

Before the man could answer, Ellis began swiftly walking toward the elevators. He exited at his floor and moved straight to the house phone on a table. If that was the man, a phone call would confirm it. There was no way two people would have the same name.

"Yes, could I get the room of Nephilim Logan, please?"

After spelling it for the hotel operator, he waited, praying to hear that nobody by that name was registered. Instead, he heard the phone start ringing. He swiftly hung up before anyone could answer.

He leaned against the table, feeling faint. The man was clearly here because of him. But how? Where had he gone wrong? There was no way the guy could know about the transfer of equipment, and Han had told him the camera had no film. But maybe it did. Maybe the man had it. Then why not just confront him? What's staying at the same hotel going to get him? *Maybe the pictures didn't come out clear enough to finger me. Maybe it's just enough to raise suspicions, and he's waiting on me to hang myself.* Ellis ran-walked to his room, the sweat on his neck feeling clammy in the over-air-conditioned hallway.

Snatching up the pay-as-you-go cell

phone, he anxiously waited for Han to answer.

"Hello," Han said. "I'm assuming this is my twenty-four-hour call?"

"Han, no. The deal's off. I think someone's on to us."

Ellis heard nothing but breathing for a moment.

"Congressman Ellis, the deal is not off. You have been paid handsomely up front and we have worked too hard to make this occur."

"Listen to me! The guy from Cambodia is here. In Cairo. In my fucking hotel! He knows. Or he at least suspects. No way am I going to do the transfer. I'll be playing right into his hands."

Han said, "The man from Cambodia is a nobody. We checked him out. His company has no history because it's brand-new, but he did find a lost Mayan temple last year. He spent his time in Indonesia looking at old fossils. He is what he says he is."

"That's what he wants you to think! Jesus, you guys shouldn't be fooled that easily. I used to do this shit for a living, and I'm telling you he's on to me. We need to postpone."

"Listen to me closely. We will not postpone. You will bring the equipment here in

160

the next four days, or we will out you ourselves. So you have a choice; maybe get caught by this phantom because of the transfer, or definitely get caught by not doing the transfer."

Congressman Ellis couldn't believe what he was hearing. Two absolutely impossible choices. Clearly, the Chinese felt he was of no more use. *They must be looking at my poll numbers.* Ellis was in trouble for reelection and was considering simply not running again after learning how much money he could make on this score. But he had never considered the second-order effect, that the Chinese would throw him away.

He squeezed his eyes shut, running through options.

"Okay, okay. I'll do the transfer if you take care of the man. Get rid of him."

"You'll do the transfer, period."

"No! No, I won't! I *will not* call the plane. You said he was a nobody, so it shouldn't matter. Just get rid of him."

Ellis waited, praying that Han agreed.

"You will hear something in the next few days. Then I will hear you tell me the aircraft is on the way."

Ellis hung up the phone and sagged onto his bed with his head in his hands.

I entered my room on the seventh floor and found Knuckles already there.

He asked, "How's it look?"

"Not too bad. The front's got plenty of standoff for any sort of vehicle-borne IED, and the circular drive has a pretty good chicane leading up to the front door. The south side's the issue. It butts up right against an alley, with a neighborhood starting right on the other side. Easy to get a large VBIED there. What about you?"

"Interior security's pretty good. X-ray and metal detectors on all doors, and manual baggage checks for any workers coming in. I talked to the concierge. They've stepped it up some because of the guests, doubling the security force."

When Kurt had diverted us to keep an eye on Noordin, he'd also tasked us with checking out the security posture of the congressional delegation's hotel. Knuckles and I were doing that while Bull and Jennifer went to the Cairo convention center to get a handle on our target.

"So," I said, "all we need to do is make sure that none of the delegation has rooms on the south side. I'll pass that and let Kurt sort it out."

I heard someone fumbling with a card key outside and opened the door. Jennifer came through, smiling like she'd found another hominid.

"I take it things went well?"

Bull said, "Better than well. We've got him for the next few days with little work on our part."

Jennifer said, "He's going on sightseeing trips. Tomorrow's the pyramids, then a day trip up to Alexandria on the coast."

Bull said, "Koko here got us on the same trips. So we don't have to work at all to keep him in sight, *and* we get to go look at old shit. She's in heaven."

Jennifer's smile left her. "Okay, I get the use of a call sign on the radio, but would you please use my name in normal conversation. Koko's a damn gorilla."

She didn't understand that the call sign was a good thing. Something that was earned and proof of further acceptance. I let it ride.

"Did you get a facial ID?" I said, meaning did they have a photograph.

"No," Jennifer said. "But I did see him. He was wearing a name tag for the convention."

"Did he see you?"

"No. I was in a crowd walking by. No way he saw me."

"Okay, you two stand down. I don't want to risk burning you. Knuckles, head over to the convention and get a shot of everyone in his booth. We'll have Jennifer ID the right guy, then we'll all know what he looks like."

20

The bus ride up to Alexandria went the same as our entire day at the pyramids — uneventful. Noordin had stumbled around gawking like every other tourist, taking pictures and paying outrageous prices for bottled water from the swarms of Egyptians just outside the gates. I was beginning to wonder if he wasn't in Cairo on legitimate business.

Our first stop was the Library of Alexandria. Jennifer had given all of us a history lesson on how the Greeks had ruled Egypt and built this incredible library, only to see it destroyed. She was itching to get a look at the remains. Instead, we pulled up to a huge, modern-day library. We thought maybe they'd built a new library around the old one, but no, it was just a library — albeit one that commemorated the spirit of the original.

The entire bus spent about five minutes

inside, apparently wondering, like us, why the tour guide thought we might want to check out some modern-day books. Noordin bought some more trinkets at the souvenir shop and we left scratching our heads.

Jennifer said, "The catacombs had better be real."

Our next stop was a burial site called Kom el-Shoqafa. Apparently a great historical find, and something that Jennifer was looking forward to. We'd already gotten the classes on it from her.

I said, "We're probably going to a modern cemetery. Don't get upset."

The bus wove its way into a densely packed neighborhood, with the buildings an arm's length apart. We eventually stopped outside a simple metal gate. We let Noordin exit first, then followed. Getting inside, there was nothing to see. Just a ticket booth. There were some artifacts around the grounds with a couple of Asian tourists taking happy snaps of each other around them.

The tour guide led us to a circular stairwell, and before I knew it, we were about sixty feet below ground level inside what was definitely an ancient catacomb. Small hallways branched out in all directions, with the walls hollowed out at regular intervals as final resting spots. *Going to be hard to keep up with Noordin in this beehive.*

We listened to the tour guide give his class, which wasn't as good as Jennifer's, and waited for him to let us wander around on our own.

As the crowd split up, I took the first shift, bringing Bull with me and staying about thirty feet back from Noordin. He broke from the pack and began to explore by himself, forcing us to lose sight of him as he wound through the small hallways. We turned one corner and almost ran into him and another man, an Arab. The section we were in was covered in water, with planks allowing tourists to crouch over and walk without getting wet. We did a dance around them, hopping from plank to plank, and kept going. Noordin paid us no mind, but his friend did.

Once we turned another corner, I said, "You recognize that guy? Is he on our trip?"

Bull was thinking the same thing I was. "No. I'm sure he's not with us."

I immediately tried to contact Knuckles and Jennifer to get them in position, but the small covert radios we had wouldn't function in the catacombs. *Should've seen that coming.* "Shit. We need to get eyes on them."

I didn't want to risk burning ourselves, and a sure way to do that was to have the same people walk by the target over and over again. If something nefarious was going on, they'd be looking for it. I knew damn well Noordin's friend would. He just gave off that vibe.

I started walking again, saying "Maybe this thing dead-ends. That would give us a reason to go back."

It didn't dead-end, but it did get messy enough for anyone to plausibly turn back, with the decrepit boards dipping into the water.

"Okay, when we go by, I'm going to completely ignore them because I got eyeballed. See what you can see."

We retraced our steps and found them both in the same location, apparently fascinated by one of the tombs that looked exactly like every other one of the hundreds down here. Something was going on.

We slipped by them, with Bull saying, "Sorry. Don't go that way. It's blocked."

Reaching the main hall, I asked what he saw.

"When we turned the corner, the Arab handed something to Noordin. He did it quickly, like he was trying to hide it. And Noordin jammed it in his pocket immediately. They also weren't saying anything. Nothing about the tombs or other tourist stuff. It's like they shut up when they saw us."

We found Knuckles and Jennifer and laid out what we'd seen.

Knuckles said, "So you want us to take the new guy? See where he goes?"

"Yeah . . . Shit, that's not going to work. If they're up to no good, he's going to stay down here until the bus leaves. I won't be able to point him out to you because I'll be on the damn bus following Noordin."

Knuckles said, "How bad is your heat state?"

"Radioactive. Bull and I both got close enough to bump asses with them."

"Well, we could blow off Noordin. You could finger the Arab and we'd just meet back at the hotel."

I thought about it but didn't want to lose our original target. If something had been passed, it might play out today — in the next couple of hours.

"No. We'll take a risk but split the difference. Bull, you get on the bus. Jennifer, you come with me. That way I can finger him and you're a fresh face."

Jennifer and I left the catacombs, finding a café on the corner across the street with a view of the metal entrance gate to the park, currently blocked by our tour bus. We watched the group exit the park, with the tour guide rounding everyone up. We saw Bull talking to him, giving some excuse for us. When the bus drove off, we had an unobstructed view of the gate. I saw the Arab man just inside, sitting on a bench and watching the bus depart. I pointed him out to Jennifer.

She said, "You want me to close the gap on him?"

I watched the Asian tourists we'd seen taking photos drive off in the opposite direction. "Naw. Let's just wait here and see what he does."

Looking around at the grimy neighborhood, Jennifer said, "I'm not sure we got the best of this deal. I'd rather be on the bus."

I laughed, watching the tour bus reach the first intersection, having to maneuver around a parked car in the cramped confines of the street. It stopped for a second, then began to back up, the car blocking its ability to turn the corner. Something about the scene spiked in my head. Egyptian drivers were horrible. Nobody would park there and risk a hit-and-run — unless they wanted to target the intersection. I started to rise, when the bus exploded in a fierce ball of fire.

21

Reacting by instinct, I dove on top of Jennifer, the pressure wave of the blast knocking over the umbrella on our table. A split second later, I was running flat out to the bus, Jennifer right behind me.

Reaching the carnage, I screamed at Jennifer to get back, afraid there was a second bomb waiting on people who responded. She ignored me.

The badly parked car on the right side of the bus was peeled open like an empty beer can, black and burning. The bus was knocked over on its side, the middle compressed as if a giant hand had squeezed it. The smell of charred flesh and burning rubber mixed together.

I grabbed a piece of metal and began tearing into the wreckage. Once I had a hole, I started pulling out the pieces. Arms, legs, torsos, anything to clear the way for me to find my friends. *Please, dear God, be on the left side of the bus.*

A crowd had gathered and begun to help. The keening wail of someone injured sliced through the air. I kept going, now pulling out whole bodies. Eventually, I reached someone alive. I got him out, and saw Bull's jacket underneath a seat. I screamed for help and found Jennifer by my side.

"I'm going to lever that seat up. Pull him out."

I jammed a broken piece of metal underneath the frame and leaned into it with everything I had, raising the seat a foot. Jennifer dragged him out. I was relieved to see he was whole, with all of his limbs. I ran to him and began immediate first aid, checking for breathing and a pulse. He had neither.

The side of his skull was cracked open, with his brain matter falling onto the ground. I shunted the image to the back of my brain and returned to the bus, looking for someone who still needed help. Looking for Knuckles.

I was pulling another body from the wreckage, when I heard Jennifer scream my name. She was yanking on a piece of smoking metal, blood on her arms, her hair singed. Racing over, I saw my friend faceup, a vicious slice running down his torso,

172

exposing his intestines underneath. And the rise and fall of his chest.

Rafik felt the blast from inside the courtyard, the shock wave shaking a cloud of dust from the walls. He scrambled out into the street, seeing a huge plume of smoke rising to the west. He ran toward it.

Fighting his way through the crowd around the wreckage, he circled, looking for Noordin. He reached a makeshift morgue, with the bodies unceremoniously thrown one on top of the other and a small stack of arms and legs looking like cast-offs from a wax museum. He saw what might be Noordin's clothes, and moved the corpses for a clear view.

The head was missing, the neck a mass of torn tissue with the spinal cord sticking out stark white against the red, but it was him. Rafik was sure. He couldn't believe the irony. Noordin was the contact with the pilots for the aircraft, and now he'd been killed by some other group. The whole plan destroyed by an infantile attack that garnered nothing.

He let out a scream of frustration, beating his hands into the ground. The people around him looking on in sympathy, misunderstanding his rage for grief. After a moment he regained his composure, thinking through his options.

All is not lost. Noordin was dead, but he wasn't the pilot. Just the contact. The pilots were in Cairo, at the trade fair. Drinking booze and whoring around. They weren't believers and had no knowledge of Rafik, but they knew they were doing something unsavory. Rafik couldn't be sure they didn't think they were just smuggling drugs, or how they'd react if he confronted them, but he was the ultimate money man, so that would count. Especially since their employer was now dead. In the end, he needed only one pilot. If they weren't swayed by money, there were other ways.

He'd had that lesson branded on him as a child prisoner in Algeria.

22

Eating dinner on a two-story boat anchored in the Nile River, Congressman Ellis wasn't enjoying the belly-dancing floor show like the rest of the entourage. Since his last conversation with Han, he hadn't enjoyed much of anything. His appetite had dropped off to nothing, and he felt permanently sick to his stomach. He'd told his aides that he'd caught something, and they'd seemed to buy it.

He felt his phone vibrate in his pocket. Excusing himself, he went to the bathroom and read a simple text message: *Check the news. Call the plane.*

He pulled out his worldwide BlackBerry and accessed the Web. Within short order, he located the terrorist attack in Alexandria. The initial death toll read eighteen, with no mention of nationalities. *Jesus. They blew up a bus?* The magnitude did nothing to dim his relief.

Thinking a minute, he dialed his pay-as-you-go phone, waiting on the long-distance connection. His contact answered, sounding like he was speaking in a tunnel.

"Hello. Can I help you?"

"Yes, I'd like to speak with Carlton Webber."

"He's not here at the moment. Can I take a message?"

Now that they were no longer in the States, they had established a code to ensure that each was who he said he was. Congressman Ellis had no doubt that Egypt maintained a pretty healthy capability for listening in on domestic cell phone calls, so their entire conversation would be benign.

Congressman Ellis said, "Yes, tell him that he can come as planned. But I had a question."

"What's that?"

"How long can he stay?"

"He's only paid for three hours."

"I know. I made the plan. Can he stay longer?"

"Uhh . . . possibly, but it will cost more money. And he won't stay past the night. He has to be back here the following morning."

Congressman Ellis realized the pilot was afraid of being at the closed Alexandria airport when the sun came up. He wanted in and out in one night. It was the best Ellis was going to get.

"Fine. Make that happen. Call me before you cross the Mediterranean."

He hung up the phone, feeling a little release. *Barring any hiccups, I'll give Han his twenty-four-hour call tomorrow night. And be done with this.* He returned to the table and flagged an aide. Telling him about the terrorist attack, he sent the man to the U.S. Embassy for a list of any Americans involved, under the pretense of finding out if one was a constituent. After the aide left, he relayed the news to the rest of the delegation, who all immediately began banging away on BlackBerrys and talking to aides, just as he had.

Congressman Ellis heard nothing from the aide until he returned to the hotel. The man entered his room with a smile, saying, "Not your constituents. No worries."

"Were there any Americans?"

"Yes. Four on the tour, one dead, one in a hospital and expected to die."

"Then wipe that fucking smile off of your face."

The aide's glee disappeared.

"How sure are you of the information?"

Now all business, the aide said, "One

hundred percent. The embassy had the manifest of everyone who paid for the tour, and has already confirmed the information about the Americans."

He handed a sheet of paper to the congressman. "The deceased have a line through their name. The wounded have an asterisk. The Americans are fourth from the bottom."

Ellis looked at the list and felt his bile rise. There were annotations next to every name but two. Nephilim was one of them. *Jesus. He's still alive.*

This early in the morning, the Kentucky Fried Chicken was closed, forcing Rafik to hide in an alley with a view of the coffee shop. He had originally planned on giving the details of his operation to the Muslim Brotherhood contact no earlier than the day the aircraft arrived, but with Noordin dead, he would need to go to Cairo himself, forcing him to give out the information early. There was a risk the man would leak the information, but Rafik couldn't see a way around it.

At precisely nine, he watched the contact go through his ritual of signals, this time correctly. He approached and took a seat. The first words out of the contact's mouth brought him up short.

"The plane's on the way. It will be here tomorrow night."

"What? Are you sure?"

"Yes, yes. They called and asked for more than three hours. They'll be on the ground for the night, but will leave before dawn."

Well, that's something anyway. I should be able to make it back from Cairo in time.

"Did you get the uniforms?"

"Yes. Five like you asked. And the side gate is my post. That's where you'll enter. Nobody else will be there."

"I'll also need a vehicle to get to the plane."

The contact looked alarmed. "You never said that. Nobody is allowed to approach the plane. It's going to land and stay out on the runway. It's not coming into the terminal."

"I never said it because I didn't want to give you any aspect of my plan. You've already shown me your accident-prone skills. Can you do it?"

The man nervously glanced left and right, refusing to meet Rafik's eyes. "I'm just letting you in. I don't want to be a part of your plan."

"I didn't ask you what you wanted. I asked if you could do it. You are *already* part of the plan."

The man said nothing. Rafik leaned forward, forcing the contact to meet his eyes. "Can you do it?"

The contact hesitated, then nodded. Rafik smiled. "Can you remember my instructions without writing them down?"

The contact nodded again. Rafik gave him the bare minimum of information he would need to accomplish the mission.

Getting back to his hotel, he accessed his Skype account and called the one man on earth he trusted. When his face appeared on the screen, Rafik felt a calm settle over him. Kamil had bled with him in Algeria and was the touchstone he needed to keep going.

Rafik said, "Peace be upon the prophet. It's time."

"Thanks be to Allah," Kamil replied. "The men are ready."

"Did you get the weapons?"

"Yes. You were right. Al-Fayoum was the perfect place to wait. We had no trouble finding weapons."

An old oasis a couple hours southwest of Cairo, al-Fayoum had some of the strictest security restrictions in all of Egypt. In 1997 a group of terrorists had massacred more than sixty foreign tourists at the Luxor archeological site. Most of the terrorists had

180

come from al-Fayoum, and the town itself suffered the repercussions. It was a counter-intuitive choice to place his trusted friend and the team in the heavily patrolled area, but Rafik didn't worry about the security. Instead, he had leveraged the reason the security was there in the first place; the town was ripe with sympathizers.

Rafik said, "There's been a complication, old friend. I'm afraid I must put more on your shoulders than I wanted. In addition to your requirements in Europe."

23

Knuckles looked like a caricature of someone injured. He was covered in bandages from his head to his waist, with irregular red polka dots splotching through where the wounds were still seeping, like oil spots trying to join together. In the twenty-four hours he had been in the hospital, he hadn't gotten appreciably better. But he hadn't gotten any worse, either. The doctors kept marveling that he was alive at all, which was something I didn't need to hear.

The hospital in Alexandria turned out to be pretty damn good, as far as foreign hospitals go. It was very clean and modern, and handled the trauma of the terrorist attack efficiently. We had been given the presidential suite because they'd run out of room, which was small compensation. It gave Knuckles an anteroom he wouldn't use with a TV he couldn't watch.

I had been conducting a vigil since we'd

arrived, not for any emotional reasons, but because I was petrified the staff here would miss something if an alarm went off on one of the plethora of machines hooked to him. So far, we'd been okay.

Jennifer had stayed as well. I could tell she wasn't sure what to do, and was probably traumatized by the carnage she had witnessed. I knew I was being an asshole by letting her flounder, but I didn't have the energy to help her cope. It was all I could do to deal with my own emotions. Seeing Knuckles' torn body was eating into me like acid. I felt a darkness coming back.

After the murder of my family, I had lived in an abyss, full of rage and hatred. The senselessness of their deaths had consumed me, bringing on a blackness that wanted to take over my soul. Those days were now a distant memory. I had tricked myself into believing they weren't even that, but just a bad dream that had no substance. The terrorist strike that had ripped my friends apart had also awakened something, a small sliver on the edge of my consciousness asking to grow. Reminding me that my past was all too real.

Had my friends been killed or injured on an operation, in combat, I would have been able to handle it differently. I had had many friends die that way, and it was something I inherently understood as the price of my job. This was different. This was just as senseless as my family's death. A random killing of people I cared deeply about, and I could feel the beast wanting back out. I wasn't sure I wanted to hold it back.

"Pike," Jennifer said, "you should eat. You haven't taken a break since we got here. Let's go take a walk."

I thought about it and decided she was right. I needed to get out of here.

"Yeah. Okay. I want to stop by the nurses' station, though, let 'em know we're leaving."

We exited the hospital onto a tight, busy street, the buildings crammed together without any space and the sunlight blinding me. Looking around, all I saw was a small industrial area with metal workers shaping fenders on cars, and lathes shooting out sparks into the alleys.

Jennifer asked a cab driver for directions and we headed out. Four blocks later, we had left the industrial area and entered a congested shopping district. We stopped at a roadside stand and ordered some local food.

Sitting down at a coffee table, Jennifer said, "Pike, I think someone's following us."

I didn't alter my demeanor. Just asked, "Who and where."

"There's an Asian guy at your nine o'clock. He was outside the hospital when we left, and now he's across the street at the other café. I only noticed him because he *was* Asian. He stuck out."

"Can you see him by looking at me?"

"Yeah."

I didn't bother to try and ID him. "Let me know if he leaves."

If Jennifer had called it, he was probably surveillance. She had an uncanny eye for this type of thing, and I had never seen her call a ghost. We ate our lunch at an unhurried pace, staying longer than any ordinary patron would. When the man didn't leave, the chances of a mistake became smaller and smaller. We finished up and began walking away from the hospital. The man followed. We entered a pharmacy and bought some aspirin, just as an excuse, then began walking back in the direction of the hospital. The man reappeared on our tail. The glimpse of him brought irrational anger.

Dumb motherfucker's going to follow me when he sticks out like a whore in church?

"Jennifer, I'm going to find out what this guy's doing."

She looked at me sharply. "How?"

185

"There was an empty warehouse in the industrial section. When we turn the corner to it, I'm going to stop and jerk his ass inside."

She became alarmed, seeing where I was going. "Then what?"

I stopped and locked eyes with her. "Then he tells us what the fuck he's doing. Don't you think it's strange that we're following a guy from Indonesia who gets killed in a terrorist attack, and now we're being followed by an Asian guy? He's probably fucking Indonesian."

"Pike, let's call the police. I don't think this is a good idea."

We turned the corner and I stopped. "Tough shit. We're here. Go inside and see what's there."

"Pike —"

"Get inside. Now."

She opened the door and disappeared. I squeezed inside the door frame and waited on our tail, my fists clenching and unclenching spasmodically, the blackness spreading.

He came around the corner and reacted instantly, throwing his hands up and stumbling backward. I batted them away and grabbed him by his throat, slamming him against the brick wall. Then I threw his ass through the doorway. All one hundred and thirty pounds of him.

I stepped into the gloom of the warehouse and smacked him in the head, stunning him again. I ripped off a satchel he was wearing and opened it, finding a beat-up Chinese Type 67 semiautomatic pistol. The barrel had a built-in suppressor, and the caliber was unique to the weapon. It wasn't something you could buy on eBay.

Well, well. Not a coincidence he's behind us.

I checked the chamber, saw it was loaded, and pointed it at his head. "Empty your pockets."

He sat up and did nothing, just stared blankly at me. He looked familiar, and it clicked. *One of the tourists from the catacombs.* I cracked him in the head with the barrel, splitting open his scalp and knocking him to the ground again. I heard Jennifer say my name, but ignored her.

"I said empty your fucking pockets."

He still did nothing. I raised the pistol again and Jennifer moved to him, pulling on his pockets.

"Get the fuck away from him!"

She did, but said, "I don't think he speaks English. Pike, don't hurt him."

The man was now emptying his pockets onto the ground.

"Bullshit. That's the first line of defense. Play like you can't understand. He was at the catacombs when the strike happened. He knows something, and he speaks fine. I promise."

I looked around the warehouse, seeing a table and chair. I pointed the pistol at him and said, "Take off your clothes."

"Pike," Jennifer said, "what are you —"

"Quit questioning me in front of the detainee." I wanted to get the man feeling as vulnerable as possible, and being completely naked was a quick way to get there, but I couldn't tell Jennifer that in front of him.

I repeated, "Take off your clothes."

He didn't move until Jennifer mimicked unbuttoning her shirt, then he began to undress.

"Jennifer, quit playing into his hands. Let me deal with this. Go find something to tie him up with."

She paused for a second, then began exploring the warehouse.

I picked up his belongings and found a passport. To my surprise, he wasn't Indonesian but Chinese. And he had an exit stamp from Indonesia the day after I had left. I flipped a page and saw that he'd entered Indonesia a day after me as well. I motioned him over to the chair, making him sit down. His face was completely blank, without a trace of emotion. The fact that he was completely naked didn't seem to faze him. Jennifer returned with an old lamp that had about a four-foot electrical cord. I ripped it out.

"Tie his hands behind his back and behind the chair. Make sure it's good."

When she was done, I moved the table until it was about five feet away and put the pistol on it. Then I picked up a length of hose lying on the ground. It was heavy rubber, and would hurt a great deal.

I rubbed his chest with it. "You're lucky in one respect. I'm not going to beat the shit out of your face. I don't want to give you the excuse that you can't talk. And I *know* you can speak English, so save yourself the pain. I'm going to find out what you know about the death of my friend. That's just a fact."

He looked at me with that blank stare, making my rage grow. I slammed the hose against his stomach, causing him to scream. I picked up a rag and shoved it in his mouth, then swung three more times. His eyes squeezed shut and he screamed again, but only a muffled sound came out.

Jennifer shouted, "Pike! Please stop.

Please."

She looked sick to her stomach. I said, "Go to the door and watch for someone coming."

"Pike . . ."

"Go."

She left and I returned to the man. He was sweating profusely and breathing hard.

"I'm not going away. You nod your head and I'll remove the rag. We'll start with an easy one. What's your name?"

I waited for him to nod. When he didn't, I striped his thighs, feeling the rage build. Blaming him for making me give him pain. Taking out my grief over a dead friend. Taking out my rage over another friend who would probably die today. My vision blurred and I hit him again and again, almost missing him nodding. I removed the rag.

His head sagged for a second, then he whispered, "Camera."

What the fuck? Speaking gibberish to get me to stop? His pathetic attempt to act like he didn't understand broke through the small bit of sanity holding back my blackness. The beast came out, looking for pain.

Jennifer kept her eyes glued to the street through a crack in the door, not wanting to witness what Pike was doing. Not wanting

190

to be a part of it in any way. She flinched every time she heard the hose strike flesh, her conscience screaming at her to stop it, but a fear of what Pike might do overweighing her impulse.

She had never seen him like this. She'd watched him sit in Knuckles' room, morose and brooding, and somewhere during the wait, he'd crossed a threshold. For the first time, she feared him. Feared what he was capable of.

She heard Pike ask the man his name, then heard the hose whipping into his flesh, her eyes involuntarily squeezing each time. Then the sound stopped. When it resumed, it was no longer the crack of the hose, but a dull, meaty drumbeat. She turned from the door and saw Pike straddling the chair, his fists a blur as he pummeled the man's face.

Without conscious thought, she ran to him, grabbing his arms and pushing him away.

"Stop it! Stop it! You're killing him!"

She registered that the man had fallen and was writhing on the ground, snaking his hands underneath his legs, then saw him spring to his feet and run to the pistol. Before she could warn Pike, he ripped out of her grip and flung her bodily into a wall, then raced to beat the man to the weapon.

Pike reached the table a split second after the Chinese, clamping his hands on the man's wrists and forcing him to the ground. They writhed on the ground for control of the pistol. She heard the pop of a suppressed round and waited to see who was hit.

Pike rose and stood over the body. Breathing hard, he turned and looked at her, his face twisted in rage.

She got her legs underneath her and did the only thing she could.

She fled.

24

The terror on Jennifer's face devastated me, smothering the rage. I tried to talk but got nothing out before she ran. I turned back and looked at the man on the ground. He was no longer human. A body topped by a popped balloon of blood. I threw the pistol across the room in frustration.

What the fuck just happened?

I had lost control. Something that had never occurred on a mission. When I was operational, I was always — *always* — in control. It was what made me the top one percent of the top one percent in the world.

And I had just killed the only lead I had into the murder of my friend, *after* beating the shit out of him. Because I'd lost control.

Dammit, Jennifer. If she hadn't tackled me, he wouldn't have gone for the gun.

I knew blaming her was bullshit. She'd done *exactly* what I would have if the situation had been reversed. *The right thing.*

For the first time since I had come back to the Taskforce, I questioned my ability to serve my country. Maybe my psyche was too damaged to do this work. Maybe I was now too sensitive to the price the job might entail. *Maybe you can't separate the consequences from your emotions anymore.*

Jennifer's expression returned. The memory of her fear and revulsion sliced through me like a razor. She had literally run from me. Afraid that I'd hurt her.

I grabbed the man's satchel and shoved everything in it, then ran out to find her. To explain. Although I had nothing to defend what she'd seen. It was what it was.

Amazingly, the neighborhood was going about its normal business. I shoved everything but the passport into a Dumpster and started in the direction of our hotel.

As I walked, the one word the man said finally penetrated my brain. *Camera.* I had thought he'd just uttered nonsense, but now, with a clear head, I put together the utterance with his passport entries from Indonesia. *Jesus. Surely this has nothing to do with Kurt's father.* I picked up my pace.

Entering our room, I startled Jennifer. I noticed her bag on the bed, with clothes in it. I immediately held up my hands.

"Hey . . . I . . . I don't know what to say. I

lost control."

She looked at me warily, like she wanted me to give her a clear shot at the door.

"Pike, I'm going home. I don't know what that was back there, but I want no part of it."

The words drove a spike into me. "Jennifer, please. Don't do this. That guy was bad. He was in Indonesia the same time we were, and was at the catacombs two minutes before the bus blew up. He had something to do with it."

"I'm leaving." She threw a shirt into her suitcase. "I'm not like you."

She said nothing for a second, then continued, "I don't want to be like you. I thought I did, but I don't want to cross that line. Maybe it's necessary. I don't know. I just don't want any part of it."

"That wasn't me. It wasn't. I don't like it either. Something happened. I . . . I would never hurt an innocent person. I would never hurt you."

"You can't say that. You might believe it, but you can't say it. I saw you. You would have killed anyone, innocent or not."

The unspoken accusation hammered me, that the man I had killed might not have done anything wrong. "You can't believe that. The guy murdered Bull! I wasn't going to kill him. Just make him talk. You've worked with the Taskforce enough. You know that's not true."

She stopped what she was doing, facing me head-on. "Bullshit! You're all alike! I'm not sure who's the good guy and who's the bad guy. Terrorists kill people, and the Taskforce reacts, running off killing people. Maybe you both just found an outlet for your psychopathic tendencies. They use God as an excuse to bomb, and you use them. Maybe there are no white hats."

I couldn't believe what she had just said. "Jesus. You can't think that we're like terrorists? We've never driven a plane into a building, for Christ's sake. I've never enjoyed killing. We do what we do to protect people. Nothing more. If they'd quit, so would we. The opposite isn't true. If we quit, they'll just keep killing."

She backed off a little. "I'm sorry. I shouldn't have said that. I don't know what I believe, but I know I'm not cut out to be a part of it. I'm going home."

I remembered the camera, and the possible connection with the bus strike. I couldn't do what I needed to do on my own. I needed a team. And I could use Jennifer's help to get one.

I knew that was just an excuse to keep her

here, but I had to do something. She had seen something good in me a year ago, when I was drowning in the abyss, and I needed to prove she wasn't wrong. I needed some time. Some space from what had happened to mend the rip between us.

And I really could use her help.

"Okay, okay. I won't stop you, but I need you to do something first."

"What?"

"The man mentioned a camera, and his passport showed him in Indonesia at the same time as us. Something's going on here. The bus strike wasn't random. I'm going back to that convention center to find out what. I need a team on the ground, and I need you to bring them in."

"Bring them in? Why?"

"Because they'll be falling from thirty thousand feet."

25

Rafik kissed Kamil on both cheeks, saying, *"As-salamu alaikum."* He shook the hands of the men with him, then touched his heart with his right hand.

"Good to see you," Rafik said. "Any issues getting here?"

"None," said Kamil. "But I'm anxious to hear why you called us to Cairo."

Rafik told him what had happened in Alexandria, and the dilemma the plan now faced.

Kamil said, "So we need to convince these heathen pilots to continue with the plan despite the fact that their boss is dead?"

"Yes. They don't know why they're here, and will probably resist. Which is why I brought you. We need to make an early lesson."

Kamil pulled out a seven-inch fillet knife. "I can do that. What's your plan?"

Rafik pointed into the hotel. "The elevator's right past the reception desk, but we'll be taking the stairs on the other side. The head pilot's in room 232. We take him, have him call the others, then hold a meeting. There's a loadmaster and three pilots. We only need one."

Fifteen minutes later, Rafik addressed the Indonesians, holding a thick plastic trash bag, the other three Arabs flanking the group left and right.

"Noordin was paying you to fly a certain cargo from Alexandria to Prague, then onward to another country. He is no longer here, but I am the one who hired him. I wish you to continue."

The lead pilot answered, "We worked for Noordin, it's true, but we're not any more. We have another job. We're leaving tomorrow. Sorry."

The loadmaster seemed to shrink into one of the other pilots, like a small child. The pilot put his arm around him, rubbing his back. Rafik was disgusted to realize they were partners, and decided the loadmaster would be the lesson. Then he grasped that the connection could be useful later.

He said, "I'm not going to threaten or beg. I'm going to show you what will happen if you say no. I only need one pilot."

Rafik turned to Kamil and said, "The one who spoke."

Initially the Indonesians looked confused. When the Arabs pulled out pistols, they showed their first signs of alarm. But by then, it was too late, their conscious minds failing to sense the extent of the danger. As had happened throughout history, whether facing a mugger in New York City or being pushed toward a shower by a Nazi guard, they acquiesced without a struggle. Kamil grabbed the lead pilot and forced him to his knees. He shoved the man's head into the trash bag and pulled out the fillet knife. The pilot, unable to see anything, remained still. Kamil placed the knife under his neck and began to saw.

The blade bit deep. Before the pilot comprehended the danger, he was already dead. His body just didn't realize it. He began flopping around like a fish on a dock, but Kamil held him down and stroked three more times. Kamil dropped the body and stood up, watching it continue to whip, causing a spackle of red to spray out, as if someone had stomped on a ketchup packet. The sounds coming from inside the bag made the other Indonesians flinch in horror. First a wet wheeze, it grew into a gurgling rattle as the pilot's lungs fought for air through the torrent of blood. In seconds, the body was still, the only sign of life a twitching left foot.

"Now," Rafik said, "do I need to repeat this?"

The loadmaster turned his head away and buried it in the pilot's chest. The pilot said, "No. I'll fly you. Please don't hurt anyone else."

"Okay. Then everyone calm down. Harm will only come to you if you fail to accomplish this mission. What did Noordin tell you about the plan?"

"Nothing. Only that we were flying a plane."

"That's true, from Alexandria to your usual spot in Prague. As just another flight from Noordin's company."

The pilot said, "That won't work. All planes have tail numbers that show where they're from and who owns them. We can't fly another plane as if it's ours."

"You're going to repaint the number to one that Noordin owns. Then just fly it home."

"What type of plane?"

"A DHC-6 Twin Otter, registered in America."

"We don't *have* any Twin Otters. All our aircraft are built by Indonesian Aerospace.

This won't work."

Rafik grew abrupt. "Nobody's going to match the tail number with the model. It's just one flight. Once it's on the ground, you can have the Twin Otter. I only want what's inside. You can either do it and risk jail, or remain here. I have more trash bags."

When the pilot said nothing, Rafik continued, "Transfer the boxes inside the Otter to a real Noordin plane, then wait for us."

He saw the pilot's face reflect a glimmer of hope. "You won't be with us?"

"No. Two Noordin employees flying a Noordin plane won't cause a commotion, but us on board will raise questions with customs that might create trouble."

"You mean three? Three Noordin employees will be flying?"

"I mean three unless you keep questioning me. We'll fly out of Cairo and meet you in Prague. Do you understand what you need to do?"

"Yes."

Rafik took the knife from Kamil and held it up, the blood and bits of flesh still clinging to it.

"You had better be at the airport in Prague when we arrive. You make me hunt you down and I'll cut off your head only

202

after I've worked my way up from the bottom."

26

I computed the time change between Cairo and D.C., and decided I'd waited long enough.

Kurt would be in the office by now, and I wasn't getting anything at the convention center. I'd cased Noordin's booth for close to three hours and gleaned nothing. Maybe nothing was going on. Maybe Noordin was doing whatever he was doing all by himself.

The booth itself — in fact, the whole convention — was moving slow, like Vegas at nine in the morning. It stood to reason, since the terrorist strike had killed Noordin and seventeen other participants.

I pulled up our VPN on the company Web site. Once I was secure, I instant-messaged my "secretary" in the rear — really just someone who was pulling radio watch in the Taskforce headquarters. When he came on, I asked him to find Kurt, then put on the headset and waited.

It had taken a little doing, but Kurt had finally agreed to send over some more operators. The connection with the terrorist strike and his father's camera had been weak, but it was enough. Everyone in D.C. seemed to be shitting their pants over the intel indicators, and ultimately it had swayed Kurt's decision. He wouldn't give me a complete team, but he did agree to send over the rest of Knuckles' men. That was fine by me, since they used to be my team.

While none of the men were documented in my company, the primary problem was that we needed equipment — and bringing it in through customs wasn't the best idea. Eventually, we'd have the ability to do that with company infrastructure, but our problem was now.

I'd pulled the trigger on an in-extremis option that the Taskforce had never used — a high-altitude, low-opening parachute jump. The team, with one man attached to a tandem bundle that held the equipment, would exit an airplane flying at commercial altitude on an existing air route. The plane, ostensibly flying a humanitarian mission to Sudan, would appear to be just transiting Egyptian airspace.

Kurt had balked at first, because it *was* fraught with risk, but I finally shamed him by asking why the hell we did all the practice jumps if we never intended to use the method. It was designed for just this type of contingency. He'd agreed, provided I gave him an update prior to the team launching from Europe on the final leg of the flight, which was why I was calling now.

I heard a scratching through my headset, then Kurt's voice, sounding like he was speaking through a tube because of the VoIP and encryption.

"Pike, you there?"

"Yes, sir. I got you."

I gave him an update on Knuckles' status, and learned that a Taskforce casualty affairs team was on the way. From this point on, it would be out of my hands. More "employees" of my company, including now a doctor, would arrive tomorrow to deal with both the recovery of Bull's remains and the treatment of Knuckles. Taskforce capability never ceased to amaze me. Neither did the organization's desire to do whatever it took to take care of its own.

Kurt shifted to the mission. "So what's up? You still want to execute?"

"Yeah. I do. I don't have a lot to go on, but finding a thread first may be too late to get a team here. I need to be able to react as soon as I find it."

"Do you have anything at all?"

"Noordin's folks are going to the Khan al-Khalili market tomorrow. Three females. It's probably nothing, but I can't follow all three by myself. The market's a tourist-trap nuthouse."

Kurt paused, then said, "You know, if we weren't all pissing in our pants here in D.C. over the indicators of a strike, I'd cancel this. The infil alone's dangerous enough."

"Sir, I got it. But we both know there's a link to something here. Did you get the film?"

"Yeah. We developed it. Only seventeen of the thirty-six frames were exposed. All of them pretty much shot by the heat and humidity in Cambodia. We managed to get an image out of six."

"And?"

"And nothing right now. Just a bunch of shadows and light. A couple have a man in them, but nothing identifiable. We're digitally working them."

"Okay. I know it sounds nuts, but those pictures mean something."

"We'll keep working it. How's Jennifer doing?"

"Fine. She's doing the recce for the drop zone right now. I'll have the coordinates by this afternoon, before the team launches from Europe."

And she's going home after that. I realized
I couldn't keep stalling about what had happened to the Chinese man. I hadn't told
Kurt how I had made the connection between the camera and the strike, but I knew
I had to. I wasn't looking forward to it. I
knew what he'd think. *Get it over with.*

"Actually, sir, she's not fine. She's coming
home tomorrow, after the jump."

"Why? Was it Bull's death?"

"No. It's something I did. I killed a guy."

I heard nothing for a second.

"Were you in the right?"

"Well, not exactly."

I told him what had happened, leaving
nothing out, knowing I was probably cancel-
ing the jump, if not my future in the Taskforce. *Shit, maybe putting my ass in jail.*
That's just the way it would have to be. I
didn't know how the Taskforce would manage that, but I knew I'd go. I finished and
waited on Kurt to say something.

"Pike, why?"

"Sir, I don't know. I went black, like I used
to do after my family died. I guess seeing
Knuckles tore me up. I didn't mean to kill
him. It was either him or me." When he
didn't respond, I hurried to get out "It was
self-defense."

I heard nothing but breathing, Kurt going through the implications in his mind. When he came back on, he was calm, but his voice was steel. "Pike . . . you need to come home. Get the team on the ground, then come back."

He was remembering my slide into the abyss, and thinking I was just getting started on another run. "Sir, it *won't* happen again. I mean that. I realize what I did. I know it's bad."

He lost his temper. I could hear it even through the Mickey Mouse sound of the VoIP. "Bad? You make it sound like you pissed on the rug. You fucking beat a detainee. Then killed him. Jesus Christ, if we were sanctioned by the government, you'd be arrested. *I* would arrest you."

"Sir, I told you, it was self-defense, and he had something to do with Bull's —"

"Shut the fuck up and let me finish. We can't afford cowboys. You know that. We're doing enough illegal shit as it is. We *do not* lose control. And we sure as shit don't beat the hell out of people because of our own personal problems."

The silence extended out. I said nothing, knowing he was right. I'd broken the sacrosanct rule. Because the Taskforce sent men out with the authority to make decisions with national implications, they had to be implicitly trusted to do the right thing. To do what was morally and ethically just. Always. Even when no one was looking. Especially when no one was looking. We operated outside the law, and we were our own police. Kurt took that very, very seriously. Trust was the cornerstone of our existence, and I might've lost his.

Kurt finally said, "Okay, get the team on the ground. I'd pull you right now, but we're in a full-court press. Something bad's coming, and I need everyone on it. We'll talk about your future after this is over. You're lucky that fucker killed a busload of people."

I sagged with relief. "You got it, sir. I'll do what I can."

"That's not what I want to hear. Do it right. No more bullshit."

27

At precisely nine o'clock at night, Rafik pulled the nondescript van up to the south gate of Alexandria's El Nozha Airport. His calm demeanor belied the adrenaline pounding his temples. He relaxed slightly when he saw his contact exit a guard shack, carrying a garbage bag.

Within five minutes, he and Kamil's men were dressed just like the contact, as Egyptian soldiers, complete with AK-47s. The two pilots and loadmaster were cowering in the back, dressed in Noordin's travel agency uniforms.

They entered the airport and waited, checking and rechecking their weapons.

Rafik said, "There'll be another vehicle somewhere. They'll go to the plane to unload. We need to beat them to the rear of the aircraft."

They saw the lights of the runway spring to life, bathing the ground in a soft glow.

The Arabs tensed, scanning the sky for the aircraft. Kamil saw it first. A blinking dot getting closer and closer. When it began its final approach, Rafik told the contact to drive.

They paralleled the runway, watching the plane touch down, the twin propellers reversing with a roar.

Behind the driver, Kamil said, "There's the other vehicle."

Rafik saw a pickup leaving the terminal, heading toward the runway.

"When we get to the plane, act like confused soldiers," he said. "It will buy us time and lull them. Kamil and I will go inside. The rest of you deal with the truck."

The driver turned onto the runway and reached the back of the plane as the rear door was lowering. The Arabs exited, Rafik in the lead.

A Caucasian man poked his head out, warily looking at the van.

Rafik said, "What is this? You have emergency?"

The man said, "Uhh . . . no. We're meeting that vehicle." He pointed to the approaching pickup.

Rafik walked up the short stairway, forcing the man to back up. Kamil followed, while the others stayed on the tarmac.

"Meeting someone? This airport is closed. Where is the pilot?"

"Hey, talk to Mansoor. Captain Mansoor? He's your boss, right?"

The man had backed up to the cockpit, where the pilots were running through checklists, not realizing something was wrong. He got their attention. Both the pilot and copilot turned and faced backward. Rafik now had three heads in a neat row. *Perfect.*

The pilot said, "Hey, come on. You want more fucking money, or what? A deal's a deal."

Without a word, Rafik raised his AK and pulled the trigger, splitting the man's head open. He heard Kamil fire twice on his left as he shifted his aim to the copilot. The man raised his hands in front of his face, as if that would stop the high-velocity round from tearing through his brain. Rafik squeezed twice and saw the man's head snap back like it was yanked on a string.

All three men were dead, the pilots lolling in their seats as if they had fallen asleep, and the loadmaster crumpled on the deck.

Rafik lowered his weapon and smiled at Kamil. Before he could say anything, they heard gunfire erupt at the rear of the plane, the rattling sound of AK-47s on full automatic competing with a lower popping from pistols.

Rafik and Kamil threw themselves onto the deck of the aircraft and began snaking their way to the rear. In the distance, Rafik heard the Egyptian soldiers on guard begin firing in every direction, with rounds puncturing the thin skin of the aircraft.

They'll ruin the plane. "Quit shooting!" he screamed. "Stop firing!" He knew as long as his men kept pulling the trigger, the Egyptians would respond.

Someone from outside shouted, "The truck will get away!"

Kamil said, "If that truck reaches the terminal, they might be able to convince the guards to attack. It's their money the Egyptians took. We'll be fighting our way through an army."

Rafik began running toward the plane's door, hoping a lucky round didn't take him out. Kamil followed.

Collapsing behind the van, he berated the first man he saw. "How could you mess this up? All you had to do was kill the men in the truck."

"They suspected something. They fired first."

Rafik looked around the corner of the van and saw the pickup fifty meters away, the

214

nose facing the front of the plane. He could see the legs of two men underneath the chassis, near the rear wheel. As he considered his options, one popped up and began shooting. Rafik's men returned fire, followed by the distant flashes of the soldiers on the perimeter. Rounds began sprinkling around them, most striking the biggest target available — the airframe.

Every bullet that ripped through the skin caused Rafik to cringe. "Stop pulling the trigger! Now!"

Underneath the truck, he saw one man move to the cab. He'd have to crawl across the seat, but once he was behind the wheel, they'd be gone. Rafik rolled underneath the belly of the plane, stood up, and raced toward the cockpit, the airframe shielding him from the truck's view.

Circling the nose, he saw the man had reached the steering wheel. The truck sprang to life, the headlights blinding him for a second. He heard the tires squeal, and he ran out, blocking the path of the pickup with his body. He raised the weapon as the vehicle bore down, stitching the front of the windshield with multiple rounds. The truck picked up speed, right at him. He refused to move, raking the AK left and right until the magazine emptied, the bolt slamming home with a clunk. He threw the weapon at the windshield, the vehicle so close it clanged off the driver's-side mirror. The vehicle veered to the left, missing him by two feet. After thirty meters, it veered back to the right, now going fifty miles an hour. It slashed across the tarmac and slammed into a ditch, the nose crumpling inward with a shriek of twisted metal.

Rafik took a deep breath. The night became still, the only sound the hissing of the radiator of the truck. He walked back to the rear of the aircraft. The men were looking at him in awe.

"Get the Indonesians and their paint. Clean up that truck."

He walked to the driver's-side door of the van. The contact was cowering in the well by the pedals. He pulled him up by the hair.

"Go talk to the security perimeter. Tell them a story. Whatever, I don't care, as long as you tell them that the transfer was successful and we appreciate their help. Hand me my bag."

The man did as he asked. Rafik pulled out a thick wad of American dollars. "Give this to whoever is the best choice. Come back when you're done."

As the van pulled away, he turned to the Indonesians.

"Get to work on the numbers."

As all three began to move, he grabbed the loadmaster. "Not you."

The loadmaster whimpered, making Rafik want to gut him right there. The pilot who was his partner began to panic. "What are you doing? You said we'd all fly."

"No. I said you'd all be fine. And you will."

He pulled out the fillet knife, the dried blood black in the dim light of the runway.

"But if you don't meet us in Prague, I'll cause him so much pain that you'll feel it long after he's dead."

Han had just settled into his suite, toying with the idea of getting a late-night massage at the spa, when the contact phone began to ring.

"Hello. I'm assuming that *now* this is the twenty-four-hour call."

Han pulled the phone away from his ear, the shouting coming from it incoherent. Congressman Ellis sounded like he was hyperventilating, babbling about the American they'd tried to kill and the equipment transfer. Han could barely make out what he was saying. He cut Ellis off.

"Stop. Start over. What has happened to the shipment?"

"It's gone! Someone stole it! I'm not lying. It had to be that Nephilim guy. I told you to do something about him."

"What do you mean, gone?"

"The plane came in tonight. I was going to transfer the equipment to you tomorrow, but someone came in and took it. My Egyptian contacts are all saying the transfer occurred and the plane flew away, but I can't get any of my men on the phone. Neither the men who were bringing the equipment to Cairo or the flight crew. They've disappeared, and so has the cargo."

Han considered for a second. Ellis could be lying, but he didn't think the man was capable of such acting. The voice on the other end of the phone was on the verge of breaking.

"How do you know it was the American?"

"I don't, dammit! But who the fuck else would it be? You need to get it back. Get it back and kill Nephilim, before he can talk. And the woman, too."

The man Han had tasked to follow the American hadn't reported in a couple of days, but that in itself wasn't unusual. He'd been told to report only if something suspicious happened, and it appeared that the American cared about nothing but his friend in the hospital.

"Are you sure the plane's gone?"

"Yes! The Egyptians told me the plane flew away. Why would they lie?"

"So why aren't you sure the transfer happened? Maybe your men just have phone trouble."

"No, no, no. This was too important. I had three numbers. They were instructed to call immediately. I've heard nothing and had to call my Egyptian contact to get the information I'm giving you. Something's wrong, and that American is at the heart of it."

Han's voice became brittle. "Before you call me in a panic, find out the facts. All of them. I'll find the American. You confirm the loss of the equipment. For your sake, you'd better hope it's just a mistake."

Han hung up the phone and called the team leader he'd brought from China.

"Have you heard from Wan?"

"No, but the last report was nothing except back and forth to the hospital. I told him to quit bothering me with useless information."

"Find him and get the American man and woman that survived the bomb. The mission's changed. Don't kill them. Bring them to me."

"You want both?"

"No. I only need one. If you can get both, fine. But don't work too hard at it."

28

I saw Jennifer finally pull off the rutted dirt road we'd been traveling down for what seemed like days. Or nights, as it were. She flashed her brakes twice to let me know this was it, and shut off the truck. I pulled in beside her and killed the engine. If things went according to plan, we had about forty-five minutes before the team jumped. Plenty of time to get the drop zone established.

We'd rented a couple of Toyota Hilux pickup trucks, ubiquitous in the desert, and had traveled south on Highway 2, then cut east before Beni Suef on Highway 54. Jennifer had found a deserted spot about three and a half hours away from Cairo, which was harder than it sounds. She kept bumping into Bedouins, forcing her deeper and deeper into the Eastern Desert.

She'd done her usual perfectionist job, bringing me the grid references for the DZ along with digital photos, which I relayed to the Taskforce. She'd treated me with detached professionalism, like a receptionist at a dentist's office. I wanted to talk to her, to connect again, but didn't know how. For her part, she seemed to be forcing the façade. But then again, maybe I was projecting what I wanted to see.

Jennifer said, "Well, does this work?"

"Yeah. Of course. As long as we don't get company."

"That's what took me so long. There's nothing for miles around here. We're good."

I smiled at her, getting a nod in return. Without a word, she turned and began to dig into a bag. *Jesus. Melt the glacier a little.*

She pulled out what looked like a small calculator and a penlight. "You want to rope?"

"Yeah, hook up the radio."

She disassembled the antennae to her truck until she could get at the cable leading to the radio. She stripped the insulation until bare wire showed. Opening the battery box to the calculator, she pulled out two alligator clips and snapped them into the wire. She powered up the device, getting a series of ones across the screen.

"We're secure."

I dialed the radio to 88.9, hearing soft static. We couldn't talk to the bird, but he could now talk to us. He'd transmit on a standard FM frequency, which would come in encrypted but would be decrypted by the device Jennifer had just attached and come out through the stereo speakers just like a DJ.

We spent the next thirty minutes in uncomfortable silence. I was on the verge of doing a perimeter recce just to get away, when the radio crackled to life.

"Prometheus, Prometheus, this is Stork. Do you copy?"

I turned on the penlight. Nothing visible happened, but I knew an infrared beam was now stabbing into the night, looking like a spotlight at a car dealer's to the men flying with night vision goggles. I began to do slow loops in the sky, like I was working a lasso.

"Roger, Prometheus, got your rope. Stand by."

Retro saw the jumpmaster touch his wrist where a watch would be and hold up two hands, fingers spread. *Ten minutes.* He felt the adrenaline start to rise. There was always a chance the jump would be called off, but the call told him it was a go. He saw the jumpmaster key his radio, and his earpiece crackled to life. "Retro, this is Decoy, you hear me?"

"Yeah, I got you."

"Help the loadmaster with Buckshot's bundle. We're closer than I thought."

"Roger."

To his front was a six-foot-by-three-foot tube full of the team's equipment. Another man on the team, Buckshot, would strap himself to it and ride it out into the night tandem, parachuting with the entire team's gear. He saw Buckshot begin working the myriad of clips and buckles on the bundle and knew he was grinning under his oxygen mask, the whites of his eyes stark against his ebony skin. *Crazy fucker. Strapping himself to a death ride.*

Buckshot was one of those guys who loved jumping, and did it on the weekends just for kicks. Retro was not. He despised it. Even when it was just a "Hollywood" jump, with no equipment on a crystal-clear day. Especially when it was in the dead of night at 26,000 feet. With another man strapped to a torpedo. Into a blind drop zone. *At least you're not jumping equipment.* With the exception of a Glock 30 in a pancake holster on his hip, all other team gear was in the tandem bundle — ammunition, long guns, beacons, and whatever other special equipment they thought they'd need — which Buckshot would ride. In Retro's mind, there was a reason HALO parachute infiltrations were classified as a "life support activity" by the military. *Because people fucking die doing this shit.*

He cinched down his leg straps and did a final check of his parachute harness, touching his rip cord and cutaway pillow while mentally going through what he would do if his main parachute failed. The jumpmaster, Decoy, cleared the loadmaster to open the ramp. Retro watched it lower, each inch escalating the sense of dread, his breath now coming in rapid pants, his goggles beginning to fog. *Soon. Going soon.*

Buckshot tapped his arm and motioned to the small drogue parachute container on the enormous pack he wore, something that was necessary to keep him above the bundle as he hurtled to earth. Retro secured it, waiting on the inevitable follow-on commands that would cause them to leave the safety of the aircraft.

He looked out the ramp and could barely make out the distinction between the earth and the sky. The night was huge. A black pool waiting to swallow him. He saw the stars blinking, the frigid air from the altitude mixing with the sweat of his fear. He calmed himself down like he always did, by remembering he didn't have to worry about the part where he jumped off the ramp. *The two minutes of free fall are painless. It's the sudden stop at the end that hurts.*

Kneeling at the juncture of the ramp and the aircraft frame, Decoy stuck his head into the wind, making sure the pilots weren't two grid squares off. He stood up and gave the two-minute warning. Retro saw the jump light go green, and barely noticed the loadmaster unhooking his oxygen tube from the floor-mounted console, allowing him to breathe straight from the bottle on his harness. He inched forward with his hand on the drogue as Buckshot pushed the bundle toward the open chasm.

Decoy looked off the ramp again, making sure they were in the correct location for the release. He pulled back into the aircraft and extended his arm, his hand giving a thumbs-up. He bounced the hand off the floor and stood. Retro's adrenaline skyrocketed.

Here we go. Here we go.

Buckshot checked to make sure Retro still had control of the drogue chute. He locked eyes, nodded, then pushed the bundle to the end of the ramp, inches from the abyss.

Decoy looked off the ramp for the last time, then faced into the plane. He extended his arm and pointed into the night, like

Death ordering them into the grave.

Retro watched Buckshot push the bundle off the ramp like a NASCAR crew pushing a car out of pit row, the line from the drogue chute snaking out of the pack on his back. He disappeared into space, pulling the drogue chute from Retro's hands. Retro took two quick steps and followed suit, diving headfirst into the black sky.

The subzero temperature immediately turned the fog in his goggles to ice. The wind punched him, attempting to flip him on his back, and within seconds he was traveling at one hundred and twenty miles an hour. The feeling finally relaxed him — as it always did.

He located the ChemLights of the bundle, with Buckshot attached, then the ChemLight of the jumpmaster, Decoy, both farther away than he wanted. He tucked his arms into his side and began to dive, his speed increasing until he was overtaking their fall. Before he slammed into them, he spread out and arched his back, now falling flat and stable next to Decoy, the bundle below them and to the left.

Ninety seconds later, he checked his altimeter and broke away, the adrenaline firing back up. *Moment of truth.*

He waved off and looked for his ripcord, a

feeble light coming from the half-inch baby ChemLight he'd taped to it, a relic from a jump when his ripcord had floated free from its pocket, forcing him to find it while he hurtled to earth, the slim piece of metal whipping around in the darkness. This time, it was right where it was supposed to be. He hooked his thumb and jerked, then looked over his shoulder, feeling the pilot chute pull out the main. He felt the satisfying yank in his groin as he decelerated to a sane speed. He looked up and saw a perfect rectangle against the night sky.

One more piece of luck I've used up.

29

Kurt sat outside the Oval Office, waiting on President Warren to get a spare moment. He'd done this ritual more times this month than he had in his entire career, but the HALO infiltration was the topic of the day, and President Warren had demanded to know immediately if anything had gone wrong. After the secretary of state's outbursts, Kurt secretly thought the president wanted to talk about Taskforce activities outside the view of the Oversight Council and was using the parachute infiltration as an excuse to get Kurt alone.

Not a good sign. The council itself had been created by Kurt and the president to keep Project Prometheus from turning into an American Gestapo. The Taskforce was a powerful, powerful organization that operated completely outside of U.S. law. Both men knew that having it answer to a single man was asking for abuse, so they had created the Oversight Council, bringing in trusted advisors who were both for and against its use, thereby guaranteeing a balanced approach. Now Kurt worried that the president might be short-circuiting the very safety valve they had created.

He absently flipped through the pictures he'd been given just before he left his office. Six frames from his father's camera, digitally restored by the best in the business. Two were of his father's team just prior to launch, which, while grainy, had come out fairly well. One was of an open bay porch–type structure with the shadows of several men inside, looking like vague ghosts. Three were of a man standing at the front of the porch. He appeared Caucasian, but that was the extent of what could be made out.

Kurt stopped at the first one and stared hard, trying to see something that would give him a clue as to why his father had risked his life for the picture. Nothing stood out. Even the face was a no-go, with a black blotch from where the negative had been scratched on the left side of his features. He scanned the next one, then the third. None were any better. The film negative had been scratched so badly that the digital reconstruction had had nothing to work with.

He was about to put the pictures back into

their folder, when he noticed that the scratches on the negatives were in the exact same spot on the face within each frame. Which was impossible. *It's not a scratch. It's a part of the man.*

He held the picture up to the light, then saw the president standing at the door of his office. He shoved everything into his bag and stood.

"Hey, Kurt. Sorry for the wait. Come on in."

Kurt followed and got right to business, wanting to get his information out and steer clear of any discussions about operational use of the Taskforce.

"The jump went fine. Infil's complete with all equipment on the ground. Pike's got three men now, so he's just one short of a full team."

"I thought we jumped in three men. For a total of five with Jennifer."

Shit. Shouldn't have brought up numbers. Kurt didn't want to get into Pike's actions and Jennifer's reactions, unsure of how the president would react. Kurt knew Pike as well as he knew himself, and believed him when he said he was good. Pike would pull himself out of action if he thought he was endangering the mission, but Kurt wasn't sure the president would see it the same way.

Disgusted, he realized that by keeping Pike's operational fiasco a secret, he was committing the same mistake he feared in the president. One man controlling the information and thus the outcome.

"Sir, Jennifer's come down with a bug. She's got it coming out of both ends. If she's not better by tomorrow, she's coming home."

He internally cursed himself for the lie, and resolved to never do it again. *This is how it starts. This is how the Taskforce becomes a threat. Who's lying to me?* He knew that the team wasn't, because trust was a cornerstone of Taskforce faith. And felt disgusted again at his lying.

The president said, "Sorry to hear that. She's proving to be an asset. The team's enough, though?"

"Yeah. It's enough. It had better be. Doing another infil is pushing more luck than we have."

"What do you think we should do if nothing's in Egypt? What's the next thread?"

Kurt inwardly cringed. "Sir, that's a question that we should pose to the council."

The president leaned back, staring hard at Kurt. "We both know something's coming.

I'm not sure the council does. They're all worried about the focus on my reelection, and I won't tolerate American deaths because of that."

"Sir, I know. But we need to trust what we created. The checks and balances were right then, and they're right now, even with the imminent threat. Especially with the imminent threat. We need to stand by what we promised. Please."

The president sat for a second, then nodded and changed the subject. "Anything come out of those pictures?"

Kurt breathed an inward sigh of relief. "Not really."

He tossed the folder on the president's desk. "Those are the only ones that came out, and they're not that big of a help. If there was a connection to the terrorist hit in Alexandria, it died with my father."

The president flipped through the photos once, then went back. Eventually, he laid out the three of the Caucasian man, staring intently.

"Jesus Christ."

Kurt said, "What?"

"This guy's got something on his face. A birthmark."

The president looked up at him, his

complexion a little pale. "I think I know who this is."

30

Early the next morning, I knocked on Jennifer's door, not sure of what I was going to say. She had a flight in a couple of hours, but I hoped the jump operation last night might have changed her mind. I saw a shadow on the peephole, but the door didn't budge.

Shit. She's not even going to let me say good-bye.

I knocked again. "Jennifer. Please. Open the door."

After a second, it cracked a few inches. Jennifer looked terrible, like she hadn't slept. Her eyes, once gray and piercing, were now raw and red. Her hair hung limp against her scalp like a houseplant that hadn't been watered. Knowing I was the cause of her pain sent a wave of guilt through me.

"Pike, please don't do this. I'm going home."

"I just want to say good-bye. Come on."

She opened the door and walked away. She stopped at her suitcase and continued packing, not even bothering to turn around.

"Jennifer. Come on, at least look at me."

She stopped what she was doing. "You just won't get it. I'm going home. And you're not changing my mind. It's not going to happen and I don't want to fight."

"Why? Jennifer, I made a mistake, but that guy was bad. I'm not proud of it, but there's no doubt in my mind. He had blood on his hands."

She stopped what she was doing and eyed me. "Pike, that's not the point. Or maybe it's precisely the point. I can't make calls like that. I don't want to decide who gets to live and who gets to die. I'm not like you or the other operators. I can't be that violent. I just don't have it in me. I don't want it in me."

She was wrong, but she'd never believe me.

"Everyone has it in them," I said. "When push comes to shove, every human will do whatever it takes to live. It's what we are. You read about people who died on their knees and it's because they'd convinced themselves that the worst wouldn't happen. Given the chance to do it over, you bet your ass they'd fight with anything they had and kill whoever it took."

"I don't believe that." She started softly crying. "I'm sorry, Pike. I don't want to hurt you, but I can't do this. I thought I wanted to, but not if I end up like you."

"What's that mean? End up how?"

She held up her hands in surrender. "Nothing. I have to go. I'm going to miss my flight."

"Jennifer, wait! I'll quit the Taskforce. I won't do this anymore. We can go back to Charleston together. After this is over."

The words surprised me as much as her. She said nothing for a moment, the silence hanging in the air. Then she crushed me.

"Pike . . . that's not what I want. I'm sorry."

Jennifer managed to hold her composure for the drive to the airport, only breaking down as she entered the first layer of security, silently crying while the listless guards waved her through.

She had lied to Pike, and she knew it. She *did* want to return to Charleston, but only with the Pike she had known before, not the Pike inside the warehouse. That man, wherever he had come from, had scared her to her marrow and caused her to question the very essence of the organization she had worked so hard to join. Pike's only remorse seemed to be that he'd been caught.

Just because the man might have had blood on his hands doesn't mean we get to beat him to death.

She finished with the second layer of security at the entrance to the terminal and joined the cattle call moving toward the departure gates. Walking with everyone else, she was jostled by a man trying to remove his bag from the X-ray conveyer. He politely said, "Excuse me," and she noticed he was Asian and appeared nervous. He turned and ran to catch up to an Arab who was impatiently waiting. An Arab she recognized.

The man from the tombs.

She watched them link up with three other Arabs and walk briskly deeper into the airport. She grabbed her bag and followed.

She shadowed them for close to ten minutes, until they finally stopped and sat at a gate. She looked to the counter and saw a flight on Czech Airlines headed to Prague. She pulled out her phone and dialed Pike. He answered after three rings, his voice clearly happy.

"Hey. Glad you called. Listen, I can't talk now. We're at the market. I'm busy."

She remembered that the team was going

to track the remaining tourist trip to the Khan al-Khalili market in the hopes of finding a thread to pull. She was certain she was looking at the thread.

"Pike, I'm at the airport and I've got eyes on the man from the tombs. You're tracking the wrong —"

He cut her off. "Jennifer, call me back. Don't go anywhere. I gotta go."

He hung up.

He must have his hands full. She looked at the men again, then looked at her ticket. *Okay. You can always fly tomorrow.*

She spent a few moments memorizing their faces, then left the airport and flagged a cab.

"Khan Khalili market, please."

31

Jennifer survived the cab drive through the chaos of Cairo traffic, pulling into the front entrance of the market with her knuckles white against the door handle. She paid the driver, ignoring his attempts to become her personal guide for her stay. She stood on the street and surveyed the area, trying to formulate a plan. She knew that the market itself, while once the center of shopping for Cairo as far back as the fourteenth century, had devolved into a massive tourist trap. The square behind her was a testament to that, as it was jammed full of tour buses transporting people from all over the world, the tourism industry finally beginning to return after the unrest of last year.

She decided to start in the souvenir area and ignore the parts of the market that still served the locals. Noordin's people could be going to the gold section, but she'd hit that after she came up empty.

She walked past the cafés on the outskirts and entered the market proper, a rat maze of hundreds of shops, most simply stalls lined with souvenirs, a few with small courtyards and doors. She could see why Pike had hung up. Staying on someone in here without getting burned would be tough.

With every step, she was accosted by shop owners, all begging her to come into their store, regardless of what they sold. She did stop every few meters and sample the wares, not because she wanted to buy anything, but because she didn't want to step all over Pike's surveillance.

Moving down another alley, she spotted the Members Only jacket that Retro wore. *Not too hard to figure out that call sign. He needs some shopping tips.*

She ducked into the nearest shop to see if she could identify the targets or Pike. The owner descended on her like a spider on a fly.

"Handmade. All handmade."

Yeah, sure. The only time a hand has touched this stuff was when it peeled off the "Made in China" label.

She picked up a lamp, keeping an eye on the activity outside. She felt the barrel of a gun jam into her back, then a voice with a heavy Chinese accent.

"Do not move or you will die right here. I do not intend to harm you."

"Pike, this is Retro. We got someone on us."

I kept my eyes on Noordin's crew. "What? You sure?"

"I've ID'd three so far. All Asian. And all on you. I don't think the rest of us have spiked yet."

What the hell? I'm being followed again? "Okay. I'm going to draw one in and see what he wants. I'm moving into the restaurant at the end of the alley."

"What about the targets?"

"Let 'em go if you have to. Watch my back."

I wasn't too concerned about my safety. In fact, I felt blessed to have a second chance to find out what the hell was going on. *Second chance to locate Bull's killer.* Noordin's crew took a backseat to that. I knew only one man would penetrate into the restaurant to keep eyes on me. He'd try to be inconspicuous and wouldn't expect an assault. I'd get the tail alone and pump him for information — without killing him.

The hostess asked where I'd like to be seated, and led me to a table. After she walked away, I went to the bathroom.

Surveying quickly, I saw one stall, a urinal, and a counter with two sinks. I decided to stay inside. It would be a little bit of a wait, but eventually the curiosity of the guy would force him to enter. Once he saw me, he'd immediately act like he needed to use the toilet or wash his hands, ignoring me so I didn't get spooked.

I decided to stay at the sink until he came inside, then head to the door, forcing him deeper into the bathroom to stay in role. Once I blocked his escape, I'd find out what he was doing.

I saw the door open and turned off the sink. I turned around and faced an Asian man. He was staring hard at me, his face set in determination. In his hand was a QSZ-92 pistol aimed at my chest. Another Chinese model, this one not sporting a suppressor.

Well, that didn't work out like you wanted.

Jennifer remained stock-still, gripping the lamp until her knuckles were white. She heard the man say something in Chinese, then felt the barrel push her forward. He switched to English.

"Put down the lamp and leave the store. Quietly."

The owner looked confused for a moment, Jennifer's body blocking the view of the gun. He assumed the Chinese man was with Jennifer and repeated his mantra of handmade crafts.

The man said, "We don't want to buy anything." He pushed Jennifer again.

True to form all over the market, the owner suspected nothing more than a little hardball haggling. He smiled and placed his hand on the Chinese's shoulder.

"Friend, how much is handmade worth? I have the best —"

Jennifer seized the distraction, whirling around and slamming the lamp into the man's gun, sending it skittering through the souvenirs.

The owner's eyes went wide at the sight of the pistol. He fled the store, screaming in Arabic out on the street. Jennifer attempted to follow, but the Chinese grabbed her arm. She felt a vise on her elbow, then a searing pain that brought her to her knees. The man twisted her wrist and used the locked joint of her elbow to drive her face-first into the ground. She ceased struggling before he could break her arm.

Jesus. He knows how to fight.

The thought sent a stinging fear through her.

Holding the joint lock with one hand, the

man pulled a knife with a three-inch blade out of his belt buckle and put it against her neck.

The terror exploded in her, her brain flashing on an image of her sliced open like a sacrificial lamb, blood jetting out of her neck and coating the floor.

Gunfire exploded outside, startling them both. She felt him shift above her. The blade left her neck, and the lock loosened a fraction. Seizing the moment, she rolled to the right, relieving the strain and freeing her joints. Flipping onto her back, she scissored her calves around the legs of the man. Before he could react, she torqued them as hard as she could, rotating onto her face again and bringing him to the ground.

She leapt up and raced to the back of the store, looking for an exit. There was none. She whirled around and faced the man, warily watching his knife hand. He slashed a long, looping strike, attempting to rip her from the pelvis up. Having nothing else, she blocked it with her left arm, feeling the knife slice into the meat of her forearm.

She lashed out in a snap kick and connected with his thigh, forcing him back. She turned and grabbed another lamp, this one shaped like a lotus flower with heavy brass leaves. The blood running from her arm sent her into a feral state. She rotated with all of her might, connecting with his head and driving one of the leaves into his eye socket.

The man shrieked, a high-pitched wail like a child, and fell to his knees. She jerked the lamp free of his eye and swung again, knocking him onto his back. She fell on top of him, hacking with the lamp again and again, the brass leaves working like a medieval weapon. She stopped when she realized his skull had cratered, leaving a bloody bowl where his face should have been.

She dropped the lamp and rolled off the body, hyperventilating.

32

The Chinese man kicked the bathroom door closed, looking like he was about to pull the trigger. I raised my hands and said, "Whoa, whoa. Easy. Don't shoot."

He said, "I won't if you come quietly. You do anything else, and I will kill you. We only need one. You are just extra baggage."

His words hammered home. *They got Jennifer. And you fucking hung up on her when she called for help.*

The man saw my reaction and said, "There's a team outside. You can't get through us all. You fight, you die."

Before he could say anything else, the sounds of multiple weapons exploded on the street outside. The man jerked his head to the door and I struck him just above his Adam's apple with my fist, crushing his larynx. I ripped the gun out of his hand as he fell to the floor, holding his throat and gasping for air. Leaning over him, I pulled his head up by the hair.

"Oops. Looks like you're not the only one with a team."

I slammed his head into the floor and left the bathroom.

The dining room was full of people cowering and screaming, all intent on getting away from the gunfire. I waded through them, batting panic-stricken tourists aside until I reached the street. Ducking behind a concrete picnic table, I could see muzzle flashes down at the end of the alley. At least four, maybe more. People were screaming and diving in all directions to get away from the gunfire, with two bodies leaking blood onto the alley. I couldn't tell if they were alive or dead.

I sought out where I'd left the team and saw Retro across the alley, pistol raised and looking for a target.

I keyed my radio, "Retro, take your guys and flank them. Hit them while they're still focused on the alley. I'm going back into the restaurant to find a rear exit. You hit them from the left flank and I'll hit them from the rear."

Retro caught my eye across the alley, keying his radio. "Roger that. I told you we should have brought at least one long gun. Don't take too long or the fight'll be over."

I nodded at him and turned to go back inside. I saw a small child in the alley, sitting and crying. In the middle of the funnel of rounds.

Jennifer looked at the blood on her arms, not sure how much was hers. She saw a three-inch gash in the fleshy part of her forearm, sending a stab of nausea through her. It looked like a piece of steak from the butcher, her meat leaking blood much slower than she expected. She grabbed a tourist keffiyeh and wrapped it tightly around the wound, fighting back the dizziness the sight caused. The gunfire continued outside, snapping and popping in a steady stream. She duckwalked to the front of the store and peered around a shelf that served as the entrance wall.

Looking down the alley, she saw the body of the store owner faceup, blood pumping from an open head wound. Scores of people of all nationalities were cowering wherever there was cover, and a child of two or three was in the middle of the street, wailing next to the body of a woman.

She saw the team on her side of the alley, pistols raised, looking for a clear shot.

Whoever was shooting at them had no such concerns but was keeping up a steady stream of fire at anything moving, the air in front of her snapping with the crack of supersonic rounds. She counted five muzzle flashes at the end of the alley seventy meters away.

She returned to the boy, mentally begging him to run. She rose into a crouch, preparing to sprint the short distance to him, when a bullet chipped the wood next to her head. She retreated, unable to take her eyes off of the child.

Go. Get him before he dies.

Her body refused to move, the fear of her own death overriding her desire to save the child.

She caught movement out of the corner of her eye, a form sprinting through the bullets. With a shock, she recognized Pike. She wanted to scream at him to stop, but simply watched him in morbid dread, knowing she was going to witness his death.

He reached the boy and scooped him up without breaking stride, running toward her and the safety of the shop. He reached the low shelf she was hiding behind and launched himself into the air, rotating over like a high jumper, the child cradled in his arms. He landed hard on his back, right next to her, his body cushioning the boy. He lay still.

She shook his shoulders, leaning over him, "Are you hit?"

He looked at her in surprise, letting the boy scamper to the back of the store. He sat up, his face splitting into a grin. "I don't think so, but I'll be damned if I know why. What the hell are you doing here?"

She said, "I found —"

He cut her off with a raised finger, listening to his covert earplug.

"No, we aren't breaking contact. Smoke those fuckers."

He returned to Jennifer, saying, "Retro's flanking now. I want to keep them focused down here."

He leaned out and snapped off a couple of rounds, drawing a fusillade of fire in return, the wood chipping all around him. He snapped his head back.

"Jesus. He'd better hurry the fuck up because I'm not doing that again."

The words still hung in the air when the gunfight erupted, the random popping of rounds replaced by a cacophony that sounded like a string of firecrackers. In seconds it ended, the silence overpowering.

She heard Pike say, "Roger that. The guy in the bathroom had a Chinese passport as well. Everyone okay?"

He paused a second, listening, then said,

250

"Good to go. Starburst out of here before the cops show up. We'll meet back at the hotel."

Scanning the store, he saw for the first time the corpse of the Chinese man Jennifer had fought. Walking over to it, he took in the massive trauma to the head and the bloody lamp next to the body. He looked at Jennifer leaning back against the shelf, her head on her arms. He noticed the keffiyeh, a red stain in the middle.

"You okay?"

She looked at the body, then at him.

"No . . . no, I'm not."

33

Keshawn Jackson leaned up on an elbow, barely able to pick out the slumbering form next to him in the feeble light of dawn. A glance at his cheap Casio caused a spark of concern. It was past six.

Roommate will be home soon. This was a mistake.

The relationship was the one rule he had broken, the one time he had slipped in his five years of iron discipline. After he'd left prison, he had followed the proscriptions of the Muslim chaplain to the letter, both religious and operational. As the years went by, he had maintained that rigid obedience. Then he had met Beth.

A checkout clerk at a local supermarket, at first he had ignored her as just another heathen. Over time, her chipper attitude had worn him down, continually asking him questions every time he shopped, no matter how indifferent he acted. Initially acting pleasant simply to avoid drawing attention, he found himself engaging her in conversation. He knew it was a mistake — knew he couldn't do anything beyond pleasantries — but he did it anyway.

He had learned quite a bit about her during the shopping trips. She didn't drink, was a pious churchgoer and a devoted volunteer of various causes. And she was very, very pretty. Against his better judgment, he did the unthinkable: He asked her out.

They had dated for close to a year, with him following the best tradecraft he could, given the situation. He never let her go to his residence, and stayed over at her place no more than once a week. Always only on nights when her roommate was sleeping over at her boyfriend's house, and he always left before she came home. He never, ever mentioned to his contact what he was doing. He knew what would happen if he did.

He'd told himself that he'd break it off the minute he was alerted for a mission. Now, staring at her slumbering form, he cursed his weakness. He was far beyond simply being alerted, and yet he persisted still.

He was lightly stroking her face, fantasizing about bringing her with him, about converting her to the one pure religion, when she awoke.

"Hey. I gotta go. It's the witching hour."

She grasped his hand and pressed it into her face. "Just stay for breakfast this once. My roommate is beginning to think I'm a liar. Or that I'm paying you."

He laughed, using his standard excuse. "I have to get to work. You know that." He leaned over and kissed her. "I'll call you later."

She said, "Let's go to your place next. Please? I know you're embarrassed about it, but I don't care if it's just a trailer or something worse. You shouldn't care either."

He stood up and put on his clothes. "I'll think about it, okay? I promise."

She followed him to the door, wearing just a sheet. He kissed her again, and walked to his car.

He sat and watched her close the door, feeling conflicted. He had his instructions, and the time was coming closer. Today, he was supposed to rent a warehouse that would facilitate the building of the means of destruction. A warehouse with an address that could be accessed by DHL. He should have felt elation at the progress forward. Should have felt deep gratitude at the responsibility entrusted to him.

Instead, he felt only sadness that he would never see Beth again.

Beth was eating breakfast when her roommate returned, wearing the clothes she had left in the night before.

"So, Mr. Wonderful has hauled ass again, huh?"

"Lay off of him, Kristy. He has to get to work. He's not avoiding you."

Kristy sat down, pouring herself a cup of coffee. "Bullshit. Beth, I don't like this guy. He's hiding something. Something illegal."

"No, he's not. He's just shy. He's a good man. Pure."

"Yeah. Probably selling drugs."

Beth flared in anger. "He doesn't even drink! He's Muslim! He's very strict about those things."

"Well, that's something else that's fucking weird. Are you sure he's not in some sort of cult? Maybe he wants to suck you in. Maybe that's why you never get to see where he lives."

"Stop it! You don't even know him. And anyway, I'm going to surprise him tonight. I'm going to his house."

"How?"

"I'm going to follow him home from work. He's just ashamed of where he lives. He doesn't make any money at his job. I'll show him I don't care about those things."

Kristy's eyebrows shot up. "You be careful with that, you hear me? Call me when you go."

Beth left the apartment without answering.

She bought a small batch of flowers on the way to the supermarket, then spent her entire shift glancing at the clock on the wall. Her replacement showed up early just as she'd promised she would. Beth gave a hurried thank-you and raced out of the store.

She arrived at the BGE district office a little unsure of herself. After much prodding, Keshawn had told her where he worked but hadn't given a firm address, only saying it was on the west side of Baltimore, outside the 695 beltway, at a vehicle barn that housed BGE trucks. She had Googled and found quite a few locations, but had narrowed it down to this place, a large building with a truck barn. She wasn't sure it was correct.

She circled the parking lot, growing more and more leery until she spotted Keshawn's beat-up Honda Civic. She smiled. *Whew. Kristy would really go off if I couldn't even find his place of work.*

She parked her own car away from his,

hidden between a pickup and a large SUV. Her dash clock told her she had only about ten minutes before his shift was up. She watched every truck that returned, finally seeing Keshawn driving one through the chain-link gate.

Fifteen minutes later, she was following him south down the beltway, staying discreetly four cars back. He drove into southeast Baltimore, toward the port and the industrial area. Driving past tow yards and scrap metal recycling facilities, she hoped he didn't live anywhere near here.

Eventually, he pulled into a large, prefabricated storage facility, with a sign out front proclaiming self-storage units, individual office space, and small warehouses for rent.

What's he doing here?

She drove by, did a U-turn, and parked in the next building over. She saw Keshawn in the front office talking to what looked like a manager. Eventually, they disappeared through a back door, then reappeared at the front of a small, stand-alone building with a roll-up door. They both disappeared inside. Five minutes later, they returned, with Keshawn shaking the man's hand. She watched him writing on some paperwork, then shaking his hand again before heading to his car.

What in the world is that all about?

She followed him back the way they had come, eventually traveling past the exit to the BGE office and continuing north. He exited the beltway near Towson, getting into the strip mall suburbs, with Barnes & Noble, movie theaters, and Cheesecake Factory restaurants dominating the drive.

After a few minutes, he pulled into an apartment complex, fairly new with a NOW LEASING sign out front. The cars in the parking lot were all late-model, with a smattering of relatively expensive foreign ones. It didn't look like a place to be ashamed of.

She stayed well away from him, pulling into the first spot she could find and watching. He parked, then went to the second floor. When she was sure he was inside and settled, she grabbed the flowers and went up, feeling anxious at her little treachery.

She knocked on the door and waited, wondering if he was staring at her through the peephole. When the door swung open, she knew he hadn't bothered to use it by the look of shock on his face.

"Hey, honey. Surprise!"

He stood still for a minute, his face flashing first anger, then sadness. "What are you doing here? How'd you find me?"

She handed him the flowers. "I followed you home. I know you don't want me to see where you live, but it's not bad at all. What're you afraid of?"

He said nothing.

She knew something was wrong, but put it down to her little detective work. She tried to lighten the mood.

"Can I come in? Or is the inside a real ghetto?"

He stood back from the door. "I wish you hadn't done this. I would have come for you when the time was right."

She kissed him on the cheek, saying, "I know how you are. The time will never be right unless I make it so."

Inside was a studio apartment with very little furniture. Just a small table with two chairs and a futon on the floor. Not even a TV.

"Wow. You live spartan. No wonder you like coming to my place."

"Yeah. That's what I mean. I can't afford any furniture. I was going to show you the place after I got some. I just rented this a few months ago."

She put her arms around his neck. "You should know me well enough by now. I don't care about that stuff." She panto-mimed sniffing him. "Wow. You stink . . . let's go clean you up."

He said nothing for a moment, seeming

to think it over. Then he smiled and relaxed, "Well, as long as you're here."

He followed her into the bathroom. When she saw the large Jacuzzi tub that came with the apartment, an impish grin slipped out. "Looks like it's big enough for two."

She turned on the water, then began to undress him. While the water filled, she said, "Hey, what's up with the storage place? What're you doing there?"

The happiness fled his face, replaced with the sadness she'd seen at the door.

"It's nothing. Just something a friend wanted me to check on."

She ignored the look, determined to prove her trick wasn't a mistake. "You get in first."

She undressed while he slipped into the water, then sat between his legs, turning on the jets. He began to rub her shoulders, just like he did when they were at her place. The tension left her body. *This is more like it.*

She closed her eyes and said, "Why don't you forget about saving for furniture? We could get a place together. With our combined income, we could afford it."

She thought she'd missed his answer over the sound of the jets. She opened her eyes and turned around to face him. She saw tears falling down his cheeks.

"Keshawn? What's wrong?"

He said nothing. He simply raised his hands to the top of her head and pushed her under the water.

34

Jennifer sat alone on the bed in her hotel room, not wanting to join the team next door. She had the shades drawn and the lights out, with the only illumination coming from a crack in the bathroom door. She could hear the men through the connecting door, laughing and joking.

"I thought we were breaking contact when I saw you running away from the fight like a spotted ape."

"I wasn't running, jackass. I was doing my duty. Protecting civilian lives."

"Yeah, sure."

"The kid was in front of you, and I've seen you shoot. I figured he was in danger. . . ."

She tuned them out, remembering the child. *I should have done something. I was closer.*

Upon their return to the hotel, the first thing the team had done was a hot wash, examining all aspects of the gunfight to see what they could have done differently or better.

It had been brutally critical, with Pike bearing the brunt. The team had hammered him for saving the child, saying he had put them all at risk by forcing them to assault with one less man.

The conversation had shamed Jennifer, making her wonder if anyone had seen her paralysis of fear. The memory alone caused her to tremble. *Why didn't I go?*

She heard the door open and saw Pike in the feeble light.

"Hey," he said. "You okay?"

"Yeah. Just tired."

"Adrenaline will do that. How's your arm?"

She flexed her hand, saying, "Good. Buckshot did a great job. The stitches itch, but that's about it."

"Well, he's had enough practice. He used to be an eighteen Delta in fifth group." Remembering she had no military experience, he added, "A medic. A Special Forces medic."

She nodded and said nothing. Pike came inside and closed the door.

"You sure you're okay?"

"Yes." She waited a beat, then said, "Why did you save that child?"

He leaned against the door, looking confused. "Uhh . . . I don't know. It just seemed like the right thing to do."

Right thing to do.

"But there was no way you should have lived. You had to have known that. Why?"

He became embarrassed at the attention. "Look, I was too stupid to realize that. Trust me, I wouldn't do it again."

She stood up, searching his face for deception. "Really? You wouldn't?"

Pike glanced away for a moment, the returned her gaze. "No. Not really. I'd do it again. That kid was going to die because someone was trying to kill me. I was the cause. I couldn't let that happen."

"But the team . . ."

"Yeah, well, they have a point, but it's the score that counts. They did fine without me, like I knew they would."

She looked down at the floor. "I should have run to him. I was closer. I could have protected him and you could have gone with the team. But I was afraid."

"Cut that shit out. You can't second-guess what you did. You had just finished a fight for your life."

The destroyed visage of the Chinese sprang into her mind, the split skull, the flying bone and brain matter as she struck him again and again. She felt a wave of nausea and sat down again, putting her head into her hands. Pike sat down next to her and rubbed her back, talking softly to her.

She lifted her head and said, "I feel dirty. Like I've crossed a line and I can never go back."

He spoke gently. "I know. It's not easy. Especially with what you were forced to do. You'll have dreams. Bad ones."

His words brought a measure of calm to her, his empathy soothing in the darkness. She reached out and squeezed his hand, wondering if she would ever figure him out.

This was the Pike she was drawn to, a man who risked certain death for an unknown child, but somewhere inside him was the monster from the warehouse. The Pike she didn't know. She flashed again to the body in the souvenir shop. *What about the Jennifer you don't know?*

"Do you get dreams? I mean, still?"

"Yeah. I do. I think it's the body's way of dealing with the stress. Eventually they'll go away and get replaced by good dreams. It just takes time. I used to get them pretty bad right after an action, but within about three to six months, they'd be replaced by dreams of my family. I guarantee I'll dream about that kid and —"

He caught himself and said nothing for a moment, then finished his thought. "And that guy in the warehouse."

She was surprised by the admission, thinking he was different. Stronger or harder. A machine. She changed the subject to get away from the talk of death. "Do you still dream about your family?"

"I used to every night. Like clockwork. Not so much anymore, since Guatemala and Bosnia. Since I ran into you, really."

She was surprised again, and showed it on her face. She knew how deeply the loss of his family had affected him, and couldn't believe that their adventures last year had altered that. "You don't dream about your family anymore? What do you dream about instead?"

He blushed, and looked away. "Nothing really. I just don't dream about them as much anymore."

The truth sank in with a small measure of flattery and a large amount of confusion. *He dreams about me.*

She considered forcing him to say it, just to embarrass him, because she knew he'd do the same to her. The idea caused her to smile as she realized she was thinking of him like she had before the warehouse killing. And that he'd managed to take her mind off the market and her actions there. She squeezed his hand again.

"Thank you."

"For what?"

"For being here. For being yourself, I guess."

He stood up with a little evil grin. "Well, as long as I'm being myself, I have to say I told you so."

"Huh? What do you mean?"

"When push came to shove, you didn't go out on your knees, begging for your life. You may not like it, but you're a meat eater."

She sat for a minute with her mouth open, not believing he'd actually said what he had after she'd opened up about how the death had affected her.

"Jesus, Pike, it's not something to brag about. It's not something I'm proud of. I don't want —"

"Wanting's got nothing to do with it. Some people have it, and some don't. No different from a higher IQ or the ability to run fast. It's a talent, nothing more." He pointed to the next room. "And they don't brag about that shit either, but they do respect it. Which might end up saving their lives someday because they won't be guessing on how you'll react."

It clicked that he was talking as if she was

going to stay with them, as if the killing she'd committed had changed her mind to continue. That wasn't going to happen.

"Pike, I . . . I think I'm going to —"

She was cut off by a shout from the other room. "Pike, you'd better get in here. Kurt's sent a message, and it's about as fucked up as a football bat."

Pike held up a finger to her and said, "Hold that thought. Looks like we get more fun."

She watched him leave the room, the conflicting emotions bouncing through her.

35

The customs agent didn't appear to be particularly vigilant, but looks could be deceiving. Standing behind a party of four from the United States, Rafik felt sweat drip down his side. He silently cursed, knowing no matter how well he pretended to be calm, his body could still give him away. He studied the agent to see how closely the man scrutinized the passports.

Rafik knew his was perfect. A copy that couldn't be discerned from an official Algerian one. It was the Czech Republic tourist visa that concerned him. He had no idea what a real visa looked like and had nothing to compare his against. He'd looked at the loadmaster's passport, but the man had a work visa for his job with Noordin's travel agency. It was similar, but different enough to be of little use. With dark humor, he supposed this was a good test. The same people who were providing him with explosives that could slip through customs had made the visa. *If this fails here, then the explosives will fail to get through customs as well. Might as well find out early.*

Before he knew it, he was being called forward. The agent smiled perfunctorily and said, "What brings you to the Czech Republic?"

Rafik beamed and said, "A visit. My first visit to Europe."

The man took his passport, Rafik waiting on the inevitable barrage of questions, but none came. Before he knew it, he was through and headed to the baggage claim, the stamping and swiping happening so quickly he didn't have time to realize he was holding his breath. He stopped on the far side to watch the loadmaster.

Because four Arabs with tourist visas and one Indonesian with a work visa traveling together would cause questions, they had placed the loadmaster in between them. He was the next in line, and if he was going to sound an alarm, it would be to the customs official.

Rafik watched him lean into the window, apparently talking. Rafik gauged the distance to the baggage claim door, calculating his chances of getting out. When he turned around, he saw the loadmaster walking

270

stiffly toward him. He kept the relief from showing on his face, but the incident drove home how much this operation depended on luck, how many single points of failure littered his operational plan. *All it will take is one link to fail. And I have so many more links to build.*

He knew it was a single link — a courier — that had killed Osama bin Laden. A single thread that had unraveled, leaving the sheik to face the barrels of the Great Satan's commandos. He buried the doubts, saying, "Good, you get to live another day."

The loadmaster said nothing, simply stopping and staring at the other passengers.

"Go get your bags. Call the pilot and tell him to meet us at the plane. Wait for us outside."

Before he could leave, Rafik touched his arm.

"Please don't cause unnecessary bloodshed. Wait for us."

The loadmaster jerked his arm away as if he'd brushed a stove, then walked through the baggage claim door.

By the time Rafik and the others had collected their bags and processed through customs, the loadmaster had made contact.

"He'll meet us at the plane in fifteen minutes. It'll take that long to get there."

"Where is it? At another airport?"

"No, it's technically at this airport, but all private and general aviation aircraft go to terminal three, which is separated from the main airport by the tarmac itself. It's about a mile away, but we'll have to drive out of the airport and down the highway to get there."

Rafik hailed a cab, having a little trouble explaining to the driver that they wanted to go from terminal two to terminal three. Finally convincing the man that he wasn't misunderstanding Rafik's English, they pulled out of the airport.

Reaching the exit for Prague, the driver made one last attempt to ensure he wasn't making a mistake, pointing at the sign showing the city to the left. Rafik pointed to the exit on the right, reading TERMINAL THREE.

The driver shrugged, and followed directions. Winding down a graffiti-painted four-lane road, terminal three came into view. Consisting of several three-story buildings, some modern, others resembling relics from the Cold War, it appeared more like an office park than an airport. As they hit a roundabout, Rafik saw the pilot waiting on the sidewalk and pointed him out to the driver.

The pilot smiled nervously as they approached. When he saw his partner, his face lit up with real joy. He helped them with their bags, saying, "The plane's here. No trouble. We had no trouble."

Rafik said, "Where is it?"

The pilot led them into the building, winding down hallways until they could see the tarmac on the other side through the windows. He showed his badge to a man at a desk and exited the building again, turning left toward the general aviation section. Rafik saw the stolen DHC-6 Twin Otter on a pad next to another cargo plane, a Casa 212. Both with the same tail numbers.

"You didn't repaint the tail?" Rafik said. "Idiot. What if someone sees the two numbers?"

The pilot looked like he had sucked a pickled egg. "Wait. I can't paint the thing right here. That would only highlight the number. It needs to be brought into scheduled maintenance, inside a hangar."

He paused, waiting to see what Rafik would do. When no violence or threats erupted, he continued, "I'll do it this week. I have it scheduled."

"That may be a problem."

"Why?"

Rafik glanced at Kamil and said, "You're going to Montreal, Canada. With some cargo I need."

The pilot paled. "I can't do that. I . . . I —"

Rafik faced him and bared his teeth. "Shut up. You *will* do it. File the flight plan."

The pilot stuttered, his mouth working but no words coming out. Eventually, he said, "When?"

Rafik looked at Kamil. "It depends. We have a call to make. Show me the cargo."

Walking up the staircase of the Twin Otter, the pilot popped the clasps on two pelican cases, both four feet by four feet. Rafik opened the lid of the first one. Inside, seated into foam receptacles, were what appeared to be simple metal disks. He pulled one out. Eight inches in diameter, it was slightly curved and would have looked exactly like a lid off of a soup pot except it was much thicker.

Opening the other pelican case, he pulled out a plastic container. This too was eight inches in diameter and about eight inches deep, looking like a soup pot made for the lid he held in his other hand. He lined up the holes on the outside of the lid with the holes on the edge of the pot, the curved side down. The match was perfect, as he knew it would be.

He smiled. "Such a simple-looking thing.

With so much destructive power."

Kamil said, "The Great Satan's own technology will be their downfall. It's a shame that they spend so much time and money creating these weapons only to have them used against themselves."

Rafik laughed. "Not a great deal of shame. Not at all."

Rafik placed the pieces back into the cases. Turning to the pilot, he said, "I need to find an air express service. One that will go to the United States."

"Both DHL and FedEx fly right to this terminal. They have an office downstairs, but I don't know if they'll take a shipment from here. You might have to take it downtown first."

"That's stupid. Go figure out how to schedule this cargo for shipment. Tell them it's from your office. I'll give you an address when you get back."

Kamil waited until the pilot had left, then said, "I don't think we should send the package from here if that's not what's usually done. We should get it into the system without shortcuts so it's harder to track. And no way should that pilot get the address. We should do it ourselves."

Rafik whipped his head around, incensed at Kamil questioning his authority. He was about to tear into him when the logic of his statement sank in. Kamil refused to break eye contact. Rafik patted his face. "Always looking out for me. For the mission. Okay. We'll do it your way. Get the information when the pilot returns. Before that, though, call the *kafir* here. Set up the meeting like we discussed. Be sure you actually see the explosives. Those men would sell us a crate of clay. Islam won't help you, no matter how much they say otherwise."

Kamil pointed at the loadmaster. "What about him?"

"Keep him. There's no telling where you'll have to meet them. An aircraft may be useful, and I want to give this pilot a reason to transport you to Canada. I'm taking Farouk. I'll leave Adnan. Use his expertise in explosives to inspect the cargo."

Kamil said, "What do I do if this contact fails? They aren't the most trustworthy of people and have no allegiance to our cause."

"Get the explosives. Don't let it fail. Do what you need to do."

Seeing Kamil's reticence and knowing the source, he said, "Old friend, we do what we must. I know how you feel, and maybe someday we'll get the chance to teach them the true meaning of Islam. Stay focused on the goal. Using them is no different than using the weapons on this plane."

36

The Marine staff sergeant on duty at Post One kept eyeballing Retro and me, like he thought we were going to steal the ashtray in the lobby. We'd done nothing wrong, and told him we were simply meeting someone, but he clearly thought we were suspicious. I decided to wait outside. Better for him not to remember who we met. Motioning to Retro, I walked out into the courtyard.

"Man," Retro said, "you'd think that guy'd lay off a little with all the security around this place."

He had a point. The U.S. Embassy in Cairo had pretty much taken over the neighborhood, with all the streets blocked off and guarded by Egyptian police. The only people allowed in the neighborhood were those who lived there. If you got past that, you still had to contend with both an outer and inner embassy wall, each complete with a security checkpoint just like an airport, before getting inside to the Marine manning Post One.

"He's just doing his job," I said. "I don't know what the hell's taking that agency guy so long."

"Maybe he didn't get the word how important we are."

I laughed. "Bullshit. You heard Kurt. I guarantee that guy got a call straight from the seventh floor."

The message Kurt had sent stated that the picture on his father's roll of film might belong to a man named Richard Ellis, a United States congressman. The kicker was that he was currently in Cairo. I'd immediately called Kurt through the VPN and put him on conference, wanting to confirm the information and what I was supposed to do. At the end of the call, the consensus was to simply confront him — to shake the tree and see what came out. We both thought something was awry, and decided to let him tell us what it was.

The problem was precisely that he *was* a United States congressman and would have to be handled carefully. If we were wrong about the picture, we needed to leave the congressman without any impression that he was being investigated. To that end, we'd come to talk to the CIA and get a little help with the "interrogation."

Mixing the Taskforce with CIA personnel was risky, and the reason we didn't want to sign in with Post One, but apparently the president himself was involved. That sort of overcame any bitching we had. No doubt he put out some tough love, which is why I thought the director of the CIA — a member of the Oversight Council — would be calling from his seventh-floor office at headquarters.

I saw a middle-aged man exit the door next to Post One and head our way.

"You guys here to meet someone from the State Department?"

"No. From another agency."

He smiled. "We going to dance all day?"

"Depends on who called you."

"How about the president? That good enough?"

I was a little startled. "The president called you?"

"Naw. But he might as well have. Big shit storm apparently."

It would be embarrassing to spill my guts to some State Department weenie, so I pushed just a little further to be sure. "And you are?"

"Mack Gleason. I'm the head honcho here. Look, I don't know who you are and I was told not to ask. No record of us meeting. That's fine with me, but I'll need something to go on. I have no idea what this is about."

That was enough for me. I hadn't expected the actual chief of station, but I suppose I should have, given the level of interest. I told him everything I knew, which raised his eyebrows.

"Holy shit. You think Ellis is a traitor? I'm supposed to see him tomorrow."

"I don't know what to think. There's definitely some sort of Chinese connection, but it beats me what it is. On top of that, this whole thing is tied into an Indonesian terrorist. Either way, I want to find out what's going on."

"But why me? I don't have any arrest authority. This is a job for the LEGATT. It's for the FBI."

I couldn't tell him that the adjutant general of the United States wasn't read on to the Taskforce, unlike the director of the CIA, and so the FBI's legal attaché wasn't someone we could use. Hell, I couldn't even tell him my name.

"You've been pulled in because this is very, very sensitive. Very political. We're not sure of the information, and need to find out discreetly. This is exactly what you guys do, and not something I'm very good at. We need some help. If it ends up being something, it's all yours. You pull in the LEGATT and we disappear, never to be mentioned. Okay?"

He was easygoing, like most of the CIA folks. He rolled right into the mission.

"Okay by me. So what's the play? What are you going to do?"

"Shit, man, that's why I'm here. I don't know. My plan was to knock on his hotel-room door and beat the shit out of him, but that didn't go over so well at home, given the political stakes. We're looking for ideas. You guys are the experts at nuance."

"Well . . . like I said, he's coming here tomorrow for a briefing. From what I got from headquarters, he used to work for the CIA as a case officer, and he's now on the Intelligence Committee. He likes to flaunt that by hitting up the station of every country he happens to visit. Makes him feel important to leave his fellow congressman at the door as uncleared."

I rapidly analyzed the gift just dropped in my lap. The congressman himself had just taken a huge burden off of my shoulders, since we wouldn't have to set up some phony meeting that would raise his suspicions. If he was innocent, we could get away clean.

I said, "How do these briefings go? Are there a lot of people in the room?"

"Yeah," he said. "At least initially. We give a one-over-the-world, then, when it's time to get down to truly secret stuff, we take him alone to a secure room and continue."

I said, "What's the briefing on?"

"Nothing important, really. He didn't ask for a specific topic. We're just going to give him our standard dog and pony show, letting him feel like he's getting secrets. Now I'm not so sure that's smart."

"No, no. That's perfect. Sway the briefing to include a bunch of Chinese stuff. Throw it in midway, completely out of synch with the rest of the briefing. Get a feel for his demeanor during the first half of the briefing, then see if it shifts when the Chinese are mentioned."

Mack thought about it, then said, "Yeah, I can do that. I'll get a case officer in the room and introduce him as an analyst. He can focus on the congressman and knows what to look for. But I'll tell you, that's exactly why this won't work. The congressman used to be a case officer. He's trained to detect deception, just like my guy. He'll know how to hide everything we're going to be looking for. If he's really a traitor, he's been pretty damn good at it to stay out of sight all these years."

"I'm not so sure about that. If he's bad, he's got something to do with that terrorist strike in Alexandria, which means he's willing to take drastic action for something. It also means he might be desperate. He might be able to hide his reaction if he knows he's going to be questioned, but he'll be off guard here."

"Yeah, well, I suppose it won't hurt to give it a shot. What do you want to do if he spikes?"

"Bring him alone to the secure room. Retro and I will be waiting. When he sees us, we'll get a reaction. If he's bad, he tried to kill me, which means he knows what I look like. We'll take it from there."

"And if there's no demeanor break during the briefing?"

"Text us. We'll vacate the room, and you just go on with your briefing."

37

Congressman Ellis was enjoying his time in the embassy, forgetting for a moment the stress of the transfer. His background as a case officer, along with his standing on the Intelligence Committee, allowed him greater access to CIA stations than most any other elected representative, but in truth, he just liked getting close to the field again. He enjoyed the back-and-forth with the chiefs of station, even though he knew the briefings were all sterile and made for public consumption. It allowed him to feel like he was on the inside. Still a case officer like Mack, the one doing the briefing. Very few other representatives could make that claim, and he enjoyed the notoriety.

As Mack continued with the political situation, Ellis threw a few softball questions his way, probing his opinion of the still struggling government after the fall of Mubarak. Mack gave him a softball answer, and Ellis ratcheted it up a little bit, having done his homework. He enjoyed watching Mack's reaction, realizing he wasn't dealing with an idiot. The banter continued back and forth, with Ellis feeling more and more in control of the conversation.

Mack finished the political overview and started into domestic threats. He gave a fairly innocuous overview of the Muslim Brotherhood, detailing the radical elements that were hidden inside the relatively new political party, along with the threats they posed to the fragile stability of the country. Ellis found himself growing bored with the presentation. Everything being briefed was something that could be found on the Internet within three minutes. Mack flipped the slide to a picture of carnage, a bus strike in the north. Ellis recognized the photo and felt his pulse quicken a tad. *What's his take on this?*

He snorted, saying, "These guys need to get a handle on their own domestic problems, or they're going to lose their tourism industry forever."

"We're not sure this is domestic," Mack said. "There's some indication of foreign influence."

Ellis heard the words, feeling a trickle of adrenaline. "Are you talking al Qaeda?"

286

"No. China or Indonesia."

The words sliced into his brain, his involuntary reflexes draining his face. He controlled his response immediately, reverting to training long since gone. *Get stable. Get control. Find out what they know. You are not the enemy.*

He said, "That's the craziest thing I've ever heard. Why would the Chinese do that?"

Solemn as a priest, Mack responded, "I'm not at liberty to say why in this room. I'll fill you in later, in the confidential briefing. But it's not a simple terrorist strike."

Ellis nodded, feeling the heat in his face. *Jesus Christ. They know something is screwy with that attack. They* know.

The brief continued, with Ellis throwing out useless questions to appear as if he was still engaged. He appeared outwardly calm. At least as calm as he could project, but inside, his stomach was churning as he dissected what possible connections could be made to him. None, as far as he could tell, and the fact that he had been briefed at all on the station's suspicions indicated he was not in the crosshairs. He calmed down, thinking he needed to make a call. Now.

It took the congressman a pregnant second to realize the briefing had ended. He focused on the chief of station and found everyone in the room looking at him expectantly. *Shit. Get control.*

Mack said, "Ready for the good stuff?"

"I need to make a phone call before we continue."

"I'm sorry, sir, but no cell phones are allowed in CIA spaces." He smiled. "Technology's changed since you worked the streets. If you wish, you can return to Post One for the call. We'll wait."

Congressman Ellis debated, then said, "No, that's all right. Let's continue. I'd like to hear about the Chinese."

Ellis failed to see the man at the back of the briefing hit the send button on his cell phone.

I felt my cell phone vibrate and looked at the message on the screen.

"Showtime. We're a go."

Retro and I positioned ourselves on the left side of the door so we wouldn't be seen until the congressman had already penetrated into the room, allowing Mack to close the door behind him. The congressman thought he was coming to a secure facility to discuss classified material, but in reality, we were simply in an office down the hall from the conference room, on the other side of the courtyard of the embassy. Since he'd never been to the Cairo embassy, I had no fears that Ellis would realize he wasn't headed to the CIA office space, and it kept us from having to go through Marine Post One. It also allowed us to keep our cell phones.

I really hoped that Mack had called it correctly and that Ellis was bad. Once he came through that door, we'd be seen and have to be explained. It was a dangerous game, and I was unsure what I would do if he had no reaction to our presence. It was a make-or-break line I would have to cross. I felt like Tom Cruise about to accuse Jack Nicholson of conducting a Code Red.

I needn't have worried. The door opened, and Congressman Ellis strode in, wiping his forehead with a handkerchief. He saw me and stopped short. He heard Mack close the door and whirled around.

"What's the meaning of this? Who are these men?"

Not the reaction of an innocent man. I decided to go the Tom Cruise route.

"Sit down, Congressman. We just have a few questions."

He regained his composure. "I'm not here to answer questions. I'm here to ask them. Let's get this briefing going."

I stood up and advanced toward him. "I said sit the fuck down. And you *will* answer our questions."

He did as I asked, but remained defiant. "Do you realize I'm a United States congressman? I have no idea what government agency you work for, but wherever it is, I'm going to find out and have your ass."

"That's going to be a problem," I said, "because I don't work for the government. So save your threats."

I saw a flicker of fear for the first time. He went through his pockets rapidly, then remembered.

"That's right," I said. "No cell phones allowed in here. It's just you and me."

"I'm still an American citizen. Just because we're in Egypt doesn't mean you can sit here and accuse me of some bullshit charge."

I heard him say "accuse," and knew he was guilty. I lost all compunction about being polite. He had something to do with the death of Bull and the wounding of Knuckles, and would now pay the price. Retro came to the same conclusion I had.

He moved behind Ellis. Speaking quietly, the venom dripping out, he said, "We can do whatever the fuck we want. And right now I want you to look at a picture. Make no mistake, your life is over. The only question now is how it will end. You fuck with me and it will be a world of pain before the lights go out."

I saw real terror begin to grow in his eyes, tinged with desperation. He jumped up and strode over to Mack.

"What the hell is going on here? I want my cell phone. And your supervisor's number. I'm a *United States congressman*. Do you know what that means?"

Mack stood by the door, mute.

Ellis turned to me. "I'm through here. I'm leaving. You try to stop me and I'll have the Marines here lock you up forever."

His face was a sickly green, with a fine mist of sweat on his brow, as if we were in a rain forest instead of the desert. His breath was coming in shallow pants, his eyes flicking from me to Retro. He made a move to the door and I threw the photo from Kurt's father on the table. He caught the movement and looked down.

"Tell me about this."

The quality was absolutely horrible, with a vague figure standing on the edge of a lanai somewhere on the earth. To me it meant nothing at all. To the congressman, it meant everything. As soon as he saw it, he gave a strangled little squeak, swayed a bit, then sank into a chair, his head in his hands.

Still not knowing what I held, I gave Retro a questioning look. He ran his fingers across his throat, the implication clear. *Crush him now. Don't give him any time to think.*

I grabbed a headful of hair, pulling up his face.

"Give me when and where."

His eyes had a glassy stare, no comprehension in them at all. I lightly slapped his face.

"Wake the fuck up. When and where?"

He snapped back to the present, focusing on me.

"I . . . I . . . that was a long time ago . . . I didn't tell anyone . . . you can't talk about it . . . it's secret . . ."

He was babbling and I wondered if he was about to have a real breakdown. Retro circled around behind him again and I shook my head. I didn't want him going over the edge. On the other hand, I didn't want him to have time to come up with a story. *Need to keep the pressure steady.*

"Vietnam is over, Congressman. There's no secrets left from that war. Chris Hale is dead."

I don't know if it was the mention of Kurt's father or Vietnam itself, but it was enough. The words convinced Congressman Ellis that I knew a helluva lot more than I did. He slumped back in his chair and eyed me.

"Okay . . . okay. You know where it is. What do you want from me?"

"I want you to tell me the story. Now."

And surprisingly, he did. After burying himself as deep as he possibly could, cementing his future, he quit. He looked at me expectantly, like he'd now earned something in return, but he hadn't said a damn thing about what was going on here.

"I got all that. I want to know what you were doing with the Chinese in Egypt."

His face showed confusion, as if I *should have known* what had happened.

"You . . . you took the shipment here. That's all I was doing. That's it."

"What shipment?"

He squinted, his brain beginning to realize he may have made a huge mistake. *Can't lose momentum.* I closed into his personal space and locked eyes with him, speaking softly.

"Congressman, let me explain something to you. Right now, you're wondering what to say, what to protect. You're thinking that maybe if you shut up, you'll save something a lawyer can use to plea bargain, but that's not going to happen."

I snatched his thumb and quickly bent it

backward, stopping just short of breaking it. He screamed, a short, sharp sound that echoed in the room. I continued speaking calmly.

"I told you, I don't work for the government, and you've had a hand in the death of a friend of mine. What you need to be concerned with right now is how painful your death will be."

The little droplets of sweat on his brow grew larger, until they trickled down his face. I released his thumb and he jerked his hand away, massaging his thumb. He began talking.

"I had a shipment of EFPs to transfer to the Chinese. Last night someone attacked the shipment and took them. I thought it was you."

Explosively formed penetrators were powerful shaped charges designed to penetrate armor at a distance. Basically just a metal dish on top of some explosive material that, when fired, warped the dish, turning it into a bullet of molten metal with aerodynamic properties traveling at hypersonic speed. They had played hell on our troops in Iraq, easily defeating even our best armor systems. While a simple concept, it required a great deal of technical capability to execute properly. The shape, diameter, thickness, and type of metal were mathematically intertwined with the ignition system and the amount and type of explosive material. Any small variant would destroy the aerodynamic properties or render the charge no more potent than shrapnel from a mortar round. Even so, EFPs had been around since World War II, and the construction parameters were widely available. It wasn't rocket science. Even if it was, the Chinese *had* rocket scientists. It didn't make sense.

"Why would the Chinese risk so much for EFPs? They can already make them."

Ellis said, "You know anything about shaped charges?"

"Enough to know that the Chinese don't need American technology to make their own."

"Not like these. The average EFP with a copper or iron plate can penetrate half of its diameter through armor steel. You have an eight-inch plate, you can penetrate four inches of armor. Change the plate to tantalum and it goes one-to-one.

"These plates were made with nanotechnology. The grain structure of the tantalum was altered at the molecular level specifically to enhance its potential as an EFP. It worked better than anyone predicted. Now, instead of halving the diameter, you square it. Up to an eight-inch plate. Then it begins to fall off again."

What he said sank in. While the EFPs in Iraq were deadly, they were also large, cumbersome things. In order to defeat an M1A1 Abrams tank, the insurgent had to lug around something that weighed damn near a hundred pounds with a width like a turkey platter. These EFPs could do the same damage with something as small as an eight-inch plate. And the little traitor wasn't finished.

"The nano work also increased the aerodynamic properties. Instead of a range of one hundred feet, the spall flies accurately up to one hundred meters. It's a true standoff attack capability."

I'd heard enough. "What did you give them? Just the plates? You couldn't fly in here with completed EFPs. You'd never get out of the U.S."

"The entire effort was an enhancement of the M303 Special Operations Demolitions Kit. It'll be in the U.S. inventory in a couple of years. The Chinese wanted to see if they could reverse engineer the plate."

The M303 SODK was a do-it-yourself explosives kit consisting of all the components needed to destroy just about anything.

Bridges, roads, aircraft, you name it, there was something in the kit that could be used. All it was missing was the explosives. We used to joke about the old commercials that said "just add water" because the kit was idiot-proof, complete with instructions for each device. You just packed the explosives into the chosen container according to the directions, installed an initiation capability, and followed the instructions for implementation.

"You mean you gave them the complete charge container, aiming devices, everything?"

I was hoping this bastard had transferred only the plates. While they were a large part of success, they were still just a part. Without knowing specifically how much explosives to use and how shallow or deep to form it behind the plate, the EFP would still fail. If he gave them the kit, that was worked out ahead of time. All that had to happen was jamming the explosives into the container that was already mathematically mated to the plate.

"Yeah. I was bringing the complete set, but I told you, I didn't get a chance to give them to anyone."

"What happened?"

He gave me what he knew, telling me what

he had planned and what had actually happened. He ended by saying that he'd thought I was behind the theft. He didn't have any idea who else it could be, but I did. *That guy in the tombs. This idiot just outfitted a terrorist with our latest technology.*

Mack pulled my sleeve. "Can I see you outside for a minute?"

"Sure." I looked at Retro. "He does anything but sit in that chair, kill him."

"How about I just kill him anyway?"

I saw the congressman scooting back as I left the room.

Once the door shut, Mack said, "What do you want to do with this guy?"

"I told you, that's your call."

"Well, I was thinking of turning him. Get him to go back to the Chinese and say he was wrong, that the airplane was delayed or some other bullshit. Then pass them faulty plates. Worse case, they figure it out and end up with nothing. Best case, they reverse-engineer the faulty plates and fill their armories with crap."

And that's why he was the chief of station. My imagination ended with beating the man to a bloody pulp. His allowed him to see an angle in this disaster that could prove to be as big a positive as the loss of the plates were a negative.

"Can you do that? I mean get something that'll pass muster that quick?"

"Won't know until I try, but it's worth a shot."

"What about the dead Chinese? We killed a few at the market because that asshole fingered us, and their boss may still want some payback."

"That was you? Jesus, you've got the entire agency spinning their wheels trying to figure out what the hell happened."

He turned away, thinking for a moment, then said, "I'll come up with a story and feed it to them. I can make that work. Are you on board?"

"Yeah, but the minute this guy quits being an asset, he gets burned."

When we reentered the room, I half expected to find Retro branding the guy's face with the coffeepot. Instead, the congressman was sitting where we'd left him, looking sorry for himself. Mack took the lead and explained what he wanted to do.

The congressman's eyes got wider and wider until he finally said, "This won't work! They'll never believe it. They'll kill me when they find out I'm trying to trick them."

I said, "Looks like you're dead either way, then, because if you don't do it, I'm going to throw your ass off the roof. So you want to give it a shot and extend your life, or save us all the exertion by choking yourself to death?"

38

"Jesus Christ! He's a fucking traitor? How are we supposed to deal with that?"

Kurt remained calm, letting Secretary of State Brookings blow off some steam, knowing President Warren would rein him in if necessary.

It was clear that Brookings was becoming an issue on the Oversight Council. A man more concerned with the effect on his career should the Taskforce become public knowledge than any judgment about how best to secure the nation. The mixing of traditional counterintelligence, a near-peer competitor like the Chinese, a U.S. congressman, and Project Prometheus was scaring the hell out of him. *And he has a point. We're on the ragged edge of this whole thing showing up on Fox News.*

The director of central intelligence said, "Let me deal with that." He addressed the president. "Sir, I'd prefer to talk to you off-line. It's not Taskforce business and doesn't need the Oversight Council."

Brookings rolled his eyes again. "The old 'sources and methods' excuse?"

The DCI said, "Actually, yes. There's a reason that rule was put in place. Usually because pompous asses like yourself caused the death of someone."

The president raised his hand. "Enough. Ordinarily I'd agree, but since everyone here now knows the congressman's status, let's hash out what we're going to do about it. I don't want a bunch of guessing the next time he's on TV."

The DCI grimaced, but relented. He relayed the plan with the faulty EFPs and the fact that the CIA would wring out of him anything and everything he had ever done against the United States.

President Warren asked, "And after that? Are we going to arrest him or what?"

"No, sir. If we did, the Chinese would suspect the plates. I'm also afraid that the whirlwind of media will uncover Pike and Decoy's little interrogation, and we can't have that come to light. Congressman Ellis has agreed to resign after we're through with him and an appropriate time has elapsed."

Kurt said, "Are you kidding? That's it? He

leaves office?"

The DCI smiled. "Yes. After we 'find' child pornography on his government computer. Then find more in his house. He's agreed to plead guilty to kiddy porn charges and go to jail. If he decides not to, he knows we'll be seeking the death penalty for his treason. It's a good trade."

Kurt blurted, "That fucker killed my father! What kind of 'good trade' is that?"

"Kurt," said President Warren, "I hear you. I really do, but you know the stakes. Killing him won't bring back your father, but this might save someone else's life. Don't jeopardize the Taskforce on a vendetta that will do no good."

Kurt said nothing.

President Warren took the silence as acquiescence, telling the DCI to execute the plan, then turned back to Kurt. "Let's get back to the current threat. What about the EFPs? Who has them?"

Kurt struggled with what to say next. It took a great effort, but he ripped himself away from the congressman and thoughts of his father, knowing the president was right. He exhaled and returned to the EFPs. "We don't really know. The team has an idea, but it basically ends with a dead Indonesian terrorist and three Arabic-looking gentlemen. We believe they've flown to Prague."

"Why?"

"Jennifer was in the airport with them at the same time. She's the one who reported it. We'll know more when the team gets to Prague."

Secretary Brookings cut in. "Prague? Who gave you permission to do that? You've moved a team without Oversight approval?"

He turned to the president. "Sir, I demand they return. We haven't done any analysis on the Czech Republic at all. Project Prometheus is getting looser and looser. Why even have an oversight council if this guy" — he jerked a thumb at Kurt — "can ignore us?"

Kurt said, "All I did was get them a Task-force aircraft. They had to have a way to get their kit through customs and we don't have a lot of time to screw around. They won't do anything until we give them the execute order. They're just preparing the battle space for follow-on operations. *If* you give them permission."

Secretary Brookings scoffed. "What the hell does that mean? 'Preparing the battle space'? That's just bullshit DOD mumbo jumbo. Like saying 'kinetic option' when you mean put a bullet in someone's head."

President Warren said, "When will Jennifer get here? Can she appear before the Oversight Council for a firsthand debrief?"

Kurt inwardly cringed at the terminology. *Appear before the council? You mean can she come talk?* The way the president phrased it sounded like the council was going to start chopping heads, like all the other witch hunts that happened after 9/11.

"Sir, she's with the team."

"I thought she was coming home because she was sick?"

"She was, but she's the only one who knows what they look like. Pike's convinced her to stay."

President Warren took that in, then said, "Okay, what's the team going to do when they get to Prague?"

"Pull the thread on Noordin's Prague office, if you give permission. It's all we've got."

The director of the CIA spoke. "Sir, I say let them investigate further. What we know for a fact is that a planeload of highly sophisticated demolitions is now out of U.S. hands. From the evidence, I think Pike's on to something. Let 'em go."

Brookings chimed in. "Why? They've got no evidence at all. Just a random sighting in an airport. Even the *suspected* terrorist we were originally tracking is dead. Let's say they do have the EFPs — and I'm not saying I think they do — what's the big deal? It's not like they're running around with a nuclear weapon. We need to use conventional assets. The threat's not worth the risk. Mark my words, this is going to end up on the front page of the *Post*."

The DCI leaned across the table until he was inches from Brookings' face. "Shut the fuck up. There's an attack on the way, and you know it. The intel is incontrovertible. If these guys have a way to stop it, let them go. Quit worrying about your own sorry ass."

President Warren broke in. "Stop it. We're all under the gun here, but there's no reason to start acting like this is our first dance."

Kurt watched the DCI lean back in his chair, his face a mask of calm. The subtle admonishment had accomplished the president's goal. Even with the stakes, nobody wanted to be remembered as the guy who couldn't handle the pressure. Least of all the director of central intelligence.

The DCI said, "It may not be nuclear, but trust me, it's bad."

President Warren said, "What do you mean?"

"Remember the covert action we did in

Sudan a couple of years ago? The one where the 'rebels' managed to destroy a Chinese oil refinery?"

"Yes. What's that got to do with this?"

"My operative used one of these EFPs to get it done, while it was still in testing. It was chosen because of its standoff capabilities. We didn't really look at its destructive power, but it ended up being significant. It ripped through the entire refinery."

"I thought you just took out a critical component, and the rebels did the rest?"

"We *targeted* a critical component. The EFP took out the *refinery.* Trust me, these things are deadly. If the terrorists are creative, we're looking at damage that rivals a WMD."

"Jesus Christ. Why wasn't I told about this?"

"Uhh . . . well, you *were* briefed on the damage and the impact. We don't usually brief you on the tactical details. It wasn't kept from you intentionally. We did report the results to DARPA for further development."

The president closed his eyes, letting the statement sink in, then said, "I want all intelligence related to the EFPs in the system, yesterday. I don't care how you do it. Wash it of Taskforce fingerprints, but get

it out there. FBI, ATF, local law enforcement, *everyone.*"

39

I was thinking about ordering another drink to give me a plausible reason to remain at my table, when Jennifer called, her information surprising the hell out of me.

"Got one of them. He's leaving the hotel now. Picture's on the way."

I pulled up the imaging software on my phone and saw an Arabic man with a thin, acerbic face and prominent ears that jutted out from the sides of his head like small wings.

"Which way?"

"Hang on. . . . Okay, he's headed east."

"Good work. See if you can get a facial ID on the others — break-break — Retro, he's coming by you. Pick him up and slave his phone. Everyone else stand by."

I was sitting at an outside patio just down the street from the suspected terrorists' hotel, with the rest of the team at various other nearby locations, waiting to take over surveillance when I directed. I knew they were amped up, because there was no way we should have found the terrorists on our first attempt.

As soon as we'd landed in Prague, I had the team start working Noordin's office. We didn't have authority to do anything overt, but I figured necking down the terrorist's location fell under the rubric of "preparing the battle space." Naturally, I didn't ask permission. It was easier to ask forgiveness, and I knew by the fact that Kurt hadn't demanded an ops update that he didn't want to know what we were doing.

We'd usually send a situation report when we hit the ground, but in this case Kurt would be forced to tell me to stand down, so we both acted like a report wasn't necessary. Which was really stretching things, because we'd done quite a few operational acts in a short span of time.

First, we'd taken a snapshot of the cell activity in and around the building that housed Noordin's Prague office. As expected, there were a bazillion cell phones in use, but running a reverse lookup left only a dozen or so that were pay-as-you-go and not tied to a human. Once we necked those down, we simply analyzed which phones were talking to each other, figuring that the terrorists had to be in contact. That left four phones, all interconnected.

We could have picked a phone and done some black magic to get it to tell us where it was located, provided it had a GPS, but the activity could be detected by the cell service provider and might lead to questions and an investigation into *our* cell phones. Especially in a city with well-developed infrastructure, such as Prague. It was better to leave that as a last resort, so we did it the hard way.

We spent a day looking at historical location patterns of the cell phones, plotting on a computer map each tower they talked to. We found that two spent the night within a tower footprint near several hotels. The other two had disappeared while we worked, either because they were turned off, had a dead battery, or — worst case — had left the area.

Early this morning, we'd received execute authority from the Oversight Council to "develop the situation," which was military speak for "I don't know what the hell to tell you. Figure it out." I had no problem doing that, since it pretty much gave me carte blanche to do whatever I thought was necessary, as long as I didn't get caught. My plan was simple: Locate the Arabs, then follow them until we could confirm or deny terrorist activity.

We took our best guess at which hotel the men might use inside the cell-tower footprint we'd found, then put Jennifer in it, the one person who knew what the suspects looked like. I figured it would take several stakeouts at different hotels before we hit the jackpot and had planned for a week to simply locate them, but we'd gotten lucky on our very first one.

My little hands-free earpiece crackled again. "Pike, Retro. I have eyes on Jug-ears."

Kamil broke out onto the street and was blinded by the sunlight. He waited a bit, letting his eyes adjust from the gloom of the cheap hotel they'd found.

The man on the phone had given him strict instructions to follow, a connect-the-dots travel pattern designed to sniff out whether he was helping the police, either wittingly or unwittingly. He didn't mind at all, and in fact appreciated the professionalism being shown for their initial meeting.

His first task was to board the metro at the Namesti Republiky stop, headed toward Zlicin. Apparently, it was somewhere nearby, just through a hideous black monolith of stone called the Powder Tower.

Finding that was easy enough, as the tower dominated the landscape. Passing through the gate, walking on cobblestones from the thirteenth century, he ignored the calls from the barker, dressed ludicrously like a soldier from the Middle Ages, urging him to see Prague from the top of the tower. Entering a large square bustling with people from all nationalities, he spotted the Republiky metro sign across the street.

Retro waited until the Arab was past him, facing away, before getting up and following. Staying a good distance back, he never once paid any overt attention to the man. Once they were through the square and across the street, both walking with the natural flow of traffic on the cobblestone sidewalk, he pulled out his phone and began manipulating the touch screen.

The phone itself looked exactly like an Apple iPhone, but the similarities ended after the Apple logo. Instead of Facebook or YouTube, the phone had a wealth of applications designed to enhance Taskforce capabilities. One was a Blue Force Tracking program interconnected with all team phones, which allowed anyone on the team to know in real time where the rest of the team was located, thereby facilitating rapid decision making on the fly. A new addition to the application was the ability to covertly inject it into another phone via a Bluetooth wireless connection, whereby that phone would appear as an icon as well on the scalable moving map.

Retro figured he could make a fortune if he sold it on the open market. *Surveillance? Why, yes, there's an app for that.*

Getting within thirty feet of his target, he started the scan and picked up more than forty cell phones within range. Scrolling down until he found the terrorist's number, he locked onto it, interrogating the phone for Bluetooth connectivity. In short order, it registered, and he hit the key sequence to inject the application.

His target reached a corner and turned right, causing him to lose visual contact. He quickened his pace, but not so much that he'd stand out. Reaching the corner, he rapidly searched the area, knowing that if the target phone got too far away, it would break the Bluetooth connection and thus the download. He caught a glimpse of his quarry getting on an escalator to the metro. He waited a beat, then followed.

He entered a well-lit tunnel on possibly the longest escalator he had ever seen. It stretched so far out in front of him, it gave him vertigo. Ten steps below him, he saw the Arab. Worried about losing the cell signal underground, he gave a verbal update.

"Jug-ears is headed down to the metro. Republiky stop. I might lose coverage down here, but I'll be able to complete the download while we ride together."

Pike came back. "Roger all. I'll leapfrog to the next station headed south. Buckshot, you take the station to the north."

Retro heard Buckshot acknowledge, then noticed a man standing at the bottom of the escalator, at what still seemed like a football field away. The metro itself was deserted, with nobody coming up on the opposite escalator and only him and the target going down. The man was looking at them both.

Shit. Perfect location to see if he's being followed. He's being washed.

He came back on the net. "Pike, Pike, target might have help. I'm being eye-fucked hard."

"You burned?"

"Not yet, but I will be. I'm at turn two. If this guy's deliberate, he'll know something's up if I stick with Jug-ears."

Retro knew the easiest way to spot surveillance was simply to see the same person over both time and distance. He'd now made two deliberate decisions along with the target, but luckily the metro was a focal point that could explain both of them. Getting on the metro with Jug-ears would be okay, but getting off and continuing to shadow the target would be turn three and four, and if this man *was* conducting countersurveillance, the game would be up.

Pike said, "Okay, I'm at the Mustek station. If he comes this way, I'll get on and pick up the target. You get off. Buckshot, you do the same if he heads the other way. Copy?"

"Roger all."

Retro finally reached the end of the escalator, buying time by acting a little confused and looking at the wall map until Jug-ears had committed to a train line. Finally, he went left, toward the Mustek stop. Retro gave him a moment, then followed. Behind came the man at the escalator.

Hmmm. Stand at the bottom doing nothing, then decide to ride?

He checked the download bar on the phone and saw that he'd injected only half of the application.

Shit. I need to pass this phone to Buckshot or Pike. When he left the metro, the connection would be broken, and the download would have to be started all over again.

Luckily, his phone maintained a cell signal even in the tunnel.

Only the three of them were waiting at the metro stop, so he texted Pike to avoid being overheard, studiously ignoring the target and the other man. The text was routed to every member of the team, just like a radio call, alleviating gaps in information.

Mustek's the stop and I'm fairly sure the other guy's countersurveillance.

A second later, his phone vibrated.

PIKE: No issues. I have a signal down here. I can see you on the map. I'll meet you coming off the metro. Any idea about the CS?

RETRO: No. He's not Arab. Looks Eastern European. Need to pass you phone. Downloads still going.

PIKE: K. Brush pass coming off metro.

Retro tapped "QSL" and waited for the train to arrive.

40

I received the QSL, which was old-fashioned radio shorthand for "message received and understood," used originally during Morse code days, then later during data-burst transmissions from cold-war radios. Now in use again for texting. *Talk about old-school. Screw all that LOL shit.*

I had no idea how our little band of terrorists had managed to integrate into some sort of Eastern European countersurveillance network, but it was just one more data point in the string of things that had made no sense, starting with Johnny's mission in Indonesia and ending with a traitor in the U.S. Congress. All we could do was continue what we were doing. Sooner or later, it would sort itself out. I would have liked a full-on support package, but this operation was way outside the standard Taskforce template. Which was to say that we didn't usually pull everything out of our ass.

I knew I'd have very little time when the metro doors opened. Retro'd get about a half second to pass me the phone as he walked by. Done right, nobody would know something had occurred. Done wrong, and we'd signal to the world that we were involved in amateur-hour illegal shit. And I hated amateur-hour shit. Illegal or otherwise.

My phone vibrated with another text message. Apparently, the unknown counter-surveillance guy had now made physical contact with the target, sitting down and giving him instructions. It looked like Retro had managed to deflect attention from himself.

Five seconds later, I got a text saying that Jug-ears had stood up, intent on getting off the metro. *Shit . . .* How in hell was I supposed to do a brush pass, picking up the phone and entering the metro while Retro left, when the target was now leaving? I'd be stuck riding the metro while Jug-ears went on his merry way. The countdown timer for the arrival of the next train showed forty-five seconds.

This is like the damn Amazing Race.

I texted Retro, asking what the CS was doing.

RETRO: Sitting still. Probably waiting on me to make a move.

PIKE: Stay on. Drag him with you. Get off couple stops later.

RETRO: K. What about download?

PIKE: I'll just start again. What car?

RETRO: 2nd from front.

I felt the breeze of the approaching train, the wind growing with a howl as the air was pushed out of the tunnel and into the station. I positioned myself at the far end of the platform, looking to anybody watching like I wanted to board.

The cars squealed to a halt, then disgorged their passengers in a flurry. Since Mustek was a transfer station for both the A and B lines, there were a lot more people getting off, allowing me to integrate into the flow with little effort. I took one last look at the photo of the target, this time to get a fix on what he was wearing, then headed to the escalator with everyone else.

Halfway up, I saw a brown jacket topped by a black head of hair. I didn't bother trying to close the gap because I absolutely didn't want to spike anyone else helping him.

Getting to the top of the Disneyland-length escalator, I had two choices — either go outside or transfer to the B metro line. I chose outside, knowing if I missed him I could redirect Buckshot to the next stop on the other line and hopefully pick him up again. Worst case, we still had the anchor of the hotel.

The Mustek stop exited right out onto Wenceslas Square, a walking promenade that a couple of decades ago had filled to capacity with angry mobs marking the end of communism in the Czech Republic without a shot being fired, but nowadays was the heart of shopping in Prague, full of cafés and department stores. It was a beautiful day, the air crisp enough to make me appreciate the warmth of the sun on my face. The square was teeming with shoppers and tourists, causing a sliver of alarm.

Too many people. I'll never know if he took the other metro line. I considered going back down to the train, but decided to check out the area first. I pulled the trigger on Buckshot, getting him in position at the Staromestska stop near the Charles Bridge, then did the same with Decoy on the other end.

The only good thing was that the same crowds that made it hard for me to track Jug-ears made it very, very hard to do surveillance detection work. No way could they be sure someone wasn't just a dumb-ass tourist bouncing around.

Which means they'd have given him directions out of this place.

I rapidly looked around and saw multiple little alleys leading away from the promenade. I took the first one I could see and began winding my way through the maze that was Old Town Prague, with single-lane roads, cut-throughs, and cobblestone alleys the norm. I was sure I'd missed him, when I saw him lazily strolling down a side street that had to be as old as the tombs we'd seen last week.

I braked a little bit and matched his stride, causally noting anyone who might be watching his back trail. We walked by several outdoor cafés, all with people in them, so it was impossible to tell, but I was sure someone was checking me out to see if I was tracking the target. There was no other reason for him to be channeling and stairstepping like he was. It was all designed to flush out surveillance, and all I could do was continue to follow, maintaining my demeanor and ignoring the target as much as possible.

I saw nothing unusual. The people were all laughing and talking, enjoying the sunshine. I had the same surreal feeling I always got on operations such as this.

I'm out here tracking a killer, and everyone else is drinking beer.

It seemed like there was a pub every fifteen feet, all with outdoor patios. There was no way I could ascertain if anyone was working with him, although if they were, they were probably drunk.

I got within thirty feet of the target and interrogated his phone. I achieved a lock with his Bluetooth, starting the application download again. He continued his little stroll, eventually breaking out into the tourist Mecca of the Old Town Square, with the Astronomical Clock and Old Town Hall, along with dozens of locals begging for attention at various attractions. He went through it to another small alley, heading toward a booth that advertised bus tours.

I let him get inside the alley but didn't follow when he stopped at the booth. No sense in pushing my luck, since there wasn't anything else in the alley and I'd stick out like a hippie at a corporate retreat. I stopped short at the square, next to a local beggar on his elbows and knees, prostrating himself in stoic silence, his grimy hands outstretched.

I dropped some coins into his cup and watched the target. He was talking to the man in the booth more than was necessary for a bus tour. Eventually, the man handed him a map of some kind. I checked my phone and saw the download was just about done. Out of the corner of my eye, I sensed rapid, hostile movement. *The beggar.*

I whirled, raising my arm against my head and ducking, but not quick enough to evade the strike of the beggar's coffee cup shattering against my skull.

I reeled back, out of his range, clearing my head before he got a chance to hit me again. He closed the gap, seemingly for the kill, but I was ready now. *And the drunk's going to regret picking this fight.*

As soon as he came within range, I batted his hands away and stunned him with four rapid jabs to his face as if I were working a heavy bag — left, right, left, right — popping his head back and forth like a paddleball on a rubber band. I followed up with a side kick to his upper thigh, using all of my weight behind it. He bounced off the wall he'd been kneeling against, the pain radiating through his face. He looked over my shoulder at something. *Bum Reinforcements on the way.*

I rotated until my back was to the wall, seeing nobody else coming to help.

He pantomimed a fake, like a high school

kid, alternating his hands back and forth as if I would fall for something that stupid, then looked down the alley again. Inexplicably, he took off running.

What the hell?

I did nothing to stop him, more concerned with whether I'd spooked my target in the commotion. When I looked down the alley, he was gone, and it dawned on me how stupid I'd been. I glanced at my phone. *At least the download completed, you jackass.*

"All elements, this is Pike. Target has active countersurveillance now. I was just given a diversion while he slipped out. The phone's loaded, but I'm burned. Pick him up, but stay very, very loose."

I passed the code to unlock the target on our Blue Force application, then waited to see who'd get to him first. Minutes later, my headset sprang to life.

"Pike, Buckshot. He's headed across the Charles Bridge. I've got him on the map and can see him walking away."

"Use the map to maintain situational awareness. If you lose him visually, let him go until you can reacquire without getting burned. All other elements vector in."

"He's stopped and receiving a call. . . . Okay, now he's dialing someone else."

I was sure he was getting the next instructions, but with the application it wouldn't matter now. *Run around all you want, asshole.*

Jennifer came on. "Pike, other targets are leaving the hotel."

Oh boy. Here we go.

"Get a photo and launch it to us."

"Already done, but they've got bags. They're leaving for good."

Motherfucker. We were now losing our anchor spot, leaving us with Jug-ears for a thread. A single point of failure that I didn't like, but I didn't want to spook the other targets.

"Let them go. Don't burn yourself. We've still got Jug-ears. They'll link up again."

Three minutes later, Buckshot came back on.

"He's getting into one of those open-air tourist cars on the other side of the bridge. He's being taken somewhere."

"Fine. Let him go. Regroup back —"

"Pike, the driver just took his phone. He threw it in the street. They're driving away."

Our single point of failure just snapped.

"Break-break, Jennifer, interrogate the other target's phone. Get on them."

I knew it was too late but figured it was worth a shot. She came back sounding like it was her fault.

"They're gone. I've lost them."

I felt like punching the wall next to me. Not only had we lost our targets, and maybe our only chance to recover the EFPs, but now they knew we were tracking them. And they'd thrown away the cell phone, so we couldn't even use the high-risk technical capability we had to track the Arab. I was hard-pressed to imagine how it could get any worse, and I had nobody to blame but myself. I wished I'd really taken it to the fake bum. *Meet his ass again and I'm going to rip him apart.*

41

Suffering the indignity of a full-on body search, Kamil offered no resistance, noting the security surrounding the person he was to meet. All were rough-looking men, and none had lowered their weapons, even after he had given them the introduction letter provided by Rafik. *Paranoid.*

He was deep in the Czech Republic countryside, one hour outside of Prague, the only structure a large stone house rising through the morning haze a quarter of a mile away. Completely on his own. He could feel the sweat build under his arms despite the morning chill. *They could bury me out here and no one would ever know.* But the man he was to meet was worth the risk. Without him, Rafik's grand operation would be stillborn.

By all accounts, Draco Ljustku was a ruthless killer, a leader in the Albanian mafia precisely because no other challenger could match his amoral ferocity. But it hadn't always been that way.

Originally a farm boy living in central Kosovo, he had become a fighter in the Kosovo Liberation Army after his family was slaughtered by Serbian Special Police. Through that quirk of fate, he had learned that he not only had a talent for violence, but also a taste for it.

The KLA itself was inexorably intertwined with crime; it was one of the few ways for the rebellious force to gather income for their fight. Drug running and prostitution were as much a part of their makeup as any nationalistic tendencies against the Serbs. When the conflict finally ended, the organized crime did not.

Draco's skills on the battlefield had proven to be useful in this arena as well, and he had worked his way up until he was the kingpin of a vast territory that included the city of Prague. But such distinction came with a price, namely the threat of a violent end, so Kamil became as compliant as possible lest one of the thugs around him decided he wasn't worth the trouble. Everything went fine until he was addressed by a man with a lazy eye.

"Give me your cell phone."

Kamil reflexively looked behind him, as

the man's eye was focused over his shoulder, and he'd already had his phone taken from him. The man snapped. He grabbed the back of Kamil's head, holding it in place while he forced the barrel of a pistol into his mouth.

"You think you're funny, sand nigger? You want to laugh at me?"

Kamil gargled, feeling a tooth chip on the front sight post. Unable to talk, he desperately waved at his original driver, convinced he was about to die.

The leader of the security force intervened. "Enough. I had the driver from Charles Bridge throw it out. He doesn't have one. Load him up."

Lazy Eye removed the pistol from his mouth and glowered, a comical look given his bouncing focus, but Kamil dared not break a smile. He followed the leader into the first vehicle, watching the man talk on a radio and probing his tooth with his tongue.

They wound down a gravel road to the stone house, Kamil in the middle with a man on either side. Reaching the circle out front, Kamil saw three men standing on the front stoop. The car stopped and Kamil was treated to a façade of welcome. Exiting the car under his own power, without being pushed or dragged, he was immediately hugged by a bear of a man, then kissed on both checks.

"Welcome to the Czech Republic. I am Draco. I trust your travel was uneventful?"

Kamil found himself staring into the piggish face of a man a head shorter than himself. His eyes were sunk back into his head, like a couple of turtles withdrawing into a shell. His right cheek had a puckered scar that ran through his upper lip. The repair to the wound had been crude, with the lip slightly uneven, giving him a permanent snarl.

Kamil grasped his outstretched hand and was startled to find the man was missing the last two fingers. He covered up the surprise, determined not to make the same mistake he had with Lazy Eye. Draco still caught it, but only made a little joke.

"Yes, a gift from the Serbian Police. Their way of saying hello. It's okay, though." He pointed his index finger at Kamil and mimed shooting a pistol. "I still have the important finger. The one that pulls the trigger."

He then laughed as if it was the funniest thing he had heard in a long time. Kamil chuckled along with him, wondering how on earth Rafik had become associated with this man.

"Come inside. Let's talk about your troubles and how I can help. You and I are very much alike, and we Muslims must stick together."

Kamil fought to prevent his disdain from showing. *I have more in common with the Great Satan's soldiers than I do with you.*

Draco continued while they walked, saying, "Someone followed you today, I pray not because you wanted them to."

Kamil snapped his head around, remembering why he was here. "Followed me? Are you sure?"

Draco smiled at the reaction. "Yes, I'm sure. And they were very good. If I hadn't sent my men, more than likely you'd be captured now. But no worries. They have nothing to go on."

"That's why you had me call my men. Change hotels."

"Yes. And you'll need to do that each night if you wish to continue with me."

Passing through the foyer, Kamil found the house dripping in opulence, a testimony to the empire Draco had built. Winding through a maze of hallways, they eventually entered a large study with an oak desk studded in leather and several comfortably overstuffed chairs. Draco circled behind the desk, saying, "Have a seat. Can I get you something to drink? Perhaps some pleasure while we do business?"

Like magic, a man appeared bearing a tray with an assortment of alcoholic beverages. Behind him another man led in five girls, teenagers from the look of them, none older than nineteen.

Kamil felt his temper flare but maintained his composure. "No, thank you. I'm sure you understand."

"Come on. You're not at home and I've seen how the Saudis act once they're out of the kingdom. Don't feel like you owe me. It's my pleasure. If you don't like what you see here, I can bring more."

"No. I'd prefer not. Can we please discuss why I came?"

"Suit yourself. You won't mind if I do, though?"

Without waiting for an answer, he pointed at a brown-haired girl. She shrank into the wall until prodded by the man who'd brought her in. She slowly made her way around the desk, then sank from view. Kamil could hear the rustle of clothing and the soft clink of a belt buckle. He could barely see the top of the girl's head. The other man, along with the girls, left the room. He began to feel sick to his stomach.

Draco sighed and looked at the ceiling.

"You really should try this. They're still very fresh. Not like that trash you find in the city. If you don't like what you saw here, I have quite a few more downstairs."

Kamil found himself unable to speak, the rhythmic motion of the girl's head disgusting him. *Allah the merciful, what have we done?* He felt unclean, and wondered if the end result of their operation would be enough to overcome the means they had used. For the first time, he feared for his future in the afterlife.

Draco leaned over and whispered something in the girl's ear, her head never stopping its hypnotic motion. He then said, "Okay, now how may I help. I've been told through my friends in Pakistan that you require explosives. Is this true?"

It took a moment for Kamil to realize he was being addressed. He felt his fists clench. He couldn't believe the man was talking about operational matters in front of the girl. Then the implication sank in, sickening him further: She was going to die, her only transgression being that she was forced to service this monster. With superhuman effort, he restrained himself from launching across the desk and killing Draco with his bare hands.

Draco saw the object of his attention and

said, "Ah, you're reconsidering my hospital-
ity?"

"No," Kamil managed to squeak out. "No,
no, no."

"A pious one, huh? I can respect that. I
wish I could have the strength you and your
kind possess." He patted the girl's head.
"But I'm afraid I'd be a hypocrite."

Hypocrite? You're an apostate.

Kamil said, "We do need explosives. And
a way to get them into America."

Draco said nothing for a moment, his eyes
closed. He allowed the girl to work for a
moment longer before stopping her.

"I can get all the explosives you may need,
thanks to the Serbian pigs that were stupid
enough to try to fight us. Artillery rounds,
detonation cord, you name it. Getting it in
to the United States is a different matter,
though. The KLA used to be loved, but
now, thanks to you and your brethren, not
so much."

"We can't use improvised explosives like
those pried out of an artillery round. We
need plastique. Composition C-4. Can you
get that?"

"No. No way. Maybe eight years ago,
when America still had a large presence in
Kosovo, but not now. I can get SEMTEX,
however. It's the same thing as C-4, with

the same burn rate and initiation methods. Will that work?"

Kamil thought about it. The demolition kit was made for use with C-4, the American plastic explosive, but SEMTEX should work. He didn't know enough about explosives to be sure, but the man he had brought with him did. He decided to agree to the SEMTEX, then talk to Adnan, the explosives expert, to see if it would work with the EFPs.

"Yes, that will be fine. How will we get it?"

"You'll have to pick it up in Budapest. How you get it out is up to you."

"Budapest? Can't you bring it here? I don't have a visa for Hungary."

"No problem. Take the train. Your visa for here will carry you through any EU country. You won't have an issue, and I'm not bringing the explosives here. Others in my organization have it. They're willing to sell, but don't push your luck. You want it, go get it."

"I was told you could prepare it for shipping in a manner that would fool immigrations and customs. Complete with all the forms we would need. Is that not so?"

"Yes, yes, I can do that, and I will for an additional charge. But not for here. You know the saying 'Don't shit where you eat'? And not for America. I can get it into Canada, and that's all."

Rafik had told him that Montreal was as close as they would get, and had prepared other methods for onward travel of the explosives to the United States, so Kamil didn't push the issue.

Draco patted the girl on the head, drawing her down again, then said, "The explosives are located at a house in the countryside. Much like this place. Do you know Hungary?"

Kamil found it hard to listen, even as Draco recited an address. As he finished with the directions, Draco's face clenched up. He grunted twice, then allowed the girl to rise to her feet. She kept her eyes downcast and scurried from the room. Kamil's revulsion was palpable, a physical thing he had to fight to contain.

Draco rose, zipping up his pants. He extended his hand, the same one that had held the head of the girl.

"*Insha'Allah,* I'll see you in Budapest."

Insha'Allah . . . If God's willing. But how could he be now? Kamil was sure they had soiled the means of victory by using Draco, that they were now no better than the infidels they chose to fight.

He shook Draco's hand, looking the man in the eye but seeing the face of the child. The expression of fear and shame burning into Kamil's soul. He said a silent prayer.

Allah the Merciful, grant me the strength to live through our strike at the Great Satan. Allow me to return and wipe this abomination from the earth. Allow me to redeem my place at your side.

42

The chirp of the keylogger brought me out of my doze. I rubbed my eyes and focused on the laptop in front of me. The image on the screen woke me up like a shot of cold water. Whoever was on the computer was finally typing something we could use.

After the fiasco at Old Town, we'd repeated the operation from Indonesia by breaking into Noordin's office, only with much less drama. We'd found next to nothing, either in the office itself or in the aircraft with his company name. The office wasn't really designed for commercial business at all. Just a two-room suite located at the general aviation section of the Prague Airport. Apparently, its only use was to give the pilots some rest between flights. It held a single computer, and although it was on a network, the fifty-pound heads at Taskforce headquarters could glean absolutely nothing suspicious from the hard drive.

When they came up empty, we'd gone back in and placed a wireless keylogger on the system. A simple device that was inserted between the USB port and the USB plug of the keyboard, it would transmit everything that someone typed on the keyboard, along with a screen shot of what he or she was looking at, to a collection device just outside the office. We'd dialed into the collection device through the cell network, allowing us to see the activity in real time.

It was a lot of effort for potentially very little payback, but we were out of options and grasping at straws. Until now, because it looked like it might have worked.

"Retro. Get in here."

I leaned the monitor back so he could see it. "Looks like someone's filing a flight plan."

"Where to?"

"Budapest, supposedly. Wonder if that's where he's really going?"

"We could slap a beacon on it."

I tried to see the downside, but short of never seeing the beacon again, I couldn't find one. "Yeah, that's a good idea. Give Buckshot a call. Tell him to get his ass out to the tarmac."

"How much time's he got?"

"Hang on, the time of departure and tail number's coming up."

Thirty seconds later, the information appeared on our screen, scrolling across letter by letter, eerily looking like a ghost was typing.

"Damn," I said. "He's leaving in the next three hours. With preflight, Buckshot's got about thirty to forty-five minutes. Get him moving."

Retro relayed the information, while whoever was at the computer submitted the flight plan and began typing a short e-mail. It was random bullshit, with nothing that raised my eyebrows. Eventually, he closed out of that as well, leaving us nothing to do but wait. Twenty-two minutes later, my phone rang.

"Pike, it's Jennifer. Buckshot's prepping the Diamondback down on the tarmac, but we've got a little problem. There are two planes with the tail number you sent."

"Two? Of the same kind?"

"Nope. One's a Casa 212, the other's a Twin Otter."

The duplicate numbers were going to force me to make a choice, but at least now we knew something shady was going on. We were on to something.

"Take the Twin Otter. It's got better range.

If they're transporting our cargo, that's what they'll use."

"Okay. Just so I'm sure — you want Buckshot to diamond the Twin Otter?"

I went back and forth in my mind, knowing if I was wrong, there was no way to correct it once the pilot showed up. I looked at Retro. He was a big help. He shrugged with his hands in the air.

I said, "Yeah. That's it."

Jennifer called back a short time later telling me the beacon was emplaced and that they were going to hang around to see which plane left. Minutes after that, she called to kick me in the gut.

"Pike, the Casa's rolling toward the runway."

Fuck me. These guys are the luckiest bastards alive.

"All right . . . wait until he's airborne, then retrieve the beacon."

As soon as I hung up, Retro said, "Wrong plane?"

"Yeah. Story of my life. Is there anything else on that e-mail he sent?"

"Not really. It's a bunch of 'how's it going' stuff. The only thing mentioned is something called the Drenica Group."

"Get it to the Taskforce, along with the e-mail addresses. Hopefully, it ends up being some sort of front import-export company. Tell 'em to get us an address, preferably in Budapest."

By the time we got an answer, Jennifer had returned with the other two guys. We read the screen together, the information not at all what I expected:

Drenica Group: An Albanian organized crime cabal.

* Named after the Drenica region of central Kosovo, where it was formed.

* Tightly interwoven with the Kosovo Liberation Army(UCK-KLA), a radical Muslim extremist group formed to counter Serbian aggression in the 1990s.

* Through KLA connections, some indicators of interface with other Muslim extremist groups, such as al Qaeda.

* Primarily known for their ruthlessness, both with law enforcement as well as with other factions that threaten their territory or perceived business expansion opportunities.

* Connected with organized crime in the Czech Republic, Hungary, and Bulgaria.

* Cells worldwide, to include New York City, Los Angeles, Paris, Berlin, and London.

* Primarily concerned with the distribution of heroin. Potentially on track to become the number one wholesaler of heroin worldwide.

* Secondary efforts include white slavery, prostitution, arms trafficking, and extortion.

"So," Buckshot said, "our terrorists are into drugs as well? What're we going to do with this information? Look up organized crime in the local phone book?"

"I was thinking of making them come to us." I smiled at Jennifer.

"What?" she said. "Why are you looking at me?"

"How'd you feel about becoming a prostitute?"

43

I watched Decoy crank his binoculars to their highest power. "Wow, she's got a great rack. I heard about her when she was going through Assessment, but nobody ever said what a hammer she was. We should've had her dress like this the whole time. I'm getting a tent pole just sitting here."

Jesus. Am I going to have to listen to this shit all night?

Our rental van was parked in a seedy area of Prague, in the closest thing we could find to a red-light district. I'd had Jennifer dress up like a tart and tossed her out onto the street, with the plan being that we'd piss off some other hooker enough to call her boss. According to the Taskforce intel weenies, the Albanians owned all the prostitution here, so that should pique someone's interest.

When he showed up to chase Jennifer away, Decoy and I would confront him, tying him up in a little argument while Buck-shot and Retro beaconed his car during the commotion.

Maybe get some damn use out of the Diamondback.

The beacon itself was a satellite feed and would have worked perfectly on an airplane because — by definition — it would always have a view of the sky, but it would probably have some gaps in coverage when used in a car. That was okay, because everything was a trade-off with technology. Hollywood notwithstanding, there were no magic bullets.

The good thing about the Diamondback, and the reason I stuck with it here, was that the battery life would exceed a week, something we might need as we continued to try and figure out where the EFPs had gone. Intermittent gaps for over a week were better than perfect coverage for forty-eight hours.

I watched Jennifer stalk a real prostitute, this one much younger than her. She put her hands on her hips, turning her back to us and apparently giving the young street-walker a piece of her mind.

"Holy shit," Decoy said. "I can't take this. Check out that ass. Man alive, her legs go on forever. Maybe we should have given her a script for a catfight with the other whore."

I gritted my teeth, watching the real prostitute walk away talking on a cell phone.

Decoy was new to Project Prometheus. Well, new since I'd left. He was a SEAL, like Knuckles, which is probably why Knuckles had hired his chauvinistic ass. He was a little bit of an anomaly in the SEAL world because he'd learned to swim *after* joining the Navy. Coming from the back-woods of Tennessee, he'd gotten his call sign when his teammates took him on his first-ever duck hunt. At least the first ever where hunger wasn't the point of the hunt. He'd blasted the first decoy he'd seen floating on the water, thinking it was real. In his mind, the goal was food on the table, not sport.

He had a solid reputation in a gunfight — as well as a solid reputation as a man-whore. Like he was worried he'd be forced to marry some bucktoothed hillbilly, so he was going to bed as many women as he could until that time. And he was apparently pretty good at it, which didn't help my attitude any.

He said, "Hey, you wouldn't mind if I tried to tap that, would you? I mean, she's not yours or anything, is she?"

Enough.

I snapped my face an inch from his.

"Decoy, you and I are going to have a serious issue if you don't start showing her some fucking respect."

He backed up until his head was against the door glass. "Whoa, easy, man. I didn't know you had a thing with her. I didn't mean anything by it."

I sputtered for a few seconds, trying to find the right thing to say, finally getting out "That's not it! She deserves the same respect you'd give a male operator. She's not 'mine,' you ass."

"Uhh . . . sure. Whatever you say . . ." I saw his eyes go wide at something over my shoulder. "Shit! It's showtime and we're late!"

A Mercedes had pulled up while we were arguing, and two men were now bearing down on Jennifer and the prostitute. As we piled out of the van, one of the men struck the young prostitute in the face, knocking her to the ground.

The other thug attempted the same thing with Jennifer. She blocked with her left arm, redirecting the energy from his slap outward in a circular motion while she snapped an uppercut to his face. The blow popped his jaw closed with a rifle crack, shattering teeth and dropping him to the ground. We were still fifty feet away, running flat out.

*This just got lethal. All because you got jeal-
ous at Decoy's bullshit.*

We reached the melee just as the first thug
drew his arm back to pile-drive Jennifer. No
slap this time. Decoy caught him at the
elbow and rotated him backward, flipping
him to the ground. I immediately put a knee
on his chest and my barrel on his nose.
Decoy frisked him, throwing a cheap CZ
pistol down the alley and pocketing a cell
phone. He then turned to the thug Jennifer
had thumped, doing the same thing while
the man rolled around holding his bleeding
mouth. The man under me screamed in a
language I didn't understand.

I said, "Hey, hold on there, big guy. Calm
down. We just didn't want you to hurt us."

He looked confused for a moment, then
said in broken English, "You will die for
this. Let us go now and maybe it will be
quick."

"Wow. That's my choice? Are you fucking
nuts? I'm holding the gun here, asshole."

He glared at me, signaling he was about
to try something. He was brave, I'll give him
that. I pushed the barrel into his eye socket
to calm him down.

"Stop it. I don't want to hurt you. All we
were doing was pulling a little scam. We
didn't want to cut into your business. We

349

were just going to do a little fleecing of American tourists. We didn't know this terrain was owned."

"You have no idea who you are dealing with. We can reach you in any country on earth. Leave now, and I won't hunt you down."

My earpiece clicked twice, telling me that the Diamondback was in place. *Time to go.*

"Okay, okay. We're out of here. Sorry for the trouble."

I backed up, keeping the weapon on his head. Decoy did the same. We pulled abreast of Jennifer.

"Get the van running and bring it around here."

Jennifer said, "Pike, the prostitute's coming with us."

I glared at her for a split second, seeing the young woman cowering behind. "What the hell are you talking about? Go get the van. And leave her here."

"No. I talked to her before she called those assholes. She's from France. She was kidnapped." Jennifer touched my arm. "She's a sex slave, Pike. There's no way I'm leaving her here."

I kept my gun trained on the thugs, knowing we were running out of time.

"Jennifer, I'm really sorry to hear that, but

we're executing a plan. That's it. We can't save the world. Just our part of it. Now go get the van."

"Pike, I can't. I promised. She's scared out of her mind, and she asked for my help. If we throw her back now, they might kill her for trying to get away. And the whole point of this thing was to get them to go to a leader. You know taking one of their little slaves would do that."

I turned to rip into her and was drawn up short by the fear pulsing out. Her eyes were large, the hands on the girl's shoulders trembling. But overriding all of that was her expression, an unspoken question of what I stood for.

Shit.

"Go get the van. Before I change my mind."

I heard her running behind me, the small clicking of her ridiculous high heels sounding dangerous on the cobblestones. Seconds later, she pulled the van up next to us. I waited until everyone was loaded before I jumped in, finding myself face-to-face with the rescued woman. A seventeen-year-old girl shaking in fear. Looking at me as if I was going to save her world.

44

Sitting in the van thirty minutes later, I felt Buckshot staring at me, trying to get my attention without saying anything. I ignored him, keeping my eyes glued to the laptop screen and the beacon track.

When we'd linked back up with him and Retro, they'd both jumped in the van, grinning and laughing about Jennifer's knockout punch. Right up until they saw the girl. All I'd said was "Don't ask."

Since then, I'd pretended to be engrossed in the little blinking icon on the screen. In the back, I could hear Jennifer softly whispering to the girl in French.

One more surprise. I had no idea she knew the language. She was clearly less than fluent but was getting by. Finally, Retro had had enough.

"Is someone going to tell me what the fuck we're doing with a Czech hooker?"

I said, "Ask Jennifer. It's her lost puppy."

Before he could say anything, Jennifer spoke up. "Pike, we have a problem here."

"No shit. Like where are we going to drop off the girl? Or what the hell was I thinking about?"

She said nothing for a few seconds, letting my comments settle in the van. I knew she was pissed, though, because she crossed her arms across her chest and eyeballed me.

Oh shit. Here it comes. I was used to her ideological rants, but what she said surprised even me.

"No, like we need to go help these girls. All of them."

My mouth dropped open. "Are you serious? How?"

"I don't know, but this girl's been kept as a slave for over a month. She says there's about twelve other girls with her. She was supposed to 'learn her trade' here before being sold to some pig. The girls come and go all the time at that place. She thinks she's due to go in a day or two."

I glanced at the girl and found her staring at me again. A young, black-haired little thing who should have been beautiful, but looked broken instead. Greasy hair and grimy nails, wearing a dress that was filthy. Scared out of her mind. Like my daughter would have looked if this had happened to her. *Stop that shit.*

"Jennifer, there's no way we're going to do anything about the girls. I'm sorry, but that's it. We don't have the authority, and we don't have the means. We're not the Justice League, for Christ's sake. This isn't a comic book. We have our own mission to do."

Her expression was pleading. "That's not true, Pike. We *are* the Justice League. At least the group I wanted to join is. Nobody else *can* help them. She thinks the police are aware of the place, but they don't do anything. This is no different than that child you saved in the street. It's what we do. Isn't it?"

"No. It *is* different. You're talking about altering the entire mission. We have the beacon. We're just going to track it, then release the girl, like we planned."

I turned to Decoy for help. I knew he wouldn't stand for any risk to life, limb, or mission just for some women. *Shit, he'd probably stop and ask the Albanians for business tips first.*

His face was grim. "I wouldn't mind dinging these guys up a little bit."

What the fuck? "Have I entered the twilight zone? You ripped my ass for saving a kid in Cairo, and now you want to risk the entire mission so we can go rescue a bunch of women we don't even know? We need to find the Arabs. Period."

The girl, apparently picking up on something I'd said, became animated and rattled off at Jennifer in French.

Decoy said, "Jennifer translated a little of what the girl's been through. These fuckers need to die. One way or the other."

I looked at him with a new understanding. *Man-whore's nothing but an act.*

Jennifer spoke. "The girl knows where the Arabs are."

I exploded. "Jesus Christ! She speaks English? Everyone shut the fuck up. Retro, take her out of the van."

I waited while they left, building up anger. I was more pissed at myself than anyone else. I'd laughed at the exact same mistakes before, having guys talking in English in front of detainees about operational matters, only to find out the terrorists spoke English as well. *Now I'm the jackass. . . .*

After the door closed, I said, "I thought she only spoke French?"

Jennifer just shrugged.

I sighed. "Okay, what was that about?"

"She says that an Arab man came to the house she's held in. Her friend was in the room with them. The friend knows what was

355

said, and because of it, they all think she's going to get killed."

I rolled my eyes. "Oh, so if we save the friend, we get the information?"

"That's what she said," Jennifer snapped. "I'm not making it up."

"Look, we've got the beacon. We know that thing works. That's the reason we came here in the first place, not to rescue a bunch of kids. I'm not going to risk this mission based on a story from a crack whore."

"She's *not* a crack whore!"

I held up my hands, attempting to calm her while imparting some reason. "Jennifer, remember we have absolutely no cover for action here. We're lucky we got the go-ahead to do some snooping around, but there's no way we can do something like a building assault. You're asking me to jeopardize our cover and the Taskforce for something that's not related to our mission. Let's use the beacon. Like we planned."

"*You're* the one who preaches that cover is just a tool, not the mission. You're the one who almost had a friend die because someone was too worried about their cover. Now this girl's friend is going to die for the exact same reason. And it *is* part of our mission. She'll be able to tell us a helluva lot more than that damn beacon."

She crossed her arms and glared at me. I pondered for a few seconds, then shook my head. "Okay, okay, get her back in here. Ask her why a master terrorist and an Albanian mafia lord would discuss operational stuff in front of a whore. I'll bet the answer is 'uhh . . . I just made that up.' "

After they were settled in the back, Jennifer spoke to her calmly, questioning slowly. As the answers came out, Jennifer's face became more and more enraged. She asked the same question a few different ways, making sure her fledgling grasp of French was capturing accurately what the girl said. Eventually, the prostitute broke down and began to cry. Jennifer stopped the questioning and stroked her back, telling us what she had learned.

The story sickened me.

I could tell it shocked the rest of the team as well. I looked each man in the eye, getting a nod, one by one. I said, "Okay, Jennifer, we'll do it. But you need to understand something."

"What?"

I locked eyes with her. "We don't live in a comic book. We go in, and it's full force. You remember the Bible verse on Johnny's hat in Indonesia? The one you asked me about, wondering if Johnny was religious?"

She nodded.

"It's Romans 3:8, and it says 'Let us do evil that good may come.' It's an inside joke and an unofficial Taskforce motto. In Cairo you said you weren't sure of the difference between the good guys and the bad, and there's some truth to that if you're on the outside looking in. We don't arrest people. We don't play fair. We solve problems through violence. No judge. No jury. It's against everything America stands for, and the reason for the inside joke. We do it because it's necessary. It's not something the average American understands sitting in his La-Z-Boy, drinking a beer."

I paused a minute to give her a chance to say something. She didn't.

"If we go in there, a lot of people are going to die. Based on your say-so. I don't have enough men to dominate the place, and these guys know how to fight. They cut their teeth killing Serbians in Kosovo. We aren't going to shoot at legs or run around shouting, 'Freeze!' Anybody that's a threat will be eliminated. Killed. No questions asked."

I spoke softer, about something only she and I would know. "You remember Guatemala? What you saw there? That's what's going to happen here. You good with that?"

She grew distant for a minute, thinking of the maelstrom of violence she had experienced in Guatemala, the graphic images of the men I'd slaughtered to save her flitting through her mind.

She contemplated the child prostitute, reaching out and brushing a tear rolling down her cheek. The girl didn't understand enough English to follow, but she sensed the lives of her friends hung in the balance. She squeezed Jennifer's hands, a tentative smile on her face. Jennifer tried to smile back, but it came out as a grimace, like she was smiling through an injury to prove she was all right.

She said, "Okay. Let's go do some evil."

45

The image on the laptop looked like a black-and-white negative, with everything reversed. It was startlingly clear, allowing me to make out the individual limbs of trees even in the total darkness. Anything generating heat showed up as light shading. Anything cold showed up as dark. I spun the ball around, catching the van with Buckshot and Retro behind me, the hood pure white from the engine heat and the glass of the windshield looking like black sackcloth.

The image, fed to the laptop through fiber-optic cable, was produced by a thermal device made by FLIR industries. Called a Blackjack, it was based on the MarFLIR Talon, a nine-inch thermal and infrared sensor used in airborne and maritime environments. Of course, we took the best of that design and created our own sensor. Mounted on gimbals, it was gyrostabilized like the Talon, allowing it to be used on the move without the user getting seasick. It also maintained a healthy optical zoom capability, along with the Talon's laser pointer capability. We kicked out everything else in order to get it small. Geo-location marking, laser range finder, lowlight CCD TV, all of that went to the curb. Our sensor was much less capable, but also a hell of a lot smaller, at only six inches in diameter. Which made it much easier to sneak through customs, like everything else we had on us.

As soon as we'd made the decision to take down what we were now calling the slave house, I sent Buckshot and Retro to our aircraft while I took Jennifer back to the hotel to change into something more suitable for an assault. While we waited for the kit, Jennifer had taken the girl into the shower and cleaned her up. I noticed that Decoy had hovered around, doing whatever Jennifer asked to make the girl more comfortable. Whatever he had acted like when we first met, something in his past had triggered a protective instinct like I'd never seen.

Eventually, Retro and Buckshot had returned from the airfield, bringing with them an arsenal of weapons and tools that would, hopefully, give us an edge on the assault.

The team equipment that had come in on the jump would have been very useful if we'd remained in Egypt, but posed a serious issue getting into Europe. Luckily, Kurt had sent us a Gulfstream G4 with very special adaptations. The plane was built with a plethora of removable panels that would conceal Taskforce kit. On the outside — or inside — it looked like an ordinary airframe, but the walls themselves housed everything Buckshot had jumped in with. It caused an issue with noise isolation because the insulation had been removed to hold the kit, but that was a small price to pay.

While the G4 itself was a godsend, it did create potential risk, because my nascent company had miraculously acquired a lease on a multimillion-dollar aircraft. The plane itself was now permanently attached to our company, which was cool, but any in-depth investigation would reveal inconsistencies in the lease that potentially would cause problems. The Taskforce was big on not doing exactly what we were now doing, preferring to solve problems with a long-term solution, getting everything perfect for outside scrutiny before employment. Just like the enemy we hunted. Nothing to be done about it, because we needed the kit, and the EFPs weren't something we could wish away.

Retro had come back with four H&K UMP assault rifles, four Glock 30s, and one H&K 416, along with a host of other unique items like the Blackjack. The UMPs and Glocks were tricked out with small red-dot sights and suppressors, but were chambered for .45 caliber, an age-old, distinctly American round. Plenty of modern cartridges beat it out in wound ballistics and carrying capacity, but it had one distinction that none of the others held: It was subsonic.

In the movies, all the actor has to do is slap a suppressor on a weapon and he's now banging away without making any noise, but the truth of the matter is that, while the muzzle blast and explosion of the round can be effectively suppressed, all combat rounds will break the sound barrier with a loud crack, rendering the suppression useless in a clandestine assault where any noise will give you away. This forced most close-combat weapons to use special subsonic rounds in a clandestine assault, which detracted from the very capabilities they originally presented, along with altering the ballistic track of the bullet from what one had trained with. The .45, while old, didn't have that problem. And make no mistake, it would knock a man down.

The 416 was for Jennifer. It fired a 5.56 round, just like the mainstay of the U.S. Army, and would be loud as hell, but it's what she'd been trained on. She would be pulling security out front while we were in the house, and I wanted her comfortable with the weapon she had to use. There would be no second chances. And if she was cracking rounds downrange, it meant that the clandestine side of things had gone to shit, so a little noise wouldn't matter.

I swung the Blackjack around with my joystick, surveying the area. Mounted on a mast, it stuck up about fifteen feet from the roof of the van, giving me a clear view of what we faced. The vehicle with the Diamondback beacon was parked out front, so the girl's information had panned out so far. I zoomed in on the house, the lights outside generating white-hot heat with darkness surrounding it. No other heat sources. *So, no close-in security.*

I panned back out, surveying the long drive toward the solitary road we were now parked on. As I got to the intersection, I saw a heat source. Zooming in, I made out two men sitting outside of a guard shack. One had a cigarette in his mouth, which caused the screen to white out, blocking his features. The other was methodically cleaning a weapon. His eyes were black pools, something I always found disconcerting when looking through thermal imagery. It made a man look like he had no soul.

"Retro, I got two targets. About two hundred meters away at the entrance to the compound."

"Roger that. Light 'em up. Buckshot and I will take care of them."

"Everyone in my van. Final check."

Retro and Buckshot entered the sliding door while Jennifer took the prostitute to the rear van. When she returned, I went over the rules of engagement and assault plan one final time, asking about the girl first.

"She going to be okay back there?"

"Yeah. She's calmer than I am. She wants some payback. She can't do anything but run away anyhow. She'll stay until someone comes for the van."

"She knows the signals?"

"Yeah. Someone comes to the van without flashing her twice with a white-lens flashlight, and she's gone."

The signal was a worst case. If it didn't come, it meant we were all dead, but it was the best I could do. If things got that bad, I had no doubt she'd be dead as well.

I turned to the team, throwing down a sack with black Nomex balaclavas in it.

"Okay. Remember what we discussed. No talking at all. No English in the presence of anyone still alive or conscious."

Buckshot said, "Do we really need to wear the damn ski masks? They're hot as shit and it'll affect our assault. Everyone's going to be dead anyway."

"No. Not everyone's going to be dead. I know what I said earlier, but we're only going to kill when there's a distinct threat. You find someone who's not a threat, take him out, but don't kill him. I don't care about the damage you have to do, but we're not slaying everything that moves."

I saw the look on the faces of the team and cut it short. "You fuckers are the best in the world. You want to go inside like a bunch of gang-bangers on a drive-by, go back to where you came from. It ain't happening here. We don't know what we're going to find. There might be some innocents mixed in with the trash. Either way, we need the masks. When we're done, the girls will still be alive. I don't want anyone to know what we look like."

I waited for a nod from each man, relieved that they didn't push the issue. "Okay, we clear from top to bottom. We need to clean out the entire house before we can do hostage recovery. First man to a stairwell leads the way. We keep it clandestine as long as possible. Hopefully, we secure the house before anyone even realizes we're there."

I turned to Jennifer. "You good with your job?"

She cradled the 416, a little nervous. "Yeah. Anyone comes up the drive, and I block their advance."

She worked the bolt of the weapon, checking to make sure it functioned smoothly, riding it back and forth to see if there were any problems. She flipped the safety lever up and down until she was sure it wouldn't hang up in a crunch, then turned on the EOTech sight, checking the reticle. She finished by seating a magazine and loading a round. When she was done, she looked up, ready. I saw the rest of the team watching and relaxing at her practiced moves. They had to rely on her with their lives, and I couldn't have scripted her actions any better.

I pretended not to notice any of the activities, saying, "That's right. We hear you fire, and it's game on. We'll be in a world of hurt, so don't miss."

She nodded, her eyes wide at the responsibility.

I smiled. "Don't worry. If it comes to that, we still have more skill than anyone else on this continent. You included."

I addressed the group. "Kit up. Let's do this."

Decoy brought out two duffel bags, with the men reaching in and pulling out ordinary-looking backpacks like college kids used. Each one unzipped to reveal a small arsenal of breaching charges and flash bang grenades, along with inserts that housed Kevlar plates for protection and Velcro belts that held magazines for the UMPs. When we were done, we looked like something out of *The Boondock Saints,* with makeshift assault kit that gave up ease of use for clandestine camouflage, and Nomex hoods that made us look like thieves.

Decoy strapped a thirteen-inch double-barreled shotgun to his thigh, the barrels themselves flattened out to spread the buckshot in a horizontal arc. The weapon was definitely not surgical. More like something that would kill everyone in its path. He saw me looking at him and said, "You never know when a room clear might be necessary. Mister Duckbill here will be just the ticket."

I hesitated, then nodded, knowing that thing wouldn't come out unless we heard Jennifer start banging away and things had gotten desperate.

I caught the eye of each man in turn, making sure they were ready. We had all done plenty of assaults like this in the past, before we joined the Taskforce, but always with the mighty green machine of the U.S. government behind us. Now we were on our own and doing something that was way outside of our mandate. We got in trouble here, and we'd be dead.

I said, "Last chance to reconsider."

Nobody said anything for a second. Then Buckshot said, "Cut the fucking drama. Let's go do some damage."

I smiled and turned on the laser pointer, centering the beam on the head of the man at the guard shack, cleaning a weapon. Retro and Buckshot stared at the screen for a moment, then slipped into the night.

The pointer itself was infrared, which meant they couldn't see it, but with his PVS-21 Night Observation Device on, Retro could. Nobody liked wearing NODs in an assault because it hampered the ability to index a weapon, but in these situations, it made you a god. Personally, I preferred the older ANVS-9 aviator NODs, but these could transition seamlessly to areas with light, unlike the older nines that would white out, forcing you to take them off. Something that would come in handy on our assault of the house. Here, it didn't matter. All Retro had to do was follow the beam like a sadistic rainbow, until he reached the treasure at the end.

With the wide-field on, I saw Retro and Buckshot begin the stalk. They moved slowly and carefully, two white blobs closing in on the men like bacteria on a petri dish. When they got within thirty feet, they slowed to a standstill, moving a foot every twenty seconds. The beam was still centered on the head of the man cleaning the weapon, who was completely unaware of the death stalking him. As my team closed the gap, I zoomed in, keeping the four on the screen. By the time the team was ready to assault, they were all within a ten-foot square, and I could once again make out facial features of the men.

Retro circled around behind the man cleaning the weapon, while Buckshot did the same to the cigarette smoker. They paused for a moment, getting ready. Both rose like wraiths from a horror movie, collapsing on the targets, the blur from the thermal imaging blending the forms together. A white-hot jet spurted out of each man, coating the ground like lava on my screen before fading to black. *Blood. Warm blood.*

I heard a gasp behind me and turned to see Jennifer ashen faced. The young whore behind her had no such reaction, either because she didn't realize what she was seeing or because she did and didn't care. Jennifer clenched her jaw, then nodded at me.

Buckshot came on my radio.

"Entrance clear."

"Rolling," I said.

46

We moved the van forward, getting to within two hundred meters of the house before stopping. I'd milked the girl — Jennifer told me her name was Maria — for all the information on the target I could get, and she'd given us the entire layout of the house, along with the alarm systems used. I didn't question her loyalty. She clearly wanted us to succeed, but we took what she said with a grain of salt because the worst thing we could do was base our entire assault on her memory, only to find out it was wrong.

Looking through the Blackjack, I saw the first part of her recollection was correct: There was an infrared trigger across the drive to signal an approaching vehicle. Which meant the door alarms were probably real as well. The good thing about the setup was that it was designed to prevent anyone escaping, not for keeping people from breaking in. According to Maria, the alarm contacts were *inside* the house, on the doors leading down to the basement, where the girls were kept. Which is why we'd hit that last, after everyone hostile was killed or captured.

We exited the vehicle and used the shadows to snake our way to the front door. I pointed out Jennifer's position, inside the shrubs, and continued on, glancing back over my shoulder to see if she was okay. She was already in the prone with the 416 aimed down the drive, wearing the PVS-21s, which looked like those ridiculous Venetian eye masks people wore on Mardi Gras, only instead of feathers, it had black plastic.

We crept up to the porch, avoiding any window observation. Retro placed a small object the size of a brick against the wall. Called a Radar Scope, it was basically a motion detector that could see through walls up to twelve inches thick, telling us whether anyone was in the room. It didn't matter if the person was playing possum or not. Breathing alone would be enough motion for it to detect. We would use the scope as we cleared until we hit resistance. From that moment on, we'd assume we were compromised, and move as fast as possible.

In seconds, Retro signaled that the foyer just beyond was clear.

Buckshot began working the door, unlocking it in a matter of moments. He looked at me, black ski mask and Venetian eyewear, and I nodded. He turned the knob and we entered, silently moving forward with all guns taking a sector of security.

In front was the stairwell, just like the girl had said it would be. Retro took up a position at the bottom, and we began flip-flopping up it, the low man pulling security while the high man went forward. When we reached the second floor, Retro went to the first room in the hallway, using the scope.

According to Maria, this floor was used for "training," with about five or six bedrooms left and right down the hallway. Retro used the scope and shook his head at door one. We got the same at door two and three. We moved across the hall to door four. I watched the scope and saw it light. *Someone's in this one.*

Retro shoved the scope in his pack and got ready to fight. Buckshot twisted the door handle, then leaned out of the way. We silently went inside, guns trained to shoot any threat that presented itself.

The room was illuminated with candles. The only thing in it was a bed, which had a teenage girl on it. Retro closed the gap to her and pinned her, gagging her mouth. The rest of the team looked for additional threats. In the corner was another door, which the girl was staring at hard. I moved to it. Before I reached it, the door swung open and I found myself face-to-face with the fake bum from Prague. He was wearing nothing but his underwear, and his brain was trying to compute what he was seeing. Before he could react, I jammed the suppressor of the UMP into his forehead. I got him on his knees and signaled Decoy. Circling around him, Decoy pulled out a small metal baton covered in a thin rubber coating. He hammered the man right above his ear, dropping him like a stone.

Retro was making shushing noises to the girl, keeping her calm. I signaled him to flex-tie her, then signaled the same to Decoy. We couldn't take her with us and couldn't risk her running around yelling, compromising the assault, so we'd tie and gag her here and come back for her later. The fake bum would get the same treatment, in case he woke up.

We exited the room and began clearing step-by-step, no longer using the scope but still moving as quietly as possible. All other rooms on the second floor were empty until we entered the last one, seeing a girl on her hands and knees with a man behind her.

He caught the movement of the door and looked up in surprise, one of his eyes staring off into space over my shoulder. Decoy put two rounds into his head, spackling the wall with brain matter, the only noise the hollow clanking of his bolt.

Jesus. The girl.

She had fallen onto her stomach and was trying to roll over. I broke silence.

"Get on her! Don't let her see the body. She'll be fucked up for life." *If she's not already.*

Buckshot threw the body on the floor, covering it with a blanket, while Retro collapsed on the girl, trapping her as she attempted to escape. I locked eyes with Decoy.

"What the fuck was that? He was no threat."

He didn't back down an inch. "He sure as shit was a threat to her."

I glared at him for a second to show him I was pissed, but I couldn't argue with the logic.

"Control yourself. This isn't a vendetta."

Retro had finished flex-tying her, smiling all the while to keep her calm, although the effect came out a little twisted given the mask and NODs. She looked confused, but didn't try to fight. Exiting the room, we went back down the stairwell to the first floor. We'd removed two from the equation, which left anywhere from four to eight still out, based on Maria's description.

We cleared room after empty room, causing the tension to build in the team. We'd rather hit the enemy one at a time, but every empty room lessened that chance. Sooner or later, we were going to kick over an ant pile. Flip-flopping down a hallway, I saw a door in front begin to swing open. I sprinted forward. A man came out empty-handed. I trapped his arm, locking up his joints in a come-along and driving him into a wall. Just past him in the room, I could see four other men around a card table, all looking at me in shock. They immediately began diving for weapons.

The ant pile. I kicked the man I held down the hall, raised my weapon and put two rounds into his face, then focused on the room. The rest of the team had collapsed on me, with two facing down each end of the hallway, pulling security, while one began tracking the targets in the room.

One of the men inside the room managed to get off two rounds, both wildly off the mark, before having his head split open. The others didn't fire a single shot. In the blink of an eye, all four were down, the noise of the suppressed weapons overshadowed by the bodies hitting the floor. The echo of the man's two rounds hung in the air.

Shit. Clandestine just went out the window. Retro and I entered the room and cleared it, ensuring everyone was dead. Seconds later, we were moving down the hall toward the final door, no longer trying to be quiet. The name of the game now was speed and violence of action. Retro turned the knob, finding it locked.

Decoy pulled a flex linear charge out of Buckshot's backpack, slapping it down the length of the door. We separated left and right with the door in the middle. He glanced to ensure everyone was clear and initiated the charge. It splintered the door inward, cutting it in half.

We followed the charge in before the pieces had even settled, finding one man on the floor laid out by the fragments of the door. Decoy fell on him while the rest of the team advanced.

The room was a kitchen. In the rear, by an oven, another woman cowered. This one older, with her hands raised. I moved to her while the team fanned out inside the spacious area. Gunfire erupted to my left, followed quickly by the muted clanking of the UMPs.

I reached the woman and prevented her

from moving, whispering softly to her, using soothing noises as I flex-tied her hands to her ankles in a sitting-up position. I didn't bother with a gag, because her screaming wouldn't make a shit's worth of difference after that door charge. I stroked her hair and smiled at her to let her know I meant no harm, then returned to the team.

We'd cleared the entire house, and I was pretty sure we'd eliminated all threats. Maria had said nobody ever stayed down with them in the basement, only coming down when it was time for someone to leave.

I signaled all-clear, meaning it was time to hit the basement. We raced back to the entrance, stacking on it with weapons raised. Retro opened the door to a completely black stairwell, so dark even our NODs were picking up no light. I could hear rustling down below, with the close-in stench of sweat and unwashed clothes wafting up. I ran my hands along the wall and found a switch, turning night into day. We began flip-flopping down the stairs, hearing the beeping of the alarm the girl had told us about, when the lights went off again.

What the hell?

Pulling security at the top, Buckshot turned them back on. We went a few feet, then they went out again. I halted the procession, turning on the infrared illumina-tor on my NODs. It wasn't that powerful, basically giving me a view of about five feet to my front, but it was better than the ridiculous light-switch competition. Retro and Decoy did the same, giving us a view down the stairwell like we were in *The Blair Witch Project*. Buckshot stayed at the top.

Moving slowly, we reached the bottom. To my left, I saw the girl working the light switch. Her eyes were wide open, straining for any hint of light, the IR source from my NODs making them glow like an animal in the night. Behind her were the other girls, all on the floor with their arms around their knees, shaking, completely unaware that we were there.

There were no beds. Just row after row of pallets on the floor. Apparently, the only time they felt a bed was when they were working, which for some reason struck me as particularly cruel.

The light-switch girl was shaking as well, her hand above the switch trembling so badly it looked like she was flicking water off of it. She had no way to stop whatever danger was coming down the stairs. All she could do was slow it down. But she didn't quit fighting.

It was quite possibly the bravest thing I had ever seen.

47

I turned to face Retro and Decoy, getting blinded by their IR source. I knew mine was doing the same to them, so I turned it off. I gave them hand and arm signals to get guns out into the room while I took out Miss Light Switch. I had no doubt she'd do something incredibly stupid and dangerous if the lights came on and we were standing in front of her with weapons. The girls sitting on the floor didn't pose the same threat. They'd have no time to react when they saw us, and probably wouldn't even if they could.

I slowly circled around the girl, feeling a little evil at the fact that she couldn't see me at all, while I could reach out and thump her in the head if I wanted. When I was lined up with her back, I pounced, encircling her arms and dragging her to the ground. She shrieked like a banshee, then began violently whipping around like a snake caught around the neck. She snapped her head back and slammed it into my NODs, causing them to shift and nearly knocking her out.

I shouted, "Lights! Lights!"

The room blazed into existence, blinding everyone for a moment. The girls on the floor began shrieking at the sight of the Boondock Saints pointing guns at them, but none made a move. Retro and Decoy began shouting, *"Ami! Ami!"* then "Friend! Friend!"

The screaming turned into whimpers, with the girls packing together like a flock of sheep cowering together at the threat of a wolf. The one in my arms was woozy from her attempts at harming me. She'd have a knot on her head, but appeared okay. I repeated *"ami"* over and over until she nodded her head. I let go of her and raised my hands. She scooted back to the flock, warily staring at us.

I keyed my radio. "Koko, house is clear. Bring in the girl."

I figured the quickest way to get complete compliance was to have Maria show herself, proving we were friends. From there, we'd sort out the exfil without worrying about one of them making a break for it.

I turned to Retro. "Go get the two girls upstairs and the one in the kitchen."

Decoy said, "What about the guy in the bedroom?"

"If he's still out, leave him there."

"And if he's not?"

"Put him back to sleep. *Then* leave him there." I keyed my radio. "Buckshot, get a gun out front. I don't want any surprises."

Minutes later, Retro came in with the woman from the kitchen. He cut off the flex ties on her hands and put her with the group. The girls showed her no outright sympathy, keeping their distance from her.

Decoy came over the net. "I'm going to need a hand up here. One girl's going to need to be carried, and I don't want to do that and watch the other one."

"What's wrong? Is she hurt?"

"No. At least not physically. But she's pretty much catatonic."

Retro said, "On the way."

While waiting on them, I checked in with Jennifer.

"Maria's good," she said. "In fact, she can't quit smiling. I'm moving to the house now in van one."

"Roger that. Buckshot, when she's in, go get van two. We need to clear out."

"Roger."

Decoy and Retro returned, Decoy carrying one girl while the other walked in front.

Decoy laid the girl on the ground, brushed her hair out of her face, then backed up. The group went ballistic at the sight, circling around them, all talking at once. The one on the ground was awake and responding to the treatment of her friends, apparently starting to believe that she wasn't about to die. The older woman from the kitchen hung at the back, trying to remain hidden.

Very different reaction from when she came in. Hmmm. . . .

Jennifer appeared at the bottom of the stairs with Maria, and the scene repeated, with everyone talking at once. Our girl was practically jumping up and down trying to explain who we were and what we were doing here. The rest of the girls seemed unsure of whether to believe it, like at any minute the trick would be exposed and they'd be told to saddle up.

I had Jennifer break up the old-home week, getting Maria to point out the girl who was in the room with the Arab. After a little back-and-forth, she pointed to Miss Light Switch.

Should have known.

Right behind her was the woman from the kitchen. When Maria caught sight of her, she froze for a second. Then she plowed through the crowd, pushing bodies left and right like a fullback trying to reach the end zone.

That's not good. "Decoy, stop her!"

He was close, but not close enough. Maria leapt on the woman like an alley cat, clawing great gouges in the woman's face as they fell to the floor. Before Decoy could reach her, the rest of the girls, seeing the attack and finally realizing they were no longer in any danger, lost all timidity and fell upon the woman as well, biting, clawing, and kicking. The outright savagery told me the woman would be dead in seconds.

It took all four of us to physically manhandle everyone off of her, and even that wasn't working until I shouted at Jennifer to crack a round into the floor with the 416. The explosion finally got them to stop, all panting like hyenas fighting over a kill. We got them separated and left Buckshot pointing a weapon to keep them calm.

We pulled out of earshot, taking Maria with us. In short order, we learned that the woman, far from being a captive, was one of the most sadistic people in the house. Maria began relaying horror stories that caused me to tell Jennifer to shut her up.

"I get the picture."

Decoy tossed his head at the cut-up woman. "Well, what about her? She's heard us talk. She'll know we're Americans."

"Maybe. Maybe not. Either way, I'm not going to kill her in cold blood. No matter how much she deserves it."

Retro said, "We don't have to do anything. We could just walk up those stairs for a few minutes."

"That would hurt the girls more than the woman. She'd just be dead, but they'd live with what they did forever." I felt Jennifer's eyes on me but didn't acknowledge it. "I have a better idea."

48

Keshawn kept his mind off the meeting by sweeping the inside of the warehouse. For the fourth time. He told himself it was just because he didn't like clutter, but deep down he knew it was because he was nervous. The tell was in the number of times he glanced at his watch, then glanced at the two Pelican cases at the back of the room.

What the fuck are you afraid of? You've walked with killers.

And yet he was. The man coming was someone who held a mythical place in his mind's eye. A fighter that would destroy all the rich motherfuckers in this godforsaken country. Turn it into an Islamic utopia, where everyone was equal in the eyes of Allah. No more greed, no more haves and have-nots. Just a society based on Sharia law, where the glory was dedication to the one true God instead of material, worldly goods.

But what if he's not?

What if all of this time and effort had been invested for some raghead loser? What if the promise wasn't real? For the first time in his desolate, violent life, he had a purpose that transcended himself, and he was now afraid he'd find out it was a fantasy.

A soft knock snapped him out of his thoughts, the sound cracking open a fight-or-flight response as great as if he'd heard gunfire.

He placed the broom deliberately in the corner, took a breath, and strode to the door. Standing outside was a pudgy, balding man nervously glancing left and right. He was dressed like a street bum, his clothes stained and his oversize running shoes showing holes at the toes. He stank of whiskey and boiled eggs. Keshawn felt his heart fall. Then felt a rage like never before, images of Beth's struggle in the bathtub turning his vision red. He brought himself under control.

"Yes?"

The man wiped the sweat from his upper lip. "You get a FedEx package here yesterday?"

"What business is it of yours?"

"It's my business because I know what's in it. And if you don't give me some money,

389

I'm going to let the cops know."

Keshawn was completely taken aback. This man wasn't the fighter. He was something else entirely. He didn't know how the man had knowledge of the delivery, but he did know one thing: The bum was a threat.

"What the fuck are you talking about?" Keshawn said. "Cops? For what?"

The bum was sweating profusely now, fidgeting left and right. "Just give me a hundred bucks, and I'll leave."

Keshawn stood back from the door, his mind running through options, none of which he could execute on the front stoop. "Come inside. I have some money in here."

"That's okay. I'm not stupid. Bring the money to me out here."

Keshawn looked left and right, seeing no one in the deserted industrial area. He reached back like he was pulling out a wallet, withdrawing a four-inch folding knife instead. He flicked out the blade and whipped it straight into the man's abdomen, blade up, stabbing deep and ripping upward toward the heart. He clamped his other hand on the man's jacket and held him upright while he continued to cut, finally hitting the bone of the rib cage. The man shrieked, his eyes bugging out of his head. Keshawn jerked him inside, the door slamming shut on its mechanical arm. He tossed the bum on the ground, watching him writhe around in a growing pool of blood, desperately attempting to staunch the flow. He knew the man was going to die in seconds.

He grabbed the bum's hair to get him to focus. "Who told you about the shipment?"

The homeless man gargled, holding his hands to his stomach, his eyes rolling back in his head.

"Who, motherfucker, who?"

The man was unresponsive, either dead or unconscious. Keshawn kicked him, then kicked the wall.

"Fuck!"

He heard another knock from outside. *What the hell?* He quickly glanced at himself, seeing blood on his right hand up to the wrist. He thought about jumping out of the window at the back of the warehouse, but grabbed a shop rag instead. Wiping off the blood, he cracked the door a second time.

Standing on the other side was wiry man with a hawkish nose. His complexion was swarthy, but what caught Keshawn's attention were his eyes. Black pools that reflected something dangerous. Perhaps something irrational as well. Just as he could smell a cop from across the street, Keshawn knew this man had been inside a prison. And not an easy one.

The fighter.

The man spoke calmly and lightly. "I'm Rafik. You must be Keshawn. May I come in?"

Keshawn said nothing, simply holding open the door, unsure of what he should do, his mind spinning. The simple question, given the killing he'd just done, seemed surreal.

Rafik walked inside and barely glanced at the eviscerated homeless man.

"You did well. I'm sorry for the deception, but I had to be sure of who you were."

"You sent him to me? Why? Suppose I let him go?"

"I would have killed him. And then killed you."

The confusion wearing off, Keshawn bristled, growing angry at being played like a child at a magic show. "Really? You think so? You ain't in raghead land now."

Rafik smiled, completely calm. "I asked for your forgiveness. I needed to be sure of your commitment. To be sure you wouldn't run at the first hint of trouble. We are on a path that may require sacrifice. I had to be sure you were up to the task."

Keshawn said, "You don't have to worry about me. I'm ready."

Rafik narrowed his eyes and flicked his toe at the body on the floor. "This is nothing. I mean real sacrifice."

Beth's struggle in the bathtub flashed in Keshawn's mind, her arms flailing around for leverage to raise her head, water splashing over the tub, the burst of bubbles as her involuntary response overcame her conscious attempt to stave off death, the tub growing cold as he held her limp body, one of her arms draped over the edge, the metronomic drips of water falling from a finger, getting farther and farther apart.

He felt Rafik's eyes on him. "I know about sacrifice," he said. "Believe me, I know."

Rafik said nothing for a moment, then nodded. "The time is almost here. You had no trouble with the DHL shipment?"

Glad to talk about anything to rid him of the memories, Keshawn led him to the Pelican cases. "No issues whatsoever. I haven't opened them, so I don't know if anything was lost."

"You didn't open the cases?"

"Well, I didn't know what was in them, so it made no sense to see if something was stolen."

Pleased at the obedient response, Rafik

opened both cases and smiled. "Nothing missing."

Keshawn saw only metal plates and plastic buckets. "What the fuck is this?"

"You'll find out with everyone else. You've done well with the warehouse. This is where we'll build the method of destruction and train the men. One team at a time. Is the meeting set for Richmond?"

"Yeah. Carl's got an apartment outside the airport. Everyone's traveling down there now and should be there in a couple of days."

Rafik clapped him on the shoulder. "Perfect. Let's clean up this mess and continue our journey."

The calmness of the conversation, considering the spreading pool of blood and the gutted body with its rictus grimace, sent a sliver of unease into Keshawn. *Maybe he's not firing on all cylinders.*

49

The room stank of stale designer coffee and fried rice. The conference table was littered with takeout cartons and Styrofoam cups, a large fruit bowl in the center holding the sad remnants of a bunch of grapes. Kurt supposed nobody wanted to be the one to eat the last bit of food.

He rested his head against the wall with his legs extended from his back-row seat behind the conference table, watching the members of the Oversight Council fidget while they waited on the arrival of the president. He had briefed them on the activities in Prague, filling in the holes from the information that had come out of the DOS and CIA's own intelligence apparatus. The story on the street was of a large raid by the Prague police based on the intelligence of a woman "informant" on the inside of an Albanian sex-slave ring. Kurt had cracked open the truth.

As expected, the council had been incredulous. The team had completely overstepped their bounds, potentially causing an international crisis that could destroy American credibility during a time when the United States was trying to regain its footing in the world. Truth be told, Kurt half hoped they'd shut the whole project down. The pressure on him was enormous, affecting his ability to make decisions that were in the nation's best interest. Calling his sleep fitful was being polite. His entire life had been dedicated to defending the constitution of the United States, and after 9/11 the Taskforce had seemed one more step on that road, but now things were spinning out of control.

An attack was coming, and the team was doing its best to combat it, but at what cost? When was enough truly enough? When would the council say the rule of law outweighed the death that was coming? He despised Secretary of State Brookings, thinking the weasel cared only about his own career, but he understood the reticence.

If Pike's actions in Prague became public knowledge, it would affect innumerable security arrangements on the European continent, which would inevitably trickle into trade negotiations and every other issue. Kurt understood that better than most, even while the council looked at him as a knuckle dragger. America no longer had the luxury of going it alone in the world. With globalization, everything was intertwined.

Then there was the domestic problem. If the Taskforce was exposed, nobody in the room had any illusions of how it would play out. Best case, the political apparatus would have a brief seizure, with a few weeks of twenty-four-hour talking heads frothing at the mouth and the usual rounds of congressional testimony before it faded from the national consciousness.

Worst case, the damage would be permanent.

Either way, all in the room knew it would be permanent for them. At the back of everyone's mind was the election less than six months away, with the opposition furiously trying to find something to harm the president.

On the heels of Kurt's brief was the latest intel on the attack. The chatter had continued unabated, with nothing concrete. The only new intelligence gleaned was a cryptic reference to the attackers being "homegrown," which, coupled with the lost EFPs, scared the hell out of everyone in the room.

The council was split in half on whether

to let the team follow the trail to Budapest. Like a hung jury, they had argued for the better part of ten hours, and were now simply going to toss the problem into the president's lap. Let him make the decision. Kurt thought it was cowardly, but he didn't get a vote.

Without fanfare, the door swung open and President Warren entered. Caught off guard, everyone jerked upright, some standing, others attempting to do so.

"Keep your seats. Sorry to make you wait. Other things going on."

The room gave a collective nod as he took his seat at the head of the conference table. Kurt surveyed the crowd to see who had changed demeanor at the president's arrival. None appeared to do so, probably out of exhaustion.

"Well, what have we got?"

Alexander Palmer, the president's national security advisor, was the man chosen to brief both sides of the argument. He cleared his throat and said, "Well, sir, we have a significant ability to stop the attack, but the risks may well be worse than the aftermath."

Warren took that in, then nodded for Palmer to continue. Palmer relayed all that had happened in Prague, ending with the lead on the terrorists attempting to get explosives in Budapest for the EFPs.

Warren didn't need a map drawn out. After a lifetime of politics, he instantly calculated the risks of what the team had done. As well as the rewards.

When Palmer was done, he said, "Okay. What's the vote?"

Palmer said, "Well, the vote's split. The potential repercussions are enormous. May already be enormous. But the terrorist plot is real. No doubt. Given the EFPs, they don't plan on a single assault. It's going to be big."

Warren smiled. "And you want me to make the vote."

Everyone shifted in their chairs, looking left and right.

Warren said, "Kurt, what do you think?"

Kurt pulled his head off the wall, leaned forward, and said, "I think this is why someone's called the president. Let 'em get out their views. But *you* have to make a decision."

Warren narrowed his brow. Kurt refused to glance away from the most powerful man on earth, but he softened the blow. "Sir, there aren't any easy answers. I could tell you what I think, but I'm not the president. Hear what the council thinks, then ask me."

Kurt saw Secretary of State Brookings

staring at him. For the first time without contempt.

Warren said, "Okay, give it to me."

Palmer went first. "Well, there's no doubt what they did was a good thing. I mean, Jesus, they saved twelve girls from a lifetime of pain. But they probably destroyed our entire counterterrorist infrastructure. Personally, I'd like to fucking hang Pike from the nearest tree. The guy doesn't understand what he's doing. We can't have him running around like this. Lord knows what he'll do in Budapest. He's leaving a trail that can be unraveled by anyone with an Internet connection."

The director of central intelligence cut in. "Hang on. I don't want to act like I'm on his side, but Pike's been better at this shit than anyone I've seen. He did screw up in Prague. If you can call saving twelve innocent girls a screwup. But he managed to divert attention from it. It's very, very shaky, but nobody knows who it was."

Palmer came back, now agitated. "Bullshit! So he saved twelve girls. Who the fuck cares? How many girls are there in the world getting screwed over right now? His mission is to defend the United States. Not run around saving whatever he thinks is right. Jesus, your guys go through enormous training for this very thing. Don't get involved in the source's life. Get what you can out of them. Don't get attached. Pike got attached in about fifteen minutes."

Kurt cut in. "Wait a minute. It was more than that. He found out a source inside the house had information on the Arab's next moves. That's why he did it. If he hadn't assaulted, we wouldn't be debating the next step. There wouldn't be a next step."

Warren raised his hand. "Okay, I got it. What's the status of the hit?"

Brookings spoke up. "Well, we were lucky in the regional security officer. He's a career guy who actually cares more about America than his job. Pike left the girls in a van outside the embassy, then called the RSO anonymously to let him know what he had, to include the house Pike had hit. Basically, he hand-fed the Prague police a political coup. They got to take down some bad guys that were already subdued by Pike's crew, then crow about breaking up a white-slavery ring. It's a win-win as far as anybody knows. The RSO also followed Pike's instructions about keeping it close-hold, even from the ambassador. My report from the Prague mission was exactly the cover story Pike devised. The Czech police raided the house, arrests in abundance, prosecutions forthcoming, yada yada yada. The ambassador has no idea what occurred, and neither do the Czech police. And they won't look too hard, given the penetration the Albanians had in their department. They'll pat themselves on the back and let it go."

"So we're at square one with this? No harm, no foul?"

Palmer spoke up. "Yes, in theory, but we still have Pike at the helm. This worked out. But it might not have. We need to look at the repercussions holistically. Pike saved twelve teenage girls, and that's great, but in so doing, he put this entire effort in jeopardy. I'm against letting him go to Budapest. We're on the verge of compromising the entire effort. It'll be too easy to connect the dots if we give him authority for Budapest."

Palmer quit talking but looked like he had something else to say. Warren waited a beat, then said, "Get it out. This isn't a time to go back home wishing you'd said something."

Kurt watched Palmer look his way, and knew it would be bad.

"Well, if we decide to do this, we need to face the repercussions. If it blows up, we'll be crucified — and I'm not talking about our careers. That's a given. We might stop this attack, but we won't stop the next one.

Or the one after. In fact, if this operation gets out, we might very well be *driving* the next attack. Taskforce operations will fuel conspiracy theories for decades. We have enough trouble trying to fight bullshit propaganda on the Arab street with normal operations. It isn't pleasant, but morality is on a scale. Nobody would say saving those girls was wrong, but Pike's operation might have cost us many more deaths, because we need to protect the Taskforce. We might need to let this attack occur so that we can prevent the next one."

Nobody said anything, the truth of the statement speaking for itself. Kurt wondered how it had come to this. How everything he had done to prevent just this problem had proven insufficient.

"Either that," Palmer continued, "or prepare a story ahead of time if things go bad. Mitigate the damage to the greatest extent possible."

Whoa. What's that mean? Kurt knew that any story would have to be backed up with sacrificial lambs. He'd seen it firsthand last year when they'd thrown some bad folks to the wolves to protect the Taskforce.

Warren addressed the secretary of defense. "What do you think?"

"Sir, I think we let them go. We know two

things: There's an attack coming, and the method of the attack involves explosives gleaned in Budapest. Without the explosives, the EFPs fail. We don't know where the attack is going to occur, but we can affect the acquisition of explosives. Pike's methods have proven risky and unpredictable, but in the end, he's all we have. I say let them continue." He paused for a minute, then said, "And I mean for the record, as the secretary of defense, I say let them continue."

Brookings and Palmer began to talk over each other at his statement, causing the secretary of defense to raise his hand. When the room was quiet, he said, "Please. Let me continue. We can't predict the future. We might all be in jail in six months, and our entire counterterrorist infrastructure could be gutted. But we don't know that. What we do know is that the attack's coming. We don't know the form or the time, but we know it's imminent. We have the ability to stop it. Right now."

He went face-to-face around the room. "I say stop the attack. If it goes bad, it goes bad, but there's no way I can sit here and say let it go so we can prevent the next one."

The silence extended from the SECDEFs statement, nobody willing to offer another opinion. Kurt watched Warren consider all that was said, glad that he wasn't in the president's shoes. Warren tapped his fingers on the table for a couple of seconds, then looked up.

"Okay. Everyone understand that this is my decision. For the record, you all disagreed vehemently. And I mean that." He looked at Kurt. "No more Taskforce activity without council oversight. Interdict the explosives and nothing more. That's the mission. I don't give a shit what they find out, that's all they do."

Stone-faced, Kurt said, "Yes, sir."

Warren's expression softened. "Kurt, I know this sounds like I'm looking for a reason to hang them out to dry, but that won't happen. I trust you. I trust them. Get them back in the fight."

Warren looked at the pad of paper on the desk, clenching his fists around the pencil in his hands. The pencil snapped under his grasp, surprising the room at the loss of control.

He looked back at Kurt. "Stop this attack. Do what you were designed to do. No fingerprints. Kill those motherfuckers."

50

Sitting on a small ridgeline overlooking the Budapest farmhouse, I had begun to wonder if we weren't wasting our time. We'd had a mobile observation post outside the place for damn near two days after the original meet time given to us by the girl in Prague, and so far nothing. I hadn't worried at first, because every action has a reaction, and our assault in Prague to get the information was bound to have repercussions that would cause a shift as the Albanians dealt with the problem. Naively, I hadn't thought that the threat extended across the ocean.

Kurt had called me to give the Oversight Council go-ahead for Budapest, then cryptically asked if I was alone. When I told him I was, he had said, "Watch yourself. Don't leave any fingerprints."

"Of course. I never do."

Kurt had laughed, then said, "Bullshit. You left a ton of fingerprints in Prague." He paused, then said, "But that's not what I mean. People are antsy here. It's gotten political because of the election. Even in our world. The hit's coming, and we have about a fifty percent chance of stopping it. We don't do it and I'm no longer sure you guys will be shielded. Watch yourself."

"Whoa. Is the team in the crosshairs? What are you saying?"

I could almost hear Kurt go back into commander role, knowing he'd said too much. "No . . . no, of course you're not in the crosshairs. Just don't leave any fingerprints. You read me?"

My mind running through the implications, I said, "Yeah . . . yeah, I get you."

"Pike, it's good. The president himself backed you up, but everyone's on edge. You got the ball. Just don't screw it up."

I didn't really care about myself, since I was quasi out of government service and a little bit untouchable, but the team was still in the military and could be hung out to dry if things went bad. Which they might.

"I won't fuck up. You know that. But I need to know how far to push this. You want it stopped even if it means compromise, or you want me to back off? What's the cut line?"

"Stop it. Fucking stop it. If it goes bad,

I've got your back."

"Will that be enough?"

To his credit, he didn't lie. "I don't know."

And now I sat on a ridgeline eating cold pizza and drinking bottled water, hoping and not hoping that something would happen.

We'd had eyes on the place forty-eight hours after our assault on the slave house, so we'd had plenty of time to assess it. And the results were pretty grim. While it looked like every other ancient farmhouse out here, this one had a pretty sophisticated security apparatus. Offset from the main road and tucked into a little valley with a creek at the rear, it had cameras on both corners out front and over the main door, roving security patrols, guard posts on the road leading in, and no doubt a full-on alarm system on all entrances. It was a mini compound. Besides the main two-story house, there was a one-story carriage house located directly behind it, and a barn kitty-corner to the carriage house. The only good thing was that there weren't any neighbors nearby. The closest house was located behind our ridgeline observation post, about a half mile away.

After the meet time had come and gone, we'd simply rotated people through the OP, with the remaining members of the team catching some rack in the other van down a dirt road in the tree line. After two days of waiting, having had time to let Kurt's conversation percolate, I was toying with the idea of going home. *Maybe this thread's pulled out.* Maybe our hit alone had stopped the transfer of explosives and stopped the attack itself. *Not to mention, we're all getting a little ripe.*

I perked up when a car wound down the drive to the house, one of many that came and went each day. I trained the Blackjack on the car, zooming in until I could make out anyone who exited. The image wasn't perfect, but it worked pretty well in daylight with the thermal turned off, even given the twilight of the setting sun. Enough to let me look at the place from over a quarter of a mile away and see anything suspicious. And, hooked to our computer system in the van, it had one benefit that our sorry-ass human eyes didn't: the ability to do a screen capture and run the image through a facial recognition program.

Two men exited the car, and I began firing away with the Blackjack. It took ten frames a second, isolated the facial features of everyone in the frame, and fed that into the computer with facial recognition software. Compared against the cell phone photos that Jennifer had taken at the hotel in Prague, we hoped to get a hit. It wouldn't be a black-and-white yes-or-no answer, but it would give us a percentage of probability.

Facial recognition was very hard to do with natural photos. The computer would have only what we gave it, so it would be comparing everything with the cell phone image. Thus, any difference in profile, lighting, or size would throw it off. The software program would mitigate that to its best ability by taking the multiple pictures fed it and isolating the ones that most resembled the pose of the cell phone before it started comparing. But it wasn't foolproof by any means.

While the Blackjack took the photos, I kept an eye on the video image. Two men exited the car, both looking like Arabs to me. *Come on. Turn and face the camera. Give me a smile.* One scanned the area, providing me a full-on face shot. The other just looked at the house, at best giving me a profile. They were met by security and searched. *Which means they aren't part of the family.*

I gave a warning order to the other van. "Get everyone kitted up. We might have jackpot."

I got an acknowledgment as I watched the men disappear into the house. Two minutes later, the computer spit out its prediction. Seventy-two percent chance on one, fourteen on the other.

Seventy-two. Good enough for government work.

I got on the radio. "Bring up the van. It's showtime."

51

Kamil and Adnan were led into the house by two large men, neither making any effort to hide the weapons on their hips, or any effort to act civilly. Kamil felt like he was starting all over again, having to prove he was trustworthy. Which made him uneasy, especially since Draco had called off the initial meeting at the last minute for no reason whatsoever.

The entourage led them through the simple farmhouse to the rear, stopping at a rustic den with a large glass window facing the carriage house and barn in the rear, the sun already dipping below the horizon. Draco was seated on a couch, giving off a glowering anger instead of the insincere happiness from their first meeting. The security men simply pointed at the chairs opposite the couch.

Sitting down, Kamil said, "Thank you for seeing us again. I hope the profit we brought will help with the inconvenience."

Draco ignored Kamil, addressing Adnan instead. "What do you know of Prague?"

Kamil saw Adnan look to him for guidance, but he didn't know where this was going. He said, "Draco, Adnan is just my explosives expert. He —"

"Shut the fuck up and let him answer." He returned to Adnan. "What do you know of Prague?"

"Uhh . . . I know nothing. I stayed in a hotel and moved when I was told. I don't know what you're asking."

"Who has your friend here met with?"

"No one besides you. We left the city after his first meeting, just like you told us to."

Draco lied, "Suppose I told you I had planted a tracking device on your friend here, and I know where he went. What he did. And now suppose that if you lie to me again, I'm going to cut your throat. Will that change your answer?"

"No."

Draco flicked his eyes at the security men, who descended on Adnan, one holding him in the chair while another brought out a knife. A third drew a pistol and aimed it at Kamil when he leapt up.

Kamil shouted, "Why are you doing this? What have we done?"

"My transit point in Prague was raided. After your visit. Given your reluctance with my product, I'm thinking you had something to do with it."

"No! We had nothing to do with it!"

"We'll know soon, I'm sure."

He nodded at the security men. The one holding Adnan in place torqued his head to the side, exposing the carotid artery. The other placed the knife against his neck.

Draco said, "You have one chance, my friend. Who did Kamil talk to after he left my house?"

Adnan said, "You have the tracker. You know. Nobody." He quit struggling and closed his eyes. "Do it."

Draco took in Adnan's willingness to die, then assessed Kamil. He waved off his men.

"Understand this: I don't trust you or your group. I think you had something to do with my losses, either directly or indirectly. If I see you again after tonight, I will consider you an enemy. And make no mistake, if something else happens to my enterprise because of your visit, I'll hunt you down wherever you are."

Kamil simply nodded.

"Did you bring the money?"

Kamil said, "Yes. Your men took it."

Draco waited until it was retrieved. When

the case was opened, he smiled.

"Well, at least you didn't lie about the cash." He addressed one of the security men. "Bring in the box."

Waiting on the team, I watched the sun sink below the horizon and thought about our chances. The house itself was smaller than the slave house, with about the same amount of manpower. But it was still daylight, and this house had a helluva lot more electronic security.

The mission was to stop the attack, and looking at it logically, the only way we were going to do that was to hit the meeting itself. If we waited until the Arabs left, we'd get them, but we might not get the explosives. Odds were they weren't going to drive to the airport with them in their car, and we still had two terrorists unaccounted for. We couldn't take a chance that they'd simply make arrangements to ship the explosives, forcing us to hit the house anyway.

Ordinarily, we'd just recock and keep on truckin', running down the threads, but not with the knowledge of the EFPs and the intel on the impending attack. We needed to knock this out right now. Which, given our manpower, sucked beyond words.

Life was much easier when I used to just hammer the shit out of a target, slicing through and overpowering everything in my path with a squadron's worth of killers. Now, once again, our entire assault was predicated on nobody knowing we were there. On silently clearing rooms and taking out targets before the next one knew there was a threat. That wasn't a problem when we were hunting an individual man in a specific hotel room. It was a little bit different taking on an entire force spread out over a building. With a single team. Not impossible, but damn well harder.

I heard the van door close and turned away from the Blackjack screen.

"Well, here we go again. The targets just entered the house."

Nobody said anything. The men looked grim, knowing exactly how hard this would be. Jennifer looked a little sick, reminding me of the opening scenes from *Saving Private Ryan.*

I used the Blackjack image on the laptop screen to brief. "We do a dismounted approach, sticking to the wood line here in the east. We enter the house from the door here on the eastern side, leaving Jennifer in the wood line for security."

Retro said, "What about the cameras?"

"From their angles, I'm pretty sure they're focused on the roadway in and the front of the house. I think we can bypass them by coming in through the wood line. They don't have three-hundred-and-sixty-degree coverage."

Decoy said, "And the alarms?"

"Well, no SCADA tricks here. From a scan, we've picked up a ton of RF coming from the house and isolated a couple of signals to the cameras outside. That leads me to believe the alarm system's wireless. We'll get to the door, isolate the signal there, and jam it."

An alarm system, by its very nature, has a single point of failure; when a breach occurs, it sends a specific signal delivering that message. So, to work around that, you can either trick the system into thinking a breach hasn't occurred or hijack the signal before it gets to whoever's looking — either a human or a mechanical device designed to start squealing. We always opted for the latter. Much easier to stop the signal than to memorize eight thousand different types of sensor systems and how they alert — motion detectors, magnetic plates, acoustic triggers, you name it. At the end of the day, all would have to send a signal. With a wireless alarm, we could stop it from broadcasting by simply overpowering the radio transmission with a signal of our own, basically making the receiver deaf.

"Of course, it's more than likely got a sensor fail-safe, so once we jam, we'll probably get ten minutes max before the control panel misses a self-test handshake with the door sensor. From there it's game on."

"What if that sensor's next on the handshake list?"

"We get about ten seconds."

"Fucking great."

Decoy asked, "Still going top to bottom?"

"No. We're looking for the Arabs and the explosives, and I doubt they're on the top floor. We don't need to secure this place, just stop the transfer. Once that's done, we haul ass the same way we came in, running the wood line back to the vans."

Retro said, "Is the house designated hostile?"

I hesitated. I didn't want to do it, but I just didn't have the force to accomplish a surgical hit. After the Prague operation, these men would be on edge, expecting an assault and trigger-happy. Looking for a fight. We wouldn't be catching anyone with their pants down like last time, and unlike the Prague hit, there were no known friendlies inside. I caught Jennifer's eye.

"Yeah. It's a hostile force. My call."

She knew it meant everyone inside who had the misfortune to cross our path would be dead, no matter if they were a threat or not, but she nodded, accepting it.

She said, "What about me?"

"Same plan as before. You stay in the wood line and interdict anyone coming down the drive. I want you to discriminate, however. I don't want to kill police or any other coincidence that might occur. If they aren't hostile, just alert us by radio. If they come out to play, light 'em up."

She nodded, her eyes wide, but showing more confidence than she had last time.

"Anything else?"

When nobody spoke, I said, "I want to be in and out in less than ten minutes. Fast and quiet. Find the terrorists and explosives, then run like hell."

I positioned Jennifer and waited in the gathering gloom for the roving patrol. We were forty meters from the side door, hidden in the brush at the edge of the wood line. From our survey over the last few days, we knew the guard would circle about once every ten minutes. After we took him out, the clock would be ticking. The good thing was the roving patrol invariably used flashlights, which meant we'd have plenty of time to see them, and they'd have no night vision.

Soon enough, we saw the bobbing light come around the back of the house. There was still enough twilight to make out the man without the aid of NODs, but he apparently felt the need to use the flashlight.

He passed our position. Two shadows separated from the wood line at a sprint, closed on him and brought him to the ground. In short order, the body was dragged into the brush. I patted Jennifer on the shoulder and signaled the team. We crossed the open area to the door.

Decoy brought out a spread-spectrum scanner and quickly isolated the nearest signal, which should be the door sensor. He identified the frequency and dialed it into a small device the size of a billiard ball. He attached it to the wall and pressed a button. It softly chirped, then apparently did nothing, but I knew it was now blasting out a signal on the same frequency the door sensor used, overriding its ability to communicate with the control panel.

Within seconds, Retro and Buckshot had the door unlocked. Guns ready, we held our breath. Retro swung it open, and we went inside. No alarm sounded.

Retro led the way, moving to the first door he saw. He opened it to find a bathroom, empty. We kept going down the hallway, almost at a jog. Decoy pulled security on a door to the right while we opened a door to the left. Sweeping inside, we eliminated two men immediately, dropping them before they had a chance to react, the only noise the thump of their bodies hitting the floor. We exited and stacked on the other door, finding the room empty. We took a left turn and entered a wide hallway that led back to a room in the rear. I could hear men talking, at least three. A door to the left halted our advance. There was no way we were going to leave an unsecured room to our rear. We entered, found the initial room empty, but saw another door on the right wall of the room.

Then the alarm went off.

52

Adnan picked up a brick of SEMTEX and tested its consistency, ensuring it wasn't just a block of flour. He nodded at Kamil and counted the blasting caps, checking that each one was capable of setting off a charge. He picked up a roll of time fuse, cut off a section, and threaded it into a fuse igniter. He pulled the metal ring on the igniter, hearing a pop and the hissing of the fuse burning down, the room filling with an acrid sulfur smell.

Satisfied, he said, "This will do."

Draco said, "Of course it will do. Did you think I would sell you junk?"

Kamil said, "What about the shipping labels? And the special containers? This does us no good if we can't fly it out of here."

"Don't worry about that. It will —"

Draco's words were drowned out by an earsplitting alarm. He snarled, "I fucking knew it!"

He drew a pistol and fired twice into Adnan's chest, Adnan holding his arms up to ward off the impending death, his eyes wide. Kamil dove into the nearest security man, wrestling him for control of his gun. Draco whirled from Andan and fired at the pair, hitting his security man in the back. Kamil rolled out from under him with the pistol and began firing wildly, hitting the other security man in the leg and causing Draco to dive to the floor. Kamil put two more rounds into the writhing bodyguard, silencing him, then moved around the couch, seeing Draco bear-crawling toward the door. He kicked Draco's arm out, knocking the pistol away and dropping Draco on his stomach.

Draco rolled over to find Kamil's pistol aimed at his head in a two-handed grip.

Draco spit into his face. "You fuck. Even your God won't help you now. You're fucking dead."

Kamil said, *"Insha'Allah."*

And pulled the trigger.

Jennifer heard the alarm split the night and fought to control the urge to flee. She silently begged the team to come running back out. When she heard gunfire explode inside the house, she knew things had gone terribly wrong. Her adrenaline skyrocketed, her breathing coming in short gasps. Then she caught the flash of headlights on the road.

Oh no. Please don't come here.

The car made the turn at a high rate of speed, the headlights sweeping across the house as it bounced down the drive. The driver slammed on the brakes, skidding to a stop in the gravel.

The doors swung open and four men spilled out, all armed. There was no indication that the car was from any government agency. No lights, no sirens, no insignia. *Not friendly.* The men huddled by the car for a pregnant second, then raised their weapons and began jogging toward the front door fifty meters away. She knew there was no way she could kill all four before they located her position. And eliminated her.

Pike's command echoed in her mind. *Light 'em up.*

She took two deep breaths and settled the EOTech sight on the rear man. She tracked him for a split second, her mind going blank. She squeezed the trigger. He dropped like a puppet with the strings cut. A detached part of her brain was surprised, as if it were a science experiment. She expected some dramatic death dance like she'd seen in the movies, but the man simply rolled forward as if he'd gone unconscious while running.

She rocked back with the recoil, working with it, just like she had been taught on the steel plate range. The weapon tracked to the next man. A squeeze. Recoil. Another drop. The third man turned at the noise of her weapon. Breathe. Squeeze. Recoil. A mist formed around his head as he was flung backward. The fourth man began running back toward the cover of the car, firing at her muzzle flash. The noise and impact of the bullets around her didn't alter her aim. She felt nothing but the rifle.

Breathe.

Squeeze.

Recoil.

The man collapsed to the ground like all the others. A sack of flesh with no control.

A split second later, her body was on fire with adrenaline. She was trembling so badly she couldn't hold the weapon straight, her body shaking as if she had entered a freezer.

Get the hell out of there. Please get out.

53

We ignored the alarm and cleared the final door in the room, finding a walk-in closet, empty of people. I heard gunfire down the hallway.

What the hell?

"Game on. Move to the sounds of the guns."

We got weapons out into the hallway, the team splitting left and right pulling security as we advanced at a jog to the back room. I saw a man pick up a chair and throw it through a large window at the rear of the room, then jump out and race away. I snapped off a couple of rounds but knew it was wasted effort.

We entered the room, finding three dead bodies and a crate on the floor.

"Search them."

Inspecting the crate, Decoy said, "Found the explosives. SEMTEX. Complete with initiation capability."

Retro said, "Got an Arab. Passport from Algeria. Nothing else but a room key to a hotel."

I said, "Get a profile from him. Skip the iris capture. I'm not sure that'll work on a dead guy."

While Buckshot finished searching the others, Retro used a HIIDE biometric scanner to get fingerprints and much better facial recognition data than our cell phone pictures, which we'd eventually put into the system for clues as to who he had been.

Searching the other bodies, Buckshot said, "Just a bunch of thugs. Nothing interesting."

Before Retro could finish fingerprinting the Arab, we were peppered with rounds through the open window. Hitting the floor, I counted at least five muzzle flashes and saw a dozen men boiling out of the carriage house.

Holy shit. I grabbed one end of the crate, shouting, "Move, move!"

Decoy entered the hallway to a fusillade of automatic fire, bouncing him back into the room.

"Hallway's blocked with three men, armed with assault rifles."

Through the window, I could see a platoon of shooters advancing.

Retro and Buckshot suppressed their fire with well-placed rounds, but we were now in a standoff. Which we would lose. I heard Buckshot shout and saw him snap back, holding his left arm. The situation crystallized in my mind. Even if we smashed the logjam in the hallway, we wouldn't be able to outrun the mob from the carriage house. They'd overwhelm us as we tried to get to the vans.

Time for drastic action.

I snatched the roll of time fuse and cut off what I thought would be three minutes. Jamming it into a blasting cap, I crimped it closed with my teeth, hearing my instructor from years ago in my head. *"It can be done, but it's not the preferred technique."*

I shoved the cap into a block of SEMTEX, screwed on an igniter, and pulled the ring.

Decoy smelled the burn and turned from the doorway. "What the fuck did you do?"

"Avalanche," I said.

"Are you fucking crazy?" he said. Then he repeated the code word for immediate evacuation through the radio. "Avalanche, avalanche, avalanche."

Buckshot and Retro closed on the door, eyes wide, still returning fire.

"How bad?" I asked Buckshot.

"Just a graze. I'm still in the fight."

Retro simply asked, "How long?"

I squeezed off three rounds through the window, seeing a shadow drop. "Three minutes, give or take a minute."

He looked at me like I'd lost my mind.

"Hey, it's old commie shit. I can't predict the burn rate."

Decoy unstrapped the duckbill shotgun from his thigh, muttering, "Crazy mother-fucker."

He tapped each man on the shoulder, saying, "We get one chance. Once I pop both barrels, I need all guns putting lead down the hallway."

We backed up to him until we were all touching. When I felt him move, I rotated around, putting my barrel over his shoulder.

He entered the hallway low, the duckbill extended in front. The shotgun was deafening in the confined space, both barrels spewing out their load of buckshot in a horizontal arc that eviscerated the men we faced.

Retro and I fired at the same time, shredding the remaining man still standing while Buckshot kept a steady stream of fire to our rear. We didn't stop to survey our damage.

Jennifer heard the avalanche call and

couldn't imagine how the assault could go any more wrong. It was the code word for evacuation at all costs, meaning something worse than the men shooting was inside the house. Something immediately deadly.

What the hell is going on?

She leapt to her feet, her adrenaline demanding action without a clear path to follow. She certainly couldn't go *into* the house after the avalanche call, but running to the vans without the team was out of the question. Even though that's what the call dictated.

She heard a distinct double boom, then rapid automatic fire. She caught movement through the windows and saw the front door fly open. Relief flooded through her when she recognized the team running onto the porch, followed by a blinding flash that launched the team into the air.

She threw herself onto the ground and covered her head from the falling debris. The shock wave of the blast subsided, leaving behind a steady ringing in her ears. She jumped up and ran to the team, thankful to see them rolling back and forth on the lawn.

She saw Pike pull up to his knees, his backpack with the Kevlar plates skewed off his shoulders. She shook him, shouting, "Are you okay?"

He nodded. She counted heads and saw the rest of the team moving, disoriented but alive. They slowly regrouped, checking to ensure they still had all their limbs and that they functioned. She went from man to man, ensuring they didn't have some catastrophic wound hidden by adrenaline. Outside of some cuts and bruises, they seemed to be okay, with Retro's Kevlar back plate cracked from taking a hit of something flying through the explosion.

Pike stood and looked at the house, now burning furiously. "Give me an up on weapons. We need to clear out."

Jennifer went behind Retro and began swatting his smoldering pack, asking, "What happened? Did the terrorists have a suicide vest?"

On his knees, Retro spit out a blob of black phlegm. Decoy simply pointed at Pike.

54

Slowing to a ragged jog, his breath coming in gasps, Kamil heard the explosion and saw a flash of orange light in the distance behind him. He stopped and leaned against a tree, his mind trying to assimilate the disaster. Adnan dead. The explosives gone. And Rafik counting on him.

How did this happen?

He picked up a fast walk, moving across a small ridgeline in the direction of Budapest. Breaking into a clearing, he saw two vans near the edge of the wood line on a dirt road. He watched for a minute, seeing no movement.

Running up to the vans, he tried all the doors, finding them locked. He hammered the door of the last van in frustration, then began a light jog down the dirt road. His mind returned to the debacle. Somehow, they had been found out. Draco had been convinced that he and Adnan were out to get him and had even mentioned him being followed on their first visit. *Which is something to be explored.*

He reached the paved highway that had led him to the house and began walking back the way he had driven just thirty minutes ago, still trying to understand. To make the connection. Nothing happened without reason. And something had caused their plan to fall apart.

He came up completely empty. The only outside influence had been the pilot and loadmaster, and they'd been under his control the entire time. *Except . . .*

A fact clicked. *I've had the loadmaster, but the pilot was left to his own devices, supposedly planning the trip to Montreal.*

And he remembered something else. The pilot had checked in once a day, to ensure that his disgusting partner was okay, and had shown deference on each visit. *Until the last one. This morning.*

The pilot had come in acting extremely nervous, stealing glances at the loadmaster as if he wanted to signal something. Kamil hadn't really paid attention, more concerned with preparing for the meeting with Draco, but, in hindsight, one instance came back vividly: When he'd come out of the bathroom, he found the pilot right next to the loadmaster, and both had jumped as he came around the corner. He'd thought nothing of it, because Adnan had been in the room, albeit on the computer, but now he wondered.

Had the pilot come up with some way of rescuing his partner? Instead of planning travel, had he planned on a way for the police to attack the house while Kamil was in it?

Only one way to find out. He saw vehicle headlights coming down a dirt road perpendicular to the paved one he was on. A dirt road just like he'd taken to find the highway. He began jogging toward the vehicle.

We made it back to the van without any issues, although everyone's bell had been rung. While I moved out, I had noticed four bodies strewn around the yard that weren't as lucky as we had been in the explosion. They lay unmoving, either unconscious or dead.

Jogging to the wood line, I had heard Retro on the radio. "Jesus, that was close. All four of these fuckers got the short end of the blast. I had no idea they were so close behind us."

A second later, Decoy, bringing up the rear, came on. "Pike, they aren't burned.

And all have head wounds."

Jennifer was right behind me, but she didn't say a word. I caught her eye and knew in an instant what had happened by her expression. She shook her head, not wanting to talk on the open net. Maybe not wanting to talk at all because it would make the killings real.

I keyed my radio, "Get in the wood line. Let's haul ass. They're no threat."

Jennifer nodded and gave me a tight smile.

Decoy came back on. "Pike, someone else could be out here. What did Jennifer see? Did she see what happened?"

Still moving toward the vans, knowing I was about to have a break in contact as my entire team moved at a snail's pace, looking for the boogeyman while Jennifer and I kept running, I gave Jennifer a little apologetic shrug and said, "Koko killed them. Keep moving."

Decoy came back. "Pike, not trying to be an asshole, but there are four bodies out here. Four dead with head shots, and we didn't get a single radio call? Is she next to you? Is her radio out? Why didn't she call? Make sure."

I stopped and looked at Jennifer. For a split second, I saw a flash of indignation.

Finally.

I clicked back on, giving them my irritation since Jennifer didn't seem to mind the insult. "Get your ass moving, Goddammit. Yes, she killed all four. No, she didn't call on the radio. I guess there wasn't a fucking reason since they were all dead and our assault was protected. You copy?"

Nobody said a word.

Collapsing into the first van eight minutes later, the men all looked at her. They wanted her to talk, to say something that would give them an out for the usual ration of shit they wanted to throw her way. Cloaked compliments of her capability, and a highly selective opening of their world for her to enter. Something that was expected. She refused to say anything. I waited a beat, then gave out rapid orders.

"Jennifer, you got van two. Follow us to the hotel. Decoy, do what you can with the key you found. Figure out where it's from. Get the hotel, then get a data dump on where it's at. Retro, collate the biometric profile of the dead Arab and get it to the Taskforce before we forget."

I waited until I saw Jennifer's lights come on, then said, "Let's roll. I want a location to hit by the time we reach Budapest."

55

The loadmaster regained consciousness with a flutter of his eyelids. He cracked them and saw Kamil's back at the computer. His hands were still handcuffed to the radiator pipe, and his lap was covered in blood. His shirt clung to his body, soaked in sweat. He saw his pants were still yanked down around his knees, and his thighs had more slices on them than he remembered before he passed out.

Kamil had come back in a rage, slapping his unprotected face and shouting nonsense about the police. When the loadmaster had no answers, Kamil had turned cold and clinical. He'd gone in the kitchen and returned with a knife and a shaker of salt. He'd made multiple small incisions on the loadmaster's thighs, all just splitting the skin. He'd then begun to apply the salt, still asking questions about the police, alternating between Arabic and English.

The pain had been incredible. The load-master had screamed through the gag in his mouth until his voice had quit. Luckily, Kamil hadn't asked about plans for escape. Only about the police. Even so, the load-master had almost told him about the cell phone. About the pilot's plan. He had come close. Very, very close. Wanting to say anything to stop the pain. Through super-human effort, he had kept the secret, knowing letting it go would cause his death. He had passed out before he could utter anything traitorous.

Keeping his eyes slitted, he heard Kamil talking to the computer. Luckily, because of the connection, both men were speaking slowly and distinctly, allowing him to comprehend the Arabic with his basic skills.

"I don't know how it happened. Maybe it was just a coincidence. The loadmaster knows nothing, and he would have talked."

The voice coming out of the Skype connection sounded mechanical. "I'm sorry about Adnan, but I'm relieved you have lived. That is the important thing. I'm going to need your help to accomplish our goal."

"How? How can we continue? We've lost the explosives. Without them, the EFPs might as well be junk steel."

"No, you're wrong. The EFPs are the

technology we need. It's true we've been set back, but there are many ways to get explosives, and we have the patience to wait for another chance. This is a setback, but not failure."

"What do you want me to do?"

"Come to America. Meet me in Richmond in two days. The rest of the men are moving there now. I'll have a meeting with them and decide what to do. It may mean simply waiting for a new opportunity. Our visas are good for six months."

The loadmaster felt a moment of relief. Maybe these madmen would let them go. There was no need for an aircraft now, and they had nothing else to offer.

Kamil said, "I'll get tickets tomorrow, but first I need to clean up the loose ends here. I have the loadmaster, so that's not a problem, but I'll need to set up a meeting with the pilot. I don't want to bring him back here. This place is going to be messy enough."

It took a moment before the meaning of the last sentence sank into the loadmaster's head.

Standing in a courtyard off of Hajos Avenue, I hoped we were in the right place. Like a lot of buildings in the eastern bloc of the old soviet sphere of influence, this one was an imposing four-story structure that dripped despair. Nothing but concrete and iron, all circling around a depressing inner courtyard that would never have enough light to grow anything. The bottom level housed what could charitably be called honest businesses but were more than likely fly-by-night tourist fleece jobs. I only cared about one thing: The courtyard was surrounded by balconies, giving anyone who walked out the ability to see us.

The key we had found had a brass plate on it with an engraving of the Budapest Opera House on one side, and a room number and "if found, please call" phone number on the other side. Doing some quick research on the phone number, we had come up with a broker of apartments in Budapest who rented to travelers looking for a cheap stay. Further research had located a stretch of apartment rooms he maintained one block from the fabled Budapest Opera House on Andrassy Street on the Pest side of the Danube. We'd been able to glean photos of the building, along with check-in/check-out procedures, but outside of the engraving on the key, we really had no way of knowing if we were in the right place. The broker might have used the same engraving for all of his keys, regardless of location.

It was past midnight, but Andrassy Street was still rocking a block away. Jennifer had dropped us off there, right next to the metro stop, and we'd moved straight to the building we had found from our research.

A lot of people were moving around, even here, off of the main thoroughfare. I would never have expected this Eastern European country to be such a hotspot for nightlife, but apparently it was, which would work in our favor. The building, after all, had at least a few apartments rented by tourists, so it wasn't like a stranger would be out of place, and with the traffic coming and going, we'd be just one of many. Even so, a fight in here would be hard to escape from. One way in and one way out, along with the fact that we'd be running down four flights of stairs. We couldn't afford a shoot-out, regardless of the fact that we would win. *If* this was the right place.

There was a group of people in the courtyard, clearly drunk, and we matched their attitude when they hollered at us, giving them the impression that we were tourists who'd had too much to drink as well. Besides helping us blend in, it would give us an excuse for any mistakes we made looking for the right door.

Moving up the stairs, I saw that there wasn't any surveillance effort here. No cameras at all, which was odd in this day and age, but a strong indicator that we were in the right place. The Arabs wouldn't want that.

We found room 406 and staged to fight. Decoy slapped on the radar scope, and we came up negative. I slotted the key, half expecting it to fail, but it slid in easily. I nodded. *Right room.* I rotated the key and opened the door, leaning back as the team entered, pistols drawn.

I followed in after the last man. While they cleared the apartment, I saw the damage. A man handcuffed to a radiator pipe. His eyes half open, his head lolling to the side, his pants down to his knees. The obscene view of his genitals overshadowed by the barbaric damage to his legs. The torrent of blood from his throat puddling around his waist.

The room stank of meat. Of packed steaks that had lost refrigeration. I waited for the all-clear, unable to take my eyes from the body. The blood off of his neck had black-ened, but the pool around his waist was still liquid. I turned away, not wanting the im-age to become a fixture in my head for later dreams, although I knew it was too late.

Buckshot returned and gave the all-clear, looking at the body.

"What the fuck is going on?" he said. "That's the guy from Jennifer's cell phone picture."

I said, "We've got little time. The Arab's cleaning house. Search the room and body. Find something we can use. But watch yourself. Don't leave any evidence that can be used against us."

The team went to work, wearing latex gloves and moving gingerly around the room. It would suffice for a quick check, but I knew it wouldn't withstand scrutiny if someone really wanted to do an in-depth analysis.

Buckshot turned from the body. "I've got a card here. Not sure what it is."

He held up a small piece of heavy bonded paper the same size as a plastic hotel key card. It had nothing on it but a red arrow pointing to one end and a magnetic stripe down the side.

Decoy said, "It's a locker rental card. I've used them before. You stick that into a slot instead of a key, and your locker opens."

I said, "Where? Where's it from?"

"Doesn't have anything on it," Buckshot said. "Nothing other than the arrow."

Decoy said, "Mine was from a train station in Vienna. Probably the same thing here."

Retro said, "There're only three train stations in Budapest."

"We just going to hit all three," Decoy said, "hoping to luck out?"

"Might as well," I said. "We have nothing else to go on."

Jennifer dropped Decoy and me off at the Keleti pu, or eastern railway station. It was our second stop, the first being the western station called Nyugati pu. We'd found some lockers there, but they used old-fashioned metal keys. No help.

Walking up the steps to the entrance, I didn't have much hope that this card would pan out. After all, for all we knew, every bus station in Budapest had lockers as well. Even that might be irrelevant. Maybe no lockers in this entire city used a computer key card. It was a pretty modern technology compared to the iron curtain amenities I'd seen so far.

The station itself was huge, with an imposing nineteenth-century Victorian look on the outside. Inside, it was a smoky, confusing mash of Cold War construction grafted onto one-hundred-year-old granite. We were in the main hall, with the train platforms straight ahead, and even at this hour, people were coming and going. We went to an information booth on the south end, which was closed, but we could see a man inside. Tapping on the window, I got his attention. He looked at us suspiciously, two older Americans asking about lockers in the middle of the night, but he pointed at the large staircase that dominated the entrance, leading to a basement level.

His gesture appeared simple enough, but there was a ton of construction going on, with plywood walls everywhere and no signs in English. Eventually, after bumping into dead ends like rats in a maze, we found the lockers. A bank extended fifteen feet with an ATM-like digital display in the center, an incongruous bit of modernity housed in the stark surroundings.

Decoy slipped in the card, and the screen flashed twice with a number. To our left, one of the upper locker doors popped open.

We both remained still for a second, completely surprised by the success, then raced each other to be the first to see what was inside. It was empty except for a cell phone. Turning it on, it had one number in the contact menu.

Decoy said, "Jackpot."

Fifteen minutes later, Decoy was slapping

the van seat in frustration. "What the fuck! This guy's phone has less capability than the damn Jitterbug phone I bought my grandmother last year."

I'd given the go-ahead to track the number with our technical capability, figuring it was worth the risk since we were reaching an endgame, but that relied on the target phone having specific capabilities, namely a basic software package and the GPS chip that came with just about every cell phone on earth. This one, however, was a pathetically cheap version that did something that no other modern cell phone did: It made calls alone.

Retro said, "What now? We want to dial it?"

I considered the idea. The man in the hotel had been tortured, then killed, which blatantly showed that the Arab was trying to get information, information that could possibly be used against him. The fact that the cell phone in the locker even existed, and hadn't been taken, indicated that the dead man was, in fact, doing something outside the Arab's purview. The contact number might be the key, but it would have to be handled carefully.

"I think we have Jennifer call. A woman on this end might give us an edge before the guy hangs up. Let him know we're friends, and that the Arab is dangerous. Maybe we'll get something."

Everyone in the van agreed, and we spent a couple of minutes war gaming and rehearsing, going over what we knew. Then Jennifer dialed.

She hung up in seconds, saying, "Straight to voice mail. No answer."

Retro threw the water bottle he was holding. I took a deep breath, then said, "Track its usage. If it's been turned on at all, it's talked somewhere in this city."

Decoy said, "Already working. It's an active number, but it shuts down each night, coming on every morning about eight. All tower registers are inside the city, on this side of the Danube, with most popping downtown within two miles of us."

The timing news actually made me happy, because it didn't force us to jump through our ass tonight. We needed some rest, and this provided the excuse.

"Okay. Let's get to a hotel and grab some rack. Plot its habitual track, and we'll stage there before eight tomorrow."

56

The pilot shivered, telling himself it was the morning chill and not his nerves. He took a sip of his coffee and tried to relax, to appear as calm as the few other patrons around him at the café.

Kamil had called him last night and set up this meeting, but he hadn't said what it was about. Kamil also hadn't said why he couldn't return to the apartment. A part of him wanted to believe the meeting was simply to give them the final instructions for their flight to Montreal, but the location raised his suspicions.

He felt his phone vibrate in his pocket. *Calling to cancel the meeting?*

Pulling it out, he was puzzled to see nobody on the other end, then he felt another vibration in his pocket. With a shock, he realized it was the other phone. The special one.

He frantically ripped it out before it went

to voice mail. He saw the number and immediately hit the connect button, saying hello in Indonesian.

A woman's voice came through, telling him it was a wrong number.

"Hello? Can you speak English?"

But it couldn't be. It was the right *number.*

He hesitated, half wanting to hang up and half wanting to know how this woman had the phone he'd planted for his partner. In the end, his partner won out. However bizarre it appeared, it was a link that he couldn't sever.

"Yes. I speak English. Who is this?"

"I'm a friend of a friend. He asked me to call."

The pilot felt a bump of elation. "He's free? Let me speak to him."

"He *is* free, but he's not with me. He gave me the phone and asked me to warn you."

"Warn me? Who is this? Put my friend on the phone or I hang up."

The woman began speaking rapid-fire, almost overwhelming his grasp of English.

"Don't hang up! There's an Arab man that you both know. He's dangerous. Your friend wanted you to stay away from him. He asked us to pick you up."

The pilot began to feel light-headed, unsure of what to believe. He swiveled his head looking for Kamil. The man would be here at any second.

He said, "I'm meeting him now. At a café."

The woman became agitated. "Where? Where are you?"

The pilot hesitated. He had no idea who this was. After the last few days, his ability to trust anyone he didn't know had evaporated. He needed a cut line, something he could anchor against. He asked a simple question.

"What's my friend's name?"

He thought he heard whispering in the background, and a rustling of paper. Then, "I can't pronounce it. It's Indonesian."

Can't pronounce it? She's trying to read the name. She hasn't talked to him.

Which scared him, but also told him she had something from his partner. And, since she wasn't with the Arab, the fact was something to consider.

He said, "I'm not going to tell you where I am, but I'll meet you. You tell me where I can see my friend, and we'll do it that way. Some place public."

The woman backed off, saying, "Okay, okay, we can do that, but you are in danger now. I mean right *now*. Get out of there."

The pilot felt a hand on his shoulder, and looked up into the flat eyes of a killer. The same man who had sawed through a crew-member's neck with all the emotion of cutting up a chicken for dinner.

Thinking fast, the pilot said, "No, no. Don't file the flight plan yet. I don't know when I'm departing. Leave the date open."

And hung up.

Kamil placed a hand on his other shoulder, standing behind his chair. He leaned in and whispered into his ear. "Sorry I'm late. Where did you get that cell phone?"

Jennifer put the phone down and said, "We've lost him. The Arab's there."

Retro said, "How do you know? What happened?"

"He started babbling nonsense about flight plans, then hung up. He was trying to cover who he was talking to."

I said, "He's got about six minutes to live. The Arab gets him into a car, and we lose. We know from the tower track this morning he's in a footprint within a half mile of here. What else do we know? How can we find him? Think, people."

Finger raised, Jennifer said, "He's at a café. He said that."

She was so sure of herself, yet the information was so vague, it hit my funny bone.

"Jesus, why didn't you say so? I can't be

expected to plan without all the information. Are you hiding a holocaust cloak as well?"

Jennifer got the reference to *The Princess Bride,* the single movie we both enjoyed, and rolled her eyes.

Decoy said, "Wait, she's actually on to something. The Arab knows as much as we do about Budapest, and he'd want a location that would be easy to find. He wouldn't pick some obscure local place, where he'd stand out. He'd pick a tourist area."

"Yeah," I said. "So what?"

"Well, right around the corner is a little promenade that's lined with cafés on both sides. That's where I'd plan a meeting."

I looked at him, waiting on an explanation.

"Hey, I had a life before the Taskforce. On the teams, we used to call this place Booty-Fest."

"Huh. Your man-whore days might pay off. Lead the way."

Decoy led us to a park called Jokai Square, a promenade full of gardens and statues. Actually, a pretty cool area that I'd like to come back to when I wasn't under the gun to stop a terrorist. It had streets on the north and south sides, but the middle was basically an open grassy area, and just like

Decoy said, it had restaurants, nightclubs, and cafés lining the way.

We split up left and right, leaving Buckshot as the van driver. I took north with Jennifer. Decoy and Retro took south.

This early in the morning, we would have little trouble getting an ID, since each café had only a few people in them, and most of the restaurants and nightclubs were closed. We slowly trolled the park, Buckshot shadowing us on a parallel path one road over.

We had one false call, which was quickly eliminated when Retro transmitted a cell phone picture of two guys in a café. The team was forcing the issue, wanting to be right, but the photo contained what looked like two Cuban guys. I didn't need Jennifer to call bullshit.

We reached Andrassy Avenue with nothing.

Retro said, "What now?"

"I don't know," said Decoy. "That was the only place I can think of. I'm sure there're others. Besides the bridal salons, I didn't do a whole lot of cultural engagement."

I felt the clock ticking, knowing we were about to lose our only hope of connecting with the EFPs. The contact on the phone was about to die.

Jennifer said, "Why don't we just keep going?"

She pointed across Andrassy. "I can see umbrellas over there as well."

Decoy looked and said, "Damn, she's right. None of that shit was here in ninety-eight."

57

On the other side of Andrassy Avenue, I could see a large four-story building with some sort of latticework scaffolding built of old rough-hewn lumber, like someone had decided to work on the façade, then quit, leaving the scaffolding in place. Directly to the southwest of the building was another promenade, this one fronted by a sculpture of different-colored flowers in the shape of a cross on a shield. Past it, several statues sprinkled among the trees competed with the outdoor cafés for the attention of the pedestrians walking around. The promenade itself was much narrower than Jokai Square

"Okay," I said. "This one's a little less open. One street on the right and nothing on the left. We'll stagger by time. Decoy and Retro go first, taking the path straight down the middle and eyeing the left side. We'll give you two minutes and follow in your footsteps looking to the right. Both teams be prepared to redirect on the other's call."

While Retro and Decoy crossed the street, I contacted Buckshot and told him our position, giving him instructions to shadow us on Terez Boulevard a block to the northwest.

Jennifer and I busied ourselves looking at a statue of some old Hungarian guy to blend in while we waited. When I made some comment about how they could have picked a more attractive subject, she said, "It's Jokai Mor. The Hungarian novelist this square's named after. Do you ever do any research?"

"Just enough to get my guy. Although I was thinking about researching those bridal salons Decoy mentioned. Know anything about that?"

She glared at me, making me take a step to the right before she could do some damage. The fact that the comment had aggravated her gave me a small bit of optimism that I was making progress reversing the clock past the incident in Egypt. Before she could say anything, our radios squawked.

"Pike, Decoy. We have 'em. Pictures on the way, but it's them."

Jennifer pulled out her phone, looked at the images, and nodded her head.

"That's the Arab and the Asian man who walked out of the Prague hotel while we were conducting surveillance on the original guy."

I clicked back, "Where are you?"

"Across from a place called Café Brazil. It's the third café on the left side. Red and green umbrellas. They're outside sitting at a table. The Asian looks like he's scared."

"Can you stay?"

"Yeah, we're across the way at a park bench. We're good. They can't see us and we can trigger."

Crossing the street, I said, "Okay, here's what I want —"

Decoy cut me off. "They're standing up. They're leaving. Headed away from you, away from Andrassy."

Shit. I looked at the map on my phone, seeing Buckshot's position. "Buckshot, come down Terez and turn south on the first street you get to. It's a one-way with a big-ass Magyar name that begins with a *D.*"

"I got it. I see it."

"Stage where it curves away from the park to the southeast. That's where we'll take them. Break-break. Decoy, leapfrog to the end of the block. Get ahead of them."

"Moving. What about the targets?"

"We've got the eye. We'll be on them in seconds."

We were moving at a fast walk when Jennifer jerked my arm to slow me down. I saw the pair to our left front, weaving in and out between the tables and chairs.

"We got them. We'll bring up the rear now. I want to hit them before they get a chance to get into the main arteries of the city, while they're still here in the park."

We followed behind them for a minute or two, my brain working through options at the speed of light, trying to assess the risks and rewards of taking them down right here in public, in daylight. It could be done, I knew from experience. You wouldn't believe the things you can get away with right in front of people. The kicker was making it look natural. Plausible.

I had no doubt we could take the Asian, but the Arab was a different story. In the back of my mind was the image I had snapped of him with the Blackjack before he'd entered the house last night. Assessing his surroundings like a wolf. Looking for the weakness before he continued. He wouldn't go down easy. He had a sense for trouble.

Buckshot called, "I'm at the bend, but I can't stay here. It's a one-way road with no parking. I gotta keep going or get police attention."

I tapped Jennifer. "Keep eyes on. Don't

lose them." I returned to the radio. "What about back up the road, before you enter the square?"

"Maybe, but it's going to be close. Pike, this is asking for trouble. I think we let them go."

"Can't. He's going to kill that guy, then disappear. He's not going to bed down tonight. He's already left a blood trail, which means he has a goal in mind."

Decoy called, "We're at the end, and there's a café here. They'll be walking right by it. It's full of people. We might be able to take one, but not two. Someone's going to see the action."

I wanted to start kicking shit, but remained cool as ice on the radio. "Roger. Buckshot, circle the block and stage on the same road, keeping in between the buildings before it breaks out into the square. Decoy, Retro, find a spot for takedown right there. In between the buildings before the square. Can you do it there? What's the visibility?"

Jennifer said, "Two minutes. They reach the end in two minutes."

Decoy came back. "Got a spot, but, Pike, it's shaky. No visibility from the park, but there's a group of schoolkids looking at a statue at the entrance. They'll see the hit. *If* he comes this way."

"All right, everyone listen. They keep going straight, we let 'em go. They make the turn to Terez Boulevard, which I think they will, we take 'em. I want them alive. No killing. Get 'em in the van and we haul ass."

Buckshot said, "Roger. I'll be there in thirty seconds."

Decoy said, "Pike, the schoolkids. I can prevent anyone from the café from seeing, but I can't do shit about the kids. They have a clean line of sight to me."

I saw the street about seventy meters in front of me, the targets about thirty meters closer to the end than I was. I could see the kids, along with a teacher talking to them. *Need a diversion. Something to focus their attention away from the left.*

"Jennifer, break away from me. Go to the right of the schoolkids and get their attention."

"How in the hell am I going to do that?"

"Jesus, I don't know. Figure it out. But don't do it until you see the targets commit to Terez Boulevard. They keep going straight, let them go."

In my head I was tracking about forty different variables and knew I was on the ragged edge of causing the entire hit to collapse. Too many things to control with too few people.

She glanced at the targets, saw them still moving, and returned to me. "Pike, don't push this. Don't . . . do something we'll regret."

I had precious seconds to get her on board. I didn't want to lose sight of the targets but decided to give Jennifer my undivided attention. I stopped and took both of her shoulders in my hands. "Jennifer, we've got about one minute to make this work. If it doesn't, I'll let it go, but I need you in place. I know what you're thinking. You don't want to be here. To be responsible for what's about to happen. I know I've put you in situations before you were ready. Caused you to do things that made you question who you are, but your feelings need to take a backseat right now."

She glanced down the square toward the target, refusing to meet my eyes. I shook her. "Look at me."

She snapped her head back at my tone.

"I need you. We need you. Right now."

Something flitted behind her eyes. A brief look of resignation tinged with anger. She broke away from me without a word, headed toward the children across the square.

I picked up my pace, closing within twenty feet of the targets. "We're thirty seconds

461

out. You guys set?"

Decoy came back. "Yeah, we're set, but those fucking kids are still there."

"Don't worry about them. The targets turn the corner toward you, the kids will be focused the other way. I'll bring up the rear. We'll double-team the Arab. Who's on him?"

Retro said, "Me. Decoy's got the Asian."

"Roger all. Thirty seconds."

I glanced quickly at Jennifer, now on the other side of the schoolkids, talking to the teacher. *Jesus, I hope this works.*

The targets reached the street and immediately turned left, amping up the adrenaline.

"They're going to Terez. Ten seconds."

I turned the corner, saw the targets abreast of our van, and heard a startled yelp behind me. Buckshot, in the driver's seat of the van, came on, "Target's ten feet out. Pike, I can see Jennifer. She just went down. Something happened."

I came back, now solely focused on the hit, no emotion whatsoever. "Execute, execute, execute."

I rushed the Arab from the rear, seeing the van door slide open in slow motion. The team deployed from an alcove, pistols drawn, Decoy taking the Asian guy and Retro focused on the Arab. The Asian froze for a second, then fell to his knees with a wail. Decoy hammered him in the head, cutting off the warbling with a thump, then threw him into the van.

The Arab reacted instantly, snarling and whipping a seven-inch fillet knife at Retro's body. He jumped back, holding his pistol close to his body and shouting, "Don't, don't!"

I closed on the Arab's back, tying up his arms and controlling the knife. I kicked the back of his knee, bringing him off balance, and knew we had won. I locked up his knife arm, about to leverage him to the ground and finish the fight when he whipped his head straight back into my mouth, splitting my lips and causing an explosion of stars.

I sluggishly tried to maintain my grip, but the man was like a snake. Nothing but lean muscle that writhed and ripped out of my control. He rotated around, facing me, still snarling with spit flying from his mouth. He raised his knife hand for a killing blow, and his head exploded, spraying me with brain matter. He collapsed on my body, giving me a view of Retro standing above, his suppressed Glock still smoking.

I shook my head, trying to get my bearings, unable to get rid of the fog, but knowing we needed to leave. Retro grabbed the body off of me and shoved it into the van, then helped me up.

I piled in the van, followed by Retro.

As we started to roll, I said, "Compromise status?"

Buckshot, who'd been on lookout in the driver's seat, said, "Nothing concrete. Nobody looking. I think we're good. The schoolkids are still focused on Jennifer. The teacher's on a phone now."

My head clearing, I keyed my mike. "Koko, break out. We're good. Meet us one block south."

We passed by her, now sitting up with a smile on her face, apparently giving the teacher a story about dehydration, epilepsy, or whatever else her imagination could conjure. Either way, whatever she'd come up with had worked, flawlessly. *I owe her.*

I took a moment to gather myself, my adrenaline still running amok. We had executed a daylight hit downtown, in a vibrant city. And gotten away with it. I surveyed the team and saw all of them still panting. It hadn't sunk in yet, but we'd done the impossible.

Decoy kept his hands on the Asian, even though it looked like that guy had become catatonic. Retro glanced at me and shook his head. "You know, when you were operational, everyone used to talk behind your back about the drama you caused. How you always pushed shit to the breaking point, squeaking out by the skin of your teeth."

I pulled out a rag, wiping the blood and brain matter from my face. "Yeah? Those same pussies that never get anyone?"

Retro laughed and looked at the Asian. "Yeah. Those same pussies."

Seeing the Arab's body, I said, "Didn't work out like I wanted."

Retro became defensive. "Hey, he was about to gut you. I had to —"

"Stop. I said it didn't work out like *I* wanted, not that you did anything wrong. Thanks for saving my ass. It was my fault. I didn't tuck my head. Fucker deserved it, although we've probably lost our main connection to the attack." I looked at the Asian man. "Maybe."

I threw the rag down and squatted in front of him. The fear radiated off of him like heat from a sauna. His eyes were wide open and wet, like he was about to cry.

I patted his knee. "Hello. We just saved your ass today. Now it's time to repay the favor."

58

When the screen cleared, I could catch movement behind Kurt's head on the video teleconference hookup, making me wonder how much I could say. The screen itself cut in and out, looking like a bootleg video of a celebrity sex tape, but that was to be expected, since we were on a secure satellite connection inside an aircraft flying over the Atlantic. There was only so much technology could do.

Kurt said, "Pike, you there?"

"Yeah. I got you. How about me?"

"You look like you're talking from a fishbowl, but I got you."

"Who else is on?"

He understood the reference. "Nobody. The link's between you and me. The only other people in the room are Taskforce. Speak freely."

We'd gotten out of Budapest without issue, loading up the G4 at the airport within thirty minutes of disposing of the dead Arab's body. We hadn't had the time to give a full SITREP, since I'd wanted to get the fuck out of there immediately. All we'd sent was the information we'd gleaned from the pilot and the biometric data of the two terrorists. Now I hoped to get something we could sink our teeth into from the Taskforce analysts.

I said, "Did you get anything from Montreal?"

"Whoa. Slow down. We'll get to that, but first tell me what happened. Did you get out clean? Quiet?"

"Well . . . there aren't any fingerprints, but it wasn't quiet."

I told him the story of the house and the explosion, followed by the hit in the park.

"Holy shit, Pike! You blew up a house? What happened to *clandestine?* Have you forgotten what that means?"

"Hey, ease up. You told me to get the explosives even if it meant compromise. It's good. I promise it's good. There'll be a little bit of news about the explosion, but everyone's dead and it was a damn Albanian mafia house. There's nothing connecting us. Trust me."

Kurt scowled. "You're using that phrase a little too much. I didn't mean you get to run amok blowing the shit out of whatever you felt like. We can't afford a stink right now, even if you did get out clean. The story alone's going to piss off the council."

The comment poked a sore spot, reminding me of all the bullshit staff officers I had to contend with before I had joined the Taskforce. "Fuck that political shit! I did what needed to be done. What I thought was right. You weren't getting shot at. My team was. You used to trust me explicitly. What's happened? Where do you stand now?"

Kurt bristled. "Don't question my trust, Goddammit. There's a lot of pressure here you don't understand. Pressure that extends beyond the mission, into the heart of the Taskforce. I ask you a question, and you answer it. Period. Or get your ass home and let someone else take over who can understand the political dimensions of the fight."

He paused for a moment, then continued, "I shouldn't have said that. I do trust you. You know that. It's just that not all the enemies are foreign terrorists. You need to be attuned to that, but if you made the call, I trust it."

The outburst took me off guard. We'd worked together for years, and he was used to me spouting off, but this time it had hit a nerve. Made me wonder again what was going on above me. He knew I understood the political side of things, even while I hated it, so I took the ass chewing and let it go. "Okay. What about Montreal?"

The pilot hadn't really known a great deal. His information consisted of three points: 1. He was supposed to fly cargo to Montreal, Canada, but he had no idea what the cargo was. 2. He had a number to call once he arrived. 3. The Arabs had shipped something from Prague via DHL.

That was it. But it should be enough to get the ball rolling, with Montreal the key.

Kurt said, "We got nothing from DHL. We've tracked every single shipment from Prague into Montreal, and we've come up with nothing. If they shipped the EFPs to Canada, they did it in a manner that used a legitimate business. Every shipment checks out."

From the pilot's description of the cargo, we were sure that the DHL shipment had been the EFPs. Since the follow-on flight plan terminated in Montreal — apparently to transport the explosives — it stood to reason that the EFPs had been shipped there as well. But it looked like that final bit of deduction was incorrect.

"What about the phone number? Did we

get anything from that?"

"No. Well, not much. It's a TracFone that was purchased over a year ago. All phone cards for additional airtime were bought with cash. The phone itself was purchased with a credit card, but the store can't tie a specific card to the purchase. Just the date it was bought. We ran a check of every credit card used at the store that day and came up with one possible. A guy named Abdul-Majid Mohammed used his card in the store the same day. He's a radical that's been on the watch list for a while. The Canadians have been keeping an eye on him for his preaching, but it's never been anything big. Just the usual anti-American crap."

"Well, okay, pull his ass in. See what he knows."

"Pike, for one, he's a Canadian citizen. We can't 'pull his ass in.' For another, he hasn't done anything wrong, even if he was in America."

"Let me go after him. It's in Canada, so it's still a foreign country. Taskforce authorities still apply. I'll go wring him out. Bring it to the council and get me Omega authority."

Kurt grimaced into the VTC screen, and I knew something wasn't right. He was keeping intelligence from me.

"What? Sir, he may be the key to the EFPs. I understand it's slim, but slim's better than none. I won't kill him. I promise."

"Pike, he's not in Canada. We did get the Canadians to check up on him, and he flew out of the country two days ago."

"Shit! That's the guy! Send me wherever he went. I'll find him."

"He came here. He flew to Baltimore."

I didn't say anything for a second, trying to assimilate how pathetic our security apparatus actually was.

"Wasn't he on the no-fly list?"

"Yes. He was. Trust me, nobody's happy about it. We're working it now."

"Are you fucking kidding me? We let a terrorist get on a plane and fly *into* the United States?"

"Pike, calm down. There are thousands of names on the no-fly list, updated every single day. This guy has never done anything overt. Just a lot of smoke. He's not a confirmed terrorist. . . . Shit. I'm not going to defend it. It is what it is. The police and FBI have his name and will find him."

I was disgusted, but decided not to press the point. At least not yet. "What about the biometric profiles? Anything from them?"

"Yeah. Both of the dead guys are Algerian,

although we knew that from the passports. They have a history of extremist activity with the Algerian authorities. Both have been in and out of jail, but nothing really drastic. Mainly a bunch of conspiracy charges that the Algerians throw around like popcorn. The older one might or might not have traveled to Afghanistan to train in the camps in the late nineties. Hard to prove, but that's a little irrelevant now. They were bad guys, and nobody's going to cry over them."

"Any associations we can use? Any other names connected to them?"

"Nothing that we don't already have. The intel's incomplete. The third guy you were tracking, the guy from the catacombs, still has no name."

"He's the leader. He's the one we want. All the intel indicators show this is the hit. They line up completely. We have JI, GSPC, and al Qaeda — along with the fucking EFPs. All we're missing is the homegrown part of the equation, and that guy in Montreal is the key. I'm sure of it. If we can't find the boss, we need to find his associates. What do we know about Abdul-Majid?"

"He runs a mosque, like they all do. Truthfully, we can't even prove he's bad. He just preaches bad shit all the time. We linked him to some shady charities, which put him on the no-fly list, but there's only smoke. No fire."

"Fat fucking good that no-fly list did. Does he have any contacts in the U.S.?"

"Some with various imams in the Northeast, but they've all checked out as no threat."

"Pull 'em all in. Put the heat to them. One of them knows something."

Kurt let out his breath. "Pike, calm down. We don't do domestic operations, and the authorities have everything we can give them. It's in their hands now."

I rolled my eyes. "I know, I know. We don't live in a police state, blah, blah, blah, but that guy is the key to this whole attack. I'm sure of it."

Kurt leaned forward toward the screen. "You'd better be kidding about the 'blah blah blah.' We *don't* live in a police state, and I'm not trying to start one, especially with the thin bit of evidence we've scraped up. All we have is a TracFone number that's close to two years old and tied to nobody, along with a credit purchase in the same store for a guy who might be bad. One of five hundred that day. It's not something that'll make anyone start pulling out fingernails. Especially since you stopped the attack in Budapest by interdicting the explosives."

I backed off. For all of my bluster, I knew he was absolutely right, but it still didn't sit well. It's why I was the guy who went out and thumped heads. I just didn't have it in me to put up with the political bullshit, but I understood it.

I asked, "You got the support team headed to Ireland?"

Relieved at the change in subject, Kurt said, "Yeah. They may be a little behind you, so you might have to do a layover, but they'll take the target off your hands."

We had the pilot bound up in the back of the plane, and I really didn't want to fly into U.S. airspace with him on board. It had been hard enough getting him on the plane without anyone noticing in Budapest. Going through U.S. Customs with him in a box was a nonstarter, so I'd arranged for a Taskforce support team to meet us in Ireland.

"Pimp that guy as soon as you get him. He probably doesn't know shit, but maybe there's a clue there."

"Will do."

I asked, "How's Knuckles doing?"

"He's getting better by the day. He's talking now and asked about the team."

I smiled in spite of myself. "Tell him we started smoking the shit out of the bad guys once we got rid of his deadweight."

Kurt laughed. "I will." He paused for a moment, then said, "Pike, you did some good work over there. Nobody's going to pat you on the back, but let the team know. Those EFPs would be going off right now if you hadn't intervened."

It was a half-assed apology for his original outburst. Letting me know he still understood what happened when bullets were flying, and that he trusted the man on the ground. I appreciated the sentiment but thought it was a little early. It was only good if nobody died.

"Thanks, but this work's not finished. I looked into the eyes of the guy in the tombs. He's not some Johnny Jihad wannabe. He's a killer, and he's not going to quit."

59

Rafik looked at the circle of men and wondered if he should tell them the truth. That the explosives had been lost and they were now on hold. Having led men in combat, both in Algeria and in Afghanistan, he understood the potential impact of the setback. Sometimes a lie was better than the truth. Sometimes the lie helped earn the victory. He had no idea of the mettle of the men before him, and worried what their reactions might be. He had seen it in untested men before. Out of the six in the apartment, four were recruits from prison. One was Abdul-Majid Mohammed, the Algerian contact from Montreal, and although he professed absolute faith, Rafik was ultimately unsure about him. Only Farouk, his remaining comrade from the original cell, could be trusted.

It may be better to simply put them back into sleeper mode, waiting on my call.

In the end, he decided to tell them the truth. Whatever the reaction was, Kamil would be arriving soon to help shepherd them to victory, although he was growing a little concerned at the lack of contact with his trusted friend.

"You men were about to begin the final push against our enemies. A strike that would cause untold pain, and perhaps bring about untold rewards. But something has happened that will delay our attack. Something I couldn't have predicted."

He laid out what had occurred, speaking in generalities, not discussing the technology he still owned. When he finished, he expected to see a look of defeat on the men. Abdul-Majid looked relieved. Farouk, having already been told the news, simply sat with a grim face. Out of the four ex-convicts in the room, two did project defeat, but two — Keshawn and the man who leased the apartment, Carl — looked thoughtful.

Rafik said, "Unless one of you has an idea, I think the best plan now is to simply return to your roles in the workforce. Await my call."

Keshawn said, "I can't do that. I've already done too much to bring on heat. I have the lease for the warehouse in my name, and I've killed three people to keep our secret.

We need to push forward now."

"We can't blindly tromp forward for a pin-prick," Rafik said. "If you go to jail, you go to jail. It is a sacrifice that must be made for the cause."

"Bullshit! I'm not going to jail without doing something. If you think —"

Carl cut him off. "I know how to get explosives."

The comment brought them both up short. He continued, "We only need military-grade explosives? Is that right? Something along the lines of the SEMTEX you were getting?"

Rafik nodded.

"Would C-4 work?"

Rafik knew the EFPs were specifically built with the U.S. plastic explosive Composition C4 in mind. He felt a sliver of hope. "Yes. C-4 would be perfect. Can you buy some? Secretly?"

"No, but just down the road here is a military base called A.P. Hill. It has a huge ASP that stores all sorts of ammunition for the National Capitol Region. All of the military units in D.C. come down here to train."

"What's an ASP? And how do you know all of this?"

"Ammunition storage point. It's just a

large area full of bunkers. It's where units store their ammo for training. They don't bring it with them back and forth. The ammo stays there, and they come down and use it. I know about it because I used to work on a cleaning crew that did the janitorial services for the post. The only job I could get right out of prison."

"So how are we few men supposed to get it? Attack the post?"

"Well, yes, in a way. All we need to do is sneak onto the post after the cleaning crew leaves at four P.M., then cut the locks on one of the bunkers. I'll know which one to hit by the signs outside."

Rafik wasn't sure what to make of the information. It seemed too good to be true. Keshawn explained, "Carl did a stint in the Army before prison. His job was ammunition handler. Trust him when he says he knows how that stuff works."

Rafik slowly nodded. "Okay. How do you propose we get on the post? And deal with the alarms?"

Carl said, "The cleaning crew I worked on was a sort of jobs program for handicapped people. Some mentally retarded, others gimped out some other way. I was let on because I was down-and-out. You didn't work every day, so as to spread the wealth around. The guards are used to different people coming and going. As for the alarms, every post I worked on had the alarms feeding into the post police station. We need to hit that, then hit the ASP. The alarms won't matter then. They're silent."

"Won't the theft cause a huge manhunt? We will still need at least three days to train each crew and give them their targets. Maybe longer. That'll be done in Baltimore, at the warehouse leased by Keshawn. As he said, the exposure's too great."

Keshawn said, "I think I can help with that. A friend of mine still in prison in New York can help. I can get there and back by tomorrow morning. A little misdirection that will cause the police to chase a ghost."

Rafik said, "Why would your friend agree to become a scapegoat? I don't want to involve anyone else."

"My friend won't be the scapegoat. Someone else who fucking deserves it will be."

60

Jennifer watched the DVD playing in the headrest in front of her but saw nothing on the screen. Her mind was running nonstop through the last few days, wondering if she'd started the corrosive effect on her soul that she'd seen in the men around her. And whether it could be reversed.

She noticed a shadow to her right and looked up to see Pike standing there expectantly. He glanced at the screen.

"*The Princess Bride*. How appropriate."

She pulled off her headphones, but he continued before she could say anything. "Can I sit down? Please?"

She nodded.

He settled into the aisle seat and said, "You okay?"

"Yeah. I'm fine. Watching a movie."

"I could tell. Except the screen you were seeing was somewhere else."

He rotated in the seat to face her. "Look,

I'm sorry I snapped at you at the park. I was under the gun and needed you to perform. Like I knew you could. We really haven't had a chance to talk about what's happened over the last few days, and I want to make sure you're all right."

"I think I got everything I needed out of the hot wash."

As usual, once the team had cleared Hungarian airspace, they had conducted a blistering after-action review. In what was starting to be a trend, Pike had been eviscerated yet again, this time for spiking the explosives while they were still under fire. Continuing with the trend, Pike had sloughed it off as "All's well that ends well," but she could tell the men were a little aggravated.

As for her, she'd finally been forced to tell how she'd taken down four armed men. How she'd decided to start from the back and work forward to prevent them from realizing they were under fire for the longest possible time. How she'd simply placed the red dot over their ears and squeezed. Making it sound easy, like flipping a light switch. When she began to tremble from the memory, she'd sat on her hands.

She didn't discuss the fear of the moment. The paralyzing terror of dying. She also failed to mention the slow, dull ache she'd had ever since she'd committed an unspeakable act. Something that would make the next time easier, like a teenager working on his first pack of cigarettes — hacking and hating the first few, but eventually craving the smoke — and that just as the dumb teenager had begun an addictive destruction of his body, she'd begun a destruction of her soul.

She still didn't understand how she'd done it. How she'd managed to keep shooting under the stress, but that wasn't part of the hot wash anyway. For their part, the men had said nothing. Made no mention of her trembling. They'd listened in complete silence, staring at her with new eyes that made her uncomfortable. A group of cigarette smokers proud to have another addict.

Pike said, "The hot wash isn't what I'm talking about. I don't mean how you performed. I mean how you're doing. Inside."

She searched his face for something disingenuous, and saw true compassion. No artifice. He was worried, and not because she was simply a member of the team. He was worried about *her,* in a personal way.

She said, "I'm all right . . . I think." She hesitated for a moment, wondering if she should let out her fears, then decided to go ahead. She found herself wanting to talk. Needing to talk.

"I'm not all right. I don't think I'll ever be all right again." She reached over and stopped the movie. "I can't do this. I can't turn into a killer. I don't want to. I don't want to lose my sense of right and wrong. Like . . . like . . . those mafia guys."

Pike caught the slip, and smiled. "You mean like me?"

She smiled back, relieved he hadn't lost his temper. "Well, yes. Like you and the other guys. You talk about killing as if it's a game. I don't want to be that way. I like my sense of morality. I want to keep it. I've read about Nazi concentration camp guards and how they slowly turned into monsters. Normal family men who ended up twisted monstrosities. I don't want to become that."

"You think that's what I am?" He waved his hand around the plane. "What they are?"

"No, no, no. I don't think you are. Yet. But you can't do this without losing your sense of right and wrong. You just can't. You showed that in Cairo. I don't think you're a bad person. You *know* that. But, Jesus, Pike, you were beating that guy to *death*."

And there it was. She'd let it out. Ripped off the Tupperware lid exposing the stench of rotting meat below. She waited to see what Pike would do. He surprised her.

"Remember our talk in Cairo? About the dreams?"

She nodded.

"Well, I have nightmares every time I close my eyes. Every night. I would take that action back any second — every single second — and that's what makes me different. What makes you different. I don't justify it in my mind because that fucker killed Bull and wounded Knuckles, because that doesn't make it right. That history doesn't make me more barbaric. It makes me less. Makes me understand how close the loss of my family affects my judgment, allowing me to prevent something like that in the future."

He took her hand into his own, a tender gesture that shocked her, something she would never have expected, given the company on the plane.

"You won't lose your sense of right and wrong. You can't. It's simply there. Those concentration camp guards weren't poor souls that were corrupted. They were sick fucks from the get-go, with an evil streak looking for a way to express itself. I don't buy any of that shit about good men going bad, because I've seen nobility in the worst of situations. It's a fight, no doubt about it, but the man with the strength of character wins. The man without it turns into a monster."

"Pike . . . you *did* turn into a monster. You're saying the same thing I am. I know you're not that way, but the death and destruction has done something to you. Can't you see that?"

She was playing devil's advocate, and she knew it. She *wanted* to believe that keeping America safe was inherently good, but those feelings were overshadowed by the fear of losing her moral compass. Of beginning to believe that doing evil was doing good, and that killing was just a way to make a living. She wanted Pike to convince her.

Pike stared at the floor for a moment, then returned his gaze to her. "No, I haven't changed. I still own the difference between right and wrong."

He pointed toward the team in the front of the plane. "Don't belittle them because they have the courage to do the dirty work. We saved those girls in Prague because *you* said to. You didn't pull any triggers there, but you *did* kill the men inside. If it was right to order the assault, it's just as right to participate in it. Killing those men in Budapest doesn't make you a monster."

He looked at the ceiling. "I wouldn't say this to anyone other than you, but what I did in Cairo scared me a great deal. Made me question who I am. So don't think you're all alone on this plane beating yourself up, but in the end, I'm not a monster and neither are you. Which is why you need to stay. We need people who can see right from wrong, regardless of the situation. Who believe in it. We work without oversight. Without anyone questioning what we do. We need someone with an internal compass who doesn't need a person looking over their shoulder, ensuring the right thing is done. Someone like you."

She didn't know what to say. A part of her clung to his words like a drowning person, his explanation exactly what she wanted to believe. Another part realized they were just words. Pike might believe them, like a child believes in Santa Claus, but it didn't make them true. *It may just be his way of coping. Of convincing himself that what he does is just.*

It was something to chew on, though. A potential truth worth further reflection.

She felt Pike's eyes on her, waiting on a response, his expression earnest and raw, a vulnerability seeping out that was completely foreign. He had never given a piece of himself to her, never let anyone into his pain, and now he had, emboldening her.

She wasn't sure when his walls would clang shut, locking her out again, so she took a chance, leaving the questions of morality and digging into something she had wanted to explore for a long time.

"Why do you want me to stay so bad? Am I just some sort of experiment, like NASA experimenting with a new O-ring? Are you just testing out a theory about female operators, and you want me to stay because you invested so much effort in convincing everyone to let me do Assessment that you'll look like a fool if I leave?"

He grew rigid, the turn of the conversation throwing him off. "Where's that coming from? I've never felt that way."

"Never?"

"Well, maybe a little bit, but it's always been based on your capabilities, not what I was getting out of it."

"Just my capabilities? My ability to climb a wall? That's it? That's the only reason you want me to stay?"

He withdrew his hand from hers, and she could almost hear the walls clanging shut, the portcullis slamming down in front of his emotions. Protecting him from harm.

"What the fuck do you want me to say? Isn't that enough? That I think the world of your capabilities?"

What do *I want him to say?*

They sat in silence for a moment, him glaring at her. Daring her to continue. So she did. Getting it out once and for all. Talking about the elephant in the room.

"No. It's not enough. If you weren't in the Taskforce, I would have never joined. I came because *you* asked me. Because I didn't want to let *you* down. Not the Taskforce. *You.* Truthfully, after Cairo, I'm wondering if that was a mistake. An illusion I held because you saved my life. The Taskforce alone isn't enough for the price you're asking me to pay. And I'm no longer sure if you are, either."

He sat stunned for a second, then looked away and stood up. When he returned her gaze, he was all business, but she got one last glimpse past the portcullis into the man. She saw a brief flicker of fear. Real, true fear in a man she thought incapable of the emotion. A fear of her leaving.

It was enough.

He said, "Jennifer, I can't make you do what I want. I can only ask that you hang on until this is over. You know the history of this operation, know the terrorist by sight, and know the team. I don't have any way to prove I'm not a monster, but even if you think I am, stay on to save American lives.

This isn't over, and we need you *and* your capabilities."

She pretended to consider the request for a moment, but she already knew her answer.

"Okay, Pike," she said. "Because *you* asked. No other reason. But when this is done, we need to talk about the future. About our company and the Taskforce."

He nodded and said, "As you wish."

He was ten feet away before the meaning of the quote from *The Princess Bride* sank in.

61

Keshawn sat in the passenger seat, sweating in the heat, Carl behind the wheel, the engine of the old Delta 88 idling roughly on the dirt road facing Highway 301. Crammed around him were five other men, all waiting for the cleaning van to pass. Keshawn rolled down his window to release the stench from the collective body odor of the group.

The men had conducted a reconnaissance the day before and confirmed Carl's information while Keshawn had driven all night to New York City and back again. He'd managed to link up with a mutual friend who had obtained what he wanted from inside Attica.

He could see Rafik fidgeting in the rear-view mirror, and knew he was having second thoughts.

He has no qualms about sending a bum to my door for me to butcher but now acts like a kid about to shoplift.

Keshawn knew it was simply because Rafik was no longer in control. That now he was at the mercy of the men around him.

Rafik said, "How sure are you that they'll let us back on base?"

Carl answered, "Pretty sure. The van got searched on its way in this morning. We stop it right after it leaves, keep the driver, and go right back through the gate, saying we left something. We're only two minutes from the gate, and they'll remember the van leaving and probably just wave us through. If they don't, we simply haul ass when they direct us to the search area."

"What if they don't let us leave? What if we're stopped and searched right there? They'll see the guns."

Carl turned around to face Rafik. "Hey, I know what the fuck I'm talking about. The guards are hired security at a backwater post. They won't —"

"There's the van," Keshawn said.

Carl swung around and hit the gas, causing the car to jump out into the two-lane highway. Keshawn looked to the rear.

"You're clear. No cars coming behind."

Carl rode right up on the bumper of the van, flashing his lights and waving his arm out the window. The van tapped its brake lights and slowed, then continued on at the reduced speed.

Keshawn said, "Need to get them to stop before we reach the town of Bowling Green."

Carl swung into the left lane and pulled abreast of the driver. Keshawn leaned out the open window and frantically pointed at the rear of the van, as if something catastrophic was about to occur. He saw the driver, an obese woman of about fifty, look wide-eyed at him for a second, then nod with understanding.

"Get back behind her before she rolls down the window and asks what's wrong."

Carl slowed, letting the van continue on. It traveled for about a quarter mile before pulling into a dirt road threading its way into a swamp.

Carl pulled in behind it, blocking any exit back to Highway 301.

Keshawn said, "Everyone take a weapon, but only the two silenced ones can shoot. Understood?"

The men, now grim at the coming task, nodded. Rafik started to say something when Keshawn cut him off. "Let's go."

All four doors swung open, the attackers boiling out quickly, two on the left and three on the right. Keshawn ran straight to the driver's-side door, stopping it before it could open. He dropped any pretense of a charade, pointing his suppressed Ruger Mark II at the driver's head.

"Get out of the van. I don't want to hurt you."

She threw her hands in the air, stuttering nonsense.

"Shut the fuck up or you're dead."

She lapsed into silence, her eyes wide and wet. He moved her to the rear of the van and turned her security over to another man. Walking back to the front, he saw four men on their knees with their hands behind their back. Looking closer, he saw they were really just boys. None over the age of twenty. Three black and one white. Two of them were looking around with grins on their faces, apparently unaware of what was occurring.

Carl said, "Let's get them tied up and into the woods."

Keshawn pulled him out of earshot of the boys, Rafik following close behind. "We can't just tie them up," Keshawn said. "They're not going home."

"Huh? Keshawn, those two are simple. They didn't do anything. We said we'd tie them up and do the robbery. No unnecessary killing."

"It's necessary. They've seen our skin.

They'll blow our getaway."

Carl grew agitated. "These guys are the people we're trying to help. They're not a bunch of rich fat cats. They're the people getting fucked over. The reason we're stealing the explosives in the first place."

Keshawn said, "I don't want to do it either, but your plan is the only way we will succeed now, and the plan is based on the police chasing a ghost. They've seen us. They'll be able to break the deception we want. I'm sorry."

Carl paused for a moment, then said, "I'm not killing a bunch of kids. You want to do it, you do it."

Rafik spoke for the first time. "Keshawn is correct. Sometimes the good must be sacrificed along with the bad. That's just the way of it."

His words brought back a memory of Beth, sending a bolt of rage through Keshawn. He whirled and jabbed his pistol at Rafik, holding it by the barrel.

"You keep talking about sacrifice like we don't know what the fuck that is. You're so pure, you fucking kill them."

Rafik grew rigid, staring hard at Keshawn for a moment. He took the pistol and held it in the air, the barrel pointed in between the boys on the ground and Keshawn himself, as if he were making a decision. Keshawn felt a trickle of fear, but didn't back down. Abruptly, Rafik turned and walked back to the group, kicking the nearest boy in the back.

"Get up. All of you get up. Start walking down the road."

Carl remained quiet until the group was out of sight around a bend.

"Man, I don't know about this," he said. "This isn't what the chaplain talked about."

Keshawn kept his gaze down the road where the boys had disappeared. "It's exactly what he talked about. I've sacrificed too much already. We're on the path now. No turning back."

62

Sitting in the back of the van, Rafik felt his adrenaline rise as he saw the approaching gate, feeling exactly like he had at the Alexandria airport only days before. On the short drive to the post, Keshawn had managed to get the men back under control and back on the mission. Rafik himself had wisely said nothing. He was pleased that his prison recruitment had provided so many unintended benefits, such as the knowledge of A.P. Hill, but he was growing increasingly concerned at their commitment. They had no sense of the history of Islam, no inherent belief in its righteousness, and appeared to be straddling their old world and his new one. Having not grown up in a Muslim society, they were unlike Adnan and other recruits who inherently knew Islam was the path, only needing to be convinced of the merits of jihad. It was a complication he hadn't fully considered before.

On top of that, every one of these American dogs had a rebellious streak, as if they were serving at their own pleasure instead of God's. It made him rethink the need to keep everything compartmented, even within this cell.

As the van pulled abreast of the gate guard, Rafik lowered himself behind the driver's seat, where it would be hardest for him to be seen, keeping his eyes on Keshawn in the passenger seat.

He heard the guard speak. "What're you doing back?"

The driver said, "Hey, Bill, one of my boys left his Nintendo DS at the headquarters building. Can I run back up there? We just left five minutes ago."

Rafik heard her voice quaver and warble, sounding to him about as disingenuous as possible. He wondered if she was sweating and wide-eyed at the thought of Keshawn's pistol in her belly. He tensed up, gripping his own pistol in preparation for the coming fight. Instead, he felt the van begin to roll forward, hearing Carl say, "All right! Head to the police station."

They took their first left and wound up a hill, driving past the headquarters building before stopping in front of a squat, one-story brick structure that housed the post police. In a rehearsed move, Carl and Rafik exited the rear of the van, bringing along two mop buckets and mops.

They entered the building with Carl leading the way. Ahead, Rafik could see a woman manning a central desk. Behind her he could see a man in the room Carl had described as the JSID alarm monitoring station. Otherwise, the place appeared empty.

The woman said, "We've already been cleaned today. You guys can go home."

Carl stopped with his bucket while Rafik continued past the desk to the room beyond.

"Hey, I said we've already been done today. Stop."

Carl reached down into his bucket and pulled out the other Mark II, shooting her in the back of the head, the hollow-point .22 long rifle mushrooming in her brain but not exiting the front. She dropped like a stone, the loudest noise from the assault occurring when her equipment belt cracked onto the hard floor.

Rafik continued straight ahead, entering the far room. The man inside stood up, saying, "You guys aren't supposed to clean in here. It's a controlled area. Someone should have told you —"

His words were cut off by Rafik's suppressed pistol spitting out two rounds, one cratering the man's nose while the other entered his forehead.

Rafik didn't bother checking the body. He locked the door from the inside, leaving the mop bucket and returning to find Carl moving the woman's body to a closet.

"We need to haul ass," Carl said. "Anyone comes in here while we're at the ASP and we'll be in a world of hurt."

Rafik helped him fold the body into the closet, saying, "How long?"

"No telling. Let's go."

Racing back to the van, Carl ordered the woman into the back, taking the wheel himself. Reaching the main road, he took a left instead of a right, driving deeper into A.P. Hill. Winding through the woods, they came upon an open area, where Rafik saw row after row of what appeared to be enormous dirt mounds covered in grass, the face of each buttressed with large concrete shielding. *The bunkers.*

They drove right up to the front gate, repeating the ruse they had used at the police station, leaving behind another two dead bodies. Minutes later, Rafik stood inside one of the enormous concrete structures, marveling at the treasure trove of death around him. Artillery rounds, anti-tank rockets, and case after case of other types of explosives. *If we only had something larger. It's not fair to leave this to the infidels.*

He was brought back to the present when Carl said, "Hey, they got claymore mines in here. We can use the M57 to command detonate whatever you've got. You want that instead of time fuse?"

Having left Farouk — his remaining explosives expert — behind at the apartment, Rafik was unsure how to answer. "What do you mean, 'command detonate'?"

"With the time fuse, you set it and wait for the fuse to burn down. The longer the fuse, the more time it takes. It requires a little precision cutting if you need the explosives to go off on a set schedule. With the M57, you set off the cap by electricity, letting you basically press a button for it to go off."

"Yes. That will be perfect. Let's load them up as well."

"How many?"

"Can they be used only once?"

"No. Over and over again."

Rafik paused, knowing that giving the answer would be giving away the number of teams. He decided to lie. "Load ten."

He helped the men with the explosives, sweating in the oppressive heat outside the bunker. Minutes later, they were driving away from the ASP, staying clear of the main road by winding through the various camps located within the post. Passing through one such camp, Rafik saw a flash reflect off the windshield. Looking to his rear, he was shocked to see a police car following them, its light bar flashing red and blue.

"Shit," Carl said. "Stay cool. I was in a ten-mile-an-hour troop zone. Probably just getting me for going too fast. I forgot how trigger-happy these fuckers are about speeding."

He continued on as if he hadn't noticed the police car, pulling over only after he was through the camp and back into a wooded section, out of view. He rolled down the window, asking Keshawn, "How many in the car?"

"Just one," Keshawn said. "If he comes out with his pistol drawn, we'll know it's not for speeding."

They waited, the fight-or-flight response building palpably. The police officer opened his door and began to saunter toward the driver's side, weapon still holstered. Carl leaned out and said, "Is there a problem, officer?"

Still walking, the officer said, "You work here long? You know the posted speed limit is ten miles an hour through our camps?"

When he reached the door, Carl said, "You know how stupid that fucking speed limit is, asshole? My van won't even idle that slow."

Before the officer could react, Keshawn leaned over and shot him in the face, the van jerking forward at a high rate of speed as his body folded to the ground.

They raced through the woods, avoiding all other camps, Rafik once again relieved that his recruit knew where he was going and what to avoid. They reached the back gate at the northern reach of the post, now chained shut and abandoned because of security procedures following 9/11. Keshawn exited the van and made short work of the locks with a bolt cutter, then swung open the chain-link gate. Carl drove through, winding along a dirt road until he reached the clean van they had stashed earlier.

While the vans were cross-loaded, Keshawn and Rafik took the woman into the woods, Keshawn assuring her that they were just going to tie her up like the others. She blubbered and sobbed, but walked in front of him to her death. Rafik could not understand why. He had seen it before when executing prisoners. They went meekly as kittens, preferring to believe the paltry lie they'd been told instead of the truth staring them in the face. It was why Islam would always defeat the infidel. When faced with overwhelming odds, the *kafir* simply didn't have the strength of faith to fight back.

Keshawn told the woman to kneel with her hands behind her back. Rafik saw that his eyes were watering, and wondered again about the man's own strength of faith.

The woman, only now beginning to realize her fate, began to wail, begging for her life. A hitch in his voice, Keshawn said, "I'm sorry for the sacrifice you must make. *Allahu Akbar.*"

Keshawn pulled the trigger, the small caliber of the .22 punching a pencil-size hole in the woman's forehead. She toppled over with a look of surprise on her face, as if she still couldn't believe he would kill her.

63

Sitting inside the underground parking garage in Clarendon outside of Washington, D.C., Jennifer and I had to wait until Buckshot successfully badged in through the key-card access on the first door, followed by Retro or Decoy using the retinal scan at the second door, before we could sprint through the double barrier, using their precious seconds of authorization to get inside.

It had taken longer than I'd wanted to get back home. Waiting to transfer the captured pilot, we'd been forced to spend a night in Shannon, Ireland, which would ordinarily have been an opportunity to kick back a little, but this time it felt like I was giving the terrorists an edge with every passing second. I was itching to see what Kurt and the Taskforce had learned while we were twiddling our thumbs over a Guinness, which is where this building came in. The parking garage ostensibly serviced a firm called Blaisdell Consulting but in reality was the headquarters for the Taskforce. A block long and four stories tall, it housed the brain trust of all Taskforce activities, from the hackers and analysts we leveraged while conducting operations, to the headquarters of the commander himself.

Since I was no longer an active-duty member, I technically wasn't allowed inside, but since I also used to be a team leader, we figured I could sneak in without anyone freaking out. At least, that's how I'd convinced the team to bend operating procedures. Stretching it further, I figured Jennifer had heard enough stories about the place that actually seeing it wouldn't be a breach. Jennifer, of course, felt like I had an elastic sense of the rules.

Sitting in the Suburban, moments before we entered, she said, "Pike, there's a reason I'm not cleared for this. I don't mind staying here."

"Fuck that. Come on. You've earned it."

I saw Buckshot open the first door, allowing Retro inside to the second door and the iris scanner. Decoy signaled us.

"Let's go. Stick right behind me."

Buckshot began a hand countdown, then swiped the card reader again. Hopefully,

Retro was synchronized inside, or we'd be caught. Buckshot opened the outer door, and I dragged Jennifer through, seeing the second door held open by Retro. We made it into the hallway beyond and waited for the three to catch up.

Minutes later, we entered the Ops Center, looking for Kurt. I found him talking to a couple of analysts. Or more correctly, he saw me and went ballistic.

"What are you doing in here? You can't be associated with this place!"

"Hey, calm down, sir. The G-4 has a history of flying in and out of Dulles. I couldn't simply take it to Charleston as part of my company. We need to figure out a seasoning schedule. And the rest of the team was coming here anyway."

My company had nothing to do with Blaisdell Consulting, and thus if anyone was tracking me, I could potentially cause some questions that shouldn't be asked. Since nobody was tracking me, and we had a bad-ass terrorist on the loose inside our borders, I figured the risk was worth it.

Kurt shook his head, glaring at the active-duty operators. Decoy said, "Well, we need to unload the kit and get it sorted out. See you, sir."

I watched them beat a hasty retreat.

Before Kurt could realize Jennifer was standing in the background, I said, "How's Knuckles? Is he up and moving?"

Looking like he was going to tear into me again, Kurt was brought up short by the question. "He's getting better each day. He's not out of bed yet, but he doesn't believe it. He refuses to use the bedpans and tries to walk to the bathroom."

I let out a breath, realizing I'd been afraid of what I would hear. "Thank God. What's his status? How long's he out of commission?"

"Doc's saying six weeks no activity, then another six months of physical therapy. Should be good as new. Now you need to get the fuck out of here. In fact, go see him."

"I will, I will. Later. What did you find out about the imam? Did law enforcement locate him?"

"No, not yet. We've had an event that overcame the hunt. Someone broke into Fort A.P. Hill and stole a bunch of C-4, blasting caps, and claymore mines."

"Come on, sir! That's them. I interrupted their transfer of explosives in Europe, so they stole explosives here. The imam is at the heart of this thing. We shouldn't be slacking off, we should be pressing forward."

"It's not your group. The people who did

it had inside knowledge of the post. No way is it a bunch of Arabs from Egypt. The police also found some literature inside the vehicle they used that points toward a white supremacist group inside Attica prison."

"Literature? What's that prove?"

"It was an underground newspaper for something called the Phoenix Order, run by a guy named Cyrus Mace. The police found five examples of the number eighty-eight and two examples of the phrase 'remember the fourteen words' encrypted in the text. No fucking way would an Arab be able to duplicate that. It was genuine."

"Why's that genuine? You lost me."

"Eighty-eight, as in the eighth letter of the alphabet, *H*. As in *H–H,* or Heil Hitler. Or the eighty-eight words from *Mein Kampf* where Hitler proclaims the master race. Take your pick. The fourteen words come from the original terrorist group The Order. It's basically a statement of racial purity, but it's shortened in communications to simply 'the fourteen words.' Trust me, an imam isn't going to know about that. Also, the people who robbed A.P. Hill killed some mentally handicapped and African American men on a cleaning crew to get inside, which is right up The Order's alley of racial purity."

"Well, maybe they were hired. Stranger things have happened. Remember how the PLO hired the Japanese Red Army to kill all those folks at that Israeli airport in the seventies? Maybe they're in partnership with the Arabs now."

"Pike, the group's called the Phoenix Order, as in the resurrection of the original terrorist group The Order. That group went on a killing spree in the eighties trying to overthrow the U.S. government, with a bunch of crazy talk about starting a new society in the Northwest of the United States. This group's founder, Cyrus, was just a member of the Aryan Brotherhood until 9/11. Since then, he's gone toxic, spouting the same shit as the original Order, only this time against Muslims. Trust me, he's not in cahoots with any Arabs."

I tried to come up with some other valuable reason to focus on foreign terrorists, but simply sputtered, "We need to find the imam. The Arab from Egypt is a killer, and he's here. Our only contact is that imam. Explosives or not, if we don't press, we'll lose them. They'll be safe to regroup."

"Pike, you interrupted their attack. I agree they're a threat, but the Phoenix Order is just as violent as the Arabs. Maybe more so, since they understand America and they want to overthrow the government. They're a clear and present danger, and they've got everyone on a high state of alert. The police are taking it personally, since they're going to be a primary target. We're not going to get them to shift priorities."

I rubbed my face, frustrated. "Okay, sir. I get it. Hopefully, our actions in Hungary will keep the terrorists from blowing up the Statue of Liberty. Maybe, maybe not."

Kurt stood with his hands outstretched. "Not our fight, Pike. We don't do domestic. We have enough going on as it is."

He then poked me a little to let me know he wasn't blind. "Best course of action is for you to get that woman in the back of the room, who's pretending to be an analyst, out of here. The one who looks remarkably like Jennifer — but I know it's not her, because even you wouldn't be that stupid. Get back to Charleston and let me know your plan for the seasoning of the G-4."

"All right, all right," I lied, "we're going."

I took Jennifer out of the Ops Center and gave her directions to the team rooms one floor up. I needed a place we could hide out for a few hours, and figured Kurt wouldn't be traveling up there any time soon.

"What are you going to do?"

"I have some questions I want answered.

511

Won't take but a minute."

She looked at me like I was keeping something from her, which I was, but she proceeded up the stairs to the fourth floor.

I went down the hall from the Ops Center, stopping at an unmarked door. I entered without knocking, seeing the two people inside whirl around.

The female spoke first. "Pike? Pike Logan? Long time, no see. Where the hell have you been? You finally going to pay me the twelve-pack you owe me?"

"Hey, Holly." I turned to the other person, a man. "Hey, Vic. How's the secret cell?"

The office here housed one of the most sensitive aspects of Taskforce operations, even if it was just purely analytical. Holly had first served as a Maryland state trooper, but ended up as a terrorist analyst in the Washington, D.C., police department before leaving the police for our lucrative pay. She was a five-foot-five blond spitfire dedicated to getting the job done.

Vic was retired from the FBI. He'd served as an agent, a LEGATT in an embassy overseas, and a member of their Hostage Rescue Team, which is where I'd met him originally. He'd taken an IED strike in Iraq years ago and was medically retired.

Now they both worked for the Taskforce

as our pipeline into domestic law-enforcement agencies — something that wasn't advertised and wasn't well known even within the Taskforce, given that anything smacking of domestic operations was anathema to us, which is why I jokingly called it the secret cell.

Given their experience, together they understood cop talk and all of the myriad different law enforcement databases in place. Their job was simply collating information, trying to put the pieces together to help us in our mission. They ostensibly worked for some bullshit department in Homeland Security, which allowed them to ask the questions they needed to ask. Because it dovetailed neatly with their primary job of data mining, they were also in charge of our internal biometric database. They were the people who got the data from our biometric scans of the dead Arabs in Prague and Budapest.

Vic said, "Going about as well as always. A lot of work for very little payoff."

Vic hated being behind a desk, but since he'd lost most of the use of his left leg, he was stuck with his fate. Both were officially retired because Kurt and the president felt it a bridge too far to actually recruit anyone who was active in law enforcement, from the Justice Department on down. Both thought it a travesty to have an officer who was supposed to catch lawbreakers support an activity that subverted the Constitution, the supreme law of the land. Made me feel a little bit like a whore.

I said, "Hey, you guys get the word on that imam from Canada? The one on the no-fly list who flew to Baltimore?"

Holly gave a short laugh. "Oh yeah, that caused a stink, but everything stopped after the A.P. Hill attack."

"I need to find him. In a bad way. Can you guys collate everything that was done before everyone was pulled off?"

"Sure, that's easy, because it was basically nothing."

I decided to push the issue. "Well, can you scan everything from the Baltimore area and pull up any arrests or spikes relating to Muslims?"

Vic spoke up. "On whose orders? We've got our plate full with ongoing operations overseas."

Holly heard the exchange and tossed her head. I could tell she didn't agree with Vic's pissed-off attitude. She and I got along well, with her constantly flirting with me even when my wife was alive. I threw in my cards, looking at Holly as I spoke.

"On my orders. Nobody else's. I get that some neo-Nazi group is running around with C-4, but there's a terrorist cell here, and it's tied to that imam. I'm asking as a favor. Please. You only have to stick with Baltimore, where he flew in. Just cover the last four days. Maybe something will give me a handle on the guy."

Vic said, "You can't do anything domestically anyway. What's the point?"

"Just do it, please. Nobody else is looking, and you guys have the experience. I understand it'll cost some time for a team overseas, but this is important."

I saw both of them look at each other, mulling it over.

Holly said, "We can give you the rest of the day, but we can't do anything more. Sorry."

Vic scowled, saying, "Bullshit. You want to do that, you're on your own. I've got enough work."

I broke into a grin. "Thanks, Holly. All I want to do is get whatever you find into the law enforcement system. You find some links, and they'll do the work. Nobody's looking right now because of A.P. Hill, and that imam's the key to something a hell of a lot worse than a bunch of redneck racists."

64

Rafik watched Carl load the dummy EFP with clay and set the blasting cap, then duplicate the sighting procedures, exactly as he had been taught by Farouk. His military experience was paying off, since he already knew about the dangers of the blasting cap and how to use the M57 firing device.

In fact, Rafik was surprised at how quickly all his prison recruits picked up the theory behind the EFPs. After the A.P. Hill hit, he'd separated the men, sending them to different hotels and bringing them individually to Keshawn's Baltimore warehouse to be trained. He'd planned two full days for the train-up, but Carl was the second recruit through today, and both had taken a quarter of the time he had allocated. He was somewhat taken aback by their calm acceptance of the mission, without any questions on the manner of the attack. There was something different in the Americans that he couldn't pinpoint. He'd spent countless hours training Arab recruits, and invariably they always needed a massive amount of time to fully comprehend what they were trying to do, as if they were going through the motions but not assimilating why. He had seen students do things with blasting caps that would be catastrophic in an uncontrolled environment, with the men acting nonchalant, firmly believing that Allah would protect them.

He believed in Allah as much as anyone he had taught, but it was a trial trying to get the men he trained to understand that Allah wouldn't save them if they made a mistake. It required repetitive instruction until they grasped the concepts, something that didn't seem to be an issue here.

Maybe I can speed things up. Get the attack going sooner rather than later.

He'd scheduled a full day of training per team, but after seeing them in action at A.P. Hill, he'd gone to two a day, with Carl the second one through. Now he was thinking he could train all four in a single day and begin the assault tomorrow morning, shaving three full days off of their timeline. Three days that they would need, given the media frenzy surrounding the stolen explosives.

■ ■ ■ ■

I left the secret cell and went up to the fourth floor to help the guys unload the kit we had used. I should have taken Jennifer and beat feet out of the building, but I needed to give the cell some time to find what I wanted. I knew if Kurt discovered us here, he'd blow a gasket. I was under no illusions about which straw I was placing on the camel's back.

The inventory was menial work, but necessary. We'd have to ensure we hadn't lost anything, then make sure it all still functioned correctly, so the next team could pull it out of a locker knowing it would work as intended. It was a gray area as to what would happen if the stuff was screwed up or missing, since I had been the team leader, but I was no longer a Taskforce operator. Another complication for an ex-operator running a front company. Especially since this ex-operator just ran a bunch of missions with national implications for presidential authority.

Kurt or the Oversight Council hadn't thought about it yet due to events, but I had. Sooner or later our company was going to need its own special oversight, to protect both them and us. A mandate that said it was okay for us to do more than the other cover organizations. All they ever did was facilitate the infiltration of an area. They never interfered in the action, leaving that to the operators on the ground. My company was different, with implications I hadn't considered when I'd built it.

Jennifer saw me come in and said, "What did you do?"

"Nothing. Just trying to get a handle on the imam. That's all."

Decoy said, "Pike, I don't know what you've got in mind, but leave it alone. We don't do domestic operations. There's a reason for that. You ever hear of posse comitatus?"

I bristled. "Don't tell me what this taskforce does or doesn't do. I was taking out terrorists in this organization while you were still sweating through hell week."

Retro cut in. "Whoa, hang on. What's that about? He's only saying what we all feel. Pike, you know I'd follow you into hell and back, but you've made a few decisions lately which were a little loose."

He dropped the case he was inventorying, holding up his hands. "You've done okay so far, but we're back at home now. Back under Taskforce control. It's time to get back to what's right, you know what I mean?"

I knew exactly what he meant: I was no longer an operator, and thus was no longer in charge. He was telling me to back off and let the "real" operators take over. It hurt a great deal, exposing another wrinkle related to our little business. Good enough to get the job done under duress, but no longer worth a seat at the table when it was over.

"Yeah," I said. "I get it. No issues."

Buckshot said, "Pike, it's not —"

I cut him off. "I fucking get it. Let's get this done so Jennifer and I can go home."

We spent the next four hours going through the kit, the atmosphere decidedly strained. Jennifer got the worst of it, because she wasn't sure where she stood. I could tell she wanted to be anywhere but in that room.

When we were finally done, Decoy said, "I'll get you guys out." He paused, then said, "Pike, I didn't mean what you think I meant. I know what you've done for this organization. You're a damn legend. It's just that . . . that . . ."

"That I'm now a nobody? Save the speeches. And we don't need you to show us out. If my feeble memory serves, we don't have to have badges to leave the building."

Jennifer looked appalled, like she was seeing a family self-destruct and wanted to stop it. We left without another word, going down the stairwell to the third floor. When I exited there instead of continuing down she said, "Where are you going?"

"I need to check something. Just hold fast. I'll be back in a jiffy."

"Pike . . . what are you doing?"

"Nothing. Just checking something out."

I left her and headed back to the secret cell. When I entered, Vic looked at me with distaste, but Holly smiled.

"Well," Vic said, "here you go. Everything with a Muslim angle. Thanks for wasting our time."

Jesus, does everyone here hate me?

"Did you find anything interesting?"

Holly said, "Not really. But see for yourself."

She handed me a sheaf two inches thick.

"Can I take this with me? Is it classified?"

"Nope. It's for official use only, but nothing more than you'd get as a police officer. They're all yours."

"Thanks. I appreciate it. You guys have a phone number where I can get you? I'm probably not coming back in here due to operational constraints, but I may need your help again."

Vic looked at me suspiciously, but Holly said, "Sure, here's our internal number. It's good for another five days. After that, I don't know what it will be. You know how the Taskforce changes numbers every five seconds."

I smiled. "Yeah, I know. Nothing like operational security to impede operational success."

Holly smiled back. "You said it. What a pain in the ass." She hesitated a moment, then said, "Look, I'm not trying to be mean, but don't use that number unless it's important. We do have real work going on."

So much for my operator mystique.

"Yeah, sure. I won't bug you unless it's important."

I left them and returned to Jennifer patiently waiting in the hallway.

"Let's get out of here. I've got some stuff I want you to look at. See what you can see."

Going down the stairs, she said, "Pike, I think you took all of that upstairs a little hard. They weren't saying anything bad. We're just the cover organization. You said that yourself when you got me to agree."

I stopped walking and turned around. "I don't give a shit about any of that. Those damn terrorists are inside the United States, and nobody seems to care because there's some ridiculous line about domestic operations. Because of it, someone's going to die."

I started walking again. She said, "What are you planning to do?"

"Nothing as it stands. I have these reports to go through, and I'd like you to help me."

Thirty minutes later, we were inside a hotel room near the courthouse on Clarendon Boulevard, the documents spread out on a table.

Jennifer said, "What am I looking for?"

"I have no idea. I'm hoping for a Son of Sam moment, where we get something we can use based on a traffic violation. Just see what you can find."

I began wading through the reports, all of which pretty much outlined a bunch of bullshit Pakistani taxi drivers ripping off tourists. After two hours of going through them, I was about done. I saw nothing of any interest. I attempted to pass the next five to Jennifer, only to have her intently reading one of the earlier reports.

"What? What do you see?"

"It's a missing person report."

"The one about the chick who had a mysterious boyfriend? What about it? There's nothing there about the imam."

"Yeah, but something the roommate said caught my eye. She said the boyfriend was in a 'Muslim cult.' Why would she say that?"

"Let me see it again."

The report was fresh, mainly because the police wouldn't file a missing person request for forty-eight hours, which meant she'd been gone for close to four days. The roommate was hysterical in the report, claiming she knew the boyfriend was bad because he'd never allow himself to be seen. She believed something was strange about him, and when she'd confronted her roommate, she'd been rebuffed. The missing girl's last act was to go to her boyfriend's home and surprise him. The roommate was sure the boyfriend had killed her friend for some sort of cult purposes, and she had subsequently preserved the missing girl's room for forensic evidence, which the police had obviously done nothing with, given the number of missing person reports they received on a daily basis. She'd screamed about the case for damn near four days straight, with little forward progress.

On the surface, the document showed nothing. Just another report like all of the other ones in front of me. Snagged in the secret cell's search engine because of a tangential relationship to anything with the term *Muslim.* But Jennifer had caught something. The roommate's statement about a

"Muslim cult" was a distinct turn of a phrase. And the man's actions clearly showed he had something to hide. Something that was worth looking into.

65

I knocked on the door of the ranch-style house, shielding myself from the light drizzle that had begun to fall. Nobody came to answer. It was now two in the afternoon, and I had only about three hours to work with before the girl in the police report came home. I looked back at Jennifer in our rental car and smiled, wondering if I had lost my mind. I was preparing to knock again when it was opened by a middle-aged woman wearing what looked like a Snuggie blanket-robe.

"Hi. I'm looking for Adam. I'm with J3 Special Operations at the Pentagon."

She looked at me like I was an alien from another planet, then turned and hollered, "Pinky! It's for you!"

I prayed the man who came to the door would recognize me. If he didn't, I was dead in the water. I might be anyway, given what I was trying to convince him to do. Adam was on a biometric team. He was the closest thing the Taskforce had to the CSI element from television, only his whole purpose was to catalog biometric data, not solve crimes. I'd worked with him a couple of times, but each one was under duress during the middle of an operation, so we didn't do a lot of talking. I hoped he remembered me because he was the only one I could find who was on military leave, and thus probably at home instead of overseas or at Taskforce headquarters.

The man who came to the door was about five foot four, pudgy and round. He pushed his glasses back onto his face and said, "Pike? What are you doing here?"

Whew.

"Hey, Adam. I've got a little problem and I need your help."

Two hours and fifteen minutes later, I was picking the lock of the door from the police report, feeling the press of time. From what she'd said in her interview, the roommate worked until five each day at a gift shop, and we were closing in on that hour. It had taken me way longer than I'd liked to convince Adam to come with me, and then he'd needed to go to Taskforce headquarters to get his equipment, followed by the drive to Baltimore.

I'd prayed he wouldn't encounter anyone from the team or Kurt while he was inside the Taskforce, knowing he'd come running back out with the security force to arrest me. Luckily, that hadn't happened, but Adam was decidedly antsy, clearly wondering if my bullshit story was true — which, of course, it wasn't. Getting to the apartment, I had given Jennifer a dual mission of early warning and Adam control, then had gone to work on the lock.

It popped easily, making me think of Bull for a split second, then we were inside. I went into the bedroom first, using an old Polaroid camera to get a plethora of pictures, taping each one at the position it was taken so Adam could replace everything exactly like it was before we had entered. We were probably the only organization on the planet that used the dated technology, having to get our film from a nostalgia site on the Web. When I was done, I let Adam go to work, scrubbing everything for any biometric elements he could find.

We were out in thirty minutes, with a bunch of fingerprints and bags of several different hair samples for DNA. Nothing more, but enough. I dropped Adam off at Taskforce headquarters, saying, "Process that stuff and get it to Holly. Have her run it. I need an answer by tomorrow morning."

His face scrunched in confusion, because he thought I was going to drop him back at his house and his warm little Snuggie blanket. Probably wondering how his decision to take two weeks of leave at home instead of Disneyland had gone so badly for him. I held our handshake a little longer than was comfortable for him.

"Don't fuck me on this. Get it done, and I'll buy you a beer. Or a milk shake. Whatever you want."

He nodded and walked into the building in what looked like a daze. I called Holly.

"Hey, Adam's coming up. Look for him. He's got some biometric stuff he's going to process, then I need you to run it against everything you've got."

"What the hell are you talking about? From where?"

"Don't worry about it. Just do it as a favor to me. Please. There's a chance the stuff will ping in our database or some police one. You can access the imam's fingerprints, right? Didn't he get arrested in Canada?"

"Pike, it's close to six o'clock right now. It'll take him at least four hours to process before I get it, and that's just the fingerprints. You're talking about an all-nighter."

"Holly, it's important. You get a hit and you'll finally get that twelve-pack I owe you. One more thing: Don't tell Kurt you're doing it."

"Dammit, Pike . . . you're going to owe me more than a twelve-pack."

Rafik watched Keshawn test the circuit on the M57, then simulate initiating the explosively formed penetrator. He was impressed with Keshawn's attention to detail, and mulled over the decision he had to make. Since the loss of Adnan in Budapest, he had been debating the makeup of the teams, feeling the need to wait for Kamil to arrive before initiating the attack so that each prison recruit would have at least one trusted Arab with him, but both Keshawn's and Carl's actions had begun to convince him that they could travel alone. That they could be trusted to accomplish the mission, with Farouk and the imam going with the other two men.

Keshawn rolled up the wire to the M57 and walked to Rafik, the faltering sunlight streaming through the garage windows becoming overshadowed by the flicker of the harsh fluorescent bulbs overhead.

"How many more men still need to train?"

Rafik considered lying, but told the truth.

"None. We finished today."

Keshawn's face flashed surprise. "You've given the men their targets? Like you did me? And they have their explosives?"

"Yes."

"So when do we strike?"

"If everyone makes it back home okay and goes to work tomorrow as a normal day, then perhaps tomorrow. If we have any issues with returning to work, we wait a day. The key is to conduct the attacks simultaneously. That is imperative."

"Why are you so fired up about returning to work? We have the targets. Shit, in most cases, I'm hitting the same substations you had me sketch, so it's not like I can't find them. I can't speak for the other teams or their companies, but in my case, BGE will have a GPS on my truck. Seems like a stupid risk."

The Americans always want to question. To fight decisions. Perhaps I'm wrong about letting him go as an individual.

"After the first few attacks, the authorities will react. I cannot predict how, but they *will* try to stop us. Your company truck, along with the trucks maintained by the companies the other teams work for, will be the subterfuge that allows success. It may be the only edge we get."

"That's bullshit. If they figure out what's going on, it'll be no effort at all to track us down. Shit, we'll be helping them."

"Keshawn, you have proven to be dedicated, but listen to me, please. If not because you trust me, then at least based on my experience. The chances of them penetrating our cell are much less than them extrapolating what we're after. They can't possibly protect every substation, but we might be unlucky enough to run into one that is protected after we start. Your truck will allow you to bypass."

Keshawn said nothing. Rafik considered his next words, toying with confirming that he himself would be Keshawn's partner, and that the attack would have to wait until Kamil arrived to be Carl's partner. But he was afraid that the time delay would cause discovery of the Trojan horse virus that Keshawn and the others had embedded in the power company systems.

After obtaining the explosives, he'd ordered it activated, and now it was only a matter of time before it was found. Without it, they would fail, since the grid would be able to automatically detect fluctuations and reallocate power at the speed of a computer. The virus would take that out of the equation, leaving the process manually done, at the speed of a human trying to blindly assess how to staunch the bleeding.

He broached the subject gently. "I'm thinking of sending Carl by himself. Do you think he could do that? Without any guidance from my men?"

Keshawn considered for a moment, then nodded. "Yeah. He's ready. With his military background, he won't have any problems."

"What about his commitment?"

"You mean because of what happened at A.P. Hill? I wouldn't worry about that. He was in jail for robbing a liquor store. They only got him on the robbery, because of some sort of screwup with the prosecution, but he killed three people in cold blood in the getaway. He developed a sense of justice based on your own chaplain's teachings, but it won't interfere. He'll do what needs to be done."

Rafik nodded. "And what about you? Can you get it done as well?"

Keshawn stared at him, the implication sinking in. "I thought you were my partner on this. I'm going alone?"

"If you think you can. Tell me if that's not the case."

Keshawn grinned, the thought of doing something to justify Beth's sacrifice hitting him at his core. "I can do it. In fact, I work better alone."

"Go home and get a good night's rest. If I'm contacted by all teams tonight, tomorrow will be a glorious day."

Gazing out the window, thinking of Beth, Keshawn whispered, "Judgment Day."

66

I awoke groggy, unsure what the ringing was, but sure of one thing: It was annoying the hell out of me. The clock told me it was six thirty in the morning. Way too early to be awake now that I was no longer in the military. I sat up in time to see Jennifer snatch my cell phone off of the table between our double beds.

"Yeah, yeah, he's right here."

She handed it to me with a quizzical look, saying, "Some woman named Holly."

I grabbed the phone. "You got a hit? The prints ended up being the imam?"

"No, Pike, they didn't, which is why I'm calling to wake you up to share some of the pain. The prints came up in AFIS database in New York as belonging to an ex-con. Thanks for keeping me up all night."

Shit. Nothing.

"Well . . . why did he spike as a Muslim?"

"No idea. Probably because the roommate's crazy. The ex-con's been out on parole for three years. He was in for gang violence. Accessory to murder for a couple of thugs that deserved to die anyway. He's a black guy, not Arabic. Did his time in Attica and has apparently done okay, because his rap sheet's clean since his release. Sorry."

Attica? Something about the prison gave me pause, but I couldn't put my finger on it.

"Hey, don't we have some terrorists in prison up at Attica? Why does that jail ring a bell with me?"

"Yeah, we've got some terrorists up there all right, but the Christian kind. It's where that asshole Cyrus Mace is being held. The guy who allegedly masterminded the theft of C-4 at A.P. Hill."

I bolted upright. *Way too much of a co-incidence.*

"Holly, I need you to stay there. I'm on my way."

"Pike, screw that. I've wasted enough time on your wild goose chases. I'm going home and going to bed. It'll be hard enough explaining my absence today without telling everyone I was freelancing for you."

"Holly, please. Give me an hour. One hour. After that, you can go. I'll buy you a case of that local brew you like so much.

The expensive shit."

I heard nothing for a moment, then, "One hour. And it's starting right fucking now."

I hung up and immediately dialed Retro at his hotel, waking him up as well.

"HELLO."

He was definitely annoyed. He was supposed to be on downtime after the deployment, and itching to get back home to his family in North Carolina, only waiting on final debriefings and other paperwork before he was released. *Oh well. Dive right in.*

"It's Pike. I need a favor."

"Shit. What now? It's not even seven in the damn morning."

"I need to get into the Force headquarters again. Right now."

Fifty-eight minutes later, I was sitting inside the secret cell with everyone but Jennifer oozing venom. Retro had to pull in Buckshot to get me access, and neither was very happy at the loss of rack time. For her part, Holly was packing her bags, getting ready to leave.

"Holly, come on. Ten more minutes. We can't talk to anyone at the prison until eight. You leave now, and the whole thing is wasted. I need your undercover-brother cop connections."

"An hour's an hour. Sorry. I'm out of here."

Retro spoke up. "Holly, I'm the last guy who would defend Pike's stupid antics, but he *did* get us out of bed this morning. Make it worth our while. When it ends up being nothing, we can all beat him to death."

Holly, eyes red and hair greasy, looked at him, then at me. She threw her hands up.

"All right. One phone call." She pointed her finger at me. "But you now owe me dinner at the restaurant of my choice."

"You got it," I said.

We waited until the clock struck eight, then she dialed. Before anyone answered, I said, "We need to get a handle on this guy. Find out what he was doing at the prison. See if anything's strange. Anything at all —"

She held up her hand. "Shut up."

"Put it on speaker?"

She did.

She spent a couple of minutes verifying her credentials, going through the cop-talk lingo until the man on the other end was comfortable with the conversation. Eventually, she worked her way around to the ex-con, but the guy had no idea about him. He pulled the convict's records, which didn't tell us anything at all except that he'd been

538

a troublemaker when he arrived but settled down into a rhythm where he became a model inmate, earning parole.

I whispered, "We need someone who worked with him. Someone who knows him personally."

Holly glared, but made the request. The man on the phone said, "If he was released three years ago, I'm not sure anyone will remember. We do have quite a few inmates, you know."

I heard him shuffling papers on his desk, then he said, "Well, Bobby was on his block during that time, and he's still here. Want to talk to him?"

Holly stared daggers at me, letting me know that we were now wasting the time of people in a different state. "Please. If you don't mind."

A few minutes later, a deep baritone came on. "This is Bobby; how can I help you?"

Holly went through her descriptions again, and waited to be told this was a waste of time.

Bobby said, "Oh yeah, I remember him. A real badass when he showed up, but calmed right down. He ended up being a pretty good guy. I know everyone wants to bitch about Muslims nowadays, but we got a chaplain here who calmed down a whole crew of killers like him. I'll tell ya, I'm all for that religion if it keeps the peace in here. Unlike that fucker Cyrus, spouting all his hate and stirring things up."

I felt an electric jolt. So did everyone else in the room. Holly continued, no longer pissed.

"What do you mean? He was in a prayer group?"

"Yeah, him and about twenty others. A group of them, four or five, really took it seriously. We had to get special permission for the chaplain to come more than he was scheduled for those guys. It was a no-brainer, since racial violence was subsiding no matter how much Cyrus tried to stir it up."

"Who's the chaplain? Is he still there? Can we talk to him?"

"Unfortunately, no. He was a volunteer and quit coming about a month ago. Too bad, really. Violence is back up now."

This is it.

I cut in. "Bobby, how many of that small group are still in prison?"

"Just one. The rest were paroled because of good behavior. Last one about a year ago."

I wrote down on a piece of paper, *Get the records of the parolees. All four.*

Holly nodded, getting switched back over to the administrator. In fifteen minutes, we split up the list, calling each parole officer in four separate states. All four ex-cons were now model citizens, with each parole officer gushing the praises of their wards.

All four worked for the main power company in the state where they resided.

They're going to hit the grid.

I said, "Collate that information into a single sheet. Names, addresses, supervisors, and anything else we can use to pin them down."

Holly went to work. Retro said, "What are you going to do?"

"Find Kurt. Get this out, right now. We may already be too late."

"Kurt's at the Oversight Council, trying to get Omega authority for an asshole in Oman."

Dammit. Another place I wasn't allowed anymore. More bureaucracy to fight through. The good news was that everyone who was anyone in the U.S. government would be there.

"Well, they're about to shift gears. That guy in Oman is nowhere near the threat we're facing now."

67

Keshawn drove down the deserted dirt road and pulled the truck alongside his beat-up Honda Civic. He got out and began to transfer the loaded EFPs and other equipment. He had decided to ignore Rafik's orders about using the BGE vehicle, feeling more secure in his own car. He had been pleased when he was told he was on his own, because he thought driving the company truck — with an Arabic imposter wearing a BGE uniform — was absolute stupidity. Others might blindly follow Rafik's orders, but Keshawn refused to do so.

The transfer complete, he continued down the road to his first target, a substation in the middle of nowhere. One that he'd sketched a month ago. He pulled the car around the back, hiding it in the wood line, then broke out the aiming tripod, his first EFP, and the M57 firing device from the trunk.

He found the same line of sight he had sketched before, and aimed the EFP through the chain-link fence to the extremely high voltage transformer within. He attached the two wires from the blasting cap to the M57, then tested the circuit. He got a green light. Placing the cap in the well for the EFP, he spooled the wire out to its maximum extension, having no idea how big the explosion would be. He crouched behind a large pine tree and took three deep breaths, looking at the M57 clacker in his hand.

Here we go.

He placed it between both hands and rapidly began to click the handle. On the third stroke, the air was split by an explosion, but there was little debris thrown his way. He turned and looked around the tree. The tripod lay on the ground, with the EFP tray vaporized, a small cloud of dust lingering in the air as the only reminder that it had existed. He walked out, searching the giant transformer for damage. He saw a hole in the chain-link fence, and a large tear in the metal sheath of the EHVT. Nothing else. He wondered if he'd screwed up, if maybe he'd failed to set up the EFP correctly. Then he noticed a silence for the first time. He'd thought it was because of the deafening noise of the explosion, but he could hear birds chirping in the distance. What he couldn't hear was the hum of electricity flowing into the substation. He smiled.

One down.

68

I waited impatiently at the gate to the West Wing of the White House, trying to get inside the parking area of the Old Executive Office Building where the Oversight Council had convened. As expected, it had turned into an enormous pain in the ass, with me getting pissed off enough to want to start ripping heads. Jennifer, who'd come along, kept me calm while sweet-talking the guard there so that I wasn't arrested.

Eventually, we were cleared for entrance. As I pulled into a parking space, I saw Kurt come out the side door of the building. He didn't look happy.

"What the hell are you doing, Pike? I told you to go home. Why are you still here? We're in a very delicate phase in Oman, and with the election shenanigans, your bullshit might cost us Omega authority with the council."

I jumped out of the car. "Sir, I know what

the terrorists are up to. It's not Cyrus Mace, and it's not a bunch of skinheads. It's the terrorists from Egypt, and they're about to try to destroy our electrical grid."

The comment brought him up short. He looked at me for a second, trying to decide if I was nuts or worth the risk to bring into the hallowed hall of the Oversight Council. He shook his head. "I'm going to regret this. Follow me."

We entered the conference room, and even I was a little awed by the talent around the table, starting with President Warren at the head. All were looking at me expectantly, except Brookings, the secretary of state. He was glowering like he wanted to castrate me.

President Warren said, "Hello, Pike. I understand you have something you urgently want to tell us."

I wasted no time, spilling out everything I had found. The information caused a ripple in the room. Nobody said a word for a minute, all trying to assimilate the intel. I ended with, "You need to let my team loose. Let us go get them."

That caused Brookings to come out of his coma. "Bullshit. No way is Project Prometheus doing anything domestically. We have law enforcement for this. They're already tracking the Cyrus Mace angle, with a manhunt for the explosives under way. All we have to do is redirect them."

I went from him, to the president, to Kurt. "No offense, but it took me damn near an hour to just get inside here. There's no way you can get the correct information into the system in time to stop this."

"Stop what?" Brookings said. "We have no indication you're right. Just your say-so. Even if it's true, the attack may be days away. We have plenty of time to stop it."

President Warren raised his hand, causing everyone to shut up.

"First, let's get this information out. Right now." He pointed at Alexander Palmer, the national security advisor. "Track these guys and see what they find." Palmer started to leave the room, when I held out the document Holly had created, saying, "Sir . . . here. This is law enforcement speak."

President Warren said, "Kurt, what do you think?"

Kurt said, "We need to get an assessment of our vulnerabilities. Figure out what they're actually going to hit. The grid's a big fucking thing. We need to neck it down instead of randomly guessing what they're planning to hit."

President Warren nodded, turning to the director of the CIA. "Get that egghead you had brief me a year ago on infrastructure vulnerabilities. The guy from the National Academy of Sciences. VTC him in here."

We waited while the video-teleconferencing bridge was established, me pacing back and forth while we wasted time. Eventually, the Tandberg secure VTC came to life, with a guy on the other end looking exactly like the stereotypical absentminded professor. Wild hair, Coke-bottle glasses, and a twitchy demeanor. All he was missing was a white lab coat and a pocket protector.

He said, "Hello, sir. To what do I owe the pleasure of this call?"

President Warren got right to the point. "You gave me a briefing on our critical vulnerabilities last year, but I need some specifics on the power grid. If a terrorist group was going to attack that, how could they do the most damage?"

"Well, that all depends on what they bring to the table. I mean, if they had an airplane, they could fly it into a nuclear plant, or if they had car bombs, they could —"

Warren cut him off. "We don't have time for this. Say they have multiple small teams with explosive packets and the means to penetrate any security. What would they hit?"

The egghead looked nonplussed for a moment, clearly wanting to pontificate for a while but brought up short by the urgency in the president's voice.

"Well, the best thing to hit would be our extremely high voltage transformers. You knock those out, and certain areas would be out of power for a while. But there's no way to systemically bring down the entire grid now. After 2003, we started going to smart-grid technology. They could do some damage, but the grid's fairly self-healing."

President Warren said, "What about our nuclear facilities? Seems like that would be the logical place to hit."

"Yes, sir, in a perfect world, but every nuclear plant has an enormous amount of security, and not just from someone who intentionally means harm. We built those things to withstand hurricanes, earthquakes, and anything else that can be thrown against them. In fact, the sites themselves *do* have to withstand a certain level of plane crash. The biggest problem with hitting a nuclear facility is our own government. After the Japanese tsunami and the troubles they had with their two plants, any attack, no matter how small, will cause the NRC's Nuclear Security and Incident Response office to shut down the reactor until we can be sure it is safe. The event would bring about some economic damage but recoverable fairly quickly. Trust me, they can't harm a nuclear plant."

President Warren said, " 'Fairly quickly' is a worthless phrase. Especially in today's economy. They poke enough nuclear plants, and the impact would be catastrophic even if every attack was a failure."

The egghead continued, "I wouldn't worry about a nuclear facility, if you really want to know what's going to hurt. As I said, the EHVTs are the way to go."

President Warren said, "Why? It's just a piece of equipment. Why is that so bad?"

"Because we don't have any spares."

"What do you mean?"

"EHVTs are enormous things, made one at a time, with most being made for a specific power system. They aren't built all the same, sort of like a carburetor in a car. You can't go to the NAPA auto store and say, 'Give me a carburetor.' You have to give the make and model of the car. EHVTs are the same, except there aren't any NAPAs to buy them at, and they take six months to build. We don't do that in America anymore. All EHVTs are made overseas, with a backlog of six months. Most U.S. energy companies keep a couple on hand, but if you took out more than we had to spare, you'd permanently alter our ability to provide power to an area."

President Warren said, "So that's what they'd hit? The EHVTs?"

"That would be my guess, but even then, it's small potatoes. Taking them out individually would cause local power outages, but what you'd really want is a shutdown of the entire grid, with the EHVTs being the lynchpin. That can't happen anymore."

"Why?"

"Because, like I said, we've made the grid smart."

When the scientist saw he wasn't convincing anyone, he began speaking to us like we were children. "Look. The country is split into three zones — the Eastern, Western, and Texas interchanges. It should be neat, but it's really not. Even between these zones, there are interchanges, and in fact, as we saw in 2003, our system impacts other countries, such as Canada. The problem with all of this is that electricity is an instant demand. We don't store it, like oil. It's produced and used instantly. The demand is constantly fluctuating, with the grid providing the response. If you interrupt that flow, you cause a ripple effect. If one substation that's used to distribute power is taken off-line, then the burden is switched to another substation. If you take out that substation as well, you overpower the next substation tasked with taking on the additional burden, and it takes itself off-line before it does damage to itself. When that happens, the entire flow is shifted to another station, with exponential effects. Eventually, every single substation shuts down because it can't handle the flow, like what happened in 2003."

I spoke up. "You keep mentioning 2003. Forgive me, but I was out of the country for most of that year. What do you mean?"

The egghead focused on me like I was a simpleton, and said, "The blackout of 2003? You don't remember that?"

"I wasn't here. And had other things to worry about. Like getting shot at."

"Well, I was getting to it anyway, because it's why we don't really have to worry about an attack against the grid anymore. Believe it or not, in 2003 a tree branch caused one high-voltage power line to short out, then what I just described happened. The northeastern seaboard — along with sections of Canada — went without power for three days, at an estimated cost of ten billion dollars. Along with a lot of deaths."

I said, "Why don't we need to worry about that now?"

"Because we learned from that experience and developed solutions. The old system simply shunted all power to the next available substation, which eventually became overpowered. Now we have a smart grid, wherein the system itself tests where best to put the load, then does so. No single substation is overpowered."

I said, "So even if you took out the EHVTs, you wouldn't cause a blackout?"

"Oh, you'd cause a blackout, but just not nationwide. It would be restricted to the area that was serviced. Still bad, but nothing like 2003."

I said, "Just say they could do it. That they could overcome your smart grid. What are we looking at?"

"Well, they can't, so it's like asking what would happen if dinosaurs were to attack your house."

I was about to lose my temper and my tone betrayed that. "The president of the United States is asking. What would happen?"

He snapped back at my sharpness, along with everyone else in the room. He paused for a moment, then said truculently, "Well, if by some black magic they could cause a blackout, it would be catastrophic. If they attacked the Eastern exchange and brought the EHVTs off-line, and managed to shunt the power linearly, it would shut down the entire eastern seaboard for months. Extrapolating from the three-day blackout, you'd be looking at losses in the hundreds of billions of dollars, and a huge loss of life, from simple traffic accidents to hospital deaths. But I'm telling you, that *can't* happen."

I looked at Kurt. "The terrorists would know that. They wouldn't put this much time and effort into an attack without ensuring success. They spent years recruiting American prisoners, then placing them inside power companies. The theft of EFPs was very well thought out, and geared toward this attack. We're missing something. You need to turn my team loose. We're the only ones who know what we're up against. The only ones who believe."

The egghead on the screen heard me and became shrill. "Mister Whoever You Are, I'm sure you believe there's a threat, but from where I'm at, I can tap into the power flow of the entire country. I can reach any interchange with the touch of a keyboard. We've put an enormous amount of effort into fixing the system. It's ad hoc, but still better than anywhere else in the world. Doomsday just isn't going to happen, not unless the terrorists have found a way to go back in time ten years."

Kurt began to say something, and the lights went out.

69

Rafik paid his five dollars and pulled around into a small parking lot adjacent to a pond, seeing a trail wind into the forest across a wooden walkway. It had taken him close to two hours to reach the Calvert Cliffs State Park from downtown Baltimore, and during that time his pay-as-you-go TracFone had vibrated four times. Four text messages stating success. Four in two hours. Much faster than he had anticipated. If they kept up this pace, the grid would reach critical mass within six hours. He had planned on ten, assuming he would lose one team eventually. In truth, in the back of his mind, he had planned on failure.

Maybe coming to this park won't end up necessary after all.

He was surprised at the number of people in the park, and wondered why they weren't at work or school. Couples leaving to hike the trails with day packs, families with picnic baskets, and lone fossil hunters with trowels, buckets, and brushes headed to the shore of the Chesapeake Bay two miles away.

He had done the research on the park on the Internet, convinced the place would be deserted, and now wondered about his ability to stay for the duration of the attack. Looking at it logically, he decided there wasn't a threat. Lots of cars were parked around him, and probably would be until the park closed at sunset. The only implication was that he wouldn't be able to sit inside his vehicle without drawing attention to himself.

No matter. You need to conduct a reconnaissance anyway.

He slung a day pack over his shoulder, the water bottles inside making it sag awkwardly, and walked to a map tacked inside a display case. He saw that the trail he was parked in front of led straight east, to the shore and the fossil cliffs. That wouldn't do. He needed one that went north, to his target. He located three other trails, all longer, that went north, then wound back to the east, starting at another lot farther into the park. He debated walking but then decided that he didn't want to traverse the entire parking area loaded down with explosives if he was forced to execute this plan.

Better to get as close as possible.

He returned to the car and wound through the park, passing shelters and picnic tables, all overloaded with people. He found the area he wanted, right next to a gravel access road labeled for emergency vehicles only. There were no parking spots available, but he noticed that others had taken to parking wherever there was space, with an apparent disregard for marked spots, which would work better for him. He pulled right into a grassy area at the trailhead, parking in the shade of a stand of hardwoods, and killed the engine. He debated for a few seconds about taking his sidearm, then decided against it, sliding it under the driver's seat. If he was stopped, the pistol would only confirm suspicions. The minute he fired a shot, the mission would be over. Better for him to talk his way out of trouble.

As he entered the trailhead, he compared himself to the other visitors and was pleased to see he blended in fine. Some were carrying larger rucksacks, which he would have to do to carry the EFP toward his target should his primary plan fail, a contingency that was looking more and more remote.

He walked up the access road, alongside three couples headed the same way. Feeling self-conscious, he tried to act interested in the flora and fauna, using a cheap digital camera as a prop. Eventually, the couples split off onto the shorter trails, with him sticking to the longest because it continued north toward his target. When it began to traverse to the east, he split off, marking the point on his GPS. He continued straight through the forest, hiking on the bearing he had set in his GPS earlier.

He felt his phone vibrate inside the pack, and rapidly pulled it out, anxious to see which of the four had managed to conduct a second attack so soon.

He pushed the button for text messaging, and stared at the phone in disbelief. It was the imam's team in Pennsylvania, and they weren't texting success.

70

Inside the conference room, the cacophony of voices shouting in the dim light of the emergency illumination was giving President Warren a headache. He rubbed his forehead, then ordered everyone to be quiet until the generator could kick in.

Three minutes later, it did, with the fluorescent bulbs flickering back to life. The cacophony grew again, as one by one the members of the council began to raise their voices to be heard.

"Quiet!" he said again.

When everyone was still, he said, "Okay, one at a time. Quit shouting over each other."

While the council members waited to be called on, Pike took the opportunity to start.

"Sir, they're at it now. You need to let me go. Turn my team loose. There's no way the police are going to be able to react in time. They don't have the assets of the Taskforce, and we don't have the time to waste."

Secretary Brookings said, "You aren't even a member of this council. I demand you remain silent unless asked to speak."

President Warren spoke to the director of the CIA. "Get that egghead back online. We need to assess what's happening."

Brookings continued, "Sir, you can't consider using Project Prometheus domestically. That was the one sacrosanct thing on which we all agreed. No matter what the consequences. That cure is worse than the disease."

"I'm not considering anything at this point. I need more information."

The Tandberg came to life, with the mad scientist now looking like he was going to throw up.

President Warren said, "Well, what's going on with the grid?"

"Uhh . . . it's being hit all over the Northeast. We've got multiple substations down, with others falling fairly rapidly due to the shifting of the load."

"What the fuck happened to your smart grid?"

"I don't know. They're checking now. Early assessments are a Trojan horse virus. It definitely knocked out our early warning, and looks like it's affected a majority of our real-time automated shunting."

"Speak English. What's that mean?"

"It means the power's being shifted linearly, like the old days. Directly from one substation to another. We're trying to manually redirect the flow, but without the alarm system, we're simply guessing. We're doing our best to mitigate, but if we keep losing substations, we're going to have a massive fault in the grid."

He shifted his feet back and forth, waiting to be dismissed.

President Warren said, "What do you mean by 'fault'? How massive?"

"Uhh . . . we're going to lose the entire Eastern exchange. The largest blackout in history."

It grew so quiet the president could hear the drone of the lights.

Pike grabbed the remote, muting the VTC screen to prevent the scientist from hearing what he said. "For Christ's sake, sir," he said, "let me go. Just me. I won't take a team, and I'll protect you. I'll take the fall. Nobody has to find out about the Taskforce. I'm a private citizen. I won't say a word, and you can put me in jail when it's done. I don't care, but don't let this happen by doing nothing."

Alexander Palmer entered the room, saying, "We got one. The guy working for Pennsylvania Power and Light. Tracked his GPS and pulled him over like a routine traffic stop."

President Warren said, "Are we sure they're terrorists?"

Palmer smiled. "Oh yeah. Guess who was with him? The disappearing imam from Canada, Abdul-Majid Mohammed. Along with a trunk full of some kind of specialized explosives."

Brookings said, "There. See. Law enforcement's doing fine."

Pike said, "Bullshit. That's one fucking team. We have no idea how many are out there, and the only way to find out is to catch the leader. The killer from Egypt. He'll have a plan for failure, and he sure as shit doesn't have a GPS on his car."

Palmer saw the intercom on the table blinking, and held up his finger. "I told them to patch in any updates. Hang on for a second."

He pressed the button and said, "This is Palmer. Go ahead."

A tinny voice came through. "We tracked the GPS of the guy working at Baltimore Gas and Electric. His truck was parked down a deserted dirt road, empty. The guy working for Pepco here in D.C. doesn't have a GPS on his truck, but his supervisor's trying to locate him. In some good news, the guy who works for Dominion Power is being tracked right now. He's outside of Richmond in a rural area. We have men posted at the only substation along his route with an EHVT."

"Can you patch their radio in here?"

"Yeah, stand by."

Thirty seconds later, they could hear the Virginia state trooper talking to his dispatch.

"I got a Dominion truck headed my way. I can see it down the hill."

"Roger. Be advised, the suspects are considered armed and dangerous."

"Roger. Don't worry, I've handled skinheads before."

Pike said, "What's he talking about? He's confused. He thinks he's still tracking the Phoenix Order."

Palmer held up his hand, getting Pike quiet so they could monitor the radio traffic.

". . . . he's turned on the access road. Must be the guy. He's seen me and stopped. I'm sending Billy down to him. Stand by."

Everyone in the conference room held their breath, waiting. Finally, the trooper came back on. *"False alarm. This guy's black. He's not a skinhead —"*

A muted crack came through the speaker, followed by random static. Then the trooper came back on, screaming. *"Officer down! Officer down! I need —"*

Nothing more came out.

Pike broke the silence. "They have no idea what they're up against. Sir, manhunting is what I do, and I'm fucking good at it. Turn me loose."

President Warren sat in silence, feeling the weight of the decision. Wondering, if he crossed the line, could he ever go back. He considered what Pike had said earlier, realizing that Pike thought the only thing riding on the decision was the fear of Taskforce discovery, and the subsequent fallout to everyone in the room. He didn't seem to grasp the peril of an organization like the Taskforce operating on U.S. soil. He returned Pike's expectant gaze.

A good man. But a predator. A menace to our way of life. A menace I created.

The scientist on the VTC spoke up. "Substation 416 outside of Richmond just went off-line, causing a string of shutdowns. We're at seventy percent. We lose seven more by attack, and it's unrecoverable."

Pike said, "Sir?"

President Warren watched the scientist fidget on the screen for a moment, then looked Pike in the eye.

"Go."

Brookings' mouth fell open in disbelief. Nobody in the room said a word, the implications of the decision speaking for itself. President Warren watched Pike scramble to get out the door, a predator now free to slaughter by any means he chose.

A predator I might have to put down.

He put his head in his hands, hating the decision he had just made.

71

Jennifer and I crawled our way back to Task-force headquarters, the gridlock caused by the lack of stoplights turning a ten-minute trip into thirty. I got sick of waiting and swung onto the sidewalk, blasting my horn at the pedestrians in front of me.

Jennifer threw her hand up to the roof and stomped down on an imaginary brake pedal.

"Jesus, Pike! What are you doing?"

"Getting us to headquarters. Call Retro; have him standing by to get us in."

She pulled out her phone, slapping the dash at every close call I had. After she hung up, she said, "I'm coming with you."

I considered the offer. I could definitely use the help, but I knew there was little chance we could do this clean. If she came, odds were she'd be prosecuted right along with me, because there was no doubt I was going to break the law.

"No, you're not. Jennifer, I'm going way,

way out on this. Trust me, you don't want to be a part of it."

"Yes, I do. I heard what's going on. I was in the room."

"*No,* you *don't.* I'm probably going to do some things that make Cairo seem mild. You don't have the stomach for it."

We were stopped by a throng of people exiting a Metro station, forcing us to inch along, with them flowing around the truck.

"And that's okay. The world needs more of you than they do of me. But right now, as much as you hate it, I'm the solution."

She gave me a funny look, then turned to the window, watching the people wandering around with dazed expressions, all apparently wondering what they were going to do without the Metro.

"I don't know what I was before I met you, but I know what I am now, and it's not that. I used to be like them, safe and happy while someone else kept me that way."

Her next words caused my jaw to drop.

"You called me a meat eater in Cairo after I killed the Chinese agent, and I hated you for it. Hated you for holding up the mirror. I didn't *want* to believe it, but that doesn't make it untrue. Those guys need to be stopped, and I'm the solution as well."

She saw my disbelief and broke into a

568

grin. "What? I am what I am. You're the man to blame."

I wasn't sure if she honestly accepted what her statement meant, and there was still the problem of prosecution when this was done.

"There's no reason for both of us to go to jail."

We made it through the crowd, and I swerved to avoid a moped that had hopped the sidewalk as well, forcing him to crash into a couple of plastic garbage cans.

She slapped the dash again, saying, "Nobody said we were going to jail for sure. But without me, you'll be charged with vehicular manslaughter." She smiled. "Besides, I'm not in the government either, and I'm tied to you by our company. Whatever you do will impact that, and I need to protect the investment."

"Jennifer —"

She cut me off, growing serious again. "Pike, remember that story you told me about sacrifice? How you always thought it was strange that plenty of men in the Army would be willing to jump on a grenade and sacrifice their lives, but not so many would stand up for what's right if it meant sacrificing their career? This is the same thing. It's my choice."

Wow, that's dirty pool. Using my own words

against me.

Something had definitely shifted within her. I saw the determination on her face and gave up. "As you wish."

The words startled her for a split second, then her face split into a grin. "Damn right. As I wish."

Pulling into the underground garage, I was surprised to see Decoy waiting outside the door. He smiled and gave us a thumbs-up. Seconds later, I met him and Retro in the stairwell.

Taking the steps two at a time, I said, "What are you doing here?"

"Helping you get a terrorist."

Retro said, "Me too. Buckshot's also waiting in Ops."

I exited on the second floor, moving straight to the communications cell.

"No, you're not going with me, because you don't have authority to operate domestically. Only I can do that."

Retro said, "What the hell are you talking about?"

I entered the communications cell, moving straight past the myriad of radios and telephone equipment to a back room lined with row after row of computer servers. I barked at the first person I saw.

"I need you to hack into the GPS tracking

systems of the Dominion Power company, and I need it done yesterday."

The man at the computer stuttered for a second, then said, "I can't do that. I'm not authorized to do anything to American networks."

"The president of the United States just authorized it. And if that's not good enough, I'm going to break every fucking finger on both of your hands until you're forced to hunt and peck with a permanent splint."

His eyes wide, he nodded. I handed him the information on the Dominion truck, saying, "I want a real-time fix on this transmitted to my phone within the next five minutes."

I left without another word, moving up two flights to the team rooms and the weapons lockup, Retro and Decoy hot on my heels. Five minutes later, I'd robbed one of the lockups of a full-size Glock 21, some handheld radios, and a Glock 30 subcompact, along with plenty of loaded magazines for both. When I handed Jennifer the subcompact on the way back down the stairs, Retro and Decoy about lost their minds.

"What the hell! She's coming with you, but you won't take us?"

I couldn't resist. "She's coming because she trusts me. You two can wait on a 'real' operator for your next mission."

Decoy said, "Come on, Pike, that's not fair. You take things too hard. You have to admit you leaned way, way out over the edge in Europe. We want to help."

I stopped outside the door of the commo cell, seeing Buckshot coming down the hall.

"Look, here's the truth. Jennifer and I have made a deal with the devil. We'll go get this guy, but if any stink comes out of it, we get blamed. The president wasn't willing to use an official Taskforce team domestically. We're both civilians, and easy to throw away. You guys aren't. You get rolled up in this, and you're going to be hung out to dry."

Buckshot heard the tail end of the conversation and said, "Maybe I'm okay with that. I'm from New York. Maybe I'll get to have a word with that asshole Cyrus Mace and his little white supremacist thing."

"I'm not sure traitors get put in state institutions. And that's what you'll be. I can't protect you, and I can guarantee I'm going to break quite a few laws to get these guys. I've already started."

All three stood for a second before Decoy said, "We're in."

I was surprised. "You guys haven't seen

leaning over the edge yet. You ready for that?"

"No issues."

I nodded. "Go get your kit. Bring down the keys for two Suburbans from the Ops Center. Buckshot, you're going to stay here to make sure these techies break the law when I tell them to."

"Why don't you leave Jennifer here for that?" He looked at her. "No offense."

I opened the door, seeing a roomful of techies all staring at me. "Because I'm going to need you to do things she's not capable of."

72

The two Suburbans chewed up the ground toward Richmond, going as fast as possible in the congestion of Interstate 95, spending most of the time throwing gravel on the shoulder to get around the traffic. Jennifer was driving while I got a data dump from the scientist at the Oversight Council. It wasn't good. Four more substations with EHVTs had been taken out, and we had at least two attackers on the loose without a way to find them.

We've got to get a handle on the leader. Some way to track.

The only thing we had going for us was that the cop killer was still driving his Dominion Power truck. His track showed up less than twelve miles ahead, now outside of Spotsylvania, near the National Military Park. We exited at Highway 208 near Fredericksburg and began to hunt. We took a right on County Road 613 and passed through the park. Getting to the far side, I saw the truck ahead of us.

"Retro, I've got him. We're going to take him out. Follow behind. When he's stopped, get out and smoke him."

"You sure that's him? You want me to confirm?"

"No. I just heard him kill two cops in cold blood. Don't waste your time trying to play Joe Friday. Kill him."

"What about questioning?"

"He won't respond to questions, and we don't have time to apply force. Get his phone. That will answer everything." I heard nothing back, and added, "Retro, trust me. Put a bullet in that guy's head before he can do the same to you."

"Roger."

Jennifer heard the conversation and squinted at me, knowing I'd just ordered the extrajudicial execution of an American citizen.

"What? We only have two or three substations left. This is how it's going to be. You want out, say the word."

She said, "What do you want me to do?"

"PIT him. Just like happened to you at Assessment. Bring his ass down."

She pressed the gas, closing in on the truck. She brought the Suburban right behind his bumper, close enough for me to recognize an African American in the driver's seat. *That's him.*

She flipped the blinker and began to pass. When she came abreast of his left rear tire, she swerved into it, slamming into the large truck with all of the force the Suburban could muster. We became engaged in a battle of steel, his truck refusing to break contact with the road surface and our Suburban grinding into it, trying to overcome gravity.

"Push, dammit, give it gas!"

She floored the Suburban, and I saw the truck begin to move. We continued racing down the roadway locked together, with the back end of the truck moving in slow motion. We reached the crossover point, and the back end began to slide. Jennifer expertly controlled the wheel, forcing the rear end to swing around. Seconds later, we were shooting past with the truck spinning out of control. Jennifer slammed on the brakes and I jumped out, running to the vehicle seventy meters behind.

Retro had pinned the truck with his own Suburban and leapt out, Decoy right behind. The driver fiddled with something in the front seat, then exited with a yell, firing a pistol ineffectually at their advance. Retro and Decoy both pulled the trigger at the same time, splitting his head open. By the time I reached the vehicle, he was down. And absolutely dead.

"Find his phone. Get the numbers."

I called Kurt. "We got one. Going to track the others with the numbers off of his phone."

Kurt said, "What do you mean 'we'?"

"I've got Jennifer with me," I lied. "Tell the Virginia troopers they can collect the carcass that killed their men." I gave him our location and hung up.

Decoy came up with the phone. "It's a pay-as-you-go. Only one number in it. What do you want to do?"

I called Buckshot. "Put a techie on the line."

I heard a faltering voice. "Hello?"

"I need a geolocation of a phone. And I need it in real time."

"Uhhh . . . Okay. Give me the number."

I passed it to him. He came back on. "Uhh . . . this is a CONUS number. I can't do anything with the domestic telephony. I'm sorry. It's illegal."

Jesus Christ.

"Put on Buckshot."

He said, "Yeah?"

"Hit him."

"What?"

"Hit him in the face. Right now. Then give him the phone."

I heard a smack, then screaming. When the techie came back on, he was crying.

"Okay. You're now under duress. It isn't your fault. You were forced to track the phones. You understand?"

"Ye-Yes. I understand."

"Get me the phone tracks right fucking now or I'm going to have Buckshot rip off your head."

I hung up and began ripping through the power truck, looking for anything to give us a handle on the other two terrorists. Inside was a laptop computer displaying a news page on the blackout. *Enjoying his last fifteen minutes of fame.* There was nothing else. Retro called from the back.

"Found the EFPs. He's got three in here, so we stopped at least that many attacks."

"That's good, but not good enough. We need some way to track those guys. We only have one number, and at least two terrorists running around without GPS on their vehicles."

Jennifer began going through the computer, looking for anything that might help us. She brought up the Internet history, clicking on recent pages. As I watched the screen slowly load, the Web page itself caused a flash of realization.

It's talking to the Internet. Out here in the middle of nowhere.

"Jennifer, how's that computer online? What's it using?"

She played with the keys for second. "Looks like an AT&T 3G connection."

My phone rang. I interrupted the techie before he had a chance to say anything.

"Can you geolocate a company computer using the cell network to access the Internet?"

"Well, sure. Basically, it's dialing in just like a cell phone. What service?"

"This one's AT&T, but I don't know about the one I need tracked."

"Well, AT&T is a GSM network, so all I need is the IMEI number from the device."

"What's an IMEI?"

"Just a standardized number that identifies the device over the network. Every GSM cell phone has one."

"How do I find it?"

"I can't explain it over the phone. I need to see the computer."

"Would there be records of that sort of thing? At the company? Is that something a company would keep if they issued a bunch of laptops with this service?"

"Yeah. Someone would have the number in case the computer was stolen. They'd want to turn off the service."

"Put Buckshot on the line."

When he came on, I told him to put a fire under the analysts, finding out if Pepco had computer hookups like Dominion, and if they did, to find the IMEI of the computer the ex-con had in his truck. I knew he'd have it on, doing the same thing as the man we'd just killed, enjoying the destruction he was unleashing. He clicked off, turning the phone back to the techie.

"What do you have on the phone number I gave you?" I asked.

He gave me a grid way out in the Maryland countryside, at a place called Calvert Cliffs.

What the hell?

"Put on an intel analyst."

A guy came on immediately, sounding scared. I could imagine Buckshot standing behind him with a tire iron.

"I need a search of Calvert Cliffs, Maryland." I gave him the cell phone track. "What's there? Why would one of these phones show up there?"

He tapped on the computer for a few seconds, then said, "Nothing's out there but wilderness. It's known for its fossil remnants in the cliffs. That's about it."

"Bullshit. Something's out there. What about power? Electricity? Jesus, do I need to do this myself?"

He came back immediately. "Sorry, I didn't know the search terms. Right north of the fossil park is the Calvert Cliffs Nuclear Power Plant. Two reactors butting up to the park, right on the Chesapeake Bay."

73

Rafik broke out onto another gravel road, breathing hard and sweating. He had begun to worry about running out of water, the trip taking him much, much longer than he thought it would, with the forest thicker than he thought possible. He was supposed to be on high ground, according to his research, but most of the movement had been in swamps. He yanked his sleeve out of a thornbush, causing him to lose his balance and stumble back. Steadying himself on a small sapling, he took stock of his surroundings.

The road, really just a rutted path suitable for four-wheel-drive vehicles, wound in front of him, first perpendicular to his line of march, then going the same direction he was headed. It had a six-foot chain-link gate across it, blocking the trail alone, with the wood line doing the job to the left and right. The only thing preventing his advance was a line of signs proclaiming a warning. Crossing the road, he read: NO TRESPASSING. THIS AREA IS UNDER CONSTANT SURVEILLANCE AND SUBJECT TO ROUTINE PATROLS.

The prohibition was repeated in Spanish, and staked out every thirty feet. He smiled.

Getting close.

He continued on, paralleling the gravel road until it wound out to the east and the coast. He continued straight north, finally heading uphill, until he broke out onto a spit of a ridgeline jutting into the Chesapeake Bay.

Spread below him was the Calvert Cliffs Nuclear Plant, housing two nuclear reactors that had been in operation since the 1970s. The plant space itself was massive, but the two unique concrete domes designed to protect the reactors stood out prominently, the nearest one about one hundred and twenty meters away, down in the low ground of the valley. Just beyond them, to the west, was the immense electrical transfer point for the energy being produced here, and his planned target.

He studied the myriad of components, looking for the EHVTs used, based on his historical research of nuclear facilities. He became painfully aware of the distance between his location and them. It was close to three hundred meters away, and the transformers at this distance looked like nine-volt batteries.

Too hard to hit, even if the EFP will work that far.

His Google Earth research had failed. There was no way to strike from this location.

But I can't get any closer.

He could see the chain-link electrified fence of the facility just down the ridge. Moving west, toward the EHVTs, meant moving into the security perimeter.

He scanned the compound again, being drawn to the two concrete domes that housed the reactors themselves. The closest was within striking distance.

He knew there was little chance his single EFP would penetrate the concrete sheath, since its sole purpose was to contain any radiation leaks in the event of a catastrophe.

But the protection is built to withstand a sloppy emergency, like an earthquake or plane crash.

Not designed to protect against a weapon built from the ground up to defeat the best armor on earth. The strike would definitely cause damage, and if the EFP even fractured the concrete a little bit, they'd be forced to pull both reactors off-line while they did a structural analysis. Especially after the Japanese tsunami catastrophe last year. The United States would be on edge because of that tragedy.

Not nearly the impact I wanted, but maybe all that's left.

He'd gotten the call from Carl saying that police officers had been waiting for him at the substation, which meant it was either blind luck or they had specifically tracked Carl. He was leaning toward blind luck, because the police had been taken by surprise and killed. Even so, Rafik had lost his earlier confidence. He was now unsure of reaching critical mass in the Eastern exchange, and had begun to resign himself to this final act.

He thought about the dome, and realized he was simply wishing for success. One EFP shot had little chance of doing any serious damage.

But what about two? Or four?

He began to formulate a germ of an idea. *What if I fired four EFPs at the same spot? Pounding the same fracture over and over? They're specifically designed to defeat this very thing, only made of steel. Surely repeated strikes would penetrate simple concrete.*

The silos weren't armored. Just very thick

traditional concrete. He didn't know the exact makeup of the EFPs in his control but had seen the damage done by ones made much more crudely, and the damage was impressive indeed. If he could penetrate the concrete, with one or two EFP shots actually going inside the dome, he might cause serious havoc.

He had done enough research to know that even if he got through the outer barrier, the inner reactor was protected as well, and aiming blindly outside would almost ensure a miss.

But he also knew the reactor process was a delicate one. If he managed to destroy some of the mechanisms controlling the cooling of the nuclear rods, they'd melt down, causing a catastrophic fault. *And perhaps a release of radioactive waste through the fault I create, just as happened in Japan.*

He began walking rapidly back toward the GPS waypoint he'd set where he left the trail, marking the path to his car. He toyed with calling one of the teams right now, telling them to meet him in the park. Perhaps Carl. Given his military experience, he would be the best choice to make the multiple strike work.

He reached the trailhead twenty minutes

later and felt his phone vibrate. He pulled it out and saw that Carl wouldn't be helping anything on the attack anymore.

74

Closing in on Washington, D.C., just outside of Springfield, my phone vibrated. Opening it up, I saw a blinking icon with the label PEPCO IMEI north of Fort Belvoir. Buckshot had found the other team, only five miles to our east.

Decision time.

We were hightailing it to the Calvert Cliffs State Park to take out the ringleader, but now we had a target of opportunity that we could destroy right here. I'd already called Kurt and given him an update on the threat to the nuclear facility, sending him and the Oversight Council into a frenzy of coordination for a police response. That would undoubtedly take precious time. I was sure I could beat that response to Calvert Cliffs, but bypassing the terrorists nearby might mean reaching critical mass on the power grid. It was a Solomon's choice.

I toyed with having Kurt triangulate the

police to the grid here as well, although I knew in my gut they wouldn't make it before the strike. There was just too much bureaucracy. The assholes might be lining up on a substation right now.

Retro called. "You seeing what I'm seeing?"

"Yeah. What do you think?"

"Bird in the hand, man. That's what I think."

That was enough to push me over the edge. I gave Jennifer instructions, and we began the hunt for the third team. We wound around surface streets north of Fort Belvoir, crossing Telegraph Road and continuing to the east. Eventually we ended up on a small service road for a substation sandwiched in between two older, established neighborhoods. Driving up it, I saw a large field of knee-high grass in front of the substation, along with the Pepco truck.

We stopped short, huddling around my Suburban. Decoy and Retro began checking their kit, getting ready for the fight. Seeing the armament being loaded, Jennifer began doing the same.

I said, "Okay, they're here and setting up for a strike. Decoy and Retro go left. Jennifer and I will go right. Follow the fence line until we meet up. No doubt they'll be setting up somewhere on the perimeter."

Decoy said, "Rules of engagement?"

"Smoke them. No questions. Shoot first."

I felt Jennifer's eyes on me, and when I glanced her way, she stared at me for a long pause, then flicked her eyes at Retro and Decoy. I got the hint. I told the men, "Get your shit together. We leave in one minute."

After they'd returned to their Suburban and out of earshot, strapping on magazines and checking weapons, Jennifer said, "Why are we shooting first? We're not in a car. We can surprise them. Maybe they have information we can use."

I should have realized that when she'd said she was part of the solution, she didn't understand what that meant. *I should scratch her right here.* Even after her experiences in Europe, she was living in the land of the civilized.

"Jennifer, we aren't cops, and this isn't an arrest. It's combat. Look, I get we're in the United States and it doesn't feel right, but that's what it is. We kill whoever we find. Just like Normandy. Pretend they're Nazis or something, but don't let me down. Shoot first. Can you do that?"

She gazed off into the tree line for a few seconds, making me wonder again about taking her along. She turned back and checked her weapon, saying, "Yeah. I can do that. If they're bad, they're dead. But this had better be worth it. We kill a crew of innocent power company guys . . ."

With a little embarrassment and a lot of relief, I realized I had completely missed the reason for her reticence. She had no qualms about killing the terrorists. Well, maybe some, but she was more worried about killing innocents. Something I completely understood.

After she trailed off, I said, "That won't happen. This *is* their vehicle. Look, I see where you're going, but Retro and Decoy will automatically discriminate and it'll be pretty damn clear if they're bad. Don't worry. We aren't going to kill anyone that's not a threat, but we're also not going to give them a fair chance. If they're bad, they're dead."

I signaled Decoy and Retro, then began running down the right-side fence line, Jennifer behind me. We circled the perimeter, scanning for a target. We got about halfway around before an explosion cracked through the site, on Retro's side of the perimeter.

Shit. The EFP.

I continued on, making sure Jennifer was keeping up. She doggedly followed, running with the Glock in a two-handed grip, the sights bobbing and weaving with her stride, exactly like she'd been taught.

I heard the crack of gunfire, a quick snapping, then nothing. I rounded the corner of the fence line and saw Retro standing over the body of a man, with Decoy searching him.

Then Retro's chest exploded, followed by the rapid fire of someone emptying a magazine. Decoy turned to the threat and was hit in the shoulder, spinning down next to the dead terrorist. The bullets began to come my way. I dove to the ground and rolled behind a log as rounds cracked into the earth around me. I popped my head up, trying to locate the shooter. I saw him fifty meters away in the wood line, spraying his pistol all over the place. The weapon locked open on an empty magazine, and he took off running deeper into the trees.

I rose on a knee for a shot, knowing the odds of me hitting him were very small. He pulled out a cell phone and began hitting keys, then his head exploded in a fine red mist. He snapped to the left like he was hooked to a bungee cord as two more rounds slapped him in the chest.

I trained my weapon on the source of the fire, seeing Jennifer break out of the wood line. She reached the body and kicked his gun away. She caught my eye, then bent down and began searching him.

I sprinted to Retro and Decoy, starting to triage the damage. Jennifer arrived as I was peeling back Retro's shirt.

She saw the wound and said, "Oh, God . . . Pike . . ."

75

Rafik was unloading the trunk when his cell phone went off again. He hoped he'd see success, but dreaded what he would find. It was Keshawn, sending that he'd accomplished another attack. The news brought a sense of calm.

We're close. Very close.

He packed the large rucksack with the two remaining EFP trays and pulled out the tripods necessary to aim them. He leaned them against the car, wondering how he was going to take them into the trail network without someone questioning him. He glanced around to see if anyone was paying attention. All he needed to do was get into the wood line fifty meters away, but there were many, many people coming and going in the parking lot, and he would most likely be walking with other strangers, just like before.

He saw a man walking with a tripod and a

camera. Going the other way, toward the shore and the cliffs. The sight gave him courage to dive right in. He shouldered the rucksack, then picked up the tripods, heading rapidly toward the trailhead leading back to the nuclear plant.

He made it into the woods without any undue scrutiny and began rapidly climbing back the way he had come, wanting to get the EFPs established as soon as possible.

Forty minutes into the trek, he reached the waypoint to leave the trail. He walked north for thirty meters when his phone vibrated again. He took a pause on the side of the trail, breathing hard, praying for good news. It was a simple text from Farouk, saying "done." It was the prearranged code word for a catastrophic event. The loss of the team. It was the third time he'd received it today. The text made him weak, wanting to sit down.

Farouk is dead. I've lost my last trusted man. Allah the Merciful, help me on this path.

He gained control of his emotions, clinically analyzing what had transpired.

Someone knows the makeup of the teams.

He had no idea how, but knew this wasn't simply bad luck. Someone had deciphered his plan, dissected his organization. Some predator was now hunting them. Someone with skill.

Time to go to the final option.

He dialed Keshawn, the last remaining man.

"Why are you calling? You said only use text for security. In case someone's listening."

"Get out of your truck. Right now. Someone knows our plans."

Rafik waited for a moment, hearing only breathing. Then, "What do you mean?"

"Keshawn, don't question me. Just do it. Then come to my location with your remaining devices."

"I've already done it. I never took the truck."

Rafik was initially incensed at his protégé ignoring his orders, but quickly tamped down the emotion. In this case, the rebellious streak may have worked in their favor.

"I need you to bring the remaining devices to me for a final attack."

He gave Keshawn instructions, telling him where he was and how to locate the shooting position. As he hung up the phone, he saw a Park Service ranger coming down the trail, looking at him strangely.

For the first time, he remembered he'd left his pistol in the car, and felt a bolt of fear. *Allah, why have you forsaken me?*

"Hey, where you headed?"

Remembering the man he had seen before, Rafik said, "I'm going to take pictures of the cliffs. I want to get a shot down the coast."

The ranger cocked his head, saying, "Well, you're going the wrong way. This trail goes to the cliffs, but it's the long one. Why are you going into the woods?"

Rafik rapidly walked back to the trail, looking left and right to make sure they were alone.

"I can't tell which trail goes where. The signs aren't that great."

The ranger looked at his tripods and relaxed, laughing. "Yeah, we need to fix them. The paint's pretty much gone, huh?"

Rafik closed up to him. "Yes. Which way should I go?"

"Just follow this trail the way you were going. But if I were you, I'd head back to the parking lot and take the red trail. It's the shortest. And probably safer."

"Why is it safer? Because it's shorter?"

"Uhh . . . yeah. That's it."

Rafik dropped his tripods and brought out a knife, whipping it straight into the man's chest. He bowed out, his face a caricature of shock, mouth in an O and eyes wide. Before he could realize what had happened,

Rafik pulled out the knife and raked it across his throat, splitting it wide open. As the man fell, Rafik grabbed his body and dragged it through the underbrush to a fallen log, hiding the remains from view of the trail.

He retrieved his tripods and sprinted into the forest, wanting to get out of sight of anyone who might be coming. He thought about the man's response. About the danger. It didn't make sense to say that to someone walking in the park, especially since he'd seen plenty of families using this trail earlier in the day. The Americans were petrified of anyone getting hurt in public places.

They know someone's here. I'm running out of time.

76

Jennifer sprinted back to the Suburban for a medical kit while I began conducting initial treatment of Retro. Decoy held a wad of his shirt against his shoulder wound, doing what he could to help.

"How'd they get the drop on you?" I asked. "What happened?"

"There was only one guy checking out the EFP damage. We smoked him, then this guy came out of the wood line, blazing away. We fucked up. We both thought there would be only one, like the guy in the truck. You drill his ass?"

"Jennifer did. Two in the chest, one in the head."

He raised his eyebrows, letting that sink in, then said, "How's Retro?"

"He's hit, but he's going to make it. Just needs to get to a hospital, like you."

I hoped I wasn't lying, because it was bad. Retro had a neat hole in his chest, and a ragged exit wound on his back. Jennifer returned with the medkit and threw it on the ground between us, and we both went to work. Jennifer packed the entrance and exit wounds with Kerlix, capping it off with a special rubber bandage for sucking chest wounds that incorporated a flutter valve to release air. I prepped an IV and got it going, hoping to increase the fluids in his system to mitigate the loss of blood. His pallor was gray, his lips going blue.

Jennifer said, "His pulse is thready. He's going into shock, and he's lost a lot of blood."

He doesn't get to a trauma center soon, and he's dead.

I said, "Help out Decoy. He's got an in-and-out to his shoulder."

I dialed Kurt and filled him in on what had occurred, saying, "I need a medevac right now, or Retro's going to die. A helicopter. I don't think I can get him to a hospital soon enough."

Like the good commander he was, he completely ignored the fact that two active-duty Taskforce members were out hunting terrorists with me, getting right to the heart of the issue. "Pike, I'll do what I can, but the emergency response system is overloaded. I'm not sure I'll be able to get you

600

rotary wing any quicker than driving. You need to make a hard call. You stay there, he might bleed out because I can't get anything."

"What about the fucking president? Can't he get something done?"

"You want the president to choose one life over another? He won't do that. If there's a helo available, it's headed your way, but if not, it means it's on another medevac."

"No, I don't want him to choose one life over another. I mean that the guy owns helicopters. Send me Marine One. This LZ is big enough."

I heard nothing for a split second, then, "That's genius. Stand by." I waited, the phone mute, then heard Kurt say, "It's launching right now, with the White House doc. Give me a grid."

I relayed the grid to the open area in front of the substation, then Jennifer and I moved Retro down to the makeshift LZ, getting him as comfortable as possible.

I said, "Decoy, can you handle exfil?"

"Yeah. No issues."

"It's all yours. Helo's probably ten minutes out." I smiled. "Don't forget to lock the Suburban when you leave."

He didn't smile back, and I knew he was

still beating himself up. "Pike —"

I held up my hand. "I don't want to hear it. Get Retro to a hospital. That's your mission now."

He nodded. Jennifer bent over him, tightening the bandage on his shoulder. He caught her arm, causing her to stop.

"Hey, that was some good shooting. Thanks."

She wiped his blood off her hands, looking physically ill. All she said was "I had a good teacher."

I said, "You ready for round three?"

She checked her Glock, reflexively ensuring there was a round in the chamber, then opened the driver's door to the Suburban, her face devoid of any emotion. She fired up the engine.

Decoy said, "Looks ready to me."

I wasn't so sure.

We took the beltway to Pennsylvania Avenue, weaving across lanes and using the shoulder whenever we got bogged down. Crossing into Maryland, we continued southeast down the peninsula into a rural area and away from the D.C. traffic, allowing us to pick up speed. Jennifer continued driving on the ragged edge of losing control, barreling down Highway 4 toward the nuclear plant.

Pulling up the moving map display on my cell phone, I could see the target phone was still in the park. In fact, it didn't look like it had moved much at all since we'd first locked on to it. I called the techies to make sure my data track was functioning. I got some bad news.

"Pike, the phone's GPS is disabled. He turned it off. We're only tracking it by triangulating its signal through the cell towers. It's not that precise. You're going to have a plus or minus of over four hundred meters out in that park. Sorry."

"So he's in the park, but no telling where?"

"Yeah, that's about it."

I thought through the ramifications, then called Kurt to let him know our status. "We're still about thirty minutes out. Put the Calvert Cliffs nuclear plant on high alert. I don't see how he could get through their tight-ass security and get close enough to use the EFPs against the reactors, but there's nothing else near the geolocation of the phone. We're headed there now, but it's going to take some time."

He said, "Pike, we've done a range analysis on a facility map. He can fire the EFP and hit the reactor dome from outside the fence line."

"How? It's still just an EFP, even if it's a powerful one. He'll be shooting from over a hundred meters away, outside of the envelope the congressman gave me. It won't have the power to penetrate the dome."

"A test version was used on a covert action in Sudan. I just found out it exceeded all parameters. He fires it, and not only will it hit, but it *will* penetrate."

Jesus Christ. I shouldn't have wasted effort on the other team.

I said, "I'm not going to get there in time. Where are we on the police response? Flood the damn place. Get enough in there, and they'll get it done, whether they know what they're looking for or not."

"All jurisdictions are swamped with the power outage. It's turning into chaos on the streets. Looting and other bullshit. There are no police. We're trying to break some free, and getting ones and twos from individual jurisdictions. It's not going to be coordinated and it sure as shit won't be quick. They're coming from all over. They certainly won't beat you there."

"What about the CAT team? Get their ass in the air. They're trained for this sort of thing."

"Pike, the threat against the national command authority is too great. The Secret Service isn't going to release the counter-assault team to go offensive. Their job is to protect the president, and believe me — they're taking that job seriously. This place is turning into an armed camp."

"I get that, but what about the guys off duty? Get them moving. All hands on deck. The CAT's got at least four full teams, and they aren't all manning a wall."

Kurt paused for a moment, then said, "Yes. That's true, and they've been mobilized. The only men available went with Marine One to extract Retro and Decoy."

Shit. That hit just keeps on giving.

I threw out one final idea, knowing I was sending in children to fight a grizzly. "Get the fucking forest service guys that work the park to start looking. That's where he's at. Find some high ground with a clear line of sight to the reactors. That's where he'll be. It's nothing different from countersniper work."

I ran out of stupid suggestions, and waited on his response.

Kurt said, "Pike, bottom line is you're it."

He let that sink in, then said, "Stop him. You hear me? All bets off. Stop that son of a bitch. I don't care what it takes. Pull the rabbit out of the hat. Like you used to do."

With a sense of failure building in my gut, I said, "No issues, sir. I'll get it done."

And hung up.

There was one bright point that Kurt hadn't considered: I had Jennifer with me, and we kicked ass as a team when under pressure. *Shit, especially under pressure.* As much as any man I had ever served with — even Knuckles. It was something subliminal, something that couldn't be taught or measured, but it was there, and I would need every single bit of it.

Unfortunately, right now I was unclear of her mental state. The choices boiled down to two — split up or stick together. Splitting up was the better option because we could cover more terrain, but I didn't want Jennifer to get hurt if she got caught off guard. I was having doubts that she could pull the trigger unless she was in a completely defensive, life-threatening situation. And that might cost her dearly.

I mulled it over for the rest of the ride, getting pulled out of my thoughts when Jennifer said, "This is it."

We drove up to a yellow shack and paid five bucks to a man-boy to get in the park. I couldn't tell if the uniform he was wearing was an official Park Service one or from a

Boy Scout troop. *Yeah, these guys have the attack under control.*

Winding around the parking lot, I saw some sort of playground structure made out of old tires, looking like something from *Mad Max,* with kids happily climbing all over the used rubber.

I said, "Get to the farthest point north you can. That's where he'll have entered."

She parked on a spit of grass, and we exited, looking at a map of the trail network. I saw three that sprouted from the trailhead and went generally parallel to each other. Splitting up really was the best option, because I had no idea which trail he might have taken. Two out of three were better odds than one out of three.

"Jennifer, you sure you're good going by yourself?"

"Yeah, Pike. I told you I could. Why do you keep questioning me?"

I handed her a radio that looked like an ordinary Garmin Rhino. Instead of the pathetic distance the Rhino achieved on its family radio frequency, though, these would work over much greater range.

"You see the blip on your screen? That's me. I can see you on my screen. If you find the terrorist, I want you to simply press the alert button. I'll get an alarm, and haul ass straight at you. Okay?"

She nodded once.

"All right. You take the shorter trail on the right. I'll take the one on the left. When you reach the point where the trail begins to curve back south, mark it on the Rhino and continue north. If we don't find them on the trail, they're in the woods. Keep going until you bump into the nuke plant, then loop back to the trail. We'll cloverleaf back and forth until we find them."

She started to move to the trail, when I caught her arm.

"Jennifer, when you leave the trail and the people, you pull that Glock out and have it at the ready. If you alert, I'll close in as fast as I can, but you need to be prepared to shoot, and shoot first. These guys are not going to fuck around."

She tucked the Glock into the waistband of her jeans, hiding the butt with her shirt to prevent other hikers from seeing it.

She said, "Pike, I'll be able to kill what I need to kill."

She pulled away and entered the trail network.

77

Rafik helped Keshawn line up the final two EFPs, keeping them separated by a great enough distance so the explosion of one wouldn't destroy the aim of the other. All four were targeted at the base of the nearest reactor dome, the hope being that the third or fourth would penetrate and damage some critical component.

Their primary problem was that there were only two of them, and only two M57 firing devices. Thus, there would be a volley of two EFPs, with a significant gap. They would need to fire the first volley, then prepare the blasting caps and connect the M57s to the second set. It would take time, and Rafik was worried about the possible response of the facility. He had been unable to find information on United States nuclear security on the Web, and imagined it was something robust and incredibly responsive.

He finished aiming and moved back to his

original EFP, picking up the M57 clacker in his hand. Unspooling the wire, his actions were mirrored by Keshawn. They entered the small stand of woods on top of the ridge and placed their backs against a tree. Rafik held his hands out from his body, the clacker clasped between them. He looked over at Keshawn and could see a bead of sweat rolling down his face as the man tested the circuit of the detonation system.

Rafik squeezed his eyes for a split second, his hands shaking slightly, and gave a silent prayer for success. When he opened them again, he steeled himself, testing the spring tension of the clacker. His face grim, he looked one more time at his partner. Keshawn gave him a thumbs-up.

They locked eyes, then nodded together in a simple rhythm. Once . . . twice . . . then Rafik saw movement over Keshawn's shoulder. He dropped the clacker and stood, Keshawn whirling around.

He heard Keshawn say, "Stop right there," then "What the fuck else can go wrong?"

He ran over and saw Keshawn aiming his pistol at an attractive woman and a small boy of about eight.

The woman said, "We're lost. We don't mean any trouble. We saw the signs saying no trespassing and were just looking for help."

They think we work for the nuclear plant.

Keshawn said, "What do you want to do?"

"I'll handle it."

He took Keshawn's pistol and aimed it at the pair, motioning for them to begin walking back the way they had come. The woman began to cry.

"Be quiet. Nobody's going to hurt you."

The woman nodded her head, holding the small boy's hands.

Like every other infidel sheep. Walking to slaughter.

Rafik considered his problem. He couldn't use the gun, because the noise might alert whatever magical security the nuclear plant possessed. He would have to use a knife, which meant he would need to tie them up to prevent one from running while he killed the other. He pulled out a length of rope from his pack and cut it into quarters two feet long.

He turned to Keshawn. "Give me five minutes, then initiate. I'll be back to help with the second two."

He pushed the female forward, forcing her and the boy back down the trail.

78

Keshawn watched until the group was lost in the foliage. He pulled his M57 over to the tree Rafik had used for cover, unspooling additional wire to make it reach. Sitting down with his back against the trunk, he consciously avoided looking at his watch, feeling the seconds crawl by.

He thought he heard movement in the woods, away from the direction Rafik had gone. He strained to pick up something besides the birds chirping. He heard nothing else, but the phantom noise put him on edge. Rafik had taken his pistol, leaving him feeling exposed should he be discovered. He glanced at his watch against his will and was aggravated to discover that only two minutes had elapsed. *Why am I waiting five minutes? What's the point?*

He picked up both clackers, one in each hand, testing if he could fire them simultaneously. He found the spring tension to be too strong. He might be able to do one, but both together was asking for a mistake. He looked out into the valley, in the direction the two EFPs were aimed, and decided to fire his first. He glanced at his watch again, taking in the molasses drip of the seconds as they went past three minutes and thirty seconds. He made up his mind.

Picking up his clacker, he pressed himself against the tree, exhaled, and rapidly began to squeeze. Between the second and third stroke, the air around him cracked like a living thing, spiking into his ears, the pressure wave from the explosive charge slapping the tree he was hiding behind. Without even turning to survey the damage, he grabbed Rafik's clacker and began to squeeze.

After the second blast, Keshawn rolled out from behind the tree to survey the damage. Running through the dust cloud raised by the EFPs, he scanned the dome the weapons had been directed against. He saw nothing. He began a methodical search, and caught a darkness near the base, about a third of the way up. He ran to Rafik's pack and ripped through it until he found a mini eight-power monocular. He trained it on the small stain spread against the whiteness of the concrete, bringing the scope into focus. The stain crystallized into two fractures about five feet apart, with a spiderweb of cracks flowing out in myriad different directions, connecting the two together.

His face split into a grin, then he remembered what he had just struck. He swept the monocular around the compound, looking for a response. He saw none. *But it won't be long. Need to fire the other two.* He was sure the next two EFPs would penetrate the concrete and cause havoc within.

He ran to the next EFP and wired the blasting cap onto the clacker, then tried to insert it into the well of the third weapon, his hands shaking so much he had trouble getting it seated.

Where the hell is Rafik? We're running out of time.

He managed to arm the EFP after the third attempt. He grabbed Rafik's clacker and ran to prepare the fourth and final EFP. He began to wire the blasting cap to it, when he heard a crashing in the woods, from the same direction as before. Away from the direction Rafik had gone.

79

Rafik pushed the woman and the child forward until the EFP site was hidden by the forest, then said, "Stop."

The woman turned around, tears running freely.

"Sit down."

They did so.

He threw the rope he'd taken from his pack at the feet of the woman, saying, "Tie up the boy, then tie your own feet. I'll tie your hands."

The woman began to blubber. *Pathetic.*

"Shhhhh. I'm not going to hurt you. I promise. There's sensitive equipment on site and you interrupted a test. This is for your own protection."

The woman nodded, and tied up the hands and feet of the boy. Rafik was amazed again at how these soft *kafir* wanted to believe they would live when death's noose was slowly circling their necks.

Finished with the boy, the woman hesitated. Rafik said, "Don't make me arrest you."

"You promise you're not going to do anything to us? We're just lost. We didn't do anything wrong."

He smiled and handed her a section of rope. "I promise. As soon as the test is done, you'll be free to go."

She wiped the tears from her eyes and bent down to tie her ankles. She flicked the rope out, circling Rafik's legs, and jerked upright, ripping him off of his feet.

He hammered the ground hard, the brunt taken by his upper back and head. He felt his weapon kicked out of his hands, and he rolled onto his knees.

The woman leapt onto his back, wrapping her legs around his waist and the rope against his neck. She looped it completely around, then jerked out, cinching the rope into his throat.

He lashed out with both elbows, connecting solidly over and over again, but the woman refused to move. The rope cut into his flesh, his windpipe crushing like an aluminum beer can. He began to rasp for air, and knew he was going to die.

At the hands of a *kafir.*

He staggered to his feet, the woman

locked relentlessly on his back. He slammed her against a tree, attempting to scrape her off, but all she did was grunt.

He heard the boom of an EFP, and renewed his efforts. *Victory. So close. I will not be killed by a* kafir.

He tried to claw her face, wildly swinging his arms at something he couldn't see. He could feel the woman's spittle on his neck as she cranked the rope tighter and tighter. In his last breaths, it dawned on him that he had been tricked. *He* had been led down a path, believing the woman was subdued. She had never trusted him, and he had fallen for her tears. The injustice was staggering.

Defeated by a woman.

I went as fast as I dared through the woods, trying to strike a balance between speed and security, the Glock tracking everything to my front. Jennifer's GPS signal from her alarm transmission showed her only four hundred meters from my location. I had been running for about two minutes when I heard an explosion ahead of me, knowing what that meant. *Jesus.*

I saw a clearing to my front and slowed, my subconscious screaming at me to simply plow ahead. I scanned quickly, then broke into the clearing, immediately seeing two large EFPs on tripods, both aimed at the nuclear facility. One had an M57 attached, ready to fire. I rapidly did a three-sixty, seeing no threat, but also seeing the destroyed tripods of two expended EFPs.

What the hell? I'd heard no gunfire, which was an ominous sign, given Jennifer's alarm, but clearly something had stopped the attack. *Where's Jennifer?* A flash of yellow caught my eye. I jogged to it, and saw Jennifer's radio on the ground.

Shit.

I was reaching down to retrieve it when a blinding flash of pain sliced through my left shoulder. I collapsed to the ground, feeling something broken grind against itself. I rolled over and saw a giant black man standing above me, holding what looked like the steel posts used on the warning signs I had passed. He swung again like he was aiming at a golf ball, and my hand holding the Glock was hammered, sending the gun sailing fifteen feet away. Before he could recover from the swing, I snapped out with a leg sweep and brought him to the ground, then scrambled to maintain the initiative.

My left arm was numb, refusing to move, but I still had use of my right, although my right hand felt like wood. I fell on top of him and popped him twice in the face, my fist refusing to close completely, the blows ineffectual. He flung me onto my back and straddled my waist, raising the bar again.

I snaked my legs around his neck, my body now resting on my shoulders with him above me. I used my one good arm to help achieve a triangle choke with my thighs, winding my left foot under my right leg. I began to squeeze, causing his eyes to bulge.

He began huffing like a bull, but didn't drop. *Jesus, this guy is strong.*

He swam a hand in between my left thigh and his neck, achieving some relief. He began to work the hand through, creating a larger and larger gap. His other hand punched my left shoulder in light jabs that at any other time would have been a joke. Today it felt like he was working a welding torch against my flesh, each blow causing my broken bones to grind into themselves. The punishment caused me to flinch, giving him a bigger gap between my lock and his neck.

He's going to escape. And I'm going to die.

He hit me again, and my vision blurred. If he kept at it, I was going to black out.

Need to end this. Right now.

I squeezed with all of my might, giving him something else to focus on besides hitting me. When he reached up to fight the hold, I completely released, causing him to flail about to keep his balance. I mule-kicked his chest, launching him in the air backward. I leapt up and began running in the direction of the Glock. As expected, he leapt up as well, only he was closer. When his eyes left me and focused on the weapon, running full out, I changed direction and ran to the armed EFP. I rotated it on the tripod until it was aimed directly at him.

He came up with the weapon, charging toward me and firing. I dropped to the ground and scrambled down the wire to the M57 firing device, the rounds popping the dirt around me. As I reached the M57 I felt a bullet tear into my thigh. I rolled over, holding the M57 in my one good hand, see-ing him standing directly in front of the EFP fifteen feet away, drawing a slow bead on my head. I frantically squeezed the clacker, and the world ripped apart.

I gradually came back to the present, unsure how long I had been out, feeling like I was in a dream but partially awake. My head slowly cleared, but not my hearing. I saw my attacker on the ground, still alive and struggling to move. His entire midsection was gone, with the exception of six inches of flesh connecting his upper body with his lower. His mouth worked like a fish out of water for a moment, then he lay still.

I caught movement out of the corner of my eye and recognized Jennifer shouting something I couldn't hear. Incongruously, next to her was a small child of eight or nine.

I'm hallucinating. I'm hurt bad.

The Jennifer vision ran to me and began checking my wounds. I could feel the pressure of her touch, confusing me further. The ringing in my ears began to subside, and I could hear Jennifer speaking as if through a long tube, reciting the litany of things wrong with me. She went about the triage expertly.

Just like I trained her. I began to believe it was real.

I croaked, "The Arab."

"He's dead."

"His phone?"

"I got it. Shut up and let me finish."

"Who's the kid?"

She stopped what she was doing, giving me a look of exasperation. "He's just a lost boy. I found him on the trail. We need to take him to his mother."

The comment was so crazy, yet so completely in character, I laughed out loud, sending a sharp pain through my shoulder.

She said, "What's so funny?"

"Still saving the lost puppies."

She finished with my thigh and said, "It's the other way around. If he hadn't been there, the Arab would have just carved me up. Because there were two people, he decided to tie us first, which gave me an edge."

"How come I didn't hear any gunfire?"

"Uhh . . . well, I had to keep the Glock hidden because of the boy. I didn't get a chance to draw it."

She saw me grin and cinched the sling on my left arm, causing a wince.

"What's funny now?"

"He saved your life by being there, but if he wasn't there, you could have used the pistol. Your lost puppies always seem to just barely break even."

She finished and stood up.

"Not all of them. I'm still working on you."

80

Kurt felt his phone vibrate and moved as unobtrusively as possible to a corner of the conference room. Even with the cacophony of voices, the president noticed him move away, and watched him like a hawk.

Since Pike had been released to go on his safari, the Oversight Council meeting had turned into a makeshift war room, with anyone who had any ability to help stop the attacks now plugged in with a laptop. As often happened in crisis situations, this little room had become the epicenter of the storm, regardless of the million-dollar suites specifically made to command and control just this type of contingency. Top advisors from across the political, law enforcement, and defense spectrum were crowded into the small space, all vying for the president's attention with information that positively, absolutely needed to be heard right now.

Kurt turned into the wall, away from any

ears. "Give me some good news."

He paused for a second, then said, "Jennifer? Is that you?"

He quit talking as she began to give him a situation report. He listened for close to four minutes, hearing Jennifer end with a summary of Pike's condition and what she was doing about it.

He said, "Don't take him to a hospital. Get him to the Taskforce. If what you say is true, and it's really a through-and-through wound, our physician's assistant can handle it."

Kurt listened for a second, then interrupted. "Jennifer, Pike's welfare is what I *am* thinking about. Don't take him to a hospital. There'll be too many questions with a gunshot wound. Let the PA take a look. If he says he can't treat it, *then* go to a hospital."

He hung up the phone, seeing President Warren still eyeballing him. He gave a small nod, and saw President Warren visibly relax. Kurt sat back down and waited on the official version of events at the nuclear plant to wind its way through the system. Ten minutes later, a call came in from the emergency response team at the Calvert Cliffs nuclear plant.

"We had an attack, but it was unsuccessful. They hit one of the domes, but then screwed up the daisy chain for the repeat attack to penetrate the concrete."

Phil Spallings, the team leader deployed from the Department of Energy's Nuclear Emergency Support Team, took the call. "What happened? How sure are you that there's no second attack?"

"Very sure. It wasn't a diversion, unless these guys are way, way more dedicated than we think."

Spallings said, "Assume they are, dammit! Don't let down your guard. We don't know the extent of the attacks. There could be others."

The tone of the man on the phone caused Kurt to smile. Like soldiers throughout history, he was on the ground but being questioned by a pinhead miles away. The man remained professional, but the sarcasm crept out. "They had a misfire. One of the devices blew up, cutting a guy in half. The rest of the devices are here, now rendered safe. I suppose they could have planned to kill him in a spectacular manner so we'd let down our guard, but, in my *professional* opinion, the attack failed."

The men and women around the conference table collectively let out their breath. Spallings paused for a minute, apparently trying to think of something heroic to say, settling with, "Good work. Keep us in the loop."

President Warren spoke to the scientist still on the VTC. "What's the status of the grid?"

"We're okay, for now. We get one spike, and we're in trouble, but right now it's contained."

"What's the assessment of the damage?"

"Well, it'll take a few days to really sort out, but off the cuff, I'd say we're looking at rolling blackouts in four states until we can replace the EHVTs. That, coupled with the loss of the Calvert Cliffs reactor until it can be certified as safe, will put a severe strain on production, but we can manage unless we get something else during that time, like damage from a natural occurrence. We can handle the load, but not if anything, and I mean *anything,* interferes."

"Well, then, make sure that doesn't happen. I'm counting on you."

The scientist looked at the president in confusion, wondering how on earth he'd be able to prevent a lightning strike. He was about to say something to that effect when he realized he'd been dismissed.

President Warren spoke to the room at large. "Well, looks like we dodged a bullet here. Good work, everyone. Keep up a full-court press; make sure we don't have anyone else out there."

The director of the FBI said, "You got it. I'll let you know if anything else spikes."

President Warren nodded, and said, "If you're not directly involved in this event, if you're not law enforcement or with the power companies, clear out. Give the people who have real work to do some room."

As the people directed to leave stood up, President Warren stopped Palmer, the national security advisor, and said something to him. Kurt watched Palmer thread his way through the people exiting and stop several, whispering in their ears.

He's rounding up the Oversight Council. Kurt waited, and eventually Palmer got around to him. "Head to the conference room down the hall. The president would like a word."

Kurt trailed the cattle call of men and women out the door, then went left instead of right, following a much smaller group. When the door closed, the president said, "Let's hear it."

Kurt relayed what he knew, including the fact that Pike and Jennifer had found the leader's cell phone, and that the owners of all the numbers within it were either dead or captured. The information caused every-one to visibly relax.

President Warren said, "Okay, that's great news. What's the damage to the Taskforce? Where do we go from here?"

Kurt said, "No damage that I can see. It's contained. No need to throw Pike to the wolves."

Secretary Brookings' jaw dropped. "What? How can you say that? It's a debacle. We've got three Taskforce members in the hospital, and Pike broke just about every privacy law on the books. Not to mention the murder of U.S. citizens. It's going to get out. We need to burn him."

When Brookings' words sank in, Kurt snapped forward against the table, leaning over it until he was close enough for the secretary to feel the spittle off of his words. "Murder? You sanctimonious little fuck . . ." He backed off, realizing he wasn't going to win by rage. "Pike broke some laws, that's true, but if he hadn't, the entire Eastern seaboard would be roasting hot dogs in their fireplaces. He stopped the damn attack. There's no reason to crucify him. Nobody knows about the Taskforce involvement. Nobody can connect the dots."

Brookings said, "Are you out of your mind? We commandeered the presidential helicopter to save two Taskforce members. You don't think that's going to make the news? You just told us about a fucking eight-year-old kid who saw the final action at the nuclear plant. You think he's going to remain quiet?"

Kurt turned cold. "What are you saying? You want me to smoke the kid?"

Brookings looked like he'd been punched in the gut. Before it could turn more contentious, President Warren held up his hands. "Stop it. This isn't helping."

He looked at Kurt. "Tony has a point. How are we going to prevent Taskforce disclosure, given what's occurred? I don't want to burn Pike any more than you do, but we need something."

Kurt said, "You sent Marine One with CAT guys, didn't you?"

President Warren's eyebrow's furrowed, seeing where he was going. "Yeah, there was no way the doctor would go without protection, and the counterassault team was all that was available."

"Well, there you go. Those guys are trained for this very thing. I mean, they're trained for a counterassault against a direct threat to your life, but it's not a stretch to say they went out to capture some terrorists that may have been hell-bent on killing you. And they're Secret Service. You control them. You can write the story. Like Kennedy and Marilyn Monroe, only for a good reason."

Kurt watched the president consider, and knew he was close. "Nobody knows anyone was injured out there. We can write the press release any way we want. Give the credit to the CAT guys and the Secret Service. They took down the terrorists."

Kurt saw Brookings look from the president to him, and knew he realized he was losing the argument. They both understood that the Secret Service story would look like the president himself had directly averted disaster with his own team, and would be something very appealing.

Brookings said, "Sir, there's no way you can contain this. It isn't 1962. We live in a world of transparency, with Internet bloggers and instant news. There'll be a History Channel special on these attacks in four months, and it'll be down to the minute. They'll know everything there is to know, and broadcast it every hour for a month."

Kurt snarled, "Bullshit. I've seen the History Channel crap. Watch the one on the capture of Saddam Hussein and you're left believing it was a fourth infantry division operation all the way. We *can* contain this."

Brookings spat back, "This isn't a war

zone, *Colonel,* it's America. You don't get to control the news here. Shit, we couldn't keep anything secret when we killed bin Laden. The entire operation was on the news in hours, and this will be no different. The truth of the matter is that Pike needs to be put down. He's a fucking menace. He's done whatever he thinks is right regardless of what we say. He's exactly why I didn't want to start this organization. Exactly the reason why it will go wrong. One man who thinks he knows better than anyone else. We need to make an example of him to other Taskforce operators —"

The tirade sank into Kurt's head and he lost control. He leapt out of his chair, crossing the table and snatching Brookings up by his hair, using his momentum to slam Brookings into the wall. He locked up Brookings' elbow and leaned into his ear.

"You fucking miserable piece of shit. Pike saved your life last year. Your *life.* Does that mean nothing to you? He just averted a national tragedy, using skills that *we* gave him, and authority that *we* blessed. He's a man doing what is best for the country. Because *we* asked him to."

President Warren said, "Kurt! Stop. Right now."

Kurt looked at the president, then at

Brookings' trembling face. He raised his voice so that everyone could hear. "Okay, sir. You want to burn Pike, so be it. But I want Mr. Secretary here to know that if Pike goes down, I'm going to put him in the hospital. You can arrest me later."

He cranked Brookings' arm, eliciting a squeal. "You get that, Mr. Sanctimonious? Pike goes to jail, for whatever reason, and I'm hunting you down. Make sure your fucking health insurance is up to date."

He released Brookings, panting a little from the adrenaline rush. The secretary sank onto the floor, rubbing his arm, looking for sympathy. President Warren ignored him. "I get the point. Calm down."

Kurt returned to his chair.

President Warren said, "Look, we can make the substation hit work. I agree with that, but what about the kid? There's no way we can cloak that."

Kurt said, "I know. Jennifer said she'd convinced him not to say anything, but he's been through a traumatic event. He's going to talk. The question is whether anyone will believe him. And if they do, if it will reach the media."

President Warrant waited, then said, "So? That's it?"

"It's a risk, but some things are worth the risk. Pike is one of them."

81

I woke up a little disoriented, confused for a second about where I was. The drive from the nuclear plant was a splintered dream, Jennifer spending her time weaving across lanes as she talked on the phone and tended to me. I was now in a bed, swathed in bandages, and it clicked that Jennifer had managed to get me inside the Taskforce, to the little medical department we kept for injuries that couldn't go to a hospital.

I heard the door open, hoping it was Jennifer, but seeing Kurt instead. Then I remembered that Jennifer wasn't allowed in here. *Great. Probably won't see her until the arraignment.*

"How're you feeling?"

"I'll live."

Kurt smiled. "You're a hard man to kill, I'll give you that. Broken clavicle seems to be the worst of it."

I didn't return the smile. "So what's

my status?"

"Don't know yet. The politicians are monitoring the press. I got the president to hold off on anything hasty. If something pops, they'll decide whether to throw you under the bus."

I nodded. "That's fine. I'm ready for whatever. I only ask two things."

"What's that?"

"Number one, you let Jennifer go. There's no reason for two folks to go to jail. I'm enough. Can you make that happen?"

Kurt paused a second, considering, then said, "Yeah, I can get that done. What's number two?"

"The president comes in here before I go to jail and gives me a fucking thank-you."

"Uhh . . . I don't know about that one. You might have to settle for me."

I laughed, then grimaced at the pain in my shoulder. "I know. A man can hope, though."

Kurt said, "It's not as bad as you think. We've got a pretty good plan in place." He told me the cover story involving the Secret Service CAT team and the "misfire" at the nuclear plant, which was good, then the fact that nobody could predict the actions of the boy, which was bad.

"It's holding up so far, though, so maybe

it'll be okay."

Before I could answer, Holly entered the room with a bunch of balloons and flowers, like I was twelve and just had my tonsils out. She was followed by a nurse, who went straight to the machines monitoring my status.

"What the hell is this shit?" I said. "Are you kidding me?"

Holly said, "Cut the crap. It's a girl thing. We're just happy you're alive."

She put the balloons next to the bed, a DVD on my lap, turned to Kurt, and said, "Sir, I've got something a little urgent to show you. Sorry to interrupt."

Kurt said, "No problem. We were just bullshitting anyway. Pike, I think you'll be good. You mentioned a thank-you, and you're on to something. The president's a good man. He'll remember what you did. I'll make sure of it."

I rolled my eyes, letting him know what I thought of that little bit of hope. He smiled and left the room, followed by Holly. She paused at the door for a second, waiting until Kurt was in the hallway, then turned to me and stage-whispered, "You owe me more than dinner now."

What the hell is she talking about?

I looked at the balloons next to the bed,

thinking she'd lost her mind if she believed I was going to owe her something for bringing me that crap. I picked up the DVD and turned it over.

The Princess Bride.

The nurse spoke, and I realized what the payback was for.

"Still trying to piss off the boss, huh?"

Jennifer was smiling, and looked very, very good. I smiled back. "How'd you get in here?"

"Holly and I are best friends now. She helped me break in, along with telling me some stories about you that probably should be kept hidden."

"Really. Breaking the rules. What's that about?"

She came around the bed and took my hand. "Well, someone told me that the rules only applied if you let them. I thought I'd check out that theory."

"Sounds like a genius. How's it working for you?"

She gave me a crooked grin that cut straight to my core. "Pretty good so far. I'll let you know in a couple of weeks."

"Don't worry about that. I'm the only one in danger now." I told her about my conversation with Kurt, then noticed the baseball cap she was wearing. It had Romans 3:8

stitched on the back, the Bible quote we used as an inside joke.

"Where'd you get the hat?"

She turned her head left and right, showing it off. "You like it? Turbo gave it to me."

"Turbo? Are you kidding me? After all of his crying about Assessment?"

She blushed slightly. "Nope. I went to see how Decoy and Retro were doing, and a bunch of guys were already there. Word's spread about stopping the attack. You guys suck at keeping secrets, by the way. Anyway, Decoy thanked me for saving his life — which isn't true, of course, but they all seemed to believe it — and Turbo gave me the hat. Probably just because he was afraid you were going to kick his ass again, but it's still pretty cool, huh?"

"Very cool. If they gave it to you, they meant it. Don't blame me for your mistakes. How's Retro doing anyway?"

"He looks terrible, but they say he's going to be fine." She snapped her fingers. "Oh, I saw Knuckles! He's doing much better, and asked about you. Well, about us and our situation with the president. They all think it's a crock."

"Glad to hear he's coming around. Maybe I'll visit his sorry ass as well." I paused, then said, "What is our situation? You still planning on leaving? Going back to being a professor of anthro-psychology or whatever the hell it is?"

She cocked her head, apparently considering how to respond. "Let's not worry about that right now. Let's figure out if I'm going to be mailing you a file inside your birthday cake in prison."

She leaned forward and kissed my forehead. "I've got to get out of here before Kurt comes back. They said you're healthy enough to leave here today. I'll see you this afternoon."

82

Five days later, I glanced reflexively at the "cleared list" for Delta Airlines. I had a confirmed seat on the same flight tomorrow, but Kurt had called this morning and said the president had decided I was free to go. Not wanting to see if he would change his mind, I'd hauled ass straight to Reagan National Airport to try my hand at a standby flight. Well, *hauled ass* was a relative term, since I needed to use a cane, and my left arm was strapped to my chest to prevent movement.

I'd left the Taskforce medical facility the same day I talked to Kurt and Jennifer, and had gone to the same hotel as Jennifer. Since then, other than visiting Knuckles, Decoy, and Retro in the hospital, I'd simply sat around, watching breaking news stories, praying some junior Woodward and Bernstein wasn't looking for a scoop, but so far the Secret Service story, along with the "misfire" at the nuclear plant, seemed to be holding up.

One thing that was definitely working in my favor was that the entire nation was fixated on the attacks. It had, naturally, become the center of attention, and the successful resolution had pretty much guaranteed the president's reelection. Originally elected on a platform of national security, President Warren had been getting hammered lately because of the economy, and it was looking like a pretty good bet that he'd be a one-term president. Now the campaign had become dominated by national security, with the president looking like a savior, and there was little chance that would change so close to the election, which is what Kurt had meant in my hospital room. Without saying a word, I knew President Warren understood who he had to thank. And it also meant at least another four years of Taskforce operations, if something else didn't come along to shine a light on the president's little secret.

For her part, Jennifer had left without giving me an answer to where she stood both with the Taskforce and with our company. I'd broached the subject again as she packed to go back to South Carolina, afraid that she'd already made up her mind and just didn't want to voice it out loud because it would be a double kick to my balls if I went to jail.

I was certain she was upset at my call to shoot Americans first and ask questions later. Certain she couldn't see the necessity of the action and was holding it against me, regardless of what she'd told me in the car prior to the killings. I had tried to defend my decisions.

"Jennifer, we didn't do anything wrong. Everyone we killed deserved it. I don't want you thinking that you did something immoral. Those men dug their own graves by their actions. There's no such thing as reading a terrorist his rights when he's in the middle of an attack, even if it's inside the United States."

Jennifer had stopped packing and sat down on the bed, searching my face for something. "What would make you think I was upset about that? I was upset about the damn blood and the fact that Retro was dying, but not what we did. Sorry. I guess I'm not a hardened commando yet."

I plowed ahead, not even listening to what she had said. "It wasn't murder. Even if it was in the United States. People don't follow the rules just because they're here, and sometimes you have to play on the field that they built. Had we waited, it would have been a larger attack than 9/11. We did the right thing."

Her eyes flashed anger, and I'd realized I'd overstepped. Misjudged her again.

"I *know*," she said. "Jesus, is that what you think of me?"

She saw my embarrassment and said, "That *is* it, isn't it? Because I got upset with what you did in Cairo, you think I'm some kind of peace freak, don't you? That's why you kept questioning me. Asking if I had it in me to get the job done."

She stopped, wringing a shirt in her hand as if she were trying to squeeze out poison. "You, of all people, know better than that. I may not like running around shooting everything that moves like you guys, but I understand it's sometimes necessary. I've learned a little bit about real-world justice. I mean, really, I killed a man with a rope."

She threw the shirt into the suitcase. "I also understand that just because it's done under the umbrella of the United States, it's not necessarily right. I can see the difference between right and wrong. I'm not so sure about you."

The comment hit me like a slap. "Jennifer, we talked about Cairo. . . ."

Her expression told me she'd regretted

what had just slipped out of her mouth. "I know, I know. I'm not saying you don't consciously wish you could take that back, but you've got some sort of prehistoric subconscious thing going on that doesn't care about the distinction between right and wrong. It's like . . ."

I waited on her to finish, but she said, "Never mind."

I said, " 'Never mind'? You can't leave that out there hanging. What were you going to say?"

She cocked her head, searching my face again.

"You know, I've spent a lot of time trying to figure you out, and I have a theory."

Oh boy. Psychobabble time.

"Everyone operates on some scale of morality. Most people live on the positive side of things. Some operate way, way above, and can do heroic acts as normal events that others would not attempt. Some people, like Hitler or serial killers, operate way, way down on the scale, probably never reaching the positive side at all. Whatever it is, your range on the scale is pretty much firm. A serial killer will never do anything heroic, and a truly heroic person has some built-in stopgap that keeps him from doing vile things."

She paused. I saw where this was going. *She thinks I'm evil because of Cairo — and it's permanent.* I suddenly felt nauseous. She was going to leave the company. *Leave me.*

"You, however, are an anomaly. You can, and often do, act very heroically. You have a capacity that very few people on earth possess, but it works both ways on the scale. I think the death of your family destroyed whatever stopgap you had, and now you have just as large a capacity for evil as you do for good."

She touched my face. "And you need to find that stopgap again."

Her words sank in, and I felt an enormous sense of relief. I sat on the bed next to her. "So, if I contain myself, we're good? If I don't kill anyone who doesn't deserve it, if I prove I'm really on the positive side of the scale, you'll stay?"

She smiled and patted my hand. "We'll talk about that later. It'll take more than just you saying it. I'm not sure what I'm going to do, and like I said at the Taskforce, it may be moot anyway. Although I do sort of like this hero stuff."

That had been four days ago, and now that I wasn't worried about going to jail, I was surprised at the level of anxiety I felt flying home to Charleston. To the answer.

I saw my name scroll on the screen. I had made the flight. I went down the gangway, feeling as nervous as a kid on his first date.

Jennifer went through the office with a dust mop one more time. Pike would be home any minute, and she wanted the place to look perfect. He had called earlier in the morning, from inside the airplane of his connecting flight in Atlanta, letting her know he'd managed to snag a standby seat. She'd felt a little thrill just hearing his voice, and it had sunk in for the first time that the feeling was genuine. His absence the last four days had solidified something; it wasn't about anything he had done for her in the past. The thrill wasn't misplaced gratitude to him for saving her life. It was what it was: an attraction to the man himself.

She still hadn't made a decision on what she was going to do about the company. She'd thought of little else since her last conversation with Pike, and had realized that it was really up to him. She knew in her heart she couldn't stay if he didn't find a way to control the blackness he held. She'd end up hating him, and she would leave first to prevent that.

She went into their office bathroom, checking one more time to see if something nasty had magically appeared in the toilet in the last ten minutes. She heard the front door open and someone shout, "Hello?"

Her face split into a smile, and she ran out, shouting, "Pike!"

Standing in the doorway was her ex-husband, Chase. All six feet four inches, oozing false charm.

"Hello, baby. How's it going? I told you I'd be coming by."

She felt the terror seize her, and circled the desk, putting it between them. She sat down so he wouldn't notice her trembling.

"What do you want? I told you not to come here."

"I just want a little help. Is that too much to ask?"

He clapped his hands, causing her to jump. He smiled at her reaction, making her feel weak and cowardly. *You're not the same girl. You are* not *the same girl.*

He kept his hands clasped, pretending to survey the office.

"You're doing pretty well for yourself, I see."

The door opened behind him and Pike entered the office, awkwardly walking on a cane. Jennifer saw his smile melt into confusion. *Oh no. This just got bad.*

"And you must be the partner," Chase

said. "Really good to meet you."

Pike shook his hand, saying, "And you are?"

Jennifer said, "Pike, this is Chase, my ex-husband."

She saw Pike's face harden, and knew that Chase was now in serious danger. Jennifer had told Pike everything her ex-husband had done, a sort of therapy to excise the fear she still held because of the beatings she had taken at his hand. It had been a mistake. Pike had become enraged, wanting to fly to Texas and confront her ex. She had stopped him, but she feared what he would do now. *He might kill Chase. Literally.*

Pike said, "Why don't you just get the fuck out of here, while you can still walk."

Jennifer shouted, "Pike! This isn't your business. Go. Please."

Chase said, "Yeah, you ought to listen to her. I don't really give a shit about your injuries. I'm just here for what's rightfully mine. You say anything else to me, and you'll have both arms in a sling."

Like a child poking an alligator lying in the sun, Chase had no idea of the danger he was in. Jennifer knew Pike could kill him easily, even with only one good arm.

She saw Pike begin to close the distance and shouted again, "Pike! Stop! Now!"

He did, although she could tell it was taking all of his self-control.

"Please leave," she said. "I can handle this."

Pike's glare remained fixed on Chase. "You sure?"

"Yes."

With what looked like superhuman effort, he slowly turned toward the door. She could sense the pain he felt at the act. *But he's doing it.* She felt a sliver of relief, then realized what had just happened. He was leaving because she'd asked. No other reason. He wanted to beat Chase within an inch of his life, probably wanted to punish him more than anything else on earth, and he was leaving.

I'm his stopgap.

For reasons she couldn't explain, the fear left her.

He had his hand on the knob, when Chase said, "That's a smart decision. This isn't your business anyway."

Jennifer said, "Pike?"

"Yes?"

She tried to remain serious but couldn't prevent a smile from leaking out. "I've changed my mind. I think I could use a little help here. To keep the fight fair."

The pain on Pike's face drained away,

replaced by a smile that matched her own. Instead of turning the knob, he locked it.

"As you wish."

ACKNOWLEDGMENTS

The prologue of this book is fiction, but there is a ring of truth. The one-one of the team was named for my cousin, SGT Dickie Thomas. He was killed running recon for CCS in Cambodia on January 9, 1970, on a mission not unlike the fictional one I portrayed. He was twenty-two years old.

He and men like him in MACV-SOG were and are some of the bravest soldiers this country has ever had, and their story is largely untold. Conducting missions that were damn near suicidal, they went across the fence into denied countries time and time again, developing tactics, techniques, and procedures that are still used by Special Operations Forces to this day. Chris Hale's actions in the book sound like fiction because it's hard to believe that such selfless courage exists, but the story is true. SPC5 John J. Kedenburg, a one-zero for a CCN recon team, received a posthumous Medal of Honor for the actions I attributed to Chris Hale, sacrificing himself to save the life of his team member — a Vietnamese.

Before I get a bunch of e-mails about how I've put American lives in jeopardy by blue-printing how a terrorist could attack our power grid, the Fort A.P. Hill Ammunition Supply Point, and/or the Calvert Cliffs Nuclear Power Plant, rest assured I didn't. Explosively Formed Penetrators are real, of course. We are, in fact, conducting research into nanotechnology to make them more effective. I have no idea, however, how effective, because all that stuff's top-secret, and I'm not privy to it anymore. It's fiction in this book. Fort A.P. Hill is also real, as is the ASP. About 90 percent of what I wrote is accurate, but there are a few red herrings in there that are not. Try attacking the place like I described, and you'll fail. For instance, the first thing you see when you go in the police station is not a desk in the open; it's a man behind a layer of bulletproof glass. I won't tell you the other red herrings, but people who work there will know. Finally, the Calvert Cliffs Nuclear Plant is also real, as is the state park. The difference is that the park doesn't butt up to the plant. There's about a mile of civilization between them. It would be impossible to attack the place like Rafik does.

Writing of any sort is a collaborative effort, and anyone who says otherwise is either a genius or a liar. Since I'm neither, I owe a debt of gratitude to a plethora of people who helped me with this story. In no particular order, here you go: Bruce, for the information on oil refineries. A chemical engineer for an oil company, and the husband of my wife's friend, he saved me about ninety hours on the Internet for no other reason than I asked. Lunchbox, for screening my first draft of the Tandem HALO jump. He's a Tandem jumpmaster who knows more about military free-fall operations than anyone else in the Department of Defense, and he fixed all of my little mistakes. I did, however, change some back for literary reasons. The mistakes are mine, not his. Poacher, for coming up with some cool call signs. I was on a contract with him and complaining about how hard it was to invent call signs that weren't already used when he started spitting some out. I told him to hold on and grabbed a pen. Finally, a huge thank-you to Tami, a close friend who really took a liking to critiquing Jennifer. Her guidance swung between "Jennifer wouldn't do that, she's not a man," to "Jennifer's a crybaby. Give her a spine." It caused me to pull my hair out, but at least Jennifer's someone Tami would hang out with now.

To my agent, John Talbot, and the entire Dutton team for the phenomenal effort you all put forth on my behalf. I've told most of you in person, but one can never say it enough. Ava, my publicist, who is relentless at getting my books and me exposure. Your work ethic is remarkable and very much appreciated. The entire sales force for amazing me with your ability to penetrate just about every single market. And last, but certainly not least, my editor, Ben Sevier, for the guidance and friendship in not only crafting the manuscript, but in helping me navigate this new world. Your instincts are always correct, even if I initially fight them.

Finally, a huge thank-you to my family for putting up with me writing at all hours. My kids have become experts at making me feel guilty ("But, Daddy, I thought you left the Army. Can't we go play?") while also letting me work. And to my wife for going through this manuscript almost as much as I did as a first-line reader of some really rough drafts. She would roll her eyes after she corrected a grammatical mistake, and I would claim (incorrectly) that she was wrong. If you find a mistake in here, rest assured she found it before you, but I was too stubborn to change it. As an example, when she was editing these acknowledgments, she added this last sentence: *She's my rock, and I love her.* I don't have the courage to change that . . .

ABOUT THE AUTHOR

Brad Taylor, Lieutenant Colonel (ret.), is a twenty-one-year veteran of the U.S. Army Infantry and Special Forces, including eight years with the 1st Special Forces Operational Detachment — Delta, popularly known as Delta Force. Taylor retired in 2010 after serving more than two decades and participating in Operation Enduring Freedom and Operation Iraqi Freedom, as well as classified operations around the globe. His final military post was as Assistant Professor of Military Science at The Citadel. His first Pike Logan thriller, *One Rough Man,* was a national bestseller. He lives in Charleston, South Carolina.